DECISION POINTS

DECISION POINTS

Edited by
Bryan Thomas Schmidt

WordFire Press
Colorado Springs, Colorado

DEDICATION

To my nephew, Griffin Melson, who graduates from high school the same week this book comes out. Now is a time of many decision points for you. Please know that whatever paths you take, I'll be proud of you.

CONTENTS

Introduction

Bryan Thomas Schmidt

On every journey there is a path you choose to follow or the path you choose to make.

Decisions, decisions—life is full of them, and many stories revolve around them. Hence the concept for the anthology you hold in your hands. The idea was gifted to me by my friend and fellow editor, Jennifer Brozek, whose own story herein is one of my favorites of her stories ever. I expanded the concept to cover a range of time and genres—not just stories of science fiction but also fantasy, dark fantasy, and horror—as well as writers both known for writing young adult stories and writers who aren't. Before YA became a genre designation, there were always stories about young people—some called them "juveniles" or various other titles. And the stories you'll find here include some really good ones involving such characters, but because not all of them might be stocked in a bookstore as specifically YA, you might miss them. Twelve of the twenty stories here are making their first appearance in an anthology with this collection. Six are brand new originals, others are reprints. All have in common decision points that affect their outcomes.

The stories include some from popular series such as Lois McMaster Bujold's long running Vorkosigan Saga, Orson Scott Card's Ender series, Jonathan Maberry's Rot and Ruin series, and Steven Gould's Jumper series. Then there are stories from newer series like my own Saga of Davi Rhii space opera series, Kate Corcino's Spark series, and K.D. McEntire's Lightbringer Urban Fantasy series, inspired by Peter Pan. Others stand alone, including several from very popular young adult authors like Alethea Kontis, Cory Doctorow, Nnedi Okorafor, and Eugene Myers. All have been chosen for their variety in tone, plot, and even moral (if they have one). The idea here is to give you choices as well about what you're in the mood for each time you pick up the book. Or perhaps to just guarantee you a different reading experience each time you decide to open these pages. However the book touches you, I hope it's as rewarding for you as it was for me during the three years I spent putting it together.

The decision point is now yours—you already made one by deciding to open this book. More decisions follow—some thrilling, some frightening, some heartwarming, some more somber. All of them enjoyable in their own way. This book is intended to offer a lot of variety, not just to make you think and question, but to entertain you; to be the kind of book you can pick up and read one story a day and find a different experience each time. So allow me to step back out of your way and let your journey begin. I hope you find it an enjoyable one.

Bryan Thomas Schmidt
Ottawa, Kansas
January 2016

We begin with a long awaited origin story from Jonathan Maberry's bestselling Rot and Ruin series, wherein two sisters face the kind of impossible choices that those living in a zombie-infested world must face as they fight to survive.

SISTERS
(A STORY OF THE ROT AND RUIN)

JONATHAN MABERRY

-1-

It rained the day the world ended.

That's how she remembered it.

The rain fell cold and hard. That day and every time the world ended. For Lilah there wasn't just one apocalypse. They kept happening to her.

And each time it was raining.

-2-

The first time was when she was little. Too little to really understand what was happening. She was just learning to speak, barely able to walk, hardly able to form the kind of memories that could be taken out later and looked at. She remembered a woman's face. Her mother's, but Lilah didn't really understand what that meant. George had to explain it to her later.

Lilah remembered her mother holding her, and running. And other people holding her. And running.

And the monsters chasing.

Grabbing. Tearing. Taking. Biting. Eating.

Always.

One of them had bitten Mom. Lilah had seen it happen but did not know what the bright colors and loud shrieks meant. Not then. Not until later.

She remembered the house where her mother and the other grownups had hidden. She remembered her mother screaming. Mommy, with her big, swollen belly. Screaming.

That's when Annie was born.

Lilah did not understand birth, either.

Or the death that followed.

Or what happened when Mom woke up.

She saw what the others did, though. She understood it on some level that ran so deep age didn't matter. She screamed louder than the newborn Annie. She screamed louder than the people who swung clubs and pipes as Mom tried to bite them.

She screamed so loud it made her spit red.

After that Lilah didn't have much of a voice. A whisper. The first words she learned to speak were said in that whisper, and every word since then. Every single word.

It had been raining that night, the drops thudding on the roof and tapping on the windows and knocking on the door. The rain hissed in the trees outside. Lilah recorded it without having labels for any of those things. Despite the rain, those memories were burned into her. She was too young for any of it, but the world ended anyway.

-3-

It rained the day George went away.

George.

Lilah never knew his last name. Last names didn't seem to matter much. People in books had last names, and people in the stories George told. And maybe he even told her his last name, but she forgot because there was no need to remember it.

George was the last of the grownups. The one who didn't die.

The others did. They went out of the house, one by one, over the weeks. Looking for help. Looking for answers. Finding nothing, it seemed, except the end of their own stories.

George stayed with Lilah and the baby. He named her Annie. After that it was Lilah, and Annie, and George for years.

And years.

Sometimes George did go out, but never too far and never for too long. He waited for times when the biters weren't so thick around the house and then he'd slip away, quiet as a mouse and vanish in the tall grass. Those were bad times. At first. Lilah would try hard not to cry because it scared Annie when she cried. So Lilah forced her raspy voice to be still, blinked her tears away, held the screams in, and waited.

George always came back. He was the only one who ever did. Pushing a wheelbarrow full of cans from someone else's kitchen. Bringing clothes and toilet paper and toys and books. Always books.

Bringing weapons, too.

Never bringing other people. There were none. They were all sure of that. No one but George, Lilah, and little Annie.

Childhood was learning to be quiet, learning to hide, learning to trick the dead. George taught them to fight as soon as they could hold tools. They spent long nights together turning wood and duct tape and kitchen knives into weapons. Quiet weapons. George wasn't a fighter. He told the girls that he used to sell shoes. He wasn't a hero like the princes and champions in the books he taught them to read. He wasn't big and full of muscle. He wasn't as handsome as Prince Charming or Aladdin or Captain America. He never took karate or anything like that. Everything he taught them was what he could make up, and some stuff he learned from books he found that weren't Disney books or comics. They all read as much as they could. They read everything. It was how George taught them about the world that was. A world Lilah and Annie would never know. Could never know because the dead rose and ate it all up.

Eight years. Just the three of them.

When Lilah was ten and Annie was eight, George met a man in the woods. Not another biter. A living man. He was dressed like a hunter from pictures they'd seen. Camouflage clothes. But he smelled like one of the biters because he smeared something on his clothes that made the monsters think he was like them, and they didn't eat each other.

George almost killed the man because at first he couldn't believe that he was alive. He *couldn't* be alive because the world had ended and everyone died. Every single person except the three of them.

But the man was alive. Really and truly alive.

When George realized that, he went running from cover and grabbed the man and embraced him, weeping, kissing his face and hands, sobbing out loud.

The hunter was happy to see him, too, but unlike George he hadn't believed the world was destroyed. Not completely.

"There's a lot of us left," he said. "We're taking the world back from these zoms."

Zoms. He called them zoms. Short for zombies. A strange word that Lilah had read in books and which didn't seem to fit. Zombies were dead people brought back to life to be slaves. These dead people ate the living. George usually called them biters or ghouls. Zoms was a new word.

George was so happy that he brought the hunter back to the house to meet the girls.

Lilah remembered that. She was absolutely terrified of the big man with all the guns and knives who smelled like a biter. And he was strange looking. The man had the palest skin, almost as white as a corpse, and he had one blue eye and the other was as red as blood. He had lots of scars and he smiled all the time.

Lilah hated him and tried to stab him with a spear. Annie threw stones at him. It took George a long time to convince them it was safe.

Safe.

Funny word.

For Lilah "safe" meant the three of them inside the house with the doors and windows shut. That was safe. It was the only safety she'd ever known.

After a long, long time of talk and promises and even some yelling on George's part—something he almost never did—Lilah stopped fighting. It took Annie a little longer to settle down. Unlike her big sister, Annie had never seen any adults other than

George. They'd all died when she was a baby.

They all sat in the living room, and the big hunter with the red eye sat on the floor. He'd taken off all of his weapons and given them to George to hold, just to prove that he wasn't going to hurt them. Lilah and Annie crouched like dogs on either side of George, ready to run, ready to bite.

"It didn't all fall down," said the big man. "We lost a lot of land, sure, but we're taking it back. This is one of the last areas that hadn't been cleared out yet, but my guys are out here doing just that."

"Your guys…?" asked George, and as she squatted next to him, Lilah could feel him tremble with excitement.

The hunter took a couple of candy bars from his pocket and reached over to offer them to the girls, but Lilah recoiled. Annie hissed at him. The man's smile flickered and he placed the candy on the floor and shifted back away from them.

"They haven't had much candy," said George. "And I trained them to be careful."

"Stranger-danger," laughed the big man. "I get it. It's cool, and that's smart. Big ol' dangerous world and you can never be too careful."

The candy bars lay there, untouched.

"You said you have people out here?"

"Sure. Part rescue team and part hunters. We're quieting the last of the zoms as we go."

George repeated the word, "Quieting."

"Yeah, it's what we call it when we put the zoms down. Bullet in the motor cortex or a blade through the brain stem. Only way to get 'er done."

"Quieting," murmured Lilah, and then Annie repeated it.

"Look," said the big hunter, "these woods are still pretty thick with zoms. Not safe for you to be here. My camp's a few hours walk, but we have food, a stockade, horses, and a hell of—oops, I mean a heck of a lot of guns. We could go there and get oriented, then I can have a team take you and the kids to the closest town."

"Town …" said George and he swayed as if he was going to faint.

"Yeah. Towns all over. Closest is Mountainside, which they set up just after the problems started. Built around a reservoir and backed up against a mountain. And it's up high because the zoms won't walk uphill unless they're chasing something. Big fence and a lot of people. That's one of the places I hang out, but there are other towns. Like I said, we're taking it all back."

George began crying again. Annie, always so sensitive, wrapped her little arms around him and started crying, too. Lilah did not. She read a lot of fairy stories that had happy endings, but she never believed that any of those stories ever really happened. There were no happy endings.

In the morning, George agreed to go with the big hunter. He filled his wheelbarrow with food, the girls' favorite toys, some of their precious books, and lots of weapons. The hunter seemed to be impressed with the handmade weapons. "You some kind of ninja?" he asked, bending to inspect the spears and other deadly tools.

George laughed. "Not even close. I figured it out as we went. Try something on a biter and if it works you try it on another one. You don't need to know a lot, but you need to be good at what you do know."

"Ain't that the honest truth," agreed the hunter.

"George says we're not supposed to say 'ain't'," said Annie, and that made the Hunter laugh out loud.

"Well, I guess Mr. George is one-hundred percent correct, little sweet pea," he told her. "I never did have much schooling, but it looks like you learned your lessons."

"I taught them as best I could," said George, his face flushing with embarrassment.

The hunter nodded and then turned sharply to Lilah who was reaching for her favorite spear. "Whoa, now, kiddo, you shouldn't play with grown up toys."

Lilah snatched the spear up, spun the shaft faster than the eye could see and passed the tip of the blade through a loose fold of the big man's shirt. Then she held the spear ready, feet wide and braced, weight on the balls of her toes. Ready.

The hunter's smile vanished to be replaced with a snarl that was as cold and mean as a hungry bear. "I can see you learned more than your ABCs from ol' George. That's mighty interesting. Now put that toothpick down before I—"

George, greatly alarmed, stepped between them. "Oh, god, I'm so sorry! She doesn't know any better. You're the first adult she's met since … since …"

The smile came back slowly. "Hey, it's all good," said the hunter. Then he chuckled. "Truth to tell I'm pretty impressed with little spitfire here. She's something to see, yes she is. How old is she? Ten? My, my, pretty as a Georgia peach and mean as a snake. Got to love that combination. Yes, sir, Miss Lilah, you can go far in this world. Even in a world as big and bad as what we got."

"What we *have*," said Annie.

The big hunter guffawed. "Got me again. Haw! Not too many people pull a fast one on ol' Charlie Matthias," he said. "No sirree bob, and here I am having a ten-year-old kid cut her mark on me and her little sister correct my grammar. I am humbled. I truly am."

He laughed until tears ran down his cheeks. He was still chuckling when they opened the back door and stepped out. There were biters out there because there were always biters. Seven of them. George edged up with his own spear, but Charlie waved him back. "Don't get your panties in a bunch," he said. "I got this."

He had a thick leather gauntlet on his left arm that covered him from fingers to shoulder, and with his less heavily padded right he drew a broad-bladed machete. Because he still smelled of rot the biters didn't swarm him, and even seemed bemused while Charlie waded into them. The big hunter used his armored left to grab the zoms and hold them still for the whistling blade of the machete. He moved with the effortless efficiency of someone who'd done exactly this a thousand times. Or ten thousand. In seconds the zoms were cut to pieces. Most were still alive, but none were whole. None were a threat.

George looked down at the twitching torsos and snapping jaws and raised his spear to finish them.

"What for?" asked Charlie, annoyed.

"To give them peace."

Charlie laughed as George, Lilah and Annie quieted the dead. Killing the dead was important, almost a ritual for their family.

George told them that ever since the plague started everyone who died, no matter how they died, came back as a biter. Every single person. It was important to give everyone who needed it a chance at real peace. Even the biters, whom they all feared. After all, it wasn't their fault they'd become monsters.

George looked uneasy because of Charlie's laughter, but he shook it off. Then they took their wheelbarrow and followed the big man through the woods. His camp was five miles away and it was starting to drizzle by the time they got there. Even with the rain Lilah could smell the smoke from cooking fires, and soon they saw the plumes of smoke rising into the cloudy sky.

There were forty men in the camp.

All of them tough-looking, big, brutal, and smiling. They milled around George and the girls, laughing, slapping Charlie on the back, staring at the little girls, appraising George.

One man, a massive man with immensely broad shoulders and a badly scarred face pushed his way through the crowd. He had matched automatic pistols at his hips and had a long length of bloodstained black pipe swinging from his belt. He stopped next to Charlie, one hand on the big hunter's shoulder and studied the girls.

"What've you got here, Charlie?"

"A couple of fighters."

"Do tell?"

"The tall one's quick as lightning," said Charlie and he showed the cut on his shirt. "Never even saw that blade coming. Rattlesnake quick."

"Nice," said the other man, who some of the others called "the Motor City Hammer," or just "the Hammer." "You thinking of training her some more or putting her right into the games?"

"Oh, the games, no doubt," said Charlie. "Raw talent like that? Shoot. She's ready to rock and roll."

Lilah had no idea what they were talking about. These men didn't seem to be the kind who would want to play games. Not Monopoly or dolls or Legos. And, besides, what did that have to do with fighting?

George caught it, too. His smile faded. "What are you talking about? Games? What's that mean?"

Charlie squinted up into the rain, which was beginning to fall heavier now, fat drops popping on the leaves of the trees around the camp. "Storm's coming," he said. "Could be bad."

As if to emphasize his observation lightning forked across the sky and thunder rumbled like laughter behind the trees. Lilah glanced up, too. She'd rarely been outside during the rain because it was hard to hear the biters during a storm. Because she was looking up she never saw who it was that hit George.

She heard the sound. Heavy and wet and wrong, and then George fell against her, slumping, collapsing, his weapon falling away, his flopping hands knocking the spear from Lilah's hands. His improbably heavy weight dragged her down into the mud. Lilah hit her head the ground, jolting her neck, making stars explode in her eyes. She heard Annie scream.

Then there were hands on her, grabbing her wrists and elbows and ankles. Someone forced a thick pillowcase over her head. She caught one last glimpse of George, his face wet with rainwater and blood, sprawled on the ground.

That's when the world ended again.

And it was raining.

Because it always rained when the world ended.

-4-

It was starting to rain.

"We have to try," said Annie. "He'll be back soon."

"Shhh," Lilah said, "let me think."

The girls knelt by the door and looked out through the bars. The hall was empty. The guard's chair stood against the hall wall, a magazine opened face down on it, a beer bottle half-empty on the crate he used as a table. Lilah knew the routine. This guard, Henry, drank too much and he went out to the bathroom at least six times during his shift. Lilah had no watch, but she'd learned to count time. After all these months here she'd learned the feel of seconds and minutes and hours. They crawled like worms over her skin. Familiar and yet hateful. Another of the prisoners here—one of the few adults who lived in a cage down the hall—called it stacking time. You took those increments of time and built walls around you. Lilah understood it. The more time here in the cages the more she understood this world and what it was. In a way it was like reading a book because she learned something new every day.

Not just the rules of the games, but other stuff. How to watch. How to understand what she saw. How to understand the guards and what they wanted and what they thought. Knowing what the guards would do if Charlie and the Hammer let them. Knowing which ones might even have let them go if the world was a different world. Knowing which ones would do bad things to them if they could. Lilah and Annie knew all about those bad things. They'd seen them happen, and it had torn holes in the version of the world they'd always understood. Some of that stuff wasn't even in the books George let them read. It was sick stuff. Bad stuff. Awful stuff.

It was stuff that *might* happen to Annie and her if they started losing their fights down in the pits. Charlie told them that. So did the Hammer. They knew it made them want to fight harder. They knew it made them cooperative. It was simple math, too. Go into the pits and fight the zoms with whatever weapons they let the girls have, or get beaten up and handed over to the guards. No third choice.

Annie was nine now and Lilah was eleven, at least by Lilah's reckoning. As best she could estimate they had been here in Gameland for eleven months. Maybe a full year. It was cold again and the rains had started the way they usually did in January and February. It had been three weeks after New Year's Day when George had met Charlie and decided to bring him back to the house.

There had been two weeks of travel with Charlie's hunting party. Terrible days marked by beatings and starvation to teach manners. Then Charlie had learned that if he threatened Annie then Lilah would do anything, follow any order. After that there were fewer beatings but a lot of threats.

Except for the escape attempts. There had been savage beatings after those. Twice Lilah peed blood, and that scared her and Annie so bad they couldn't speak for days.

Experience is a great teacher. That's one of the things George had said a long time ago. Lilah made sure she learned from everything they experienced. Every single thing.

Like the timetable of the guards posted here in the Fighters' House. That's what they called it. From what Lilah had been told by other prisoners, the Fighters House used to be the Funhouse of an amusement park. Those were things the girls had read about. Places where people went to be shocked and scared for fun. How weird was that?

"He's going to be back soon," whined Annie.

"I know," said Lilah, keeping her voice low. "It's still early. He hasn't had that much to drink."

"But—"

"We have to wait until he goes for a long bathroom break."

"He doesn't always do that," protested her sister.

Lilah wrapped her arm around Annie's thin shoulders. "He does most of the time. He will tonight."

"How do you know?"

"I know," lied Lilah. Actually, she hoped she was right. Most nights Henry went out for a longer break, and when he did, he took his magazine or a book with him. Pee breaks were too quick. If he took something to read he'd be gone for at least twenty minutes, sometimes more. This was a new magazine for him, one Lilah hadn't seen. Maybe he'd settle down on the toilet and read it for a while.

The rain pinged against the plywood walls of the Fighters House. In the other cages she could hear kids crying or talking or snoring. One of them, a boy who had nearly lost the last couple of fights in the pits, kept talking to himself in a language of made up words. Lilah almost envied him. His mind was broken and he'd escaped into a nonsense world. Maybe he thought he was dreaming.

There was a fourteen-year-old girl in the cage next to them who was shivering in her sleep. The guards thought she'd gotten through her two-on-one pit fight without getting hurt, but Lilah knew better. The girl had been bitten and the fever was taking her. Maybe the guards would come for her tomorrow and open the cage without checking first. That would be nice. It would be even nicer if it was Charlie or the Hammer, but Lilah didn't think they'd be fooled. Not them. They were smart. Not book smart like George had been, but animal smart.

She glanced at the shivering girl in the next cage. Her name was Christine and she'd been hiding with a group of nuns in a building in the hills. Lilah heard rumors of what had happened to the nuns. She really hoped Christine got to bite someone after she turned.

A sound made Annie tense and Lilah looked up to see the door at the far end of the hall open and Henry come back in. He was whistling a song that Lilah didn't know. It was a happy song, and that made Lilah really hate him.

Henry walked down the hall to the T-junction where the two sisters were caged. He looked up and down the side halls, nodded to himself, and walked back to his chair.

Annie hung her head and clenched her fists. "We should have gone."

Lilah kissed her on the head. "We will, I promise."

"Tonight?"

Lilah studied Henry and listened to the rain. If the storm got heavier the noise would help them. She usually hated the rain, but not tonight. She waited until Henry was concentrating on what he was reading and then she pushed lightly on the door. They'd spent hours and hours very quietly filing at the metal, and all they needed to do was give it one or two good kicks to pop it open. It would make noise. The rain whispered to her that it was going to help her this time. It promised that it was her friend this time.

"Yes," she said.

-5-

Henry did not move for over three hours. By then the rain was hammering on the walls and ceiling and the noise was deafening inside.

Perfect.

When he finally got up, he folded his magazine and tucked it under his arm, gave the cages a quick inspection, then walked toward the exit, once more whistling that song. The door banged shut behind him.

"Now!" hissed Lilah. She and Annie lay on their backs near the door and bent their knees. "Three, two—*go!*"

They kicked out with all their strength.

And the door shuddered but did not open.

"Hey!" yelled someone else. The adult in the cage down the row. "Keep it down … some of us are trying to sleep."

"Again," growled Lilah, and they kicked once more.

A third time. A fourth.

"Yo! What the heck are you doing down there?"

Five. Six. Seven.

"You're going get us all in trouble."

Eight. Nine. Annie was crying, her kicks becoming wild, desperate, sloppy. But Lilah was getting mad. She ground her teeth together and kicked, kicked, kicked.

Fourteen, fifteen.

And *bang*.

The door flew open so hard it slammed against the outside wall and whipped back to crunch against their feet. Annie cried out in pain, but Lilah just snarled. She grabbed her sister, pushed her up and shoved her out of the cage, then swarmed out after her. The thunder outside was a continuous bellow and the rain hammered down. Even so, Lilah crouched for a moment and listened for Henry's footsteps, listened for him to yell.

Nothing.

The kids in the other cages stared at her. A few reached out between the bars with desperate fingers, clawing at the air as if they could pull themselves out. Annie and Lilah stared at them.

"Can we get them out?" whispered Annie, her words nearly washed away by the storm.

"No," said Lilah.

Saying that word hurt as bad as getting punched in the chest. It hurt her heart to say it. It hurt worse to know that it was true. They had no tools other than the small metal rasp they'd used on their own bar and it would take as many days to free even one of them as it had to cut their own lock. There was no time and no way. Lilah grabbed Annie's hand and pulled her away.

"I'm sorry!"

Annie's cry was as sharp and high as a gull's call. The kids in the other cages began to scream. Not yell. Scream.

Those screams chased the girls down the hall. They rose like the cries of storybook banshees to fill the night and howl louder than the storm itself.

"Hey!" came the muffled voice of Henry from the other side of the building. Even with all of the rain and thunder he'd heard those screams. "Hey, what's happening in there?"

Lilah pushed Annie toward the outside door. There was a fire axe hung on the wall held by metal clips. Lilah paused and tore it free. It was far too heavy for her, clumsy and awkward. But it was a weapon. She stared for a moment at the wickedly sharp edge of the blade. Then she whirled and ran after her sister who was already out in the rain.

Gameland was a massive sprawl of buildings, disused rides, concession stands, and other buildings whose nature Lilah didn't know or understand. There were big tents near the center of the park and the girls ran away from them as fast as they could. Those tents had not been part of the amusement park but had instead been erected later. Scavenged, Lilah had been told, from a circus where everything—human and animal—had been consumed by the biters. Now the big tents rose above the trees, enclosing bleachers for paying customers who would sit and hoot, cry, call, boo, and cheer at the action. And that action took place inside any one of a dozen wide, shallow pits. Fighting pits. Kids—almost always kids—would be lowered down into the pits and zoms would be shoved over the edge. Sometimes the kids were given weapons, but not always. Sometimes all they had were their hands, their fear and whatever skills they had managed to learn.

Lilah and Annie had survived those pits for months. Even little Annie had killed down there. Killed and killed and killed. There were times she would be pulled out of the pit covered from head to toe in black blood, madness boiling in her eyes but a killer's grin on her mouth. Lilah worried about her sister. She knew that ever since George had agreed to leave the house with Charlie, Annie had become strange. Scared at nights in the cage but fierce and maybe crazy down in the pits.

Lilah wondered if she, too, had gone mad. She did not come grinning from the pits, but she fought with a savagery that surprised even herself. With blades or hammers, with golf clubs or a tennis racket, with a screwdriver or her own bare hands, she had fought the biters and killed them.

One hundred and nineteen so far.

More than anyone else in Gameland.

With each kill she felt herself grow stronger and felt herself grow colder. Meaner. Stranger.

She wondered what it would do to her when she killed her first living person. She thought of Charlie and the Hammer. She wanted to use the axe on them so badly that it made her sick. It also made her excited in ways that she had never felt before. She was free. *They* were free, she and Annie, and Lilah had a weapon.

They ran through the rain, which pounded down in sheets. It turned the ground to mud that was as cold and which clung to their feet, slowing them, trying to stop and hold them.

"Keep going," cried Lilah every time Annie slowed down or stumbled. "Don't stop."

The best path out of Gameland was to the north, but it was a long slope uphill to the trees. Hard-packed dirt and lots of rocks. Annie fell over and over again, and Lilah had to haul her up time and again until finally they staggered forward at little more than a slow walk. Water ran downhill like a small river, chilling them to the bone.

Suddenly the air above them flashed white and they looked up to see something rise into the night sky. A flare. It cast everything into a glow of ghostly white, and painted them like black bugs against the slope. Off in the distance, Lilah heard someone yell. Henry? No. The Hammer.

"There!"

"Run, Annie ... *run*!"

"I ... can't...." Annie cried, but she tried. And fell. Got up. And fell again. Lilah hooked her under the arm and dragged her to her feet every time.

They ran, but Annie was slipping too much. Lilah finally realized that they weren't going to make it. The men were coming.

They would catch them and they would do every bad thing they'd promised to do.

To them.

To Annie.

"God," cried Lilah, begging the rainy sky for mercy. "Please."

Lighting flashed again and again, the bolts coming one after another, and in their glow Lilah saw something off to the left hand side of the road. It was an old abandoned car, choked with weeds, rusted, sitting on rotted tires. Beyond it were others. Fifty, maybe a hundred of them. Without a moment's hesitation she pushed Annie toward them.

Back on the road there were big shapes moving their way. She saw the distinctive bulk of the Hammer leading them. No time, no time.

"W-what—?" asked Annie, her teeth chattering from cold and fear. "What are you doing?"

"Get in there," snapped Lilah, pushing her toward one of the cars. It lay on its side, crushed up against a tree. The trunk hung open. Lilah shoved Annie inside and then tore wet shrubs and branches to cover her. "Stay here and be quiet."

"Wait!" cried the little girl. "Don't leave me. You can't!"

Lilah knelt quickly by her sister. She caressed her cheek and kissed her forehead. "Shhh, you have to be quiet. I'm not leaving you, Annie. I'm going to play a trick on the men."

"A trick?"

"I've got to lead them away, like George used to lead the biters away from the house. Only instead of using noise, I'm going to leave a fake trail. You understand?"

Annie clung to her. "Please don't leave me alone. I'll go with you. I can help."

"No. You know I'm faster alone. You need to stay here and be quiet. The biters can't find you here and the men will follow me," Lilah said, having to lean close to be heard with the noise of the storm. "I'll lead them way up the road and then cut back through the forest like George taught us."

"But—"

"Trust me, Annie. I'll be back for you," Lilah said. "You'll be safe here."

Annie stared at her with terrified eyes. "You won't let them get me?"

"I promise, Annie. I swear to God and cross my heart."

"You won't leave me ever?"

"I won't. You know I won't."

"Never ever?"

"Never ever."

"Say it, Lilah," begged Annie. "Say you promise."

"God, I promise to never ever leave you. I'll keep you safe always and forever." She kissed Annie's cheeks. "But I have to go do this now. I promise I'll be right back. Just stay here and wait for me."

Annie promised her, but she was crying when she made that promise. And Lilah was crying when she closed the trunk lid and moved off. The sobs hurt her so deeply. But they also made her clutch the axe with greater strength. The thought of what would happen to Annie if she did this wrong turned the cold of the rain into fire. It filled her chest and burned in the back of her throat.

She ran through the rain.

-6-

George had taught the girls a lot about the woods. About the forest, and about tracking. As he learned it from books and firsthand, he shared it with his adopted daughters, rediscovering the ancient sciences of tracking and woodcraft, of stealth and deception. Lilah used everything she'd learned and she put her own thoughts into it. She was a natural at it because she had been born into a world of hunting and killing, and of thwarting hunters and not being killed.

She let herself be seen on the road, waiting for lightning flashes so they could spot her. And then when the darkness fell, she ran off the path and circled back and laid false trails and broke branches so they could see the path of her flight. The Hammer led the chase, and he sent men along eight different false trails. Lilah could feel the seconds and minutes burning off, but she knew she was doing it right. The men would never give up, she knew that much. They hated her and Annie for making fools of them; and if they didn't drag them back to the cages it would be harder to control the others. They had to win. And some of them probably ached to be part of the punishments. Not all of the men were that evil, but enough of them were.

Enough.

Lilah encountered two biters in the woods, but they were no problem. She had the axe and she had her rage. She left the bodies where they could be found and where they would mark false escape routes.

The storm got heavier still, as if the universe itself was an audience at a new kind of Gameland, cheering on the winners and the losers with equal mad intensity.

Finally, when the storm was at its wildest, Lilah left the road and went into the forest, working a long, random path back to the abandoned cars. Back to Annie. She had already worked out their real escape route. It was risky but the men would never expect the girls to circle around Gameland and head south. That way was filled with biters and the slopes down the hill were difficult. For them, definitely, but for two girls willing to take risks and who were as strong as life could make them ... maybe not. Lilah thought they could make it. Down south there was a river, and if they crossed that then not even a pack of dogs could track them. There would be houses and buildings where they could hide, and animals to hunt in the woods. They would survive. She believed that with all her heart.

Lightning whitewashed the forest and she saw it gleam off the curved corpses of the cars. Her heart lifted because there were no men around. Except for the rain it was quiet and still. Gripping the axe, Lilah crept forward, moving between the automobiles and trucks, moving as silently through the mud as she could until she saw the overturned car.

Then her heart seemed to tear itself loose from the inside of her chest.

The trunk lid was open.

And Annie was not there.

-7-

Lilah ran forward and tore at the debris in the trunk, but there was no trace of her sister. The mud at her feet was a confusion of puddles that told her nothing.

Nothing.

She reeled, feeling the ground under her tilt like one of those ancient amusement rides. She wanted to vomit. She wanted to die.

She tried to scream.

But as she opened her mouth, she heard Annie.

She heard Annie scream.

And she heard the harsh, grating laugh of the Motor City Hammer.

-8-

Lilah ran through the rain, tripping twice in deep puddles. The second time she fell so hard that the axe went flying from her hands and vanished into the mud. She gagged, coughing rain and dirty water from her mouth, and when she looked for the axe, she couldn't find it. The mud and puddles had swallowed it whole.

There was another scream. High and terrible. It rose and rose and then …

It stopped.

Cut short.

Lilah rose screeching from the puddle and ran for a dozen feet on hands and feet, scampering like a dog. The storm winds stole her memory of where the screams had come from and she lost her way in the dark. Then she found the road and realized that this is where Annie must have been.

The rain fell like sharp needles as Lilah staggered out of the woods and onto the muddy road. Gameland was back there, the tent and rusted rides painted white with each burst of lightning. In the distance, down the slope, she saw the Motor City Hammer walking slowly away, his black pipe club loose in one hand, swinging as he walked.

He was alone. Annie was not with him.

Because Annie was there on the road.

Lilah stood on trembling legs, staring at the scene. Reading the truth of it because it was there to be read. Annie had waited too long and gotten scared, had doubted that Lilah was going to keep her promise and come back. In her fear she'd crept to the road to take a look. And there she'd met the Motor City Hammer.

There were footprints and skid marks from scuffling feet, and as Lilah watched the rain filled them in, softened their edges, and melted them away.

Annie was there. The scuff marks showed where she'd tried to run. It showed where she'd slipped and fell.

She lay there in the rain.

She looked like she was asleep. Eyes closed, lashes brushing her beautiful cheeks, head resting in a pillow.

Except that it wasn't a pillow.

It was a rock.

Lilah felt herself fall. Her knees buckled and she dropped down beside the little body. Annie's pale hair was darker where it curled around the rock, and when the lightning flashed, the red was too red.

Too red.

Too red.

Lilah gathered her sister up in her arms and held her gently. So gently. As if afraid to wake her up from a nap. She pulled her close and rocked her, crooning a little lullaby that George used to sing to both of them. The fires in Lilah's chest burned out and the rain turned the ashes to ice, and still she held her sister.

Lightning burst above them and the thunder roared.

And still she held little Annie.

It was raining and the world had ended.

She knew what would happen next. What had to happen. George had schooled them on it. And Lilah's earliest memories confirmed it. When Mommy had died the other survivors— George included—had known, and they had used sticks and clubs. You couldn't call it "quieting" Mommy. There had been too many screams. But it was the same thing.

Annie twitched.

Tears burned on Lilah's face. They were the only heat in the world.

Annie was going to wake up soon. And she would wake up hungry. Of course she would. There were no fairy tale endings to make this all right. Annie would wake up as one of them—a biter. Then she would want to bite.

Anyone. Anything.

She would want to bite Lilah.

Annie wouldn't be able to help herself.

That was how the world was.

The rain fell and Annie twitched again. And again. The rock onto which Annie had fallen was right there within easy reach.

But, no. That was an impossible choice.

Impossible.

Impossible.

Lilah turned her face up to the rain and wondered what to do. Her heart was so badly broken that she could not bear to think of moving away from this place. Annie was here and when she woke up she would want to eat. No … she would *need* to eat. She would be a small ghost, a tiny monster. What chance would she have of ever catching food? She would wander, lost and hungry forever.

I promise to never ever leave you. I'll keep you safe always and forever.

That's what Lilah had told her, and she'd sworn to God and crossed her heart.

Annie's fingers opened and closed, but Lilah kept her pressed against her. She didn't want to see her sister open her eyes and not find Annie in there.

I promise to never ever leave you.

The rain washed over her face and stole her tears.

It would be so easy to do nothing. To let Annie wake up. To let Annie have what she needed. To be there for her sister. And, afterward, if there was enough left of her, maybe Lilah would rise, too, and they would go off together. Two sisters. They were already strange and they were already killers. Why shouldn't they be monsters together?

God, it was better than the unbearable thought of being alone. Without Annie. Without George or anyone. Alone.

Annie began to struggle now. She was awake. Her fingers clawed at Lilah, grabbing at cloth, at hair. Her mouth opened, but Lilah held her with crushing force, not allowing her to bite.

Not unless that was the right thing to do.

"Please," she said, begging the night and the storm. "Please."

I promise to never ever leave you.

"I love you, Annie," she said in her raspy, ghostly voice. "I will always, always love you."

Annie thrashed in her arms. All Lilah had to do was ease the pressure just a little. Just an inch. Make the decision and join her sister. It was the only choice that made sense. Every other choice was completely insane. She could not live without Annie. She didn't want to.

I promise to never ever leave you.

Lilah held her sister with one arm, holding on with all of the love she had left in the cold furnace of her soul.

And with the other hand she reached for the rock.

It rained the day the world ended.

* * *

Jonathan Maberry *is a NY Times bestselling novelist, five-time Bram Stoker Award winner, and comic book writer. He writes the Joe Ledger thrillers, the Rot & Ruin series, the Nightsiders series, the Dead of Night series, as well as standalone novels in multiple genres. His comic books include* Captain America, Bad Blood, Rot & Ruin, V-Wars, *and others. He is the editor of many anthologies including* The X-Files, Scary Out There, Out of Tune, *and* V-Wars. *His books* Extinction Machine *and* V-Wars *are in development for TV, and* Rot & Ruin *is in development as a series of feature films. He was a featured expert on the History Channel documentary,* Zombies: A Living History *and a regular expert on the TV series,* True Monsters. *Jonathan lives in Del Mar, California with his wife, Sara Jo.*
jonathanmaberry.com

One of the most unique voices working today in speculative fiction, and one of my favorite writers, Nigerian American author Nnedi Okorafor's stories frequently feature African culture and characters. Her latest is set in Ghana and focuses on a girl with unusual connections ... to death.

SANKOFA

BY NNEDI OKORAFOR

The moon was rising when Sankofa came up the dirt road. Her leather sandals softly slapped her heels as she walked. Small swift steps made with small swift feet. When she passed, the crickets did not stop singing, the owls did not stop hooting, and the aardvark in the bushes beside the road did not stop foraging for termites.

Sankofa was thirteen years old, but her petite frame and chubby cheeks made her look closer to ten. Her outfit was a miniature version of what the older more affluent women of northern Ghana wore—a hand-dyed long yellow skirt, a matching top embroidered with expensive lace and a purple and yellow headband made of twisted cloth. She'd done the headband exactly as her mother used to when she visited friends. Sankofa covered her bald head with a shorthaired black wig. She'd slathered her scalp with two extra coats of thick shea butter, so the wig wasn't itchy at all. Despite the night's cloying heat, the shea butter and her elaborate heavy outfit, she felt quite cool ... at the moment.

A young man leaned against a mud hut smoking a cigarette in the dark. As he was blowing out smoke, he spotted her. Choking on the last puff, he cupped his hand over his mouth. "Sankofa is coming," he hollered in Ewe, grabbing the doorknob and shoving the door open. "Sankofa is coming!"

People peeked out windows, doorways, from around corners and over their shoulders. Noses flared, eyes were wide, mouths opened and healthy hearts pounded like crazy.

"Sankofa. *Na* come!" someone shouted in Pidgin English.

"Sankofa is here!"

"Sankofa strolling!"

"Sankofa, *Sankofa*, o!"

"Here she comes!"

"Beware of remote control, o!"

"Sankofa bird landing!"

Women scooped up toddlers playing in the dirt and ushered them inside. Doors slammed. Steps quickened. Car doors slammed and cars sped off.

The girl called Sankofa walked up the quiet deserted road of the town that was pretending to be full of ghosts. Her face was dark and sweet and her jaw was set. The only item she carried was the amulet bag the juju man had given her five years ago not long after she left home. The size of a grown man's fist, it softly bounced against her hip. Its contents were simple: a roll of money that she rarely needed, a wind-up watch, a large jar of shea butter, a hand drawn map of Accra and a tightly rolled up book. For the last week, her book had been a copy of *No Orchids for Miss Blandish*, a paper novel she barely understood yet enjoyed reading. Before that, a crumbling copy of *Gulliver's Travels*.

The town was obviously not poor. There were huts but they were well built and this night, though dark as caves, Sankofa could see hints of bright light coming from within. People feared her but they still wanted to watch television. These mud huts had electricity. Beside the huts were modern homes, which equally feigned vacancy. Sankofa felt the town staring at her as she walked. Hoping, wishing, praying that she would pass through, a wraith in the darkness.

She set her eye on the largest most modern-looking home in the neighborhood. The huge hulking white mansion with a red roof surrounded by a large white concrete gate topped with broken green bottle glass was easy to see. As she approached the white gate, she noticed a large black spider walking up the side. Its stretching legs and hairy robust body looked like the hand of a ghost.

"Good evening," Sankofa said as she stepped up to the gate's door. The spider paused, seeming to acknowledge and greet her back. Then it continued on its way up, into the forest of broken glass on the top of the gate. Sankofa smiled. Spiders always had better things to do. She wondered what story it would weave about her and how far the story would carry. She lifted her chin, raised a small fist and knocked on the gate's door. "Excuse me, I would like to come in," she called in English. She wasn't sure how far she'd come. Better to stick to the language most understood. "Gateman, I have come to call on the family that lives here."

When there was no response, she turned the knob. She wasn't surprised that it was unlocked. The gateman stood on the other side of the large driveway, near the garage. He wore navy blue pants, a crisp white shirt and a blank look on his face. He had prayer beads in his hand and when he saw her, he worked them through his fingers even faster. There was a light on over the garage and she could see his face clearly. Then he turned and spat to the side, making no move to escort her to the house.

"Thank you, sir," Sankofa said, walking to the large front door. The doorway light was off. "I will show myself in."

Up close, the house looked less elegant, the white walls were stained at the bottom with red dirt, splashed there as mud during rainy season. And there were large dirty spider webs in the upper corners where the roof met the walls. A shiny silver Mercedes, a black BMW, and a blue Honda sat in the driveway. The garage was closed. The house was dark. But Sankofa knew people were home.

Something flew onto her shoulder as she stepped up to the front door. She stifled the instinct to crush it dead and, instead, grabbed it. Gently, she opened her hand. It was a large green grasshopper. She'd seen this one in one of the books she read. A katydid. She giggled, watching it crawl up her hand with its long delicate green legs.

She softly glowed a leaf green. Not enough to kill but enough to bath the grasshopper in a shade of its own lovely greenness. If a grasshopper could smile this one did. She was sure of it. Then it hop-flew off. "Safe adventures," she whispered.

She knocked on the door. "It is me," she called. "Death has come to visit."

After a few moments, the front door lights came on. She looked up at the round ball of glass lit by the light bulb. In a few minutes, insects would people the light. But not yet. A haggard-looking tall man in a black suit and tie slowly opened the door. The lights turned on behind him and she could see about ten well-dressed adults, some in traditional clothing, others in stiff Western attire, all pressed together, wide-eyed and afraid. Cooled air wafted through the opened door and it smelled like wine, champagne, goat meat and jollof rice. The air-conditioner and the house cooks were working hard tonight. The hallway was decorated with shiny red and green trimming and fake poinsettia flowers, a plastic ornamented Christmas tree at the far end.

"I hope I am not interrupting your Christmas party," Sankofa said. She blinked. Was it Christmas? Maybe it was still Christmas Eve? She felt a muffled pang deep in her chest and pushed it away as she always did.

"No, no," the man jabbered, smiling sheepishly. "Em … p-please. Come in, my dear. Happy Christmas, o." He wore a silver chain with a crucifix around his neck. The crucifix rested on his shoulder. He'd just put it on, probably as he rushed to the door. Sankofa chuckled.

"Happy Christmas, to you all, too," she said. "I won't stay long."

She slid her sandals off and left them by the door as she stepped inside. The solid marble floors were cool beneath her bare feet. The walls were covered with European style oil paintings of European rustic landscapes. Sankofa wondered what trouble these people went through to get these paintings all the way out to this small affluent town not far from Accra. And she wondered if it was worth it; the paintings were quite ugly. A large family photo hung on the wall, too. It was of a tall fat man, a fat woman with one fat son and two fat daughters. Happy content people and definitely "been-tos." If she had to guess, she'd say from America.

In the dining room, Sankofa was asked to sit at a large table laden with more food than she'd seen in weeks. It was nearly obscene. She'd never imagined that been-tos ate so many native dishes. Kele-wele, aponchi-krakra and fufu, kenkey, waakye, red red, jollof rice, fried chicken, akrantie and goat meat, too much food to get her eyes around. "Oh *charli*," she muttered to herself. Behind her, the house party came in and stood around.

A young woman set an empty plate before her. She wore a uniform similar to the gate man's—a white blouse and navy blue pants. "Do you …" The woman trailed off, her eyes watering with tears. She paused, looking into Sankofa's eyes. Sankofa gazed right back.

"I would also like a change in clothes," Sankofa helpfully said. "I have been wearing these garments for a week."

The woman smiled gratefully and nodded. Sankofa guessed the woman was about ten years older her senior, maybe even twenty-five. "Something like what you are wearing now?" the woman asked.

Sankofa grinned at this. "Yes, if possible," she said. "I like to wear our people's style."

The woman seemed to relax. "I know. We all know."

"My name is known here?" Sankofa asked, the answer being obvious.

"Very well," she said. The woman looked at the silent party. "Can someone call the seamstress?"

"It's already done," a fat woman said stepping forward as she closed a cell phone. Sankofa recognized her quickly. She looked a little fatter than she had in the family photo. Life was good for her. "Miss Sankofa," the lady of the house said. "You shall have whatever garments you like within the hour." She paused. "The town has always anticipated a visit from you."

Sankofa smiled again. "That is good."

"You would like orange Fanta, right?" the young woman in the uniform asked her. "Room temperature, not chilled."

Sankofa smiled and nodded. These were good people.

* * *

The people from the Christmas party watched Sankofa eat. Unable to sit down. Unable to whisper amongst themselves. Paralyzed. Sankofa was ravenous. She'd been walking all day.

The food was glorious. She gnawed on a goat bone and dropped it on her plate. Then with greasy hands, she took her bottle of warm Fanta and guzzled the last of it. She belched as another was placed before her. The young woman popped the cap and stepped back.

"Thank you," Sankofa said, taking a gulp. She picked up another piece of spicy goat meat and paused. She turned to the silent party. "Are there any children in the house?" she asked. "I would like some company."

She nibbled on her piece of goat meat as the adults fearfully whispered amongst themselves. It was the same wherever she visited. They always whispered. Sometimes they cried. Sometimes they shouted. Always amongst each other. Away from her. Then they went and got the children. They knew they had no choice. This time was no different.

A plump boy of about ten and an older equally plump girl about Sankofa's age, shuffled in. The girl's mother, the lady of the house, had to shove her in. They wore their nightclothes and looked like they'd been dragged out of bed. They plopped themselves across from her at the table. The boy eyed a plate of fried plantain.

"So what are your names?" Sankofa asked.

"Edgar," the boy said. Sankofa blinked. He spoke like an American. She'd been right in her assessment. Americans were always so well-fed.

The girl muttered something Sankofa couldn't catch. "What?" Sankofa asked.

"Ye," the girl whispered. She spoke like an American, too.

"It is nice to meet you," Sankofa said. "Do you know who I am?"

"You're Sankofa, the one who sleeps at death's door," Edgar said. He eyed her as he slowly took a sliced fried plantain. Sankofa took a few of the oily slices, too. They were sweet and tangy. Edgar seemed to relax when he saw that she enjoyed the same food as him.

"You should get a plate," Sankofa said. Before Edgar could look around, the young woman placed a plate before each of them. The girl took all of two plantain slices and the boy loaded his plate with plantain and roasted goat meat. Sankofa liked the boy.

"You don't look as ugly as they say you look," he said.

Sankofa laughed. "Really?"

"No," he said, biting into some goat meat. "Your outfit reminds me of my mom."

"Reminds me of mine, too," Sankofa said. "That's why I wear it."

They ate for a moment.

"So what'd you get for Christmas?" she asked.

"We haven't opened presents yet," he said, laughing. "It's Christmas Eve."

"Oh." She fixed her eye on the girl. "Ye," she said.

The girl jumped at the sound of her name.

"I'm not going to kill you," Sankofa said.

"How do I know that?"

Sankofa frowned, annoyed. "You're not very good company."

Edgar leaned forward. "We only hear about you from our cousins," he said. His eyes narrowed. "So is it true? Can you …"

"Can I what?"

He glanced at his sister. She had stopped eating and was frowning deeply at him.

"I can," Sankofa said. "You want to see?"

The party adults moaned. "This boy is an idiot," she heard one of them hiss. "You don't tempt the devil!"

"*Charli*, make him shut up!" someone else whispered. "He's going to get us all killed."

Sankofa glanced at the adults and then looked piercingly at the kids before her. She smirked. "Turn off the lights." The boy jumped up, ran, and shut the lights off. She smiled when she heard him snatch his arm from his protesting mother and take his seat across from her.

In the past, it had been difficult to control. And there had been terrible consequences. But not any longer. Since she'd turned thirteen, months ago, she could keep herself from killing by accident, as long as she was not in pain. It was like flexing a muscle.

Right there in the darkness, she glowed a dim green. Ye whimpered. Sankofa could see tears freely rolling down the girl's cheek. The boy's eyes were wide and he had an enormous grin on his face. "Real life 'remote control'!" he whispered. "Wow!"

She relaxed herself and her glow faded and then winked out. Someone flipped the lights on.

"What is this town called?" she asked getting up.

"Nsawam," Edgar said.

"Relax, Ye," she said. "You won't see me here again."

Ye wiped the tears from her face, then got up and ran out of the room. Sankofa and Edgar looked at each other.

"So where are you going next?" Edgar asked.

"Accra," she said. She smiled, glad that he had not run. She hated when that happened. It always made her feel that ache she worked so hard to mute.

"Why?"

She shrugged. "Don't know yet. I just have a feeling. But I've been walking on foot for a month."

"You really can't ride in cars?"

She shook her head.

"That's so cool," he whispered.

"Not really."

"Are you a child of the d—?"

"No," she snapped. The conversation ended there.

*   *   *

She left the house an hour later having eaten her fill, taken some leftovers, and showered. She'd traded *No Orchids for Miss Blandish* for another paper novel Edgar insisted she read titled *Mouse Guard*. He said he'd gotten it from the trip his family recently took to the UK and that it was one of the only paper books he owned. She hadn't wanted to take such a precious item from him but he insisted.

She now wore a brand new blue and white wrapper, matching top and headband. She walked with her head up and looked into the night with the confidence of a leopard. She liked to imagine that she was an Ashanti princess walking the moonlit road toward her long lost queendom. If she had to guess, her mother would have been proud of the way she chose to carry herself … despite it all.

There were footsteps behind her. She whirled around. It was the gateman from the house she'd just left. The one who had looked at her as if she were a smear of feces on some child's underwear.

"Evil witch!" he cried. *"Obayifo!"* He was sweating and weeping. "Kwaku Agya. Do you know this name? Do you remember my brother's name? Does the child of the devil remember the names of those it kills?"

"I know the name," she said. Sankofa remembered all the names.

Surprise and then rage rippled across his face. He raised something black in his hand.

Blam!

Time always slowed for her during these kinds of moments. The misty white smoke plumed from the gun's muzzle. Then the bullet, this one golden, short and dented. It flew out of the gun's muzzle followed by a larger plume of white smoke. The bullet rotated counter-clockwise as it traveled toward her. She watched this as the heat bloomed from her like a round mushroom. During times like this, it was near involuntary. From somewhere deep within her soul, a primal part of her gave permission. That part of her had been on the earth, walking the soils of the lands known as Ghana for millennia.

The night lit up.

The empty road.

The trees.

The houses and huts nearby.

The eyes of the silent witnesses.

The gnats, mosquitoes, flies, grasshoppers, beetles, some in flight, some not. The hiding, always observing spiders. The birds in the trees. The lizards on the walls. And the grasscutter crossing the road a few feet away. Washed in light that did not come from the moon.

The corona of soft green light domed out from Sankofa. To her, it felt like the shiver of a fever. It left a coppery smell in her nose. The bullet exploded feet from her with a gentle *pop!* The molten pieces flew into the flesh of a palm tree beside the road.

Sankofa shined like a moon who knew it was a sun. The light came from her skin. It poured from her, strong and controlled. It washed over everything but it was only hungry for the man who shot at her. It hadn't always been this way. In the past, her light's appetite was all-encompassing.

The man stumbled back. The gun in his hand dropped to the ground. Then he dropped, too.

Sankofa walked up to him, still glowing strong. She knelt down, looking into the gateman's dying eyes. "Your brother's name was Kwaku Samuel Agya and his cancer was so advanced that it had eaten away most of his internal organs. I did not cause this cancer, gateman. I happened to walk into the village when he was ready to die. He asked me to take him. His wife asked me to take him. His son asked me to take him. His best friend asked me to take him." Tears fell from her eyes as she spoke. Then she pushed away the pain in her chest. She muted it. Her tears dried into trails of salt as her skin heated. She stood up. "When was the last time you spoke to your brother, gateman?"

His skin crackled and peeled as it burned orange. It blackened, flaking off into dust. His entrails spilled out in a hot steaming mass when his skin and abdominal flesh burned away. Then that burned, too. The muscle and fat from his limbs flared up and then fell to ash, as well. There was little smoke but the air began to smell like burning leaves. As always, a mysterious wind came and swept away the ash and soon all that was left was one bone. It dried, snapped, splintered, and then cooled. Someone would find it.

She turned away, opened her bag and brought out the jar of thick yellow shea butter. She scooped out a dollop. She rubbed it in her hands until it softened and melted. Then she rubbed it into the skin on her arms, legs, neck, face and belly. She sighed as her dry skin absorbed the natural moisturizer. Then she walked into the night as if she were her own moon.

* * *

Nnedi Okorafor's *books include* Lagoon *(a British Science Fiction Association Award finalist for Best Novel),* Who Fears Death *(a World Fantasy Award winner for Best Novel),* Kabu Kabu *(a Publisher's Weekly Best Book for Fall 2013),* Akata Witch *(an Amazon.com Best Book of the Year),* Zahrah the Windseeker *(winner of the Wole Soyinka Prize for African Literature), and* The Shadow Speaker *(a CBS Parallax Award winner). Her adult novel* The Book of Phoenix *(prequel to* Who Fears Death*) was released in May 2015; the New York Times called it a "triumph." Her novella* Binti *was released in late September 2015 and her young adult novel* Akata Witch 2: Breaking Kola *will be released in 2016. Nnedi holds a PhD in literature/creative writing and is an associate professor at the University at Buffalo, New York (SUNY). She splits her time between Buffalo and Chicago with her daughter Anyaugo and family. Learn more about Nnedi at Nnedi.com.*

Next, award winning author Jennifer Brozek takes us to the future and a world where families live with the fear of being ripped apart by Takers, who choose children and take them away at a certain age. Is that a gift or a curse? No one is certain.

THE PRINCE OF ARTEMIS V

BY JENNIFER BROZEK

A princess is a servant to all of her people. She's supposed to care for them and never let them down. Ever," Lanteri said.

Hart nodded at his little sister. "What's the first rule of being a princess?"

"Never, ever abandon your people—for they need you more than you know," she said in a tone so serious that it would have indicated satire if it had not come from an eight-year-old's mouth.

"You're a very good princess."

"I'm trying." She smiled at her older brother. "But sometimes, it's hard."

"I know. As Dad says, 'Nothing good …'"

"'… ever comes easy,'" they both finished together and then grinned.

Lanteri bent over her pixel board and continued to draw her idea of the perfect castle. She drew each line slowly, dragging the pixel pen over the board. Whenever a line was not exactly as she wanted it, she turned the pixel pen over to erase the offending pixels, before going back to her masterpiece. She had been working on this particular picture for weeks.

Hart watched her, envying both her ability to manipulate the pixel board and her imagination. He, himself, had never had her artistic talent and had not drawn anything since that night five years ago … since Toor was Taken. Though only thirteen, Hart felt old. He felt like his parents must feel after a long day in the fields of harvesting the purpuran flower buds. He hoped that Lanteri would never have to feel the way he did right now. Especially as the double moons of Artemis V readied themselves to rise in their annual double-full arc tonight.

The opening and closing of the front door signaled the arrival of their parents. Neither child moved from their respective places in their shared bedroom. The conversation between their parents, or argument as it seemed to be, echoed through the small Company-provided house.

"They all look at me like she's already been Taken," Hart heard his mother say. He could imagine the distressed flush of his mother's face. "We've got to do something."

"The Company doesn't give a damn what happens to us. As long as the purpuran flowers are harvested and the royal dye is made, they don't care." In his mind's eye, Hart could see his father's drawn face and strength failing in his old man's body.

"We've got to do something. Anything. Stop the purpuran shipments. Get their attention." His mother's voice had softened to the whine of a wounded animal. "I can't go through this again."

"Saneri, the last time we tried something like that the Company almost starved us to death. The only thing that grows on this mudball is the purpuran flower. The Company doesn't care. The empire doesn't care. The empress herself can't know of this and even if she did, would she care? No. I don't think so. There are no rescuers. No brave guardsmen. No heroic Hedari. No stranger SLINGing in from another galaxy who'll come roaring to the rescue. We only have us to depend on. That's how it's always been."

"I can't go through this again. I can't lose her."

Hart reached over and closed the bedroom door to shut out their parents' pain and worry, and most of all, their helplessness. He hoped Lanteri had not heard their parents' despair but, as all hopes were dashed on Artemis V, this one was too.

"In my world," Lanteri said without looking up from her pixel drawing of a castle in a beautiful sunny landscape, "there are no Takers and no one's afraid of losing their children."

*   *   *

"I'm going to Nori's," Lanteri called as she headed out the door.

"Wait!" Saneri called.

Hart, sitting at the kitchen table, heard the panic in his mother's voice and hoped Lanteri would not. He also hoped that their mother would not ground Lanteri on what might be her last day alive.

Lanteri stopped, turned and gave her mother an impatient look. "What?"

"Uh, don't forget your coat."

"I'm just going next door, Mom."

"Don't you sass me. Go get your coat or you're not going anywhere."

Lanteri sighed and stomped back to the bedroom to get her coat. Hart listened as their mother paced, then fussed with Lanteri's coat. "You be back before dark. You hear me?"

"It's not like it's gonna get all that dark with the double full moon, Mom."

Hart smiled at the defiance in his little sister's voice.

"Lanteri …" Their mother's voice had a warning note in it that promised pain and punishment if she were not obeyed.

Another sigh. "Yes, ma'am. Before dark. Can I go now?" Lanteri asked.

There was a pause before their mother's reluctant answer came, "Yes. Ok. Go."

Hart knew their mother would not make that kind of fuss about him if he wanted to go over to a friend's house today. It made him hurt a little more inside. He waited for his mother to come to the kitchen.

Saneri was wiping at her face when she entered. Seeing her son there surprised her. "Hart? What's wrong?"

"You look at her as if she's already been Taken." His voice was flat and full of anger.

Saneri blinked at her eldest in shock and realization. Shock turned to anger in a tightening of her lips. "You don't know what it's like."

"I lost Toor, too. He was my brother. My twin. He was closer to me than you. You act like … like … you're the only one who lost him."

The tightened lips turned into a white line while bright splotches of red shone on Saneri's cheeks. "Don't you dare!"

"No, don't you dare!" Hart stood up, his chair falling away from him to clatter on the floor. "We *all* lost him when he was Taken. Now, you act like Lanteri's already gone."

Hart's outrage deflated his mother's anger and she slumped to the kitchen chair in front of her like a spent windsock. She put her face in her hands and silently wept into them, her body shaking with her repressed sobs.

It was Hart's turn to be deflated. He watched his mother break down in front of him for a couple of silent moments before picking up the kitchen chair, setting it right and sitting across from her. He let the worst of her grief, anguish and rage pass before offering her a kitchen towel as an apology. For several long minutes, the two of them sat there in silence. Him watching her and her wiping at her face, regaining her composure bit by bit.

"Toor," she said, "was special to me. He promised me he'd never be Taken. He promised me …"

"He was your favorite." There was no accusation in Hart's voice; just a simple knowing truth. Saneri looked away but did not deny it. This lack of denial murdered the last bit of his child's heart. He swallowed his own grief and pressed on. "Now, Lanteri's your favorite."

"She's the only girl child of age in this harvest zone. She's special."

"What about Nori?"

"Nori's too old. They haven't Taken anyone over the age of fifteen in at least twenty years."

"Then why aren't you worried about me?" The betraying words were out of Hart's mouth before he knew he was going to ask the question. But now that the words were on the table between them, he could not snatch them back. At least his mother had the decency to look shocked again.

"What? Of course I'm worried about you! What would make you think…? Why? Oh, Hart, I love you. Of course I'm worried you'll be Taken." She paused, waiting for him to respond but he just continued to look at her, stone-faced. "You're different. You're stronger. Solid. Dependable," she tried to explain.

"Not the prize that Toor was and Lanteri is?"

His mother gave him a look. "Now you're just being sullen. Stop it." She wiped at her face again but this time it was more of a nervous tic.

This casual maternal admonishment made him smile though he did not really understand why. Perhaps it was that the admonishment was a sign that she really did care about him and what he did.

Saneri took the small smile as a sign of encouragement. "I love you, Hart. You're the one I can depend on. You always have been." She paused, took a breath and then forged onward, "That's why I need you to protect your sister."

"Because you and Dad can't."

She looked away and nodded, but not before he saw the flinch of pain on her face. "Yes. You're closer to her. She idolizes you. You … I-I think you're her only hope."

Now that the truth was out between them—almost all of it anyway, Hart nodded at her, feeling better. He *was* Lanteri's only hope. He knew it. He had always known it. "Don't worry, Mom. I'll protect her. I promise." The look of gratitude on his mother's face was painful but he smiled at it. "I know what to do."

* * *

Lanteri and Hart sat in their bedroom not speaking. They both watched the window as the sun set late in the summer's evening. Their silence spoke volumes to each other in sibling-speak. They were both worried. She looked to him for comfort and he gave it in a sudden slap at the button that closed the blinds and signaled the room's automatic sensors to produce a dim light.

Then, he patted the spot next to him on his bed nearest the wall. She came willingly enough despite wanting to seem adult. There was enough of a child's need for comfort that she took it when it was offered.

They sat like that on his bed, Lanteri pressed to her brother's side and he with his arm wrapped around her shoulders in a protective embrace. When she spoke, her voice was soft. "What was Toor like?" She could not see Hart's frown but she sensed it and looked up.

He did not look down at her. "He was a lot like you. Good with animals. A dreamer. Always forgetting about the time." Hart smiled, "I was always saving him from punishment. Reminding him to do his chores. To come home on time. To remember what Mom and Dad said to do."

"I'm not like that. I remember things."

Hart looked down at her. "You're right. I guess you've got a bit of both me and Toor in you. Part dreamer. Part ... not dreamer."

Lanteri smiled a brave smile at him, "I'm a princess."

"Yes. You are." He returned the smile in kind.

The two of them lapsed into silence again, watching the minutes tick over on the clock. Hart did not know what she thought of but his mind raced. Finally, he shifted, waking Lanteri from her doze.

"What's going on? Are they here?" There was a hint of panic in Lanteri's voice.

"No, silly. We've just got to get ready."

"Oh," she yawned. "How?"

"Like this." Hart reached up to the shelf above his bed and found a small wad of dingy rope. "You're gonna sleep in your clothes tonight and on my bed with me." He tied one end of the rope around his left ankle and then tied the other end of it around her right ankle. "If they come to Take either of us, this will connect us and the pulling should wake one of us up. Then, we have to save the other one. OK?"

"I'm gonna save you?"

He shrugged. "Maybe. I don't know." He kept his head down so she would not see the look on his face. He did not want her to know that he knew what was coming.

Lanteri nodded. "I'll save you." She curled up next to him, facing the wall while he remained on his back.

"Lan?"

"Yeah?"

"What's the first rule of being a princess?"

"Never, ever abandon your people—for they need you more than you know," she said. There was a smile in her sleepy voice.

"Good. And the second?"

Lanteri's body relaxed in the comfort of the familiar game. "A princess is a servant to all of her people. She's supposed to care for them and never let them down. Ever."

"Yep. What's the third rule?"

"A princess must be kind and generous but firm because she has to make the hard decisions that others cannot."

"Because 'nothing good ever comes easy.'" He quoted to her.

There was a moment of silence before she spoke again. "Will you always be my subject?"

"Yes. Always." Hart said. He smiled to himself, allowing his eyes to close and await that which was to come.

*   *   *

They came as they had for the last five years. This was the sixth time that Hart would face them, the Takers. They came in light, sound and beauty. They looked like they could be any one of a dozen humanoid races but not. They were all beautiful. Shining. Perfect. Too perfect. But, God, they were beautiful. Hart was standing in a field of grass and flowers that could never exist on Artemis V. The sun was shining in that bright, cheerful way that made the Harvesters rush to cover the delicate purpuran flowers that could only survive in the shade.

The air smelled cool, clear and clean. There was no hint of the musty smell the permeated everything on Artemis V. He knew he was still at home in bed, but at the same time, he was also here, in this impossibly perfect place of beauty and light. There were several of them in the distance, the Takers, watching him. He wanted to go to them but refused to be moved. They had to come to him.

A boy approached. It was the same boy who had approached him every year for the last five years. This boy, with brown hair and blue eyes, grew a year older with each meeting so that he and Hart were always peers. Never one older or younger. "Hart, we're still waiting. Waiting for you."

Hart ached at the sound of his name. "I can't go with you." He saw the boy's smile falter and it hurt his soul.

"Please. Hart, why not? You deserve a better life. You deserve to play in the sun and the grass. That world is no place for a child."

Hart shook his head, "You aren't real. You can't prove you're real and that what you say isn't a lie."

The boy sighed with weariness of the familiar argument. He tried something new, "Your brother—"

"Is dead!" Hart interrupted, not willing to listen to anything about Toor. "You killed him five years ago."

The boy shook his head. "No. Far from it. He's here with us and happy. He misses you. He told me to tell you to remember the Day of Purple Hands." For once, the boy did not look happy or sad. He looked confused. "I don't know what that means and he wouldn't tell me."

Hart felt his stomach lurch. The Day of Purple Hands was the day he and Toor had decided that if they were not allowed to wear the royal purpuran purple color, they would dye their skin with it. It had been Toor's idea; a small act of defiance against the Company and the circumstances that had made their family all but indentured servants to those that employed them. They had gotten in so much trouble. They had been grounded for weeks. But both of them had considered it a victory over the Company. It was something Toor *would* remind him of.

But he could not leave Lanteri.

"It doesn't matter." Hart turned from the boy, though it was hard to turn from that light.

"But, why?" There was a desperate plea in the boy's voice. "Why can't you come with us?"

Hart's answer was a whisper. "Because a prince never abandons his people—for they need him more than he knows."

The boy walked up close behind Hart, putting his hand on Hart's shoulder. "My time is running out. I won't be able to keep coming back. You're my other half. You're the one I was meant to save. If I can't save you, I don't know what I'll do. It might kill me. *Please.*"

The feel of the boy's hand on Hart's shoulder was warm and comforting. It almost unraveled his resolve right then and there. The idea that this boy needed him and needed to save him was almost too much. Then, another sensation distracted Hart from the warmth of the boy's hand. Something was tugging at his ankle. He looked down and saw the dingy rope from his shelf that he had tied around his ankle pulled tight. It was not a part of this world. It was a part of his home.

Lanteri.

Lanteri was being Taken. From him, from his mother, from his family. Hart shrugged the boy's hand from his shoulder. "My sister needs me." He closed his eyes and groped for his sister. At first, he thought he was too late, and then his hand found his sister curled in a tight ball in the corner of the bed. He grabbed her upper arm and squeezed tight. "Lanteri, stay with us," he whispered to her, praying she could hear him.

Hart opened his eyes upon that field of beauty and light, drinking in the wonder that it was. In his hand, he could feel, but not see, Lanteri's arm. "I can't go with you. My family needs me. And I can't let you take Lanteri." He felt the boy step back from him but did not turn around. He could not turn around to see the sorrow he knew was etched all over the boy's perfect face. It would be too much to bear.

"I'll go now," the boy said. "But I can't wait much longer. We'll meet only one more time on the next double full moon. You have one last chance to free yourself of that hellish place and then, all hope is lost. Please...."

Hart squinched his eyes shut against the temptation of this place and willed that the boy with his promises of light and joy would just go away. Mercifully, the scent of that place disappeared and the boy did not speak again.

* * *

"You bruised my arm," Lanteri said as she looked at the finger shaped marks on her arm in the twilight of the morning.

Her voice was subdued as she refused to look at him.

"I'm sorry," Hart said, apologizing for more than the bruise, as he bent over to untie the rope from around their ankles. As he wadded up the rope again, he could have sworn he smelled that other world on it. He threw it from him towards the shelf and did not bother to see if he hit his mark. He looked down and saw a bruise around his ankle. "You bruised me, too."

Lanteri turned in a sudden motion, threw her arms around him and pressed her face into his chest. Her voice came out in choked sobs. "Why didn't you tell me it'd be like that? Why didn't anyone tell me they'd be so pretty?"

He hugged her to him and petted her hair. "Shhhh," he said as he rocked her. "Shhh, it's OK. You won't remember soon. You won't remember anything about it. It'll be just a dream. No one remembers, really. That's why no one talks about it."

"They were so pretty. It was just like my dream, my picture."

"I know, Lan, I know."

She pulled away from him and looked at his face, "Do they come for you every year? Is it like that every year?"

He smoothed away a tear smudge from her cheek and nodded, not wanting to lie to her again. He grimaced at the look of pain on her face.

"How do you not go? Why do you stay?"

Hart closed his eyes and wondered that himself. "I think of you," he said. "I stay because of you. You need me. And so do mom and dad."

"But, what if it's not a lie? What if … it's really what they say?"

"You can't think like that. You can't, Lanteri. Think of what it would do to mom and dad if you were Taken. If *we* were Taken. It would kill them." Hart shook his head. "Don't think like that ever." He could hear the lack of conviction in his voice and was certain that she could, too.

She frowned, "I can't remember what she looked like. I can't remember anything but the shining sun."

He turned from her, "Go wash your face and then wake up mom and dad. They'll be glad to know you're still here."

Lanteri got up and walked to the door. She paused, looking back at him, "I want to remember." When he did not answer, she shook her head and left to do as he told her to do.

He shook his own head, murmuring "No, you don't," under his breath. He did not remember most of the time. It was only in the weeks before the next double full moon that he would remember the field with the flowers and the boy. Last night was the first time the boy had given him proof that Toor was still alive and happy. Last night was the first time the boy had told him how much he needed Hart and that their next meeting would be their last.

For five years, Hart had resisted for the sake of Lanteri, if not for his parents. Now, he knew for certain the Takers wanted both him and his little sister. Next year, they both could be Taken to that place of wonder, to be reunited with Toor, and to live their lives in the sun instead of the shadows and mud. He knew it would kill their parents to lose all of their children to the Takers but, right now, Hart was not certain that knowledge would be enough next time.

Jennifer Brozek *is a Hugo Award-nominated editor and an award-winning author. She has worked in the publishing industry since 2004. With the number of edited anthologies, novel sales, RPG books, and nonfiction books under her belt, Jennifer is often considered a Renaissance woman, but she prefers to be known as a wordslinger and optimist. Read more about her at jenniferbrozek.com or follow her on Twitter: @JenniferBrozek.*

In our next tale, part of her bestselling, long running Vor-kosigan series, Lois McMaster Bujold writes of young officers sent on grisly duty—retrieval and identification of corpses across the stars. And one officer is disturbed by a another's passion for her duties—is it the nature of her job or has she lost her mind?

AFTERMATHS
(VORKOSIGAN SAGA)

BY LOIS MCMASTER BUJOLD

The shattered ship hung in space, a black bulk in the darkness. It still turned, imperceptibly slowly; one edge eclipsed and swallowed the bright point of a star. The lights of the salvage crew arced over the skeleton. *Ants, ripping up a dead moth,* Ferrell thought. *Scavengers ...*

He sighed dismay into his forward observation screen, picturing the ship as it had been, scant weeks before. The wreckage untwisted in his mind—a cruiser, alive with patterns of gaudy lights that always made him think of a party seen across night waters. Responsive as a mirror to the mind under its pilot's headset, where man and machine penetrated the interface and became one. Swift, gleaming, functional ... no more. He glanced to his right, and cleared his throat self-consciously.

"Well, Medtech," he spoke to the woman who stood beside his station, staring into the screen as silently and long as he had. "There's our starting point. Might as well go ahead and begin the pattern sweep now, I suppose."

"Yes, please do, Pilot Officer." She had a gravelly alto voice, suitable for her age, which Ferrell judged to be about forty-five.

The collection of thin silver five-year service chevrons on her left sleeve made an impressive glitter against the dark red uniform of the Escobaran military medical service. Dark hair shot with gray, cut short for ease of maintenance, not style; a matronly heaviness to her hips. A veteran, it appeared. Ferrell's sleeve had yet to sprout even his first-year stripe, and his hips, and the rest of his body, still maintained an unfilled adolescent stringiness.

But she was only a tech, he reminded himself, not even a physician. He was a full-fledged pilot officer. His neurological implants and biofeedback training were all complete. He was certified, licensed, and graduated—just three frustrating days too late to participate in what was now being dubbed the 120-Day War. Although in fact it had only been 118 days and part of an hour between the time the spearhead of the Barrayaran invasion fleet penetrated Escobaran local space, and the time the last survivors fled the counterattack, piling through the wormhole exit for home as though scuttling for a burrow.

"Do you wish to stand by?" he asked her.

She shook her head. "Not yet. This inner area has been pretty well worked over in the last three weeks. I wouldn't expect to find anything on the first four turns, although it's good to be thorough. I've a few things to arrange yet in my work area, and then I think I'll get a catnap. My department has been awfully busy the last few months," she added apologetically. "Understaffed, you know. Please call me if you do spot anything, though—I prefer to handle the tractor myself, whenever possible."

"Fine by me." He swung about in his chair to his comconsole. "What minimum mass do you want a bleep for? About forty kilos, say?"

"One kilo is the standard I prefer."

"One kilo!" He stared. "Are you joking?"

"Joking?" She stared back, then seemed to arrive at enlightenment. "Oh, I see. You were thinking in terms of whole—I can make positive identification with quite small pieces, you see. I wouldn't even mind picking up smaller bits than that, but if you go much under a kilo you spend too much time on false alarms from micrometeors and other rubbish. One kilo seems to be the best practical compromise."

"Bleh." But he obediently set his probes for a mass of one kilo, minimum, and finished programming the search sweep.

She gave him a brief nod and withdrew from the closet-sized Navigation and Control Room. The obsolete courier ship had been pulled from junkyard orbit and hastily overhauled with some notion first of converting it into a personnel carrier for middle brass—top brass in a hurry having a monopoly on the new ships—but like Ferrell himself, it had graduated too late to participate. So they both had been rerouted together, he and his first command, to the dull duties he privately thought on a par with sanitation engineering, or worse.

He gazed one last moment at the relic of battle in the forward screen, its structural girdering poking up like bones through sloughing skin, and shook his head at the waste of it all. Then, with a little sigh of pleasure, he pulled his headset down into contact with the silvery circles on his temples and midforehead, closed his eyes, and slid into control of his own ship.

Space seemed to spread itself all around him, buoyant as a sea. He was the ship, he was a fish, he was a merman; unbreathing, limitless, and without pain. He fired his engines as though flame leapt from his fingertips, and began the slow rolling spiral of the search pattern.

*　*　*

"Medtech Boni?" He keyed the intercom to her cabin. "I believe I have something for you here."

She rubbed sleep from her face, framed in the intercom screen. "Already? What time—oh. I must have been tireder than I realized. I'll be right up, Pilot Officer."

Ferrell stretched, and began an automatic series of isometrics in his chair. It had been a long and uneventful watch. He would have been hungry, but what he contemplated now through the viewscreens subdued his appetite.

Boni appeared promptly, and slid into the seat beside him. "Oh, quite right, Pilot Officer." She unshipped the controls to the exterior tractor beam, and flexed her fingers before taking a delicate hold.

"Yeah, there wasn't much doubt about that one," he agreed, leaning back and watching her work. "Why so tender with the tractors?" he asked curiously, noting the low power level she was using.

"Well, they're frozen right through, you know," she replied, not taking her eyes from her readouts. "Brittle. If you play hotshot and bang them around, they can shatter. Let's stop that nasty spin, first," she added, half to herself. "A slow spin is all right. Seemly. But that fast spinning you get sometimes—it must be very unrestful for them, don't you think?"

His attention was pulled from the thing in the screen, and he stared at her. "They're *dead*, lady!"

She smiled slowly as the corpse, bloated from decompression, limbs twisted as though frozen in a strobe-flash of convulsion, was drawn gently toward the cargo bay. "Well, that's not their fault, is it?—one of our fellows, I see by the uniform."

"Bleh!" he repeated himself, then gave vent to an embarrassed laugh. "You act like you enjoy it."

"Enjoy? No … But I've been in Personnel Retrieval and Identification for nine years, now. I don't mind. And of course, vacuum work is always a little nicer than planetary work."

"Nicer? With that godawful decompression?"

"Yes, but there are the temperature effects to consider. No decomposition."

He took a breath, and let it out carefully. "I see. I guess you would get—pretty hardened, after a while. Is it true you guys call them corpse-sicles?"

"Some do," she admitted. "I don't."

She maneuvered the twisted thing carefully through the cargo bay doors and keyed them shut. "Temperature set for a slow thaw and he'll be ready to handle in a few hours," she murmured.

"What do you call them?" he asked as she rose.

"People."

She awarded his bewilderment a small smile, like a salute, and withdrew to the temporary mortuary set up next to the cargo bay.

* * *

On his next scheduled break, he went down himself, drawn by morbid curiosity. He poked his nose around the doorframe. She was seated at her desk. The table in the center of the room was yet unoccupied.

"Uh—hello."

She looked up with her quick smile. "Hello, Pilot Officer. Come on in."

"Uh, thank you. You know, you don't really have to be so formal. Call me Falco, if you want," he said, entering.

"Certainly, if you wish. My first name is Tersa."

"Oh, yeah? I have a cousin named Tersa."

"It's a popular name. There were always at least three in my classes at school." She rose, and checked a gauge by the door to the cargo bay. "He should be just about ready to take care of, now. Pulled to shore, so to speak."

Ferrell sniffed, and cleared his throat, wondering whether to stay or excuse himself. "Grotesque sort of fishing." *Excuse myself, I think.*

She picked up the control lead to the float pallet, trailing it after her into the cargo bay. There were some thumping noises, and she returned, the pallet drifting behind her. The corpse was in the dark blue of a deck officer, and covered thickly with frost, which flaked and dripped upon the floor as the medtech slid it onto the examining table. Ferrell shivered with disgust.

Definitely excuse myself. But he lingered, leaning against the doorframe at a safe distance.

She pulled an instrument, trailing its lead to the computers, from the crowded rack above the table. It was the size of a pencil, and emitted a thin blue beam of light when aligned with the corpse's eyes.

"Retinal identification," Tersa explained. She pulled down a pad-like object, similarly connected, and pressed it to each of the monstrosity's hands. "And fingerprints," she went on. "I always do both, and cross-match. The eyes can get awfully distorted. Errors in identification can be brutal for the families. Hm. Hm." She checked her readout screen. "Lieutenant Marco Deleo. Age twenty-nine. Well, Lieutenant," she went on chattily, "let's see what I can do for you."

She applied an instrument to its joints, which loosened them, and began removing its clothes.

"Do you often talk to—them?" inquired Ferrell, unnerved.

"Always. It's a courtesy, you see. Some of the things I have to do for them are rather undignified, but they can still be done with courtesy."

Ferrell shook his head. "I think it's obscene, myself."

"Obscene?"

"All this horsing around with dead bodies. All the trouble and expense we go to collecting them. I mean, what do they care? Fifty or a hundred kilos of rotting meat. It'd be cleaner to leave them in space."

She shrugged, unoffended, undiverted from her task. She folded the clothes and inventoried the pockets, laying out their contents in a row.

"I rather like going through the pockets," she remarked. "It reminds me of when I was a little girl, visiting in someone else's home. When I went upstairs by myself, to go to the bathroom or whatever, it was always a kind of pleasure to peek into the other rooms, and see what kind of things they had, and how they kept them. If they were very neat, I was always very impressed—I've never been able to keep my own things neat. If it was a mess, I felt I'd found a secret kindred spirit. A person's things can be a kind of exterior morphology of their mind—like a snail's shell, or something. I like to imagine what kind of person they were, from what's in the pockets. Neat, or messy. Very regulation, or full of personal things … Take Lieutenant Deleo, here. He must have been very conscientious. Everything regulation, except this little vid disc from home. From his wife, I'd imagine. I think he must have been a very nice person to know."

She placed the collection of objects carefully into its labeled bag.

"Aren't you going to listen to it?" asked Ferrell.

"Oh, no. That would be prying."

He barked a laugh. "I fail to see the distinction."

"Ah." She completed the medical examination, readied the plastic body bag, and began to wash the corpse. When she worked her way down to the careful cleaning around the genital area, necessary because of sphincter relaxation, Ferrell fled at last.

That woman is nuts, he thought. *I wonder if it's the cause of her choice of work, or the effect?*

* * *

It was another full day before they hooked their next fish. Ferrell had a dream, during his sleep cycle, about being on a deep-sea boat, and hauling up nets full of corpses to be dumped, wet and shining as though with iridescent scales, in a huge pile in the hold. He awoke from it sweating, but with very cold feet. It was with profound relief that he returned to the pilot's station and slid into the skin of his ship. The ship was clean, mechanical and pure, immortal as a god; one could forget one had ever owned a sphincter muscle.

"Odd trajectory," he remarked, as the medtech again took her place at the tractor controls.

"Yes … Oh, I see. He's a Barrayaran. He's a long way from home."

"Oh, bleh. Throw him back."

"Oh, no. We have identification files for all their missing. Part of the peace settlement, you know, along with prisoner exchange."

"Considering what they did to our people as prisoners, I don't think we owe them a thing."

She shrugged.

* * *

The Barrayaran officer had been a tall, broad-shouldered man, a commander by the rank on his collar tabs. The medtech treated him with the same care she had expended on Lieutenant Deleo, and more. She went to considerable trouble to smooth and straighten him, and massage the mottled face back into some semblance of manhood with her fingertips, a process Ferrell watched with a rising gorge.

"I wish his lips wouldn't curl back *quite* so much," she remarked, while at this task. "Gives him what I imagine to be an uncharacteristically snarly look. I think he must have been rather handsome."

One of the objects in his pockets was a little locket. It held a tiny glass bubble filled with a clear liquid. The inside of its gold cover was densely engraved with the elaborate curlicues of the Barrayaran alphabet.

"What is it?" asked Ferrell curiously.

She held it pensively to the light. "It's a sort of charm, or memento. I've learned a lot about the Barrayarans in the last three months. Turn ten of them upside down and you'll find some kind of good luck charm or amulet or medallion or something in the pockets of nine of them. The high-ranking officers are just as bad as the enlisted people."

"Silly superstition."

"I'm not sure if it's superstition or just custom. We treated an injured prisoner once—he claimed it was just custom. People gave them to the soldiers as presents, and that nobody really believes in them. But when we took his away from him, when we were undressing him for surgery, he tried to fight us for it. It took three of us to hold him down for the anesthetic. I thought it a rather remarkable performance for a man whose legs had been blown away. He wept.... Of course, he was in shock."

Ferrell dangled the locket on the end of its short chain, intrigued in spite of himself. It hung with a companion piece, a curl of hair embedded in a plastic pendant.

"Some sort of holy water, is it?" he inquired.

"Almost. It's a very common design. It's called a mother's tears charm. Let me see if I can make it out—he's had it a while, it seems. From the inscription—I think that says 'ensign,' and the date—it must have been given him on the occasion of his commission."

"It's not really his mother's tears, is it?"

"Oh, yes. That's what's supposed to make it work, as a protection."

"Doesn't seem to be very effective."

"No, well ... no."

Ferrell snorted ironically. "I hate those guys—but I do guess I feel sort of sorry for his mother."

Boni retrieved the chain and its pendants, holding the curl in plastic to the light and reading its inscription. "No, not at all. She's a fortunate woman."

"How so?"

"This is her death lock. She died three years ago, by this."

"Is that supposed to be lucky, too?"

"No, not necessarily. Just a remembrance, as far as I know. Kind of a nice one, really. The nastiest charm I ever ran across, and the most unique, was this little leather bag hung around a fellow's neck. It was filled with dirt and leaves, and what I took at first to be some sort of little frog-like animal skeleton, about ten centimeters long. But when I looked at it more closely, it turned out to be the skeleton of a human fetus. Very strange. I suppose it was some sort of black magic. Seemed an odd thing to find on an engineering officer."

"Doesn't seem to work for any of them, does it?"

She smiled wryly. "Well, if there are any that work, I wouldn't see them, would I?"

She took the processing one step further, by cleaning the Barrayaran's clothes and carefully re-dressing him, before bagging him and returning him to the freeze.

"The Barrayarans are all so army-mad," she explained. "I always like to put them back in their uniforms. They mean so much to them, I'm sure they're more comfortable with them on."

Ferrell frowned uneasily. "I still think he ought to be dumped with the rest of the garbage."

"Not at all," said the medtech. "Think of all the work he represents on somebody's part. Nine months of pregnancy, childbirth, two years of diapering, and that's just the beginning. Tens of thousands of meals, thousands of bedtime stories, years of school. Dozens of teachers. And all that military training, too. A lot of people went into making him."

She smoothed a strand of the corpse's hair into place. "That head held the universe, once. He had a good rank for his age," she added, rechecking her monitor. "Thirty-two. Commander Aristede Vorkalloner. It has a kind of nice ethnic ring. Very Barrayaranish, that name. Vor, too, one of those warrior-class fellows."

"Homicidal-class loonies. Or worse," Ferrell said automatically. But his vehemence had lost momentum, somehow.

Boni shrugged, "Well, he's joined the great democracy now. And he had nice pockets."

Three full days went by with no further alarms but a rare scattering of mechanical debris. Ferrell began to hope the Barrayaran was the last pickup they would have to make. They were nearing the end of their search pattern. Besides, he thought resentfully, this duty was sabotaging the efficiency of his sleep cycle. But the medtech made a request.

"If you don't mind, Falco," she said, "I'd greatly appreciate it if we could run the pattern out just a few extra turns. The original orders are based on this average estimated trajectory speed, you see, and if someone just happened to get a bit of extra kick when the ship split, they could well be beyond it by now."

Ferrell was less than thrilled, but the prospect of an extra day of piloting had its attractions, and he gave a grudging consent. Her reasoning proved itself; before the day was half done, they turned up another gruesome relic.

"Oh," muttered Ferrell, when they got a close look. It had been a female officer. Boni reeled her in with enormous tenderness. He didn't really want to go watch, this time, but the medtech seemed to have come to expect him.

"I—don't really want to look at a woman blown up," he tried to excuse himself.

"Mm," said Tersa. "Is it fair, though, to reject a person just because they're dead? You wouldn't have minded her body a bit when she was alive."

He laughed a little, macabrely. "Equal rights for the dead?"

Her smile twisted. "Why not? Some of my best friends are corpses."

He snorted.

She grew more serious. "I'd—sort of like the company, on this one." So he took up his usual station by the door.

The medtech laid out the thing that had been a woman upon her table, undressed, inventoried, washed, and straightened it. When she finished, she kissed the dead lips.

"Oh, God," cried Ferrell, shocked and nauseated. "You *are* crazy! You're a damn, damn necrophiliac! A *lesbian* necrophiliac, at that!" He turned to go.

"Is that what it looks like, to you?" Her voice was soft, and still unoffended. It stopped him, and he looked over his shoulder. She was looking at him as gently as if he had been one of her precious corpses. "What a strange world you must live in, inside your head."

She opened a suitcase, and shook out a dress, fine underwear, and a pair of white embroidered slippers. A wedding dress, Ferrell realized. This woman was a bona fide *psychopath.* ...

She dressed the corpse, and arranged its soft dark hair with great delicacy, before bagging it.

"I believe I shall place her next to that nice tall Barrayaran," she said. "I think they would have liked each other very well, if they could have met in another place and time. And Lieutenant Deleo was married, after all."

She completed the label. Ferrell's battered mind was sending him little subliminal messages; he struggled to overcome his shock and bemusement, and pay attention. It tumbled into the open day of his consciousness with a start.

She had not run an identification check on this one.

Out the door, he told himself, *is the way you want to walk. I guarantee it.* Instead, timorously, he went over to the corpse and checked its label.

Ensign Sylva Boni, it said. *Age twenty*. His own age ...

He was trembling, as if with cold. It *was* cold, in that room. Tersa Boni finished packing up the suitcase, and turned back with the float pallet.

"Daughter?" he asked. It was all he could ask.

She pursed her lips, and nodded.

"It's—a helluva coincidence."

"No coincidence at all. I asked for this sector."

"Oh." He swallowed, turned away, turned back, face flaming. "I'm sorry I said—"

She smiled her slow sad smile. "Never mind."

* * *

They found yet one more bit of mechanical debris, so agreed to run another cycle of the search spiral, to be sure that all possible trajectories had been outdistanced. And yes, they found another; a nasty one, spinning fiercely, guts split open from some great blow and hanging out in a frozen cascade.

The acolyte of death did her dirty work without once so much as wrinkling her nose. When it came to the washing, the least technical of the tasks, Ferrell said suddenly, "May I help?"

"Certainly," said the medtech, moving aside. "An honor is not diminished for being shared."

And so he did, as shy as an apprentice saint washing his first leper.

"Don't be afraid," she said. "The dead cannot hurt you. They give you no pain, except that of seeing your own death in their faces. And one can face that, I find."

Yes, he thought, *the good face pain. But the great—they embrace it.*

Lois McMaster Bujold *was born in 1949, the daughter of an engineering professor at Ohio State University, from whom she picked up her early interest in science fiction. She now lives in Minneapolis, and has two grown children. She began writing with the aim of professional publication in 1982. She wrote three novels in three years; in October of 1985, all three sold to Baen Books, launching her career. Bujold went on to write many other books for Baen, mostly featuring her popular character Miles Naismith Vorkosigan, his family, friends, and enemies. Her fantasy from HarperCollins includes the award-winning Chalion series and the Sharing Knife series.*

Ten-times nominated for the Hugo Award for Best Novel, she has won in that category four times, in addition to garnering another Hugo for best novella, three Nebula Awards, three Locus Awards, the Mythopoeic Award, two Sapphire Awards, the Minnesota Book Award, the Forry Award, and the Skylark Award. In 2007, she was given the Ohioana Career Award, and in 2008 was Writer Guest-of-Honor for the 66th World Science Fiction Convention. A complete list may be found here: sfadb.com/ Lois_McMaster _Bujold. Her works have been translated into over twenty languages.

More information on Bujold and her books is archived at dendarii.com and her blog at:

goodreads.com/ author/ show/ 16094.Lois_McMaster_Bujold/ blog

Every teenager dreams of their first car, and Jerry is no different. Somehow he stumbles onto the perfect vehicle, too good to be true. And that's the problem. What dark secret lurks in the vehicle's past and can he ever be free of it? Or is that the price of ...

DRIVING A BARGAIN

BY ROBERT J. SAWYER

Jerry walked to the corner store, a baseball cap and sunglasses shielding him from the heat beating down from above. He picked up a copy of the *Calgary Sun*, walked to the counter, gave the old man a dollar, got his change, and hurried outside. He didn't want to wait until he got home, so he went to the nearest bus stop, parked himself on the bench there, and opened the paper.

Of course, the first thing he checked out was the bikini-clad Sunshine Girl—what sixteen-year-old boy wouldn't turn to that first? Today's girl was old—23, it said—but she certainly was pretty, with lots of long blonde hair.

That ritual completed, Jerry turned to the real reason he'd bought the paper: the classified ads. He found the used-car listings, and started poring over them, hoping, as he always did, for a bargain.

Jerry had worked hard all summer on a loading dock. It had been rough work, but, for the first time in his life, he had real muscles. And, even more important, he had some real money.

His parents had promised to pay the insurance if Jerry kept up straight A's all through grade ten, and Jerry had. They weren't going to pay for a car itself, but Jerry had two grand in his bank account—he liked the sound of that: two grand. Now if he could just find something halfway decent for that price, he'd be driving to school when grade eleven started next week.

Jerry was a realist. He wanted a girlfriend—God, how he wanted one—but he knew his little wispy beard wasn't what was going to impress ... well, he'd been thinking about Ashley Brown all summer. Ashley who, in his eyes at least, put that Sunshine Girl to shame.

But, no, it wasn't the beard he'd managed to grow since June that would impress her. Nor was it his newfound biceps. It would be having his own set of wheels. How sweet that would be!

Jerry continued scanning the ads, skipping over all the makes he knew he could never afford: the Volvos, the Lexuses, the Mercedes, the BMWs.

He read the lines describing a '94 Honda Civic, a '97 Dodge Neon, even a '91 Pontiac Grand Prix. But the prices were out of his reach.

Jerry really didn't care *what* make of car he got; he'd even take a Hyundai. After all, when hardly anyone else his age had a car, *any* car would be a fabulous ticket to freedom, to making out. To use one of his dad's favorite expressions—an expression that he'd never really understood until just now—"In the land of the blind, the one-eyed man is king."

Jerry was going to be royalty.

If, that is, he could find something he could afford. He kept looking, getting more and more depressed. Maybe he'd just—

Jerry felt his eyes go wide. A 1997 Toyota, only twenty thousand miles on it. The asking price: "$3,000, OBO."

Just three thousand! That was awfully cheap for such a car.... And OBO! Or Best Offer. It couldn't hurt to try two thousand dollars. The worst the seller could do was say no. Jerry felt in his pocket for the change he got from buying the paper. There was a phone booth just up the street. He hurried over to it, and called.

"Hello?" said a sad-sounding man's voice at the other end.

Jerry tried to make his own voice sound as deep as he could. "Hello," he said. "I'm calling about the Toyota." He swallowed. "Has it sold yet?"

"No," said the man. "Would you like to come see it?"

Jerry got the man's address—only about two miles away. He glanced up the street, saw the bus coming, and ran back to the stop, grinning to himself. If all went well, this would be the last time he'd have to take the bus anywhere.

*   *   *

Jerry walked up to the house. It looked like the kind of place he lived in himself: basketball hoop above the garage; garage door dented from endless games of ball hockey.

Jerry rang the doorbell, and was greeted by a man who looked about the same age as Jerry's father ... a sad-looking man with a face like a basset hound.

"Yes?" said the man.

"I called earlier," said Jerry. "I've come about the car."

The man's eyebrows went up. "How old are you, son?"

"Sixteen."

"Tell me about yourself," said the man.

Jerry couldn't see what difference that would make. But he *did* want to soften the old guy up so that he'd take the lower price. And so: "My name's Jerry Sloane," he said. "I'm a student at Eastern High, just going into grade eleven. I've got my license, and I've been working all summer long on the loading dock down at Macabee's."

The basset hound's eyebrows went up. "Have you, now?"

"Yes," said Jerry.

"You a good student?"

Jerry was embarrassed to answer; it seemed *so* nerdy to say it, but ... "Straight A's."

The basset hound nodded. "Good for you! Good for you!" He paused. "Are you a churchgoer, son?"

Jerry was surprised by the question, but he answered truthfully. "Most weeks, with my family. Calgary United."

The man nodded again. "All right, would you like to take the car for a test drive?"

"Sure!"

Jerry got into the driver's seat, and the man got into the passenger seat. Not that it should have mattered to whether the deal got made, but Jerry did the absolute best job he could of backing out of the driveway and turning onto the street. When they arrived at the corner, he came to a proper full stop at the stop sign, making sure the front of his car lifted up a bit before he continued into the empty intersection. That's what they'd taught him in driver's ed: you know you've come to a complete stop when the front of your car lifts up.

At the next intersection, Jerry signaled his turn, even though there was no one around and took a left onto Askwith Street.

The basset hound nodded, impressed. "You're a very careful driver," he said.

"Thanks."

Jerry was coming to another corner, where Askwith crossed Thurlbeck, and he decided to turn right. He activated the turn signal and—

"No!" shouted the man.

Jerry was startled and looked around, terrified that he'd been about to hit a cat or something. "What?" said Jerry. "What?"

"Don't go down that way," said the man, his voice shaking.

It was the route Jerry would have to take to get to school, but he was in no rush to see that old prison any sooner than he had to. He canceled his turn signal and continued straight through the intersection.

Jerry went along for another mile, then decided he'd better not overdo it and headed back to the man's house.

"So," said the man, "what did you think?"

"It's a great car, but ..."

"Oh, I know it could really use a front-end alignment," said the man, "but it's not that bad, is it?"

Jerry hadn't even noticed, but he was clever enough to seize on the issue. "Well, it *will* need work," he said, trying to sound like an old hand at such matters. "Tell you what—I'll give you two thousand dollars for it."

"*Two* thousand!" said the man. But then he fell silent, saying nothing else.

Jerry wanted to be cool, wanted to be a tough bargainer, but the man had such a sad face. "I'll tell you the truth," he said. "Two thousand is all I've got."

"You worked for it?" asked the man.

Jerry nodded. "Every penny."

The man was quiet for a bit, then he said, "You seem to be a fine young fellow," he said. He extended his right hand across the gearshift to Jerry. "Deal."

*　*　*

Today was the day. Today, the first Tuesday in September, would make everything worthwhile. Jerry put on his best—that is, his oldest—pair of jeans and a shirt with the sleeves ripped off. It was the perfect look.

He got in the car—*his* car—and started it, pulling out of the driveway. A left onto Schumann Street, a right onto Vigo. Jerry didn't have any real choice of how to get to school, but was delighted that some of the other kids would see him en route. And if he happened to pass Ashley Brown ... why, he'd pull over and offer her a lift. How sweet would that be?

Jerry came to the intersection with Thurlbeck, where there was a stop sign. But this time he was trying to impress a different audience. He slowed down and, without waiting for the front of the car to bounce up, turned right.

Thurlbeck was the long two-laned street that led straight to Eastern High. Jerry had to pick just the right speed. If he went too fast, none of the kids walking along would have a chance to see that it was him. But he couldn't cruise along slowly, or they'd think he wasn't comfortable driving. Not comfortable! Why, he'd been driving for *months* now. He picked a moderate speed and rolled down the driver's-side window, resting his sleeveless arm on the edge of the opening.

Up ahead, a bunch of kids were walking along the sidewalk.

No ... no, that wasn't quite right. They weren't walking—they were *standing*, all looking and pointing at something. That was perfect: in a moment, they'd all be looking and pointing at *him*.

As he got closer, Jerry slowed the car to a crawl. As much as he wanted to show off, he was curious about what had caught everyone's attention. He remembered a day years ago when everybody had paused on the way to school as they came across a dead dog, one eye half popped out of its skull.

Jerry continued on slowly, hoping people would look over and take notice of him, but no one did. They were all intent on something—he still couldn't make out what—on the side of the road. He thought about honking his horn, but no, he couldn't do that. The whole secret of being cool was to get people to look at you without it seeming like that was what you were trying to do.

Finally, Jerry thought of the perfect solution. As he got closer to the knot of people, he pulled his car over to the side of the road, put on his blinkers, and got out.

"Hey," he said as he closed the distance between himself and the others. "Wassup?"

Darren Chen looked up. "Hey, Jerry," he said.

Jerry had expected Chen's eyes to go wide when he realized that his friend had come out of the car sitting by the curb, but that didn't happen. The other boy just pointed to the side of the road.

Jerry followed the outstretched arm and ...

His heart jumped.

There was a plain white cross on the grassy strip that ran along the far side of the sidewalk. Hanging from it was a wreath. Jerry moved closer and read the words that had been written on the cross in thick black strokes, perhaps with an indelible marker: "Tammy Jameson was killed here by a hit-and-run driver. She will always be remembered." And there was a date from July.

Jerry knew the Jameson name—there'd always been one or another of them going through the local schools. A face came into his mind, but he wasn't even sure if it was Tammy's.

"Wow," said Jerry softly. "Wow."

Chen nodded. "I read about it in the paper. They still haven't caught the person who did it."

*　*　*

Jerry finally got what he wanted at the end of the school day. Tons of kids saw him sauntering over to his car, and a few of the boys came up to talk to him about it.

And just before he was about to get in and drive off, he saw Ashley. She was walking with a couple of other girls, books clasped to her chest. She looked up and saw the car sitting there. Then she saw Jerry leaning against it and her eyes—beautiful deep-blue eyes, he knew, although he couldn't really see them at this distance—met his, and she smiled a bit and nodded at him, impressed.

Jerry got in his car and drove home, feeling on top of the world.

* * *

The next morning, Jerry headed out to school. This time, he thought maybe he'd get the attention he deserved as he came up Thurlbeck Street. After all, even if the cross was still there—and it was; he could just make it out up ahead—the novelty would surely have worn off.

Jerry decided to try a slightly faster speed today, in hopes that more people would look up. But, to his astonishment, he found that the more he pressed his right foot down on the accelerator, the more his car slowed down. He actually craned for a look—it was a beginner's mistake, and a pretty terrifying one too, he remembered, to confuse the accelerator and the brake—but, no, his gray Nike was pressing down on the correct pedal.

And yet still his car was rapidly slowing down. As he came abreast of the crucifix with its wreath, he was moving at no better than walking speed, despite having the pedal all the way to the floor. But once he'd passed the cross, the car started speeding up again, until at last the vehicle was operating normally once more.

Jerry was reasonably philosophical. He knew there *had* to be something wrong with the car for him to have gotten it so cheap. He continued on to the school parking lot. Not even the principal had a reserved spot—it made his car too easy a target for vandals, Jerry guessed. It pleased him greatly to pull in next to old Mr. Walters, who was trying to shift his bulk out of his Ford.

* * *

Jerry was relieved that his car functioned flawlessly on the way home from school. He still hadn't managed to find the courage to offer Ashley Brown a lift home, but that would come soon, he knew.

The next day, however—crazy though it seemed—his car developed the exact same malfunction, slowing to a crawl at precisely the same point in the road.

Jerry had seen his share of horror movies. It didn't take a Dr. Frankenstein to figure out that it had something to do with the girl who had been killed there. It was as though she was reaching out from the beyond; slowing down cars at that spot to make sure that no other accident ever happened there again. It was scary but exhilarating.

At lunch that day, Jerry headed out to the school's parking lot, all set to hang around his car, showing it off to anyone who cared to have a look. But then he caught sight of Ashley walking out of the school grounds. He could have jumped in his car and driven over to her, but she probably wouldn't get in, even if he offered. No, he needed to talk to her first.

Now or never, Jerry thought. He jogged over to Ashley, catching up with her as she was walking along Thurlbeck Street. "Hey, Ash," he said. "Where're you going?"

Ashley turned around and smiled that radiant smile of hers. "Just down to the store to get some gum."

"Mind if I tag along?"

"If you like," she said, her voice perfectly measured, perfectly noncommittal.

Jerry fell in beside her. He chatted with her—trying to hide his nervousness—about what they'd each done over the summer. She'd spent most of it at her uncle's farm and—

Jerry stopped dead in his tracks.

A car was coming up Thurlbeck Street, heading toward the school. It came abreast of the crucifix but didn't slow down, it just sailed on by.

"What's wrong?" asked Ashley.

"Nothing," said Jerry. A few moments later, another car came along, and it too passed the crucifix without incident.

Of course, Jerry had had no trouble driving home from school, but he'd assumed that that was because he was in the other lane, going in the opposite direction, and that Tammy, wherever she was, didn't care about people going that way.

But …

But now it looked like it wasn't *every* car that she was slowing down when it passed the spot where she'd—there was no gentle way to phrase it—where she'd been killed.

No, not every car.

Jerry's heart fluttered.

Just my car.

* * *

The next day, the same thing: Jerry's car slowed down almost to a stop directly opposite where Tammy Jameson had been hit. He tried to ignore it, but then Dickens, one of the kids in his geography class, made a crack about it. "Hey, Sloane," he said, "What are you, chicken? I see you crawling along every morning when you pass the spot where Tammy was killed."

Where Tammy was killed. He said it offhandedly, as if death was a commonplace occurrence for him, as if he was talking about the place where something utterly normal had happened.

But Jerry couldn't take it anymore. He'd been called on it, on what Dickens assumed was his behavior, and he had to either give a good reason for it or stop doing it. That's the way it worked.

But he had no good reason for it, except …

Except the one he'd been suppressing, the one that kept gnawing at the back of his mind, but that he'd shooed away whenever it had threatened to come to the fore.

Only his car was slowing down.

But it hadn't always been *his* car.

A bargain. Just two grand!

Jerry had assumed that there had to be something wrong with it for him to get it so cheap, but that wasn't it. Not exactly.

Rather, something wrong had been *done* with it.

His car was the one the police were looking for, the one that had been used to strike a young woman dead and then flee the scene.

* * *

Jerry drove to the house where the man with the basset hound face lived. He left the car in the driveway, with the driver's door open and the engine still running. He got out, walked up to the door, rang the bell, and waited for the man to appear, which, after a long, long time, he finally did.

"Oh, it's you, son," he said. "What can I do for you?"

Jerry had thought it took all his courage just to speak to Ashley Brown. But he'd been wrong. This took more courage. Way more.

"I know what you did in that car you sold me," he said.

The man's face didn't show any shock, but, Jerry realized that wasn't because he wasn't surprised. No, thought Jerry, it was something else—a *deadness*, an inability to feel shock anymore.

"I don't know what you're talking about, son," said the man.

"That car—*my* car—you hit a girl with it. On Thurlbeck Street."

"I swear to you," said the man, still standing in his doorway, "I never did anything like that."

"She went to my school," said Jerry. "Her name was Tammy. Tammy Jameson."

The man closed his eyes, as if he was trying to shut out the world.

"And," said Jerry, his voice quavering, "you killed her."

"No," said the man. "No, I didn't." He paused. "Look, do you want to come in?"

Jerry shook his head. He could outrun the old guy—he was sure of that—and he could make it back to his car in a matter of seconds. But if he went inside … well, he'd seen *that* in horror movies, too.

The man with the sad face put his hands in his pockets. "What are you going to do?" he said.

"Go to the cops," said Jerry. "Tell them."

The man didn't laugh, although Jerry had expected him to—a derisive, mocking laugh. Instead, he just shook his head. "You've got no evidence."

"The car slows down on its own every time I pass the spot where the"—he'd been about to say "accident," but that was the wrong word—"where the *crime* occurred."

This time, the man's face did show a reaction, a lifting of his shaggy, graying eyebrows. "Really?" But he composed himself quickly. "The police won't give you the time of day if you come in with a crazy story like that."

"Maybe," said Jerry, trying to sound more confident than he felt. "Maybe not."

"Look, I've been nice to you," said the man. "I gave you a great deal on that car."

"Of course you did!" snapped Jerry. "You wanted to get rid of it! After what you did—"

"I told you, son, I didn't do anything."

"That girl—Tammy—she can't rest, you know. She's reaching out from beyond the grave, trying to stop that car every time it passes that spot. You've got to turn yourself in. You've got to let her rest."

"Get out of here, kid. Leave me alone."

"I can't," said Jerry. "I can't, because it won't leave *her* alone. You have to go to the police and tell them what you did."

"How many times do I have to tell you? I didn't do anything!" The old man turned around for a second, and Jerry thought he was going to disappear into the house. But he didn't; he simply grabbed a hockey stick that must have been leaning against a wall just inside the door. He raised the stick menacingly. "Now, get out of here!" he shouted.

Jerry couldn't believe the man was going to chase him down the street, in full view of his neighbors. "You have to turn yourself in," he said firmly.

The man took a swing at him—high-sticking indeed!—and Jerry started running for his car. The old guy continued after him. Jerry scrambled into the driver's seat and slammed the door behind him. He threw the car into reverse, but not before the man brought the hockey stick down on the front of the hood— somewhere near, Jerry felt sure, the spot where the car had crashed into poor Tammy Jameson.

* * *

Jerry had no idea what was the right thing to do. He suspected that the basset hound was correct: the police would laugh him out of the station if he came to them with his story. Of course, if they'd just *try* driving his car along Thurlbeck, they'd see for themselves. But adults were so smug; no matter how much he begged, they'd refuse.

And so Jerry found himself doing something that might have been stupid. He should have been at home studying—or, even better, out on a date with Ashley Brown. Instead, he was parked on the side of the street, a few doors up from the man's house, from the driveway that used to be home to this car. He didn't know exactly what he was doing. Did they call this casing the joint? No, that was when you were planning a robbery. Ah, he had it! A stakeout. Cool.

Jerry waited. It was dark enough to see a few stars—and he hoped that meant it was also dark enough that the old man wouldn't see him, even if he glanced out his front window.

Jerry wasn't even sure what he was waiting for. It was just like Ms. Singh, his chemistry teacher, said: he'd know it when he saw it.

And at last *it* appeared.

Jerry felt like slapping his hand against his forehead, but a theatrical gesture like that was wasted when there was no one around to see it. Still, he wondered how he could be so stupid.

That old man wasn't the one who'd used the hockey stick. Oh, he might have dented Jerry's hood with it, but the dents in the garage door were the work of someone else.

And that someone else was walking up the driveway, hands shoved deep into the pockets of a blue leather jacket, dark-haired head downcast. He looked maybe a year or two older than Jerry.

Of course, it could have been a delivery person or something. But no, Jerry could see the guy take out a set of keys and let himself into the house. And, for one brief moment, he saw the guy's face, a long face, a sad face … but a young face.

The car hadn't belonged to the old man. It had belonged to his son.

*　*　*

There were fifteen hundred kids at Eastern High. No reason Jerry should know them all on sight—especially ones who weren't in his grade. Oh, he knew the names of all the babes in grade twelve—he and the other boys his age fantasized about them often enough—but some long-faced guy with dark hair? Jerry wouldn't have paid any attention to him.

Until now.

It was three days before he caught sight of the guy walking the halls at Eastern. His last name, Jerry knew, was likely Forsythe, since that was the old man's name, the name Jerry had written on the check for the car. It wasn't much longer before he had found where young Forsythe's locker was located. And then Jerry cut his last class—history, which he could easily afford to miss once— and waited in a stairwell, where he could keep an eye on Forsythe's locker.

At about 3:35, Forsythe came up to it, dialed the combo, put some books inside, took out a couple of others, and put on the same blue leather jacket Jerry had seen him in the night of the stakeout. And then he started walking out.

Jerry watched him head out, then, he hurried to the parking lot and got into the Toyota.

* * *

Jerry was crawling along—and this time, it was of his own volition. He didn't want to overtake Forsythe—not yet. But then Forsythe did something completely unexpected. Instead of walking down Thurlbeck, he headed in the opposite direction, away from his own house. Could it be that Jerry was wrong about who this was? After all, he'd seen Forsythe's son only once before, on a dark night, and—

No. It came to him in a flash what Forsythe was doing. He was going to walk the long way around—a full mile out of his way—so that he wouldn't have to go past the spot where he'd hit Tammy Jameson.

Jerry wondered if he'd avoided the spot entirely since hitting her or had got cold feet only once the cross had been erected. He rolled down his window, followed Forsythe, and pulled up next to him, matching his car's velocity to Forsythe's walking speed.

"Hey," said Jerry.

The other guy looked up, and his eyes went wide in recognition—not of Jerry, but of what had once been his car.

"What?" said Forsythe.

"You look like you could use a lift," said Jerry.

"Naw. I live just up there." He waved vaguely ahead of him.

"No, you don't," said Jerry, and he recited the address he'd gone to buy the car.

"What do you want, man?" said Forsythe.

"Your old man gave me a good deal on this car," said Jerry. "And I figured out why."

Forsythe shook his head. "I don't know what you're talking about."

"Yes, you do. I know you do." He paused. "*She* knows you do."

The guy told Jerry to go … well, to go do something that was physically impossible. Jerry's heart was racing, but he tried to sound cool. "Sooner or later, you'll want to come clean on this."

Forsythe said nothing.

"Maybe tomorrow," said Jerry, and he drove off.

* * *

That night, Jerry went to the hardware store to get the stuff he needed. Of course, he couldn't do anything about it early in the day; someone might come along. So he waited until his final period—which today was English—and he cut class again. He then went out to his car, got what he needed from the trunk, and went up Thurlbeck.

When he was done, he returned to the parking lot and waited for Forsythe to head out for home.

* * *

Jerry finally caught sight of Forsythe. Just as he had the day before, Forsythe walked to the edge of the schoolyard. But there he hesitated for a moment, as if wondering if he dared take the short way home. But he apparently couldn't do that. He took a deep breath and headed up Thurlbeck.

Jerry started his car but lagged behind Forsythe, crawling along, his foot barely touching the accelerator.

There was a large pine tree up ahead. Jerry waited for Forsythe to come abreast of it, and …

The disadvantage of following Forsythe was that Jerry couldn't see the other kid's face when he caught sight of the new cross Jerry had banged together and sunk into the grass next to the sidewalk. But he saw Forsythe stop dead in his tracks.

Just as *she* had been stopped dead in his tracks.

Jerry saw Forsythe loom in, look at the words written not in black, as on Tammy's cross, but in red—words that said, "Our sins testify against us."

Forsythe began to run ahead, panicking, and Jerry pressed down a little more on the accelerator, keeping up. All those years of Sunday school were coming in handy.

Forsythe came to another tree. In its lee, he surely could see the second wooden cross, with its letters as crimson as blood: "He shall make amends for the harm he hath done."

Forsythe was swinging his head left and right, clearly terrified. But he continued running forward.

A third tree. A third cross. And a third red message, the simplest of all: "Thou shalt not kill."

Finally, Forsythe turned around and caught sight of Jerry.

Jerry sped up, coming alongside him. Forsythe's face was a mask of terror. Jerry rolled down his window, leaned an elbow out, and said, as nonchalantly as he could manage, "Going my way?"

Forsythe clearly didn't know what to say. He looked up ahead, apparently wondering if there were more crosses to come. Then he turned and looked back the other way, off into the distance.

"There's just one down the other way," said Jerry. "If you'd prefer to walk by it …"

Forsythe swore at Jerry, but without much force. "What's this to you?" he snapped.

"I want her to let my car go. I worked my tail off for these wheels."

Forsythe stared at him, the way you'd look at somebody who might be crazy.

"So," said Jerry, again trying for an offhand tone, "going my way?"

Forsythe was quiet for a long moment. "Depends where you're going," he said at last.

"Oh, I thought I'd take a swing by the police station," Jerry said.

Forsythe looked up Thurlbeck once more, then down it, then at last back at Jerry. He shrugged, but it wasn't as if he was unsure. Rather, it was as if he were shucking a giant weight from his shoulders.

"Yeah," he said to Jerry. "Yeah, I could use a lift."

Robert J. Sawyer *is one of only eight writers in history to win all three of the world's top awards for Best Science Fiction Novel of the Year: the Hugo, the Nebula, and the John W. Campbell Memorial Award. The ABC TV series* FlashForward *was based on his bestselling novel of the same name. His 23rd novel,* Quantum Night, *has just been published. He lives in Toronto.*
Website: sfwriter.com.

E.C. Myers made a huge splash on the YA scene with his debut novel, Fair Coin, *and its sequel. In this tale, the young protagonist seeks the devastating truth about what happened to his father and what it might bode for his own future …*

MY FATHER'S EYES

BY E.C. MYERS

My hands tremble as I swirl developer solution over the photographic paper. I've never been more anxious to see one of my pictures before. My classmates would say this is another drawback to traditional photography over digital: delayed gratification. I'll never make that technological leap; I still shoot in black and white. My father never dabbled with digital photography either, and it's because of him that I decided to become a photojournalist in the first place.

A cloudy scene emerges on the paper floating in the tray. Shapes and shadows magically replace the blank white surface, gradually forming trees and rocks. I've had this image burned into my mind ever since I glimpsed it through my lens and my finger instinctively clicked the shutter. It's a bad photo, the subject slightly unfocused and too far away, though I've blown it up as much as I can. It won't help my thesis project or launch a career, but it's the single most important picture of my life.

As I squint at it in the dim red glow of the safelight, a crouching figure fades into the scene like a ghost. His face is blurred, captured in motion just as he'd turned and darted away.

Despite the blurring, and the fact that I haven't seen him in fifteen years except in other pictures, I know he's my father. I knew it even before I unloaded the film from my camera.

In my haste to fish the page out of the developer, I fumble the metal tongs into the tray with a splash. I lift the photo out, but I don't bother to let the chemicals run off completely before dunking it in the stop bath and submerging it in the fixer.

I study the damp photograph at the kitchen table, with an old family photo beside it for comparison. My father's hair has grown long, falling below his waist and draping his broad shoulders in mangy tangles. He's bigger than he used to be, his large muscles taut and defined as he springs into motion. A bushy beard obscures much of his face, and his naked body is patched with dried mud. He seems feral, more animal than man, except for his eyes. I remember those eyes: clear, brown and sharp, like mine. When I looked into those eyes, I knew.

By the time my mother comes home from her late shift at the hospital I've made multiple prints of that photo, enlarging it over and over. I cropped many of the prints around his eyes, his most human feature. I've also scanned the image into my computer, trying to enhance it into something more recognizable as my father. He's in there, somewhere. Alive.

"What's all this?" my mother asks as she enters the kitchen and drops a bucket of fried chicken onto the table with a hollow thump. She looks around at the drying photos I have suspended on wires across the room, the warped and curling prints scattered on the table, the family portrait that was taken a little after my fifth birthday. A little before my father disappeared.

She never told me what happened to him. He was just gone; that's what my mother said whenever I asked, until I stopped asking. "Gone," she would say, which could mean anything. He left, he died, he was killed. Whatever I wanted it to mean, really. In my favorite fantasy I made him a secret government agent on an important mission. Kids want their dad to be someone they can be proud of, someone they can brag about—especially if he can't be someone they can come home to. Who thinks that his dad might be running around naked in the wilderness?

"When were you going to tell me, Mom?" I ask.

"Tell you what?" she says distractedly. She looks at the pictures, but doesn't see them. I toss her a printout of one of my best efforts and she picks it up. She drops it a moment later.

"Why didn't you tell me my father's a devol?" I ask.

"Don't use that word," she says. She sounds tired. She suddenly looks old and weary, like life has defeated her at last. Like she's given up. Maybe she has—or maybe she gave up fifteen years ago.

She sits down at the table across from me, the evidence spread between us. She covers her face with her hands, then removes them, like a game of peek-a-boo. She does it again, and now her face and palms are wet.

"What's a better word? Is this what you call 'gone'? When people go, they usually end up somewhere."

"It's all the same, Ambrose. This—" She picks up the printout and crinkles it up. "This isn't your father."

"It sure looks like him," I say.

"Your father was go—He stopped being Randall Welling a long time ago."

"Did you ever visit him at the reservation?"

"There was no reason to."

"He would've liked to see you. Us."

She shakes her head.

"Well, I'd have liked to see him," I say.

"I hoped you'd never see him like this." She bows her head, eyes shut and tears falling. "I wanted you to remember him as he was, before."

The sound of her tears dripping onto the photograph fills the silence.

"I barely remember him at all. I had a right to know!" I tell her. I stand up and leave her alone. Her sobs follow me all the way to the basement until I close the darkroom door and shut them out.

* * *

Devols, Neo-anderthals, or, to be politically correct, regressives—whatever you want to call them—have been around for almost sixty years. They all suffer from a rare form of dementia called Hollander's disease, named for Dr. David Hollander, who diagnosed it in 2017. Or maybe it was named for the first case he studied: his teenage daughter Alessandra.

Most victims of this degenerative disease, unable to function in society, end up in one of three national reservations. Some are sent to smaller asylums that specialize in managed care for devols. Dr. Hollander contributed millions to the development of the reservations; he wanted to secure a place for his daughter to live out her life as happily and naturally as she could. Years later he joined her when he finally succumbed to the disease himself, or at least appeared to. Since he died, his biographers have speculated that he wasn't a regressive at all, suggesting that he just wanted to be close to his daughter.

When my advisor proposed that I study and photograph regressives for my undergrad thesis, I was excited because there aren't many pictures or videos of them—not nearly as many as you might expect. The main reason they are kept out of the public eye is because of accusations that the reservations are a violation of human rights. Most who argue this don't have family or friends that are affected by the disease, but the fiercest opponents include families that don't want to be reminded of the loved ones they've lost to the disease. I can understand that. Seeing my father in that primitive state was painful, but I was surprised more than anything else. Even though I barely had a chance to know him, I felt his absence every day of my life—even more so because it had never been explained.

* * *

When I get home from school later that day, the house is dark. My mother has the night off, and when I pass her room upstairs I see the light of her bedside lamp shining around the cracks of her door. I stand outside, listening. I consider knocking, apologizing for my accusations, but I slink off to my room instead. Our family has always left things unsaid.

On my bed I find a stack of the photographs I had left in the kitchen—face down—and an old cardboard box marked "Christmas ornaments," spotted with mold and water stains, one corner crushed in. I sit beside the box and pull at the folded flaps, feeling grime stick to my fingertips as I open it.

My father's old camera is here, a manual Canon 35mm SLR, identical to mine. The lens is scratched and the film compartment is jammed shut; something rattles inside when I shake it. My mother had his backup camera repaired and gave it to me for my sixteenth birthday, the summer before I left for college. The gesture meant a lot: it was the first time she had openly acknowledged my father, long after we had stopped discussing him. Whenever other students—and often my teachers—try to persuade me to switch to a digital camera, I cling to that small fragment of my father, a relic of the past, and ignore them.

I rummage in the box and pull out two handfuls of plastic black and white film cartridges. A number of them have been exposed, the film leader rewound into the magazine, but they haven't been developed. I set them aside, wondering if I'll be able to coax photographs from the aged emulsions.

At the bottom of the box are several small, red leather photo albums. I open the top one and see my face, wide-eyed and pudgy, about three years old. I turn the thick plastic pages and see photo after photo of a younger me. The next book is filled with pictures of my mother, pregnant. There are images of her later, in the hospital, carrying her newborn son.

There are a lot of close-ups of my mother as a young woman, happier than I can recall ever seeing her. One picture in particular shows her posing for my father—it makes me wish that a woman will look at me that way someday. The next photo shows a complete transformation: she's crying, mascara streaks lining her cheeks. Was this when he gave her the bad news? When she realized she was going to lose him? I imagine having that same conversation with my mother one day. I don't ever want to cause someone that much pain.

I know why my father decided to capture that heartbreaking moment. My mother's face is open, her defenses are down—you can see right to the core of her. As frightened and vulnerable as she appears, I think it's the prettiest I've ever seen her.

The third album is incomplete. There's a picture of my mother and me in the park and some photos from my fifth birthday, including a close-up of me with cake smeared all over my face. And there's one picture of my father.

This last photo, only a third of the way through the mostly empty book, is taken at a skewed angle, badly out of focus and underexposed. Despite the amateurish quality, I see that he is kneeling on a boulder at the park, the beginnings of a beard growing in. It looks surreally similar to the photograph I took yesterday. I realize that this is probably my first photograph.

"I haven't seen those in years," my mother says softly.

I look up and wipe tears from my face. She's standing in the door with her bathrobe wrapped around her, her arms wrapped around that. She's been crying too.

"I've never seen them," I say. I sound harsher than I intend. This box is a time capsule, a memorial, dedicated to my father. It's also a peace offering. "Thank you."

"You're so much like him," my mother says.

"Is that why you didn't tell me?" I ask.

She nodded. "I didn't want to know … if I were going to lose you too."

I hold up the book and show her the picture of my father as a young man.

"Did I take this?"

She comes closer to study the picture then nods. "You were only five. He wanted to teach you photography, couldn't wait until you were old enough. He was planning to get you a training camera, but he was already slipping away. After that day he went quickly."

When I scoot over she sits on the edge of the bed. She rests a hand on the broken camera on the bedspread.

"I went for a blood test today," I say.

She nods. "I thought you might."

"I have to know." The thought of losing my mind like my father did is terrifying. What kind of life is left after forgetting your wife and your son, living like a savage?

"I didn't want him to go," she says. "But he decided he wanted to go to a reservation, once he found out what was going to happen to him. He made me promise. And even then I didn't let him leave until I was absolutely sure …" Her voice quavers and she looks at me, then away and closes her eyes. "Until I was sure there was nothing left."

"Are you sure?"

She flips over one of the pictures I printed, a blow-up of my father's face. "I thought I was. Until I saw this." She lays the picture in her lap. "What if I made a mistake?"

"You did what he asked, Mom." I put my hand over hers, over the picture in her lap. "There was nothing else you could do."

"When do you get the results?"

"Not for a few days." I put the photo albums back into the box, in the order that I found them. "Do you want to know what I find out?"

"I don't know."

She nods to the film rolls scattered on my bedspread. "I almost developed those, a few times, before I put them away. Your father was too confused to do them himself. He gave up after ruining a couple. But he kept shooting that camera, until the very end. Until he could barely remember how a camera worked."

I scoop the rolls up and cradle them against my chest.

"Do you think there are still pictures on them?" she asks.

"I don't know. I don't know how much is left. But I'm going to find out."

* * *

Hollander's disease has a very slow onset, resembling Alzheimer's disease at first, then progressing very rapidly.

Early symptoms include short-term memory loss, irritability, and mood swings. Long-term memory gaps and personality shifts develop, followed by disorientation and confusion. Eventually the higher faculties deteriorate—most noticeably reasoning and communication. There's an accompanying loss of inhibition and an increased sex drive, a strengthening of what are considered primal urges.

In the final stages, victims are reduced to simple speech and behavior; basically, they become evolutionary throwbacks. Cavemen.

As I stand in complete darkness, blindly guiding the film from the cartridges onto spiral holders, I think about what my father must have gone through. When I stand in the darkroom—his darkroom—I always feel close to him, closer now that I know I might suffer the same fate. He knew what was happening to him, but did he lie to himself that it was all just a phase, that he would be all right—the way my mother did? When he could no longer believe his own lies, how did he keep himself going, taking pictures and making plans for his future instead of giving in to despair? I hope his photographs will give me some of the answers.

There are eleven rolls of film in total, but only eight of them yield what could be called pictures. The rest are a waste, not because of the age of the film, but because they reveal only blurry photos of nothing in particular: impressions of grass, a cloudless sky. A full reel that looked like it was taken with the lens cap on. These are the photos of a man who is losing his mind.

I make contact sheets from the negatives and examine the miniature images, organizing them in my best estimate of chronological order based on the deterioration in quality of composition and technique. I select the best of them and develop my dad's photographs one by one, growing more despondent with each new photo I pin to the line to dry. I had imagined that I could put together a collection of his last work, but the pictures are almost too painful to look at.

The first roll is closest to my father at the height of his talent—pictures of the neighborhood, places he had been. Some of them were long drives away, back in his hometown two states away. It was like he was revisiting his life, one last time. There were also pictures of people, a lot of children in the playground, a few more pictures of me.

My father was an urban photographer, documenting the city and the people that live there, but I noticed a trend towards emptiness—a large abandoned parking lot, an overgrown field behind a chain-linked fence, and then pictures of the open country just outside the city limits.

Later, rolls seem almost random, little better than the careless snapshots of a tourist. An entire roll follows a woman walking down the streets who becomes overtly frightened of the photographer stalking her. Another shows a series of pictures of sidewalks, garbage bags, abandoned cars, piles of dog shit on the street.

The rest are simply confused. Pictures of his hand, his feet, a leg, his penis, his back reflected in a mirror. Maybe he was cataloging the parts of himself, trying to stop himself from changing in the only way he knew how, by preserving himself forever in a photograph. There is one startling shot of his eyes, as though he had held the camera the wrong way around and peered into the lens.

When I finish, exhausted from spending the whole day developing and nauseous from the chemical fumes, I leave the pictures hanging in the darkroom. My mother will find them there, though I'm not sure if she should see them or not. I finally know exactly what she meant when she said my father was gone.

* * *

There is no cure for Hollander's. There is no treatment.

Many doctors continue to study and question what caused the disease in the first place, even as the number of new cases has dropped to the hundreds each year instead of the thousands. It's a hereditary disease, but the trigger for the genes has yet to be discovered.

Some people blame the government, terrorists, or God. Others blame pollution, radiation, even cell phones. One popular belief is that it is a result of human tampering with nature; that there is no cure for Hollander's because Hollander's is the cure for *us*.

Most people simply pretend that it doesn't exist.

I'm nervous as I approach the security station. I slide the university pass my advisor arranged for me through the slot in the glass. The pass has expired, but I couldn't wait for the paperwork to be renewed. I suppose I can tell the security guard that I'm visiting my father, but that would seem suspicious if he remembers me from my visit last week, and I want to bring my camera inside with me.

"You're back!" the guard says. "You ran off in such a hurry last time. People don't know what to expect when they come here. Not everyone can handle it."

"I just realized I was late for a class." I give him a foolish smile.

The guard frowns over his glasses as he examines the pass. "This is a week old."

"I know, but …" I lean closer to the window. "This is kind of embarrassing, but I botched the entire roll of pictures I took. It was a completely amateurish thing to do, but the film never threaded into the camera."

"You're not using digital?"

"I wanted a nostalgic touch," I say. "Listen, I *really* need photos for my senior thesis …"

The guard studies me. "Well, you've already been in there once, so I guess there's no harm." He slides the pass back to me and taps the touchscreen embedded in the desk. "Check in here."

When I check in I also check out, logging a time still several hours away. If I'm lucky no one will notice that I haven't left after this guard ends his shift.

When I get inside the tall, electrified gates I walk a distance from the guardhouse before ducking into the trees. I couldn't take many photos last time because the regressives had run from me, or hidden in the forest, though one curious woman had actually edged up to me. She plucked at my loose tee shirt and sniffed at me, her body close and smelling earthy and sun-warmed. As soon as I spoke to her she bolted like a scared rabbit.

Under the cover of thick foliage I strip, folding my shirt, jeans, and boxer shorts and placing them in a shallow hole with my sneakers and a plastic bag containing my watch, keys, cell phone, and wallet. I cover them with dirt and place a rotting log across the spot. I walk a little farther to the stream, which is man-made like all the other "natural" features on this expansive tract of land.

I slap on thick handfuls of mud from the banks of the stream, shivering at the cold sliminess as I cake it over my bare skin. In preparation for this I've also grown my beard for the last three days, but my hair is still short. It's not much of a disguise, but I'm trying to pass myself off as a new arrival at the reservation; at the very least, I hope I won't spook the regressives as soon as they catch sight of me.

The only modern luxuries I allow are my camera and my camera bag, which has enough film and some provisions to last me for a week or so. After that I'll need to find food, though I doubt I'm up to hunting the wildlife they truck in here for the regressives.

I trudge through the forest making far too much noise and feeling every stone and twig dig into the soft soles of my feet. I sense eyes on me, but I don't spot anyone. Eventually I emerge into a clearing. There's a half-circle of regressives facing me, waiting.

My eyes scan their faces, glancing over their bronzed bodies and then sliding away. Their nakedness makes me self-conscious. The group is made up mostly of men, burly like the muscle-heads at my gym. The five women there are smaller, less muscled, and lean.

I stare at their sagging breasts and react in spite of myself. I'm surprised to see that two of the women are only a little older than me, reminding me that the disease targets without regard for age or sex. I recognize one of them—a pretty girl with a wild mane of reddish-brown hair, large breasts, and wide hips—as the woman who approached me before. I think she smiles a little, her head high and her nose flaring as she scents the air.

I lift my camera very slowly and peer through the viewfinder. I focus on the gathering, carefully framing the composition. When I press the shutter the click resounds in the silent forest and sends them scattering.

A rock hits a tree beside me, just missing my head. I duck, sheltering the camera with my body. I dodge behind the tree, trying to see who is attacking me and from where, and another rock glances off my right ankle. I stumble to my knees and feel a sharp stone cut into my leg.

"No!" a voice grunts. A male voice. I crawl out and see my father crouching in the clearing, his back to me. I gasp, stunned that I've found him this easily. Or has he found me?

This is the nearest I've been to him since he left. An older woman hovers beside him, one arm cast across his shoulders. I approach slowly and he turns and grunts when he catches sight of me. He stands, hunching his shoulders, then backs up towards me. I freeze as he leans close and sniffs. I haven't bathed in two days, because everything I've studied indicates that regressives rely heavily on smell for recognition, along with body language. He touches my face, rubs long-nailed fingers against my sparse beard, and I try not to flinch away. He places his hand on the camera around my neck before turning back to the group.

"Me," he grunts loudly, his arms extended with the palms facing out. He sweeps a hand behind him in my direction. "Me."

*   *   *

"Dad," I whisper, the word catching in my throat. He looks around and sniffs again. His eyes shine at me, identical to the eyes that I am used to seeing in the mirror.

"Me," he says.

Because I was so young, I can't tell which memories of my father really happened and which I have constructed over the years from stories, half-forgotten dreams, and my own imagination. I remember him lurking with his camera around the house. I remember him laughing with my mother, curling up with her on the couch. I imagine him in his darkroom, bent over the counter studying a photograph with a dissatisfied frown. We played catch as fathers and sons do, or maybe I just wish that we had. I only remember these moments as snatches of images— photographs developed in my mind, never committed to film and faded with time.

I have been living with my father on the reservation, in the cave he shares with three women: the older one I saw him with before, another who fusses over me like a concerned mother, and the attractive young redhead. He sleeps with the first two, without caring that I'm around, but the youngest has taken an obvious interest in me, and my father doesn't touch her.

One day I caught the girl looking at me the way my mother looked at my father in that photo. I hesitated, trying to decide whether to photograph her or kiss her, but the moment was lost and she stalked off. I am tempted to give into more primal urges, which feel more and more natural the longer I stay here. No one here will judge me, but I'll know better.

I have a full beard now and my hair is growing out, but it's only a matter of time before someone notices that my RFID signature doesn't belong here, if anyone's even paying attention.

I wonder how long my mother will wait for me to come home, whether she will come looking for me—for us. I left a copy of the results of my blood test with a note telling her where I planned to go. I didn't think she would understand my need to come here, especially when I barely understand it myself.

I had to experience this even though I won't get Hollander's. I won't go through the same transformations that took my father; of course that's a relief—I don't want to forget who I am—but I'm discovering that I *could* survive here. This life is as good as any other, maybe better. Life here is peaceful; the people seem happy the way they are. I want my mother to see that, too.

In the dirt at the back of the cave I discovered crude drawings my father made—just stick figures—of three people that could be a man, woman, and child. Since then I've been trying to re-teach him to use a camera. We've been taking pictures together again.

As I live among the regressives I study them, learn about our past and what might be our future. I hope my photos and experiences will show everyone a forgotten part of themselves. I want to honor those who were forced into this existence whether by divine will, evolutionary checks and balances, or simply luck. Maybe they aren't victims after all, maybe they've just been chosen.

I use my thesis to rationalize my decision to stay a little longer, but the truth is I'm finally getting to know my dad.

E.C. Myers *was assembled in the US from Korean and German parts and raised by a single mother and the public library in Yonkers, New York. He is the author of numerous short stories and four young adult books: the Andre Norton Award–winning* Fair Coin, Quantum Coin, The Silence of Six, *and* Against All Silence. *E.C. lives with his wife, son, and three doofy pets in Pennsylvania. You can find traces of him all over the internet, but especially at ecmyers.net and on Twitter: @ecmyers.*

For Sun, life as a gargoyle is a challenge, but at least he's not a Stoner or a grotesque ... the city streets can be a tough place to grow up no matter who you are in Alethea Kontis' latest tale.

Like a Thief in the Light

By Alethea Kontis

The Stoners were up to their old tricks again.

Sun downshifted the street sweeper and pulled up on the brake. He untangled his gangly limbs from the gears and stepped down, cracking his head on the doorway again. Stupid low ceiling. Stupid giant head.

Pierre never had this problem; his head just dented the doorway. But Sun was not a gargoyle, so there would be a tiara of bruises around Sun's bulbous, bald pate until he remembered how to get out of his own way. Nor did Sun have Pierre's water-summoning power, so he had to fill the sweeper's giant tanks in the Shadow Street Reservoir before making rounds on the days when Pierre was too weary to sweep. Those days were every day now.

The Stoners weren't gargoyles either, just a gang of grotesques who liked to perpetuate the lie because gargoyles had a far more romantic reputation. But their bodies were also made of stone, and they also froze into statues in the daylight—as the asshole currently blocking his sweeper demonstrated—but they had no magic over water or anything else. The only talent the Stoners had was "taking donations" from passersby. It wasn't technically stealing if the person *gave* them all their worldly goods out of the kindness of their own heart ... or from the fear of having said heart ripped out through their chest cavity by stone claws.

Sun paused before stepping all the way down to the street and leaned back into the cab. He was careful not to wake Fuzz, curled up and dozing in the passenger's seat like a long tailed black rat who wore his skull on the outside. The aye-aye was nocturnal, like ninety-nine percent of the population of Shadow Street. But Fuzz insisted on tagging along, Sun's life was easier if he didn't argue.

Sun's long white fingers silently flicked the button on the glove box and he took out the can of safety orange spray paint Pierre saved to mark road hazards for the night shift. Fuzz let out a soft whuffle of a snore. The can smelled like gasoline. There wasn't much on that ancient wreck of a sweeper that *didn't* smell like gasoline. Pierre had managed to keep the sweeper running, but one good rain would wash it into the shadows, sprockets and widgets and all.

Shaking the can was like parading a brass band down the street. The ball bearings careening back and forth inside the can echoed off the walls of the buildings on the empty street loud enough to wake the dead ... somewhere else. No dead here worth his salt would bother to rise before twilight. Nothing walked this street at noon except the loners, the shadows, and the street sweepers. Sun was all three.

The harsh light of day was unforgiving to the bricks and mortar of Shadow Street. There were no streetlights and gas lamps to take the years away, no neon to gussy up the years of cracks and scars. Daylight made all the buildings equal: from the gothic marble and limestone library to the concrete and glass of that new vampire club. At the Witching Hour, blood was love and sex and life. At noon, it was just another brown stain on the pavement.

Everything was tall and gray and unsightly in the brightness, just like him. It was the only place and time Sun ever felt like he belonged, the king of the world, quiet and looming here in the ugly truth.

Sun stopped shaking the can, and the high-pitched gunfire stopped repeating off the sun-bleached moldy walls. Hatch looked a little worse for the wear himself, now that Sun was brave enough to get a nice, close look at him. After sunset he wouldn't want to be closer than a block away from any of the Stoners, but here and now he could examine to his heart's content.

Hatch was covered in pockmarks, small divots in the rock made from time, wear, and general stupidity. One of his horns was missing the tip, giving him a lopsided look. Hatch was a wingless grotesque, with a face like a bull and the body of a lion. His feet were splayed and his arms were spread wide—he'd tried to make as large a barrier of himself as possible, and he'd succeeded. Sun would have to back the sweeper up and swing it wide to miss him, after he cleaned this section of the street by hand. Sun wished he could back up and run Hatch over with the sweeper itself, but he knew it would 1.) irreparably damage the sweeper and 2.) wake Fuzz up. Sun was far more scared of the latter.

Sun wrapped his long fingers around the ring in Hatch's nose and rapped against his bull chin. "Anybody home?" Sun giggled to himself, and then quit when he realized how pathetic it sounded. He cleared his throat and started again.

"Looking rough, man. Know what you need? A makeover. Here, let me help you." Sun shook the can a few more times for good measure, and then painted Hatch a nice, full head of safety orange hair.

"Remember, ladies. Do not neglect those eyebrows." Sun took it upon himself to attend to them on Hatch's behalf. "I do declare. You look at least two hundred years younger." Sun kissed Hatch on the cheek and stepped back to survey his handiwork.

That's when he noticed the shadow.

Everyone knows: the brighter the sunlight, the darker the shadow. What everyone doesn't know is what hides in those shadows, invisibly waiting to reach out and feed on your soul. Sun knew this because he was one of them. He could see them with his poison green eyes.

Normally shadow thieves were blind, led by way of temperature and feeding by soulsmell, but Sun was not normal. His mother had not been a shadow. He wasn't sure what she'd been, exactly, but she'd given him some green eyes and a horrible skin condition to remember her by. His father had given him a lanky build, a big bulbous head, and the ability to pop in and out of shadow without having to suck souls. But while his father and mother may have created him, Pierre was the one who had given him a home and a life and a purpose. Pierre was the only parent Sun gave a crap about.

But Pierre was sick and old and getting sicker and older. In the far too near future, Sun would lose him. He didn't want to think about it. And yet, lately it was all he could think about. Stupid thoughts. Stupid head.

A snarl and a growl at his feet snapped Sun out of his melancholy. Fuzz gnashed his scary front teeth and swiped his bony black fingers at the shadow beside them. It took a moment for Sun's brain to register that the shadow thief had slipped into Sun's own shadow and was feeding upon Sun's soul. With some effort—thanks in no small part to Fuzz's distraction—Sun jumped back away from Hatch's dark shadow and the blind, hungry thief trapped inside it.

Sun couldn't suck souls, but Fuzz could. He was the reason the aye-aye as a species had such a bad reputation in the first place. Fuzz might have been ten times smaller than Sun, but he was a hell of a lot more intimidating.

"Yeah, yeah. So you're a big shot," said Sun. "Rub it in."

Fuzz responded by displaying one of his disproportionately distended middle fingers. With a yawn, he deftly crawled back up into the sweeper.

Sun laughed, grabbed his broom, and went back to work.

*   *   *

"When I pass on, Sun, ze sweeper, she is for you, no?" It had been a long time since Pierre had left his tiny little colony on the coast of South America, but he'd never lost the accent.

"No," said Sun. He washed his hands in the basin and opened the shutters to let the twilight in. Fresh air would do Pierre a world of good.

"How can you no love ze daylight sweeper? She is a good sweeper."

"She is a fine sweeper," Sun agreed. "I just meant no, you will not 'pass on' anytime soon. Stop talking like that."

"We cannot stop ze sun from rising or ze moon from setting," said Pierre. "We do not live forever, *mon soleil*, not even these old stones. Not talking about it cannot make it so."

"Tell that to the rest of Shadow Street," Sun muttered under his breath.

Either Pierre did not hear him, or he just ignored the snarky comment. It was hard to tell sometimes. "I would like to work in ze garden today," Pierre mused.

Of course he would. Sun wondered sometimes why he ever bothered showering, since he seemed destined to be covered in dirt of some kind. Not that the dirt was the issue. The garden was to be Pierre's final resting place. Sun didn't love the idea of landscaping a graveyard.

But as Sun didn't want to appear ungrateful, he said none of this. He simply went to Pierre's side, removed the tray of untouched soup, and helped his giant stony carcass out of bed like the dutiful foster child he was.

It just didn't make any sense. If ninety-five percent of the population on Shadow Street was immortal, why did Pierre have to die? What made gargoyles so different from all the other monstrous peoples of the world?

As soon as the question was swimming around in that giant head of his, Sun knew exactly who would have the answer. "Oh, crap," he said aloud.

"Am I too heavy?" asked Pierre. He *was* leaning more of his weight onto Sun than usual, but Sun had grown stronger because of it.

"No heavier than my head, fat man," said Sun. It was a long-standing joke between them. "The 'crap' was just me suddenly regretting something."

Pierre's knowing chortle degraded into a raspy cough. Sun hoped none of that water had managed to find a way into his lungs. "We make mistakes," he said when he finally caught his breath. "What sets us apart are those of us who learn from them."

Sun only nodded; he was afraid that if he spoke it might crack his already damaged calm. He would miss Pierre's croissant-flavored fortune cookie wisdom. But Pierre was not gone yet. It was just stupid of Sun to miss him while he was still here. He blinked a few times and bit his tongue so that the pain would distract him from his sorrow. It was nothing close to the painful lesson he was about to learn.

Pierre's energy did not last long—it was only an hour past full dark before they gave up on the garden and came inside for simpler pleasures. Sun made sure Pierre was all set up in his workshop, wings deep in crystals and gauges and gears, before he called it an early night. Pierre, deep into his tinkering, merely waved him away.

It didn't take Sun long to find the Stoners. He slipped into the shadows and slunk the outskirts of the labyrinthine sewer system. Traveling as a shadow was faster than going on foot, but Sun couldn't shadowshift unless he fully stepped into darkness. He exited the sewers by the library and saw the gang a block away, "accepting donations" outside the library. More to the point, Hatch's Day-Glo orange head shone like a beacon beneath the streetlights.

Sun winced. Oh, yeah. This was going to be fun. He slipped from shadow to shadow between the chain link fence and the broken sidewalk, making sure they didn't see him until he was good and ready. He only had one shot; he had to make it count.

"Damn, Ginger, you are looking *hot*." Sun drew the word out and attached a sizzle and a hoot for good measure.

The first punch aimed at Sun's face swung through as his body, with one foot still in shadow, turned to mist.

"Grab him!" Hatch yelled through gritted teeth.

Spoiler, with his bear body and demon face, bumped Sun out of the shadows. Hinge, a hairless cat with batwings, slashed at him with his claws. Fender, a pitbull with wings, clamped his jaws around Sun's shoulder and held him down in the circle of light cast by the streetlight. There were no shadows to escape to and— even if he could break free of Fender's grip—nowhere to run.

They beat the crap out of him.

Sun's brain reminded him that if he didn't fight it, if he tried to relax and didn't tense his muscles, it would hurt less. Sun's muscles, seeing Hatch's fists and feet flying at him like stone barbells, told his brain to go screw itself and braced for impact.

He squirmed and shifted and attempted to dodge when he could, but Fender's jaws held tight. Sun also tried to get a word in between thrashings, before he lost too many teeth to be understood.

"I—" Bash to the head. Stupid head.

"—need—" Ribs cracking. One, maybe two.

"—your—" Hot lines dug with razor blade claws down his back. Fire.

"—help—" Pretty sure that last crack was his left arm bone.

"—please."

That was the word that stopped them. Sun didn't know why. He was sure some of their devoted fans had yelled the same thing while having their stuffing extracted. Perhaps it was his tone.

Spoiler's split tongue darted out. "Did he jusssst ssssay…?"

"Mm—I fink sho," Fender said before spitting out Sun's shoulder in a shower of drool. Sun's limp body tumbled to the ground. His ruined shirt caught on one of Fender's jutting fangs and ripped to shreds. He didn't have the strength to care.

"Wow," barked Fender.

"What the hell is that?" said Hinge.

"He'ssss a freak," said Spoiler.

Leave it to Hatch to be the only Stoner without ADD. "What kind of freak moron asks for help from the one kicking his ass?"

Sun hadn't really thought this far ahead in the conversation. Honestly, he'd pretty much counted on dying right there in the street, or at least losing consciousness before they could have a meaningful conversation. If one could have a meaningful conversation with a gang of ugly, blockheaded statues named after car parts. There was so much to explain. However, the Stoners had brains the size of walnuts, and Sun only had enough energy to get to the point.

"Pierre's … dying."

"That don't make no damn sense." Sun didn't try to open his eyes; even if he could, he'd be staring at blood-soaked pavement. But he could hear Hatch laughing at him. "Pierre's only from …" he snapped his fingers.

"Devil'sssss Island," offered Spoiler.

"See? There are real French gargoyles way older than him. He should live forever."

"Nobody lives forever." Fender's voice was deep and gravelly.

"Shut up, Fender," said Hatch. "You know, I bet it's all that water. All water eats away stone eventually. No getting around that."

That was possibly the most intelligent thing Hatch had said in his whole life.

"But there are other beings on this street who live forever." Hinge would know, he had nine or so lives himself.

"How—" Sun coughed and spat the blood out of his mouth to make room for his tongue. He tried to lift himself up and failed completely. That's right. Broken arm. Broken ribs. "How do you make stone live forever?" he asked into the sidewalk when he caught his breath again.

"What else lives forever?" asked Fender.

"Vampiresssss," said Spoiler.

"Too bad gargoyles have no blood," said Hatch.

Yeah, too bad, thought Sun. He'd happily donate some of the stuff he was currently leaking.

"Zombies," Hinge added with a yowl. "Or werewolves. Though you probably wouldn't want Pierre to survive like that."

"Gargoyles don't catch plagues," said Hatch.

"Ghosts!" barked Fender.

"That would defeat the purpose, muttface," said Hatch.

"Ssssshadow thievesssss," Spoiler said finally. Sun would have laughed if it didn't feel like knives. He managed to lean on his right arm enough to flip himself over. The intention was to use the streetlight post for back support, but all he managed to do was touch it with the top of his gargantuan head.

"Why do you look like somebody dropped you through stained glass when you was a baby?" asked Hatch.

"Or coughed up a crayon box," said Hinge.

The Stoners were able to see his skin now, the deformity that usually hid beneath his long-sleeved shirts. The birthmarks covered the length of his pale body—except for his head, hands and feet—patches of discoloration every color of the rainbow. It wasn't even a cool design, either; he looked more like a retarded Tiffany lamp.

"My mother … is … was"—wow, Sun had seriously taken for granted his previous ability to breathe—"not … shadow."

"That don't make no damn sense neither!" It was a good thing Sun couldn't laugh, because Hatch looked freaking hilarious with those Bozo orange eyebrows. And if Sun *had* laughed, he would've had to add himself to the list of things on this street that definitely didn't live forever.

"You're either a shadow or you ain't," said Hinge.

"Ssssso what are you, Poisssssson Eyesssss?"

He was about five minutes away from becoming another stain on the sidewalk. "I'm a freak," he said. "Just kill me already and be done with it."

Hatch nudged Sun's body with a stone toe. "Don't feel like it anymore."

"Yeah," Fender woofed. "It's no fun when they can't fight back."

Sun felt their shadows pass over him as they walked away. One, two, three …

"Hey," the last shadow said. "Freak."

Sun cracked one eye open and saw Spoiler looming above him. He felt pieces of himself dissolve into the devil's blessed shadow.

"Asssssk your dad."

"Ask him what?" There were at least a hundred questions. How he gave birth to a freak? Why he abandoned him? What he had to do with his life that was more important than having a son?

"Assssk him how to live forever," said Spoiler. "Pierre'ssss a good guy."

One of the Stoners hollered for Spoiler and all too soon his shadow was gone, leaving Sun in a pool of light and blood and pain.

Sun peeked through his lids up into the bulb of the streetlight that beamed down upon him, merciless as the noonday sun. Soon, Pierre would see a beam like this, and his soul would use it to walk from this dark world into a place of beauty and peace. There would only be a statue left in this world where Pierre had been: a statue, a few dents in the door of the street sweeper, and a hole in Sun's heart.

Sun tried to sob but his broken ribs would not let him gasp for breath. A few hot tears silently leaked out the corners of his eyes anyway, making trails in the dirt and blood on his giant head. It hurt to move. It hurt to breathe. It hurt to live.

Maybe if he stared at it long enough, Sun could make it to that place on the other side of the light first. Wouldn't Pierre be surprised when he arrived.

And then the light went out.

Sun heard the pop of the bulb in enough time to close his eyes before the tiny shards of glass and filament fell on his chest. Fuzz was the next thing to fall on his chest. Sun braced himself.

The aye-aye fell right through him and landed on the sidewalk.

Sun yelped in relief and gratitude as he slowly became one with the shadows and the pain melted away. Oh, he'd still have to heal, but at least he could do it in the privacy of his own bed instead of bleeding to death on the sidewalk.

Sun took a few gloriously deep breaths. Fuzz chittered at him.

"All right," said Sun. "Thank you already."

"You're welcome."

A match sprang to life before him and lit a cigarette. It took a moment for Sun's eyes to adjust. Before him stood a shadow thief. He was taller than Sun, skinnier, and paler. His head was just as big. But his eyes … Instead of milky white, they were completely black—blacker than shadow—the empty black of nothingness and despair. But this guy wasn't blind. He could see just fine.

This was one of the elder shadow thieves, the original inhabitants of this street. The thief took a long drag from the cigarette and exhaled. The foul gray smoke mixed with his own insubstantial shape. "Hello, Lightwalker."

"Do I know you?" Sun didn't, but he asked the question anyway. Deep down, he had a really good idea.

"No." Another drag. The cigarette's glow mirrored in those black eyes. "If you're lucky it'll stay that way."

"Why?" asked Sun. He wasn't sure which of the hundred questions he was looking to answer, but this word covered most of them.

"I'm no good, kid. I'm a monster. I'm The Bad Guy. Bumps in the night are for pussies. I suck souls and leave the carcasses for the street sweepers. It's what I do. It's who I am." Ash fell onto the sidewalk. Smoke curled up toward heaven. "Shadows don't have children."

"Then what am I?"

"You're a mistake, kid. A lapse in judgment. Darkness actually found a soul so bright he couldn't bear to take her." He tossed the cigarette into the gutter.

I'll be sweeping that up later, thought Sun.

"But I took her anyway," said the thief. "In the end, I ate her soul. Because that's what I do. It's who I am. Do you understand me?"

Sun shrugged. "Yeah."

"See, I don't think you do. I think you're still contemplating the possibility of getting the Captain here"—he indicated Fuzz— "or one of the other bats to suck Pierre's soul so that you can babysit a shell for the rest of your life."

It had crossed Sun's mind, even before Spoiler had mentioned it.

"I'm telling you right now, it's a bad idea. It's what Bad Guys do. You have never been a Bad Guy."

Sun shrugged again. How would he know?

"Don't take after me, you hear me? You let that soul find peace like it's supposed to. Just because you're not okay with the idea doesn't give you the right to change the way of the world." The wind picked up, blowing a cold eddy of street trash through the both of them. Dirt and straw wrappers stuck in the blood left on the sidewalk. "Trust me. I know." The thief's voice fell, fading. "If you love him, let him go."

Sun could not think of more perfect parting words from a father he had never known, and would likely never meet again. "Be seeing you, then."

"No, you won't." That cold metallic wind picked up again; it smelled like fresh graves and sorrow. "Keep an eye on him, Captain."

Fuzz gave a few clicks and a snort, but the thief was already gone.

With nothing left for him here, Sun slunk through the shadows behind Fuzz and the rats, all the way back to the ratty apartment. He slipped right in through the front door—he wasn't sure what to tell Pierre about this particular outing, but he didn't want to hide it from him either. Pierre deserved to know what was on Sun's mind. He deserved to be part of the conversation.

Unfortunately, it was a conversation they would never have.

Sun left Pierre's empty bedroom and walked out back to the courtyard. He tried not to think about how hard it must have been for Pierre to make it all the way out here unaided. But there he was in the center of the garden, wings unfurled, arms outstretched, head thrown back in a passionate cry, basking in the glory of the full moon. From his mouth trickled a small fountain that fed the flowers at his feet, and in each of his hands he held a crystal prism. And as the moonlight hit those prisms—Sun imagined it would be even more magnificent at dawn and sunset—the already colorful garden was blanketed in a scattering of rainbows.

Light and shadow and color. Pierre had spent his last days on this earth tinkering in his workshop, making a tribute to him, the only son he ever knew. It was a true gift of love for which Sun would never be able to thank him.

Despite Fuzz's scolding chirps, Sun stepped out of the shadow and into the moonlight. His broken bones began to ache again and his cuts started to bleed, but he needed to feel something, even if it was pain. He had so very little that mattered to him, and in his very short life he'd gone and lost it all. What did he have to look forward to? A future of long days sweeping a street clean of death so the shadows could muck it all up again? It may have been Pierre's legacy, but it didn't seem like much of a life.

A movement in Pierre's great shadow interrupted his thoughts. It wasn't a thief—didn't look like one or stink like one or slink like one. It moved more like smoke curls from a cigarette, like a clumsy butterfly flitting from one spot of rainbow to the next. Sun didn't smell a soul on it. A ghost maybe? But not substantial enough. Ah ... a wraith. Wraiths were sometimes left after a shadow thief feasted, if the soul was strong enough.

Sun decided not to frighten the wraith; it wasn't causing any trouble. Besides, Sun was enjoying his level of pain too much to move and make it worse. And then the moonlight caught the silhouette of the wraith's arm as it stretched out to touch a flower. A rainbow reflected off the shape of a wing. It was a fairy.

All the pieces fell into place. The light, the dark. The prisms. The garden. The secrets. The warnings. The rainbows. Fairies loved green and growing things. They loved colors and light. They had souls that shone like beacons. This fairy had no business being anywhere near Shadow Street, but for better or worse she had come, and met her end here.

This wasn't just any wraith. This was his mother.

And, just like that, Sun once again had something to live for.

New York Times bestselling author **Alethea Kontis** *is a princess, a fairy godmother, and a geek. She's known for screwing up the alphabet, scolding vampire hunters, turning garden gnomes into mad scientists, and making sense out of fairy tales. Alethea is the co-author of Sherrilyn Kenyon's* Dark-Hunter Companion, *and penned the AlphaOops series of picture books. Her short fiction, essays, and poetry have appeared in a myriad of anthologies and magazines. She has done multiple collaborations with Eisner winning artist J.K. Lee, including* The Wonderland Alphabet *and* Diary of a Mad Scientist Garden Gnome. *Her YA fairy tale novel,* Enchanted, *won the Gelett Burgess Children's Book Award in 2012, was nominated for the Audie Award in 2013, and was selected for World Book Night in 2014. Both* Enchanted *and its sequel,* Hero, *were nominated for the Andre Norton Award.* Tales of Arilland, *a short story collection set in the same fairy tale world, won a second Gelett Burgess Award in 2015. Born in Burlington, Vermont, Alethea currently lives and writes on the Space Coast of Florida. She makes the best baklava you've ever tasted and sleeps with a teddy bear named Charlie. You can find Princess Alethea online at: aletheakontis.com.*

At St. Agatha's Home for the Rehabilitation of Crippled Children, residents find themselves serving their own Fagin right out of Dickens' Oliver, a tough taskmaster they call Old Grinder. But instead of hoping for his eighteenth birthday and escape, a boy named Sian looks for a way out—maybe even one that can improve life for them all, in Cory Doctorow's inspiring steampunk tale ...

CLOCKWORK FAGIN

BY CORY DOCTOROW

Monty Goldfarb walked into St. Agatha's like he owned the place, a superior look on the half of his face that was still intact, a spring in his step despite his steel left leg. And it wasn't long before he *did* own the place, taken it over by simple murder and cunning artifice. It wasn't long before he was my best friend and my master, too, and the master of all St. Agatha's, and didn't he preside over a *golden* era in the history of that miserable place?

I've lived in St. Agatha's for six years, since I was 11 years old, when a reciprocating gear in the Muddy York Hall of Computing took off my right arm at the elbow. My Da had sent me off to Muddy York when Ma died of the consumption. He'd sold me into service of the Computers and I'd thrived in the big city, hadn't cried, not even once, not even when Master Saunders beat me for playing kick-the-can with the other boys when I was meant to be polishing the brass. I didn't cry when I lost my arm, nor when the barber-surgeon clamped me off and burned my stump with his medicinal tar.

I've seen every kind of boy and girl come to St. Aggie's— swaggering, scared, tough, meek. The burned ones are often the hardest to read, inscrutable beneath their scars. Old Grinder don't care, though, not one bit. Angry or scared, burned and hobbling or swaggering and full of beans, the first thing he does when new meat turns up on his doorstep is tenderize it a little. That means a good long session with the belt—and Grinder doesn't care where the strap lands, whole skin or fresh scars, it's all the same to him—and then a night or two down the hole, where there's no light and no warmth and nothing for company except for the big hairy Muddy York rats who'll come and nibble at whatever's left of you if you manage to fall asleep. It's the blood, see, it draws them out.

So there we all was, that first night when Monty Goldfarb turned up, dropped off by a pair of sour-faced Sisters in white capes who turned their noses up at the smell of the horse-droppings as they stepped out of their coal-fired banger and handed Monty over to Grinder, who smiled and dry-washed his hairy hands and promised, "Oh, aye, sisters, I shall look after this poor crippled birdie like he was my own get. We'll be great friends, won't we, Monty?" Monty actually laughed when Grinder said that, like he'd already winkled it out.

As soon as the boiler on the sisters' car had its head of steam up and they were clanking away, Grinder took Monty inside, leading him past the parlour where we all sat, quiet as mice, eyeless or armless, shy a leg or half a face, or even a scalp (as was little Gertie Shine-Pate, whose hair got caught in the mighty rollers of one of the pressing engines down at the logic mill in Cabbagetown).

He gave us a jaunty wave as Grinder led him away, and I'm ashamed to say that none of us had the stuff to wave back at him, or even to shout a warning. Grinder had done his work on us, too true, and turned us from kids into cowards.

Presently, we heard the whistle and slap of the strap, but instead of screams of agony, we heard howls of defiance, and yes, even laughter!

"Is that the best you have, you greasy old sack of suet? Put some arm into it!"

And then: "Oh, dearie me, you must be tiring of your work. See how the sweat runs down your face, how your tongue doth protrude from your stinking gob. Oh please, dear master, tell me your pathetic old ticker isn't about to pack it in, I don't know what I'd do if you dropped dead here on the floor before me!"

And then: "Your chest heaves like a bellows. Is this what passes for a beating round here? Oh, when I get the strap, old man, I will show you how we beat a man in Montreal, you may count on it my sweet."

The way he carried on, you'd think he was *enjoying* the beating, and I had a picture of him leaping to and fro, avoiding the strap with the curious, skipping jump of a one-legged boy, but when Grinder led him past the parlour again, he looked half-dead. The good side of his face was a pulpy mess, and his one eye was near swollen shut, and he walked with even more of a limp than he'd had coming in. But he grinned at us again, and spat a tooth on the threadbare rug that we were made to sweep three times a day, a tooth that left a trail of blood behind it on the splintery floor.

We heard the thud as Monty was tossed down onto the hole's dirt floor, and then the labored breathing as Grinder locked him in, and then the singing, loud and distinct, from under the floorboards: "Come gather ye good children, good news to you I'll tell, 'bout how the Grinder bastard will roast and rot in Hell—" There was more, apparently improvised (later, I'd hear Monty improvise many and many a song, using some hymn or popular song for a tune beneath his bawdy and obscene lyrics), and we all strove to keep the smiles from our face as Grinder stamped back into his rooms, shooting us dagger-looks as he passed by the open door.

And that was the day that Monty came to St. Agatha's Home for the Rehabilitation of Crippled Children.

* * *

I remember my first night in the hole, a time that seemed to stretch into infinity, a darkness so deep I thought that perhaps I'd gone blind. And most of all, I remember the sound of the cellar door loosening, the bar being shifted, the ancient hinges squeaking, the blinding light stabbing into me from above, and the silhouette of old Grinder, holding out one of his hairy, long-fingered hands for me to catch hold of, like an angel come to rescue me from the pits of Hades. Grinder pulled me out of the hole like a man pulling up a carrot, with a gesture practiced on many other children over the years, and I near wept from gratitude. I'd soiled my trousers, and I couldn't hardly see, nor speak from my dry throat, and every sound and sight was magnified a thousandfold and I put my face in his great coat, there in the horrible smell of the man and the muscle beneath like a side of beef, and I cried like he was my old Mam come to get me out of a fever-bed.

I remember this, and I ain't proud of it, and I never spoke of it to any of the other St. Aggie's children, nor did they speak of it to me. I was broken then, and I was old Grinder's boy, and when he turned me out later that day with a begging bowl, sent me down to the distillery and off to the ports to approach the navvies and the lobsterbacks for a ha'penny or a groat or a tuppence, I went out like a grateful doggie, and never once thought of putting any of Grinder's money by in a secret place for my own spending.

Of course, over time I did get less doggy and more wolf about the Grinder, dreamt of tearing out his throat with my teeth, and Grinder always seemed to know when the doggy was going, because bung, you'd be back in the hole before you had a chance to chance old Grinder. A day or two downstairs would bring the doggie back out, especially if Grinder tenderized you some with his strap before he heaved you down the stairs. I'd seen big boys and rough girls come to St. Aggie's, hard as boots, and come out of Grinder's hole so good doggy that they practically licked his boots for him. Grinder understood children, I give you that. Give us a mean, hard father of a man, a man who doles out punishment and protection like old Jehovah from the Sisters' hymnals, and we line up to take his orders.

But Grinder didn't understand Monty Goldfarb.

I'd just come down to lay the long tables for breakfast—it was my turn that day—when I heard Grinder shoot the lock to his door and then the sound of his callouses rasping on the polished brass knob. As his door swung open, I heard the music box playing its tune, Grinder's favorite, a Scottish hymn that the music box sung in Gaelic, its weird horsegut voice box making the auld words even weirder, like the eldritch crooning of some crone in a street-play.

Grinder's heavy tramp receded down the hall, to the cellar door. The doors creaked open and I felt a shiver down in my stomach and down below that, in my stones, as I remembered my times in the pit. There was the thunder of his heavy boots on the steps, then his cruel laughter as he beheld Monty.

"Oh, my darling, is *this* how they take their punishment in Montreal? 'Tis no wonder the Frenchies lost their wars to the Upper Canadians, with such weak little mice as you to fight for them."

They came back up the stairs: Grinder's jaunty tromp, Monty's dragging, beaten limp. Down the hall they came, and I heard poor Monty reaching out to steady himself, brushing the framed drawings of Grinder's horrible ancestors as he went, and I flinched with each squeak of a picture knocked askew, for disturbing Grinder's forebears was a beating offence at St. Aggie's. But Grinder must have been feeling charitable, for he did not pause to whip beaten Monty that morning.

And so they came into the dining hall, and I did not raise my head, but beheld them from the corners of my eyes, taking cutlery from the basket hung over the hook at my right elbow and laying it down neat and precise on the splintery tables.

Each table had three hard loaves on it, charity bread donated from Muddy York's bakeries to us poor crippled kiddees, day-old and more than a day-old, and tough as stone. Before each loaf was a knife as long as a man's forearm, sharp as a butcher's, and the head child at each table was responsible for slicing the bread using that knife each day (children who were shy an arm or two were exempted from this duty, for which I was thankful, since those children were always accused of favoring some child with a thicker slice, and fights were common).

Monty was leaning heavily on Grinder, his head down and his steps like those of an old, old man, first a click of his steel foot, then a dragging from his remaining leg. But as they passed the head of the furthest table, Monty sprang from Grinder's side, took up the knife, and with a sure, steady hand—a movement so spry I knew he'd been shamming from the moment Grinder opened up the cellar door—he plunged the knife into Grinder's barrel-chest, just over his heart, and shoved it home, giving it a hard twist.

He stepped back to consider his handiwork. Grinder was standing perfectly still, his face pale beneath his whiskers, and his mouth was working, and I could almost hear the words he was trying to get out, words I'd heard so many times before: *Oh, my lovely, you are a naughty one, but Grinder will beat the devil out of you, purify you with rod and fire, have no fear—*

But no sound escaped Grinder's furious lips. Monty put his hands on his hips and watched him with the critical eye of a bricklayer or a machinist surveying his work. Then, calmly, he put his good right hand on Grinder's chest, just to one side of the knife handle. He said, "Oh, no, Mr. Grindersworth, *this* is how we take our punishment in Montreal." Then he gave the smallest of pushes and Grinder went over like a chimney that's been hit by a wrecking ball.

He turned then, and regarded me full on, the good side of his face alive with mischief, the mess on the other side a wreck of burned skin. He winked his good eye at me and said, "Now, he was a proper pile of filth and muck, wasn't he? World's a better place now, I daresay." He wiped his hand on his filthy trousers— grimed with the brown dirt of the cellar—and held it out to me. "Montague Goldfarb, machinist's boy and prentice artificer, late of old Montreal. Montreal Monty, if you please," he said.

I tried to say something—anything—and realized that I'd bitten the inside of my cheek so hard I could taste the blood. I was so discombobulated that I held out my abbreviated right arm to him, hook and cutlery basket and all, something I hadn't done since I'd first lost the limb. Truth told, I was a little tender and shy about my mutilation, and didn't like to think about it, and I especially couldn't bear to see whole people shying back from me as though I were some kind of monster. But Monty just reached out, calm as you like, and took my hook with his cunning fingers—fingers so long they seemed to have an extra joint—and shook my hook as though it were a whole hand.

"Sorry, mate, I didn't catch your name."

I tried to speak again, and this time I found my voice. "Sian O'Leary," I said. "Antrim Town, then Hamilton, and then here." I wondered what else to say. "Third-grade Computerman's boy, once upon a time."

"Oh, that's *fine*," he said. "Skilled tradesmen's helpers are what we want around here. You know the lads and lasses round here, Sian, are there more like you? Children who can make things, should they be called upon?"

I nodded. It was queer to be holding this calm conversation over the cooling body of Grinder, who now smelt of the ordure his slack bowels had loosed into his fine trousers. But it was also natural, somehow, caught in the burning gaze of Monty Goldfarb, who had the attitude of a master in his shop, running the place with utter confidence.

"Capital." He nudged Grinder with his toe. "That meat'll spoil soon enough, but before he does, let's have some fun, shall we? Give us a hand." He bent and lifted Grinder under one arm. He nodded his head at the remaining arm. "Come on," he said, and I took it, and we lifted the limp corpse of Zophar Grindersworth, the Grinder of St. Aggie's, and propped him up at the head of the middle table, knife handle protruding from his chest amid a spreading red stain over his blue brocade waistcoat. Monty shook his head. "That won't do," he said, and plucked up a tea towel from a pile by the kitchen door and tied it around Grinder's throat like a bib, fussing with it until it more-or-less disguised the grisly wound. Then Monty picked up one of the loaves from the end of the table and tore a hunk off the end.

He chewed at it like a cow at her cud for a time, never taking his eyes off me. Then he swallowed and said, "Hungry work," and laughed with a spray of crumbs.

He paced the room, picking up the cutlery I'd laid and inspecting it, gnawing at the loaf's end in his hand thoughtfully. "A pretty poor setup," he said. "But I'm sure that wicked old lizard had a pretty soft nest for himself, didn't he?"

I nodded and pointed down the hall to Grinder's door. "The key's on his belt," I said.

Monty fingered the keyring chained to Grinder's thick leather belt, then shrugged. "All one-cylinder jobs," he said, and picked a fork out of the basket that was still hanging from my hook. "Nothing to them. Faster than fussing with his belt." He walked purposefully down the hall, his metal foot thumping off the polished wood, leaving dents in it. He dropped to one knee at the lock, then put the fork under his steel foot and used it as a lever to bend back all but one of the soft pot-metal tines, so that now the fork just had one long thin spike. He slid it into the lock, felt for a moment, then gave a sharp and precise flick of his wrist and twisted open the doorknob. It opened smoothly at his touch. "Nothing to it," he said, and got back to his feet, dusting off his knees.

Now, I'd been in Grinder's rooms many times, when I'd brought in the boiling water for his bath, or run the rug-sweeper over his thick Turkish rugs, or dusted the framed medals and certificates and the cunning machines he kept in his apartment. But this was different, because this time I was coming in with Monty, and Monty made you ask yourself, "Why isn't this all mine? Why shouldn't I just take it?" And I didn't have a good answer, apart from *fear*. And fear was giving way to excitement.

Monty went straight to the humidor by Grinder's deep, plush chair and brought out a fistful of cigars. He handed one to me and we both bit off the tips and spat them on the fine rug, then lit them with the polished brass lighter in the shape of a beautiful woman that stood on the other side of the chair. Monty clamped his cheroot between his teeth and continued to paw through Grinder's sacred possessions, all the fine goods that the children of St. Aggie's weren't even allowed to look to closely upon. Soon he was swilling Grinder's best brandy from a lead crystal decanter, wearing Grinder's red velvet housecoat, topped with Grinder's fine beaver-skin bowler hat.

And it was thus attired that he stumped back into the dining room, where the corpse of Grinder still slumped at table's end, and took up a stance by the old ship's bell that the morning child used to call the rest of the kids to breakfast, and he began to ring the bell like St. Aggie's was afire, and he called out as he did so, a wordless, birdlike call, something like a rooster's crowing, such a noise as had never been heard in St. Aggie's before.

With a clatter and a clank and a hundred muffled arguments, the children of St. Aggie's pelted down the staircases and streamed into the kitchen, milling uncertainly, eyes popping at the sight of our latest arrival in his stolen finery, still ringing the bell, still making his crazy call, stopping now and again to swill the brandy and laugh and spray a boozy cloud before him.

Once we were all standing in our nightshirts and underclothes, every scar and stump on display, he let off his ringing and cleared his throat ostentatiously, then stepped nimbly onto one of the chairs, wobbling for an instant on his steel peg, then leaped again, like a goat leaping from rock to rock, up onto the table, sending my carefully laid cutlery clattering every which-a-way.

He cleared his throat again, and said:

"Good morrow to you, good morrow all, good morrow to the poor, crippled, abused children of St. Aggie's. We haven't been properly introduced, so I thought it fitting that I should take a moment to greet you all and share a bit of good news with you. My name is Montreal Monty Goldfarb, machinist's boy, prentice artificer, gentleman adventurer and liberator of the oppressed. I am late foreshortened—" He waggled his stumps—"as are so many of you. And yet, and yet, I say to you, I am as good a man as I was ere I lost my limbs, and I say that you are too." There was a cautious murmur at this. It was the kind of thing the Sisters said to you in the hospital, before they brought you to St. Aggie's, the kind of pretty lies they told you about the wonderful life that awaited you with your new, crippled body, once you had been retrained and put to productive work.

"Children of St. Aggie's, hearken to old Montreal Monty, and I will tell you of what is possible and what is necessary. First, what is necessary: to end oppression wherever we find it, to be liberators of the downtrodden and the meek. When that evil dog's pizzle flogged me and threw me in his dungeon, I knew that I'd come upon a bully, a man who poisoned the sweet air with each breath of his cursed lungs, and so I resolved to do something about it. And so I have." He clattered the table's length, to where Grinder's body slumped. Many of the children had been so fixated on the odd spectacle that Monty presented that they hadn't even noticed the extraordinary sight of our tormentor sat, apparently sleeping or unconscious. With the air of a magician, Monty bent and took the end of tea towel and gave it a sharp yank, so that all could see the knife-handle protruding from the red stain that covered Grinder's chest. We gasped, and some of the more faint-hearted children shrieked, but no one ran off to get the law, and no one wept a single salty tear for our dead benefactor.

Monty held his arms over his head in a wide "vee" and looked expectantly upon us. It only took a moment before someone—perhaps it was me!—began to applaud, to cheer, to stomp, and then we were all at it, making such a noise as you might encounter in a tavern full of men who've just learned that their side has won a war. Monty waited for it to die down a bit, then, with a theatrical flourish, he pushed Grinder out of his chair, letting him slide to the floor with a meaty thump, and settled himself into the chair the corpse had lately sat upon. The message was clear: I am now the master of this house.

I cleared my throat and raised my good arm. I'd had more time than the rest of the St. Aggie's children to consider life without the terrible Grinder, and a thought had come to me. Monty nodded regally at me, and I found myself standing with every eye in the room upon me.

"Monty," I said, "on behalf of the children of St. Aggie's, I thank you most sincerely for doing away with cruel old Grinder, but I must ask you, what shall we do *now*? With Grinder gone, the Sisters will surely shut down St. Aggie's, or perhaps send us another vile old master to beat us, and you shall go to the gallows at the King Street Gaol, and, well, it just seems like a pity that ..." I waved my stump. "It just seems a pity, is what I'm saying."

Monty nodded again. "Sian, I thank you, for you have come neatly to my next point. I spoke of what was needed and what was possible, and now we must discuss what is possible. I had a nice long time to meditate on this question through last night, as I languished in the pit below, and I think I have a plan, though I shall need your help with it if we are to pull it off."

He stood again, and took up a loaf of hard bread and began to wave it like a baton as he spoke, thumping it on the table for emphasis.

"Item: I understand that the Sisters provide for St. Aggie's with such alms as are necessary to keep our lamps burning, fuel in our fireplaces, and gruel and such on the table, yes?" We nodded. "Right.

"Item: Nevertheless, Old Turd-Gargler here was used to sending you poor kiddees out to beg with your wounds all on display, to bring him whatever coppers you could coax from the drunkards of Muddy York with which to feather his pretty little nest yonder. Correct?" We nodded again. "Right.

"Item: We are all of us the crippled children of Muddy York's great information-processing factories. We are artificers, machinists, engineers, cunning shapers and makers, every one, for that is how we came to be injured. Correct? Right.

"Item: It is a murdersome pity that such as we should be turned out to beg when we have so much skill at our disposal. Between us, we could make anything, *do* anything, but our departed tormentor lacked the native wit to see this, correct? Right.

"Item: the sisters of the simpering order of St. Agatha's Weeping Sores have all the cleverness of a turnip. This I saw for myself during my tenure in their hospital. Fooling them would be easier than fooling an idiot child. Correct? *Right.*"

He levered himself out of the chair and began to stalk the dining room, stumping up and down. "Someone tell me, how often do the good sisters pay us a visit?"

"Sundays," I said. "When they take us all to church."

He nodded. "And does that spoiled meat there accompany us to church?"

"No," I said. "No, he stays here. He says he 'worships in his own way.'" Truth was he was invariably too hung-over to rise on a Sunday.

He nodded again. "And today is Tuesday. Which means that we have five days to do our work."

"What work, Monty?"

"Why, we are going to build a clockwork automaton based on that evil tyrant what I slew this very morning. We will build a device of surpassing and fiendish cleverness, such as will fool the nuns and the world at large into thinking that we are still being ground up like mincemeat, while we lead a life of leisure, fun, and invention, such as befits children of our mental stature and good character."

* * *

Here's the oath we swore to Monty before we went to work on the automaton:

"I, (state your full name), do hereby give my most solemn oath that I will never, ever betray the secrets of St. Agatha's. I bind myself to the good fortune of my fellow inmates at this institution and vow to honor them as though they were my brothers and sisters, and not to fight with them, nor spite them, nor do them down or dirty. I make this oath freely and gladly, and should I betray it, I wish that old Satan himself would rise up from the pit and tear out my treacherous guts and use them for bootlaces, that his devils would tear my betrayer's tongue from my mouth and use it to wipe their private parts, that my lying body would be fed, inch-by-inch, to the hungry and terrible basilisks of the Pit. So I swear, and so mote be it!"

There were two children who'd worked for a tanner in the house, older children. Matthew was shy all the fingers on his left hand. Becka was missing an eye and her nose, which she joked was a mercy, for there is no smell more terrible than the charnel reek of the tanning works. But between them, they were quite certain that they could carefully remove, stuff, and remount Grinder's head, careful to leave the jaw in place.

As the oldest machinist at St. Aggie's, I was conscripted to work on the torso and armature mechanisms. I played chief engineer, bossing a gang of six boys and four girls who had experience with mechanisms. We cannibalized St. Aggie's old mechanical wash-wringer, with its spindly arms and many fingers; and I was sent out several times to pawn Grinder's fine crystal and pocket-watch to raise money for parts.

Monty oversaw all, but he took personal charge of Grinder's voicebox, through which he would imitate old Grinder's voice when the sisters came by on Sunday. St. Aggie's was fronted with a Dutch door, and Grinder habitually only opened the top half to jaw with the sisters. Monty said that we could prop the partial torso on a low table, to hide the fact that no legs depended from it.

"We'll tie a sick-kerchief around his face and give out that he's got 'flu,' and that it's spread through the whole house. That'll get us all out of church, which is a tidy little jackpot in and of itself. The kerchief will disguise the fact that his lips ain't moving in time with his talking."

I shook my head at this idea. The nuns were hardly geniuses, but how long could this hold out for?

"It won't have to last more than a week—by next week, we'll have something better to show 'em."

Here's a thing: it all worked like a fine-tuned machine.

The kerchief made it look like a bank-robber, and Monty painted its face to make him seem more lively, for the tanning had dried him out some (he also doused the horrible thing with liberal lashings of bay rum and greased its hair with a heavy pomade, for the tanning process had left him with a smell like an outhouse on a hot day). Monty had affixed an armature to the thing's bottom jaw—we'd had to break it to get it to open, prying it roughly with a screwdriver, cracking a tooth or two in the process, and I have nightmares to this day about the sound it made when it finally yawed open.

A child—little legless Dora, whose begging pitch included a sad little puppetry show—could work this armature by means of a squeeze-bulb taken from the siphon-starter on Grinder's cider brewing tub, and so make the jaw go up and down in time with speech.

The speech itself was accomplished by means of the horsegut voice box from Grinder's music box. Monty sure handedly affixed a long, smooth glass tube—part of the cracking apparatus that I had been sent to market to buy—to the music box's resonator. This, he ran up behind our automatic Grinder. Then, crouched on the floor before the voicebox, stationed next to Dora on her wheeled plank, he was able to whisper across the horsegut strings and have them buzz out a credible version of Grinder's whiskey-roughened growl. And once he'd tuned the horsegut just so, the vocal resemblance was even more remarkable. Combined with Dora's skillful puppetry, the effect was galvanizing. It took a conscious effort to remember that this was a puppet talking to you, not a man.

The sisters turned up at the appointed hour on Sunday, only to be greeted by our clockwork Grinder, who stood in the half-door, face swathed in a "flu" mask. We'd hung quarantine bunting from the windows, crisscrossing the front of St. Aggie's with it for good measure, and a goodly number of us kiddees were watching from the upstairs windows with our best-drawn and sickly looks on our faces.

So the sisters hung back practically at the pavement and shouted, "Mr. Grindersworth!" in alarmed tones, staring with horror at the apparition in the doorway.

"Sisters, good day to you," Monty said into his horsegut, while Dora worked her squeezebulb, and the jaw went up and down behind its white cloth, and the muffled simulation of Grinder's voice emanated from the top of the glass tube, hidden behind the automaton's head, so that it seemed to come from the right place. "Though not such a good day for us, I fear."

"The children are ill?"

Monty gave out a fine sham of Grinder's laugh, the one he used when dealing with proper people, with the cruelty barely plastered-over. "Oh, not all of them. But we have a dozen cases. Thankfully, I appear to be immune, and oh my, but you wouldn't believe the help these tots are in the practical nursing department. Fine kiddees, my charges, yes indeed. But still, best to keep them away from the general public for the nonce, hey? I'm quite sure we'll have them up on their feet by next Sunday, and they'll be glad indeed of the chance to get down on their knees and thank the beneficent Lord for their good health." Monty was laying it on thick, but then, so had Grinder, when it came to the sisters.

"We shall send over some help after the services," the head sister said, hands at her breast, a tear glistening in her eye at the thought of our bravery. I thought the jig was up. Of course the order would have some sisters who'd had the "flu" and gotten over it, rendering them immune. But Monty never worried.

"No, no," he said, smoothly. I had the presence of mind to take up the cranks that operated the "arms" we'd constructed for him, waving them about in a negating way—this effect rather spoiled by my nervousness, so that they seemed more octopus tentacle than arm. But the sisters didn't appear to notice. "As I say, I have plenty of help here with my good children."

"A basket, then," the sister said. "Some nourishing food and fizzy drinks for the children."

Crouching low in the anteroom, we crippled children traded disbelieving looks with one another. Not only had Monty gotten rid of Grinder and gotten us out of going to church, he'd also set things up so that the sisters of St. Aggie's were going to bring us their best grub, for free, because we were all so poorly and ailing! It was all we could do not to cheer.

And cheer we did, later, when the sisters set ten huge hampers down on our doorstep, whence we retrieved them, finding in them a feast fit for princes: cold meat pies glistening with aspic, marrow bones still warm from the oven, suet pudding and jugs of custard with skin on top of them, huge bottles of fizzy lemonade and small beer. By the time we'd laid it out in the dining room, it seemed like we'd never be able to eat it all.

But we et every last morsel, and four of us carried Monty about on our shoulders—two carrying, two steadying the carriers—and someone found a concertina, and someone found some combs and waxed paper, and we sang until the walls shook: "The Mechanic's Folly," "A Combinatorial Explosion at the Computer-Works," and then endless rounds of "For He's a Jolly Good Fellow."

* * *

Monty had promised improvements on the clockwork Grinder by the following Sunday, and he made good on it. Since we no longer had to beg all day long, we children of St. Aggie's had time in plenty, and Monty had no shortage of skilled volunteers who wanted to work with him on Grinder II, as he called it. Grinder II sported a rather handsome and large, droopy mustache, which hid the action of its lips. This mustache was glued onto the head-assembly one hair at a time, a painstaking job that denuded every horsehair brush in the house, but the effect was impressive.

More impressive was the leg-assembly I bossed into existence, a pair of clockwork pins that could lever Grinder from a seated position into full upright, balancing him by means of three gyros we hid in his chest cavity. Once these were wound and spun, Grinder could stand up in a very natural fashion. Once we'd rearranged the furniture to hide Dora and Monty behind a large armchair, you could stand right in the parlor and "converse" with him, and unless you were looking very hard, you'd never know but what you were talking with a mortal man, and not an automaton made of tanned flesh, steel, springs, and clay (we used rather a lot of custom-made porcelain from the prosthetic works to get his legs right—the children who were shy a leg or two knew which legmakers in town had the best wares).

And so when the sisters arrived the following Sunday, they were led right into the parlor, whose net curtains kept the room in a semi-dark state, and there, they parlayed with Grinder, who came to his feet when they entered and left. One of the girls was in charge of his arms, and she had practiced with them so well that she was able to move them in a very convincing fashion. Convincing enough, anyroad: the sisters left Grinder with a bag of clothes, a bag of oranges that had come off a ship that had sailed from Spanish Florida right up the St. Lawrence to the port of Montreal, and thereafter traversed by rail car to Muddy York. They made a parcel gift of these succulent treasures to Grinder, to "help the kiddees keep away the scurvy," but Grinder always kept them for himself or flogged them to his pals for a neat penny. We wolfed the oranges right after services, and then took our Sabbath free with games and more brandy from Grinder's sideboard.

* * *

And so we went, week on week, with small but impressive updates to our clockwork man: hands that could grasp and smoke a pipe; a clever mechanism that let him throw back his head and laugh, fingers that could drum on the table beside him, eyes that could follow you around a room and eyelids that could blink, albeit slowly.

But Monty had *much* bigger plans.

"I want to bring in another 56 bits," he said, gesturing at the computing panel in Grinder's parlor, a paltry eight-bit works. That meant that there were eight switches with eight matching levers, connected to eight brass rods that ran down to the public computing works that ran beneath the streets of Muddy York. Grinder had used his eight bits to keep St. Aggie's books—both the set he showed to the sisters and the one where he kept track of what he was trousering for himself—and he'd let one "lucky" child work the great, stiff return-arm that sent the instructions set on the switches back to the Hall of Computing for queueing and processing on the great frames that had cost me my good right arm. An instant later, the processed answer would be returned to the levers above the switches, and to whatever interpretive mechanism you had yoked up to them (Grinder used a telegraph machine that printed the answers upon a long, thin sheet of paper).

"56 bits!" I boggled at Monty. A 64-bit rig wasn't unheard of, if you were a mighty shipping company or insurer. But in a private home—well, the racket of the switches would shake the foundations! Remember, dear reader, that each additional bit *doubled* the calculating faculty of the home panel. Monty was proposing to increase St. Aggie's computational capacity by a factor more than a *quadrillionfold*! (We computermen are accustomed to dealing in these rarified numbers, but they may boggle you. Have no fear—a quadrillion is a number of such surpassing monstrosity that you must have the knack of figuring to even approach it properly.)

"Monty," I gasped, "are you planning to open a firm of accountants at St. Aggie's?"

He laid a finger alongside of his nose. "Not at all, my old darling. I have a thought that perhaps we could build a tiny figuring engine into our Grinder's chest cavity, one that could take programs punched off of a sufficiently powerful computing frame, and that these might enable him to walk about on his own, as natural as you please, and even carry on conversations as though he were a living man. Such a creation would afford us even more freedom and security, as you must be able to see."

"But it will cost the bloody world!" I said.

"Oh, I didn't think we'd *pay* for it," he said. Once again, he laid his finger alongside his nose.

And that is how I came to find myself down our local sewer, in the dead of night, a seventeen year-old brassjacker, bossing a gang of eight kids with 10 arms, 7 noses, 9 hands and 11 legs between them, working furiously and racing the dawn to fit thousands of precision brass push-rods with lightly balanced joints from the local multifarious amalgamation and amplification switch-house to St. Aggie's utility cellar. It didn't work, of course. Not that night. But at least we didn't break anything and alert the Upper Canadian Computing Authority to our mischief. Three nights later, after much fine-tuning, oiling, and desperate prayer, the panel at St. Aggie's boasted 64 shining brass bits, the very height of modernity and engineering.

Monty and the children all stood before the panel, which had been burnished to a mirror shine by No-Nose Timmy, who'd done finishing work before a careless master had stumbled over him, pushing him face-first into a spinning grinding wheel. In the gaslight, we appeared to be staring at a group of mighty heroes, and when Monty turned to regard us, he had bright tears in his eyes.

"Sisters and brothers, we have done ourselves proud. A new day has dawned for St. Aggie's and for our lives. Thank you. You have done me proud."

We shared out the last of Grinder's brandy, a thimbleful each, even for the smallest kiddees, and drank a toast to the brave and clever children of St. Aggie's and to Montreal Monty, our saviour and the founder of our feast.

*   *   *

Let me tell you some about life at St. Aggie's in that golden age. Whereas before, we'd rise at 7 AM for a mean breakfast—prepared by unfavored children whom Grinder punished by putting them into the kitchen at 4:30 to prepare the meal—followed by a brief "sermon" roared out by Grinder; now we rose at a very civilized 10 AM to eat a leisurely breakfast over the daily papers that Grinder had subscribed to. The breakfasts—all the meals and chores—were done on a rotating basis, with exemptions for children whose infirmity made performing some tasks harder than others. Though all worked—even the blind children sorted weevils and stones from the rice and beans by touch.

Whereas Grinder had sent us out to beg every day—excepting Sundays—debasing ourselves and putting our injuries on display for the purposes of sympathy; now we were free to laze around the house all day, or work at our own fancies, painting or reading or just playing like the cherished children of rich families who didn't need to send their young ones to the city to work for the family fortune.

But most of us quickly bored of the life of Riley, and for us, there was plenty to do. The clockwork Grinder was always a distraction, especially after Monty started work on the mechanism that would accept punched-tape instructions from the computing panel.

When we weren't working on Grinder, there was other work. We former apprentices went back to our old masters—men and women who were guilty but glad enough to see us, in the main— and told them that the skilled children of St. Aggie's were looking for piecework as part of our rehabilitation, at a competitive price.

It was hardly a lie, either: as broken tools and mechanisms came in for mending, the boys and girls taught one another their crafts and trade, and it wasn't long before a steady flow of cash came into St. Aggie's, paying for better food, better clothes, and, soon enough, the very best artificial arms, legs, hands and feet, the best glass eyes, the best wigs. When Gertie Shine-Pate was fitted for her first wig and saw herself in the great looking glass in Grinder's study, she burst into tears and hugged all and sundry, and thereafter, St. Aggie's bought her three more wigs to wear as the mood struck her. She took to styling these wigs with combs and scissors, and before long she was cutting hair for all of us at St. Aggie's. We never looked so good.

That gilded time from the end of my boyhood is like a sweet dream to me now. A sweet, lost dream.

* * *

No invention works right the first time around. The inventors' tales you read in the science penny-dreadfuls, where some engineer discovers a new principle, puts it into practice, shouts "Eureka" and sets up his own foundry? They're rubbish.

Real invention is a process of repeated, crushing failure that leads, very rarely, to a success. If you want to succeed faster, there's nothing for it but to fail faster and better.

The first time Monty rolled a paper tape into a cartridge and inserted it into Grinder, we all held our breaths while he fished around the arse of Grinder's trousers for the toggle that released the tension on the mainspring we wound through a keyhole in his hip. He stepped back as the soft whining of the mechanism emanated from Grinder's body, and then Grinder began, very slowly, to pace the room's length, taking three long—if jerky—steps, turning about, and taking three steps back. Then Grinder lifted a hand as in greeting, and his mouth stretched into a rictus that might have passed for a grin, and then, very carefully, Grinder punched himself in the face so hard that his head came free from his neck and rolled across the floor with a meaty sound (it took our resident taxidermists a full two days to repair the damage) and his body went into a horrible paroxysm like the St. Vitus dance, until it, too fell to the floor.

This was on Monday, and by Wednesday, we had Grinder back on his feet with his head reattached. Again, Monty depressed his toggle, and this time, Grinder made a horrendous clanking sound and pitched forward.

And so it went, day after day, each tiny improvement accompanied by abject failure, and each Sunday we struggled to put the pieces together so that Grinder could pay his respects to the sisters.

Until the day came that the sisters brought round a new child to join our happy clan, and it all began to unravel.

We had been lucky in that Monty's arrival at St. Aggie's coincided with a reformer's movement that had swept Upper Canada, a movement whose figurehead, the Princess Lucy, met with every magistrate, councilman, alderman, and beadle in the colony, the sleeves of her dresses pinned up to the stumps of her shoulders, sternly discussing the plight of the children who worked in the Information Foundries across the colonies. It didn't do no good in the long run, of course, but for the short term, word got round that the authorities would come down very hard on any master whose apprentice lost a piece of himself in the data-mills. So it was some months before St. Aggie's had any new meat arrive upon its doorstep.

The new meat in question was a weepy boy of about 11—the same age I'd been when I arrived—and he was shy his left leg all the way up to the hip. He had a crude steel leg in its place, strapped up with a rough, badly cured cradle that must have hurt like hellfire. He also had a splintery crutch that he used to get around with, the sort of thing that the sisters of St. Aggie's bought in huge lots from unscrupulous tradesmen who cared nothing for the people who'd come to use them.

His name was William Sansousy, a Metis boy who'd come from the wild woods of Lower Canada seeking work in Muddy York, who'd found instead an implacable machine that had torn off his leg and devoured it without a second's remorse. He spoke English with a thick French accent, and slipped into *Joual* when he was overcome with sorrow.

Two sisters brought him to the door on a Friday afternoon. We knew they were coming, they'd sent round a messenger boy with a printed telegram telling Grinder to make room for one more. Monty wanted to turn his Clockwork Grinder loose to walk to the door and greet them, but we all told him he'd be mad to try it: there was so much that could go wrong, and if the sisters worked out what had happened, we could finish up dangling from nooses at King Street Gaol.

Monty relented resentfully, and instead we seated Grinder in his overstuffed chair, with Monty tucked away behind it, ready to converse with the sisters. I hid with him, ready to send Grinder to his feet and to extend his cold, leathery artificial hand to the boy when the sisters turned him over.

And it went smoothly—that day. When the sisters had gone and their car had built up its head of steam and chuffed and clanked away, we emerged from our hiding place. Monty broke into slangy, rapid French, gesticulating and hopping from foot to peg-leg and back again, and William's eyes grew as big as saucers as Monty explained the lay of the land to him. The *clang* when he thumped Grinder in his cast-iron chest made William leap back and he hobbled toward the door.

"Wait, wait!" Monty called, switching to English. "Wait, will you, you idiot? This is the best day of your life, young William! But for us, you might have entered a life of miserable bondage. Instead, you will enjoy all the fruits of liberty, rewarding work, and comradeship. We take care of our own here at St. Aggie's. You'll have top grub, a posh leg and a beautiful crutch that's as smooth as a baby's arse and soft as a lady's bosom. You'll have the freedom to come and go as you please, and you'll have a warm bed to sleep in every night. And best of all, you'll have us, your family here at St. Aggie's. We take care of our own, we do."

The boy looked at us, tears streaming down his face. He made me remember what it had been like, my first day at St. Aggie's, the cold fear coiled round your guts like rope caught in a reciprocating gear. At St. Aggie's we put on brave faces, never cried where no one could see us, but seeing him weep made me remember all the times I'd cried, cried for my lost family who'd sold me into indenture, cried for my mangled body, my ruined life. But living without Grinder's constant terrorizing must have softened my heart. Suddenly it was all I could do to stop myself from giving the poor little mite a one-armed hug.

I didn't hug him, but Monty did, stumping over to him, and the two of them bawled like babbies. Their peg legs knocked together as they embraced like drunken sailors, seeming to cry out every tear we'd any of us ever held in. Before long, we were all crying with them, fat tears streaming down our faces, the sound like something out of the Pit.

When the sobs had stopped, William looked around at us, wiped his nose, and said, "Thank you. I think I am home."

* * *

But it wasn't home for him. Poor William. We'd had children like him, in the bad old days, children who just couldn't get back up on their feet (or foot) again. Most of the time, I reckon, they were kids who couldn't make it as apprentices, neither, kids who'd spent their working lives full of such awful misery that they were *bound* to fall into a machine. And being sundered from their limbs didn't improve their outlook.

We tried everything we could think of to cheer William up. He'd worked for a watch-smith, and he had a pretty good hand at disassembling and cleaning mechanisms. His stump ached him like fire, even after he'd been fitted with a better apparatus by St. Aggie's best leg-maker, and it was only when he was working with his little tweezers and brushes that he lost the grimace that twisted up his face so. Monty had him strip and clean every clockwork in the house, even the ones that were working perfectly—even the delicate works we'd carefully knocked together for the clockwork Grinder. But it wasn't enough.

In the bad old days, Grinder would have beaten the boy and sent him out to beg in the worst parts of town, hoping that he'd be run down by a cart or killed by one of the blunderbuss gangs that marauded there. When the law brought home the boy's body, old Grinder would weep crocodile tears and tug his hair at the bloody evil that men did, and then he'd go back to his rooms and play some music and drink some brandy and sleep the sleep of the unjust.

We couldn't do the same, and so we tried to bring up William's spirits instead, and when he'd had enough of it, he lit out on his own. The first we knew of it was when he didn't turn up for breakfast. This wasn't unheard of—any of the free children of St. Aggie's was able to rise and wake whenever he chose, but William had been a regular at breakfast every day. I made my way upstairs to the dormer room where the boys slept to look for him and found his bed empty, his coat and his peg-leg and crutch gone.

"He's gone," Monty said, "Long gone." He sighed and looked out the window. "Must be trying to get back to the Gatineaux." He shook his head.

"Do you think he'll make it?" I said, knowing the answer, but hoping that Monty would lie to me.

"Not a chance," Monty said. "Not him. He'll either be beaten, arrested or worse by sundown. That lad hasn't any self-preservation instincts."

At this, the dining room fell silent and all eyes turned on Monty and I saw in a flash what a terrible burden we all put on him: saviour, father, chieftain. He twisted his face into a halfway convincing smile.

"Oh, maybe not. He might just be hiding out down the road. Tell you what, eat up and we'll go searching for him."

I never saw a load of plates cleared faster. It was bare minutes before we were formed up in the parlor, divided into groups, and sent out into Muddy York to find William Sansousy. We turned that bad old city upside-down, asking nosy questions and sticking our heads in where they didn't belong, but Monty had been doubly right the first time around.

The police found William Sansousy's body in a marshy bit of land off the Leslie Street Spit. His pockets had been slit, his pathetic paper sack of belongings torn and the clothes scattered and his fine hand-turned leg was gone. He had been dead for hours.

* * *

The Detective Inspector who presented himself that afternoon at St. Aggie's was trailed by a team of technicians who had a wire sound-recorder and a portable logic engine for in-putting the data of his investigation. He seemed very proud of his machine, even though it came with three convicts from the King Street Gaol in shackles and leg-irons who worked tirelessly to keep the springs wound, toiling in a lather of sweat and heaving breath, heat boiling off their shaved heads in shimmering waves.

He showed up just as the clock in the parlour chimed eight times, a bear chasing a bird around on a track as it sang the hour. We peered out the windows in the upper floors, saw the inspector, and understood just why Monty had been so morose all afternoon.

But Monty did us proud. He went to the door with his familiar swagger, and swung it wide, extending his hand to the Inspector.

"Montague Goldfarb, officer, at your service. Our patron has stepped away, but please, do come in."

The Inspector gravely shook the proffered hand, his huge, gloved mitt swallowing Monty's boyish hand. It was easy to forget that he was just a child, but the looming presence of the giant Inspector reminded us all.

"Master Goldfarb," the Inspector said, taking his hat off, and peering through his smoked monocle at the children in the parlour, all of us sat with hands folded like we were in a pantomime about the best-behaved, most crippled, most terrified, least threatening children in all the colonies. "I am sorry to hear that Mr. Grindersworth is not at home to the constabulary. Have you any notion as to what temporal juncture we might expect him?" If I hadn't been concentrating on not peeing myself with terror, the inspector's pompous speech might have set me to laughing.

Monty didn't bat an eye. "Mr. Grindersworth was called away to see his brother in Sault Sainte Marie, and we expect him tomorrow. I'm his designated lieutenant, though. Perhaps I might help you?"

The inspector stroked his forked beard and gave us all another long look. "Tomorrow, hey? Well, I don't suppose that justice should wait that long. Master Goldfarb, I have grim intelligence for you, as regards one of your young compatriots, a Master—" He consulted a punched card that was held in a hopper on his clanking logic engine. "William Sansousy. He lies even now upon a slab in the city morgue. Someone of authority from this institution is required to confirm the preliminary identification. You will do, I suppose. Though your patron will have to present himself post-haste in order to sign the several official documents that necessarily accompany an event of such gravity."

We'd known as soon as the Inspector turned up on St. Aggie's door that it meant that William was dead. If he was merely in trouble, it would have been a constable, dragging him by the ear. We half-children of St. Aggie's only rated a full inspector when we were topped by some evil bastard in this evil town. But hearing the Inspector say the words, puffing them through his drooping mustache, that made it real. None of us had ever cried when St. Aggie's children were taken by the streets—at least, not where the others could see it. But this time round, without Grinder to shoot us filthy daggers if we made a peep while the law was about, it opened the floodgates. Boys and girls, young and old, we cried for poor little William. He'd come to the best of all possible St.

Aggie's, but it hadn't been good enough for him. He'd wanted to go back to the parents who'd sold him into service, wanted a return to his Mam's lap and bosom. Who among us didn't want that, in his secret heart?

Monty's tears were silent and they rolled down his cheeks as he shrugged into his coat and hat and let the Inspector—who was clearly embarrassed by the display—lead him out the door.

* * *

When Monty came home, he arrived at a house full of children who were ready to go mad. We'd cried ourselves hoarse, then sat about the parlour, not knowing what to do. If there had been any of old Grinder's booze still in the house, we'd have drunk it.

"What's the plan, then?" he said, coming through the door. "We've got one night until that bastard comes back. If he doesn't find Grinder, he'll go to the sisters, and it'll come down around our ears. What's more, he knows Grinder, personal, from other dead ones in years gone by, and I don't think he'll be fooled by our machine, no matter how good it goes."

"What's the plan?" I said, mouth hanging open. "Monty, the plan is that we're all going to gaol and you and I and everyone else who helped cover up the killing of Grinder will dance at rope's end!"

He gave me a considering look. "Sian, that is absolutely the worst plan I have ever heard." And then he grinned at us the way he did, and we all knew that, somehow, it would all be all right.

* * *

"Constable, come quick, he's going to kill himself!"

I practiced the line for the fiftieth time, willing my eyes to go wider, my voice to carry more alarm. Behind me, Monty scowled at my reflection in the mirror in Grinder's personal toilet, where I'd been holed up for hours.

"Verily, the stage lost a great player when that machine mangled you, Sian. You are perfect. Now, get moving before I tear your remaining arm off and beat you with it. Go!"

Phase one of the plan was easy enough: we'd smuggle our Grinder up onto the latticework of steel and scaffold where they were building the mighty Prince Edward Viaduct, at the end of Bloor Street. Monty had punched his program already: he'd pace back and forth, tugging his hair, shaking his head like a maddened man, and then, abruptly, he'd turn and fling himself bodily off the platform, plunging 130 feet into the Don River, where he would simply disintegrate into a million cogs, gears, springs and struts, which would sink to the riverbed and begin to rust away. The coppers would recover his clothes, and those, combined with the eyewitness testimony of the constable I was responsible for bringing to the bridge, would establish in everyone's mind exactly what had happened and how: Grinder was so distraught at one more death from among his charges that he had popped his own clogs in grief. We were all of us standing ready to testify as to how poor William was Grinder's little favorite, a boy he loved like a son, and so forth. Who would suspect a bunch of helpless cripples, anyway?

That was the theory, at least. But now I was actually stood by the bridge, watching six half-children wrestle the automaton into place, striving for silence so as not to alert the guards who were charged with defending the structure they were already calling "The Suicide's Magnet," and I couldn't believe that it would possibly work.

Five of the children scampered away, climbing back down the scaffolds, slipping and sliding and nearly dying more times than I could count, so that my heart was thundering in my chest so hard I thought I might die upon the spot. Then they were safely away, climbing back up the ravine's walls in the mud and snow, almost invisible in the dusky dawn light. Monty waved an arm at me, and I knew it was my cue, and that I should be off to rouse the constabulary, but I found myself rooted to the spot.

In that moment, every doubt and fear and misery I'd ever harbored crowded back in on me. The misery of being abandoned by my family, the sorrow and loneliness I'd felt among the prentice-lads, the humiliation of Grinder's savage beatings and harangues. The shame of my injury and every time I'd grovelled before a drunk or a pitying lady with my stump on display for pennies to fetch home to Grinder. What was I doing? There was no way I could possibly pull this off. I wasn't enough of a man— nor enough of a boy.

But then I thought of all those moments since the coming of Monty Goldfarb, the millionfold triumphs of ingenuity and hard work, the computing power I'd stolen out from under the nose of the calculators who had treated me as a mere work-ox before my injury. I thought of the cash we'd brought in, the children who'd smiled and sang and danced on the worn floors of St. Aggie's, and—

And I ran to the policeman, who was warming himself by doing a curious hopping dance in place, hands in his armpits. "Constable!" I piped, all sham terror that no one would have known for a sham, "Constable! Come quick, he's going to kill himself!"

* * *

The sister who came to sit up with us mourning kiddies that night was called Sister Mary Immaculata, and she was kindly, if a bit dim. I remembered her from my stay in the hospital after my maiming: a slightly vacant prune-faced woman in a wimple who'd bathed my wounds gently and given me solemn hugs when I woke screaming in the middle of the night.

She was positive that the children of St. Aggie's were inconsolable over the suicide of our beloved patron, Zophar Grindersworth, and she doled out those same solemn cuddles to anyone foolish enough to stray near her. That none of us shed a tear was lost upon her, though she did note with approval how smoothly the operation of St. Aggie's continued without Grinder's oversight.

The next afternoon, Sister Mary Immaculata circulated among us, offering reassurance that a new master would be found for St. Aggie's. None of us were much comforted by this: we knew the kind of man who was likely to fill such a plum vacancy.

"If only there was some way we could go on running this place on our own," I moaned under my breath, trying to concentrate on repairing the pressure gauge on a pneumatic evacuator that we'd taken in for mending.

Monty shot me a look. He had taken the Sister's coming very hard. "I don't think I have it in me to kill the next one, too. Anyway, they're bound to notice if we keep on assassinating our guardians."

I snickered despite myself. Then my gloomy pall descended again. It had all been so good, how could we possibly return to the old way? But there was no way the sisters would let a bunch of crippled children govern themselves.

"What a waste," I said. "What a waste of all this potential."

"At least I'll be shut of it in two years," Monty said. "How long have you got till your eighteenth?"

My brow furrowed. I looked out the grimy workshop window at the iron-grey February sky. "It's February tenth today?"

"Eleventh," he said.

I laughed, an ugly sound. "Why, Monty, my friend, today is my eighteenth birthday. I believe I have survived St. Aggie's to graduate to bigger and better things. I have attained my majority, old son."

He held a hand out and shook my hook with it, solemnly. "Happy birthday and congratulations, then, Sian. May the world treat you with all the care you deserve."

I stood, the scrape of my chair very loud and sudden. I realized I had no idea what I would do next. I had managed to completely forget that my graduation from St. Aggie's was looming, that I would be a free man. In my mind, I'd imagined myself dwelling at St. Aggie's forever.

Forever.

"You look like you just got hit in the head with a shovel," Monty said. "What on earth is going through that mind of yours?"

I didn't answer. I was already on my way to find Sister Immaculata. I found her in the kitchen, helping legless Dora make the toast for tea over the fire's grate.

"Sister," I said, "a word please?"

As she turned and followed me into the pantry off the kitchen, some of that fear I'd felt on the bridge bubbled up in me. I tamped it back down again firmly, like a piston compressing some superheated gas.

She was really just as I remembered her, and she had remembered me, too—she remembered all of us, the children she'd held in the night and then consigned to this Hell upon Earth, all unknowing.

"Sister Mary Immaculata, I attained my eighteenth birthday today."

She opened her mouth to congratulate me, but I held up my stump.

"I turned eighteen today, sister. I am a man, I have attained my majority. I am at liberty, and must seek my fortune in the world. I have a proposal for you, accordingly." I put everything I had into this, every dram of confidence and maturity that I'd learned since we inmates had taken over the asylum. "I was Mr. Grindersworth's lieutenant and assistant in every matter relating to the daily operation of this place. Many's the day I did every bit of work that there was to do, whilst Mr. Grindersworth attended to family matters. I know every inch of this place, every soul in it, and I have had the benefit of the excellent training and education that there is to have here.

"I had always thought to seek my fortune in the world as a mechanic of some kind, if any shop would have a half-made thing like me, but seeing as you find yourself at loose ends in the superintendent department, I thought I might perhaps put my plans 'on hold' for the time being, until such time as a full search could be conducted."

"Sian," she said, her face wrinkling into a gap-toothed smile. "Are you proposing that *you* might run St. Agatha's?"

It took everything I could not to wilt under the pity and amusement in that smile. "I am, sister. I am. I have all but run it for months now, and have every confidence in my capacity to go on doing so for so long as need be." I kept my gaze and my voice even. "I believe that the noble mission of St. Aggie's is a truly attainable one: that it can rehabilitate such damaged things as we and prepare us for the wider world."

She shook her head. "Sian," she said, softly, "Sian. I wish it could be. But there's no hope that such an appointment would be approved by the Board of Governors."

I nodded. "Yes, I thought so. But do the Governors need to approve a *temporary* appointment? A stopgap, until a suitable person can be found?"

Her smile changed, got wider. "You have certainly come into your own shrewdness here, haven't you?"

"I was taught well," I said, and smiled back.

* * *

The temporary has a way of becoming permanent. That was my bolt of inspiration, my galvanic realization. Once the sisters had something that worked, that did not call attention to itself, that took in crippled children and released whole persons some years later, they didn't need to muck about with it. As the mechanics say, "If it isn't broken, it doesn't want fixing."

I'm no mechanic, not anymore. The daily running of St. Aggie's occupied a larger and larger slice of my time, until I found that I knew more about tending to a child's fever or soothing away a nightmare than I did about hijacking the vast computers to do our bidding.

But that's no matter, as we have any number of apprentice computermen and computerwomen turning up on our doorsteps. So long as the machineries of industry grind on, the supply will be inexhaustible.

Monty visits me from time to time, mostly to scout for talent. His shop, Goldsworth and Associates, has a roaring trade in computational novelties and service, and if anyone is bothered by the appearance of a factory filled with the halt, the lame, the blind and the crippled, they are thankfully outnumbered by those who are delighted by the quality of the work and the good value in his schedule of pricing.

But it was indeed a golden time, that time when I was but a boy at St. Aggie's among the boys and girls, a cog in a machine that Monty built of us, part of a great uplifting, a transformation from a hell to something like a heaven. That I am sentenced to serve in this heaven I helped to make is no great burden, I suppose.

Still, I do yearn to screw a jeweller's loupe into my eye, pick up a fine tool and bend the sodium lamp to shine upon some cunning mechanism that wants fixing. For machines may be balky and they may destroy us with their terrible appetite for oil, blood and flesh, but they behave according to fixed rules and can be understood by anyone with the cunning to look upon them and winkle out their secrets. Children are ever so much more complicated.

Though I believe I may be learning a little about them, too.

Cory Doctorow *(craphound.com) is a science fiction author, activist, journalist and blogger—the co-editor of* Boing Boing *(boingboing.net) and the author of many books, most recently* In Real Life, *a graphic novel;* Information Doesn't Want To Be Free, *a book about earning a living in the Internet age, and* Homeland, *the award-winning, best-selling sequel to the 2008 YA novel* Little Brother.

In Rebecca Moesta's charming fantasy tale, young Allie begins corresponding with a penpal via her mysteriously magical new mailbox—a penpal who is a princess in a different world ...

POSTCARDS

BY REBECCA MOESTA

Memorizing her new zip code had been the easiest part of Allie's move. After all, how hard could it be to remember five digits when three of them were sevens? The hardest part had been leaving her friends—and what seemed like her entire life—behind.

Sitting on a pile of moving boxes in the echoing, otherwise-empty living room of their new house, Allie wondered morosely whether yanking a fifteen-year-old out of school three-quarters of the way through her sophomore year could not be considered child abuse.

Raking a hand through her shoulder-length blond hair, she thought back to the night her life had changed. Allie had just returned from her fourth date with Ian Walters—*Ian Walters*, a senior and a forward on the Jackson Eagles basketball team—when her parents met her with the "wonderful news." Her father, after only five months of unemployment, had taken a new job as head of Human Resources for a regional telecommunications firm halfway across the country. He said it was a "great opportunity."

Allie knew she should have been happy for her parents. The relief was so plain on their faces. But it was obvious they hadn't stopped for a moment to think about how this would affect *her*. Just that evening, Ian had asked Allie to the prom. In a little over a month, she should have been dressing like a fairy tale princess and then dancing all evening with one of the cutest guys in the whole school. But she would miss out on that now. Barely three weeks after her father's announcement, the family had moved— leaving behind the only world Allie had ever known.

Now, Allie's black Labrador retriever Merlin chuffed, gave his tail a tentative wag, trotted to the front door, and looked back at her. Allie heaved a sigh. "C'mon, boy. We could both use a walk. I need to mail my letter to Roshanda anyway." For the moment, letters were her only means of communication. Some sort of delay had come up in activating the telephone wiring, and now the idiot phone company said it could be another *three weeks* before their phone or internet service was connected. Her parents both had cell phones, but they didn't seem to think that Allie might need one, too.

From the moving carton next to her Allie picked up a yellow envelope containing a letter to her best friend, in which she had detailed the miseries of her new life in West Nowheresville, USA. Okay, sure, her parents were delighted. It was easy for them. Their financial worries were over, and they had found a beautiful new house. Her mom was already out applying for a job and meeting the neighbors. But on Monday Allie would be forced to start in the middle of the semester at a school she had never heard of before. Who knew what classes they would try to shoehorn her into? She would be the new girl, without a friend in the entire state.

"Not a friend here but you, boy," she said, clipping the leash to Merlin's collar.

At the end of the long, curving driveway, they paused at the rural-style mailbox, which was empty, of course, since she and her parents were the first residents at this address, and nothing from their old house had been forwarded yet. Allie put the envelope in and raised the little red flag on the side of the enameled aluminum box to indicate a letter for pickup.

Abandoning herself to the dog's whims, Allie let Merlin take the lead and enjoy his explorations for a couple of miles. She paid just enough attention to their route to be sure she could find her way back to the house. The black lab romped and sniffed and peed and chased, finding wonder and delight in his new surroundings.

Allie wished she could share the feeling, but for her, life felt bleak and hopeless and lonely. The only wonder in her world was wondering why this had had to happen to her. In spite of these gloomy thoughts, a smile quirked one corner of her mouth when, after an hour and a half of rambling, they returned to the house and she noticed the flag on the mailbox was down. Good, that meant her letter was mailed, and the sooner Roshanda got it, the sooner her friend could reply. Even though she knew it was foolish, she decided to peek into the mailbox in case a letter or some piece of junk mail had found its way here already. As she had expected, the interior of the arched metal box looked empty.

But just as she was about to close the door, Allie saw a glint of something lying on the corrugated aluminum bottom of the mailbox. A sheet of cellophane perhaps? No, it sparkled too much.

Merlin wagged his tail wildly and barked twice, as if impatient to know what she was looking at. Allie put in her hand and drew out the shiny scrap of material. She laid it across her palm to study it. It was a pliable, crystalline sheet about the size and shape of a standard postcard, but that was where the similarity ended. The card itself was as clear as spring water and etched with strange symbols that did not look like any form of writing Allie had ever seen. They looked like those laser carvings of sailboats or eagles or lighthouses in blocks of Lucite that she had seen in the airport gift store.

The etched symbols seemed to float deep inside the rectangle, which was strange since the clear material was thinner than a piece of notebook paper. In fact, the more Allie looked at it, the more three-dimensional the symbols seemed to appear. The markings—hieroglyphics, perhaps?—started to swirl before her eyes, forming and unforming words that she did not recognize but felt she ought to know. As if responding to an optical illusion, her field of vision deepened, and ripples moved across the card's surface, like tiny waves on a crystal-clear mountain lake.

With one finger she reached out to touch the swirling symbols and suddenly found herself facing a life-sized, shimmering image of a girl no older than she with knee-length raven locks and a tear-streaked face. A window behind the girl framed a many-turreted stone castle standing on the shores of a sparkling blue-green lake. Allie gasped and blinked several times. The image didn't disappear, yet she could see right through it to her house and the mailbox and Merlin. It was as if she was looking at the largest, most vividly colored hologram ever created.

Allie groaned. "I've finally lost it, haven't I, Merlin? It—"

But before she could finish her sentence, the ethereal girl sat down at a desk by the window. A diminutive, kindly looking old man with a shock of fluffy gray hair handed her a long white feather, and she began writing with the quill on a scrolled sheet of brown paper. The girl spoke aloud as she wrote, and Allie found that although the language was strange, she could understand every word.

Dearest Quillfriend,

My trusted confidante Mythwell the Enchanter has encouraged me to write to you, stranger though you may be, in the hope that by sharing my woes, the burdens of my heart may be somewhat eased. Since I have no companions here of a like age, Mythwell has agreed to use his magicks to ensure that my words fall on friendly ears.

Allie realized she had stopped breathing and forced herself to take slow, quiet breaths. She didn't want to miss a word.

My situation now is more grave than thus far it has ever been in my life. Yes, graver even than on the day when the dragon Grovich flew away with me to his lair and held me captive until seven of my father's bravest knights came to rescue me.

Please, dearest friend, write to me and tell me whether you would hear of my plight. If you are disposed to do me this honor, please affix my rune crystal to your letter, and Mythwell's spell will bring it to me. I await your reply and crave any word of comfort you might impart.

Your Quillfriend (if you are willing),

Princess Avienne of Mereglade

With that, the transparent image faded to a blur of rainbow scintillation and then disappeared. Allie tried to reactivate the sparkling rectangle—the rune crystal?—by gazing into it again, smoothing it between her hands, turning it over, pressing it, folding it, and even shaking it, but the sad-eyed girl did not reappear. Next, Allie spent a full five minutes attempting to convince herself that the image had been some sort of elaborate, high-tech hoax, but found that this idea was almost as difficult to believe as receiving a magical letter from a fantasy princess. And much less enjoyable.

Merlin barked once, sniffed the air where the glittering princess had seemed to stand, circled the mailbox wagging his tail, then repeated his actions.

"So you believe she was real, huh boy? Well, who am I to argue with the great Merlin?" With a shrug, Allie decided to accept the impossible. For now. She *wanted* to believe it. She was so lonely here, what would it hurt to play along for a while? In any case, it would be at least a week before she could expect a reply from Roshanda.

After dinner with her parents, Allie wrote a note, knowing full well that mailing it probably wouldn't work. While she was writing, her mother looked in on her.

"What are you working on, dear?"

"Writing a letter to a princess."

Instead of giving her a strange look, her mom beamed. "That's wonderful. I always hoped you'd get back to writing stories again, like you used to in middle school. Can I read it?"

"Uh … it's not ready yet," Allie said. "Maybe in a few days, when it's further along. Anyway, I'm having fun just thinking about it." To her surprise, Allie found that it was true. Perhaps the note would turn out to be a silly waste of time, but it amused her. If no one wrote back, maybe she *should* turn it into a story. "Dear Princess Avienne," she wrote.

I don't know if you'll get this letter, but I had to try. I would love to be your Quillfriend. I think I would be able to understand your problems, since you look like you're about my age.

I'm 15 and my life is a mess. My parents don't even consider my feelings when they make decisions, and I have no idea what my future will be. Feel free to tell me your problems, and I'll tell you mine. I could really use someone to talk to right now. Please write soon.

Your Quillfriend,

Allie

P.S. I'm enclosing a school picture of me, so you can see what I look like.

Allie tucked the note and picture into a pink envelope, taped the rune crystal to the front, and wrote her entire return address in the upper left corner, including the zip code, just to avoid any confusion. She left the upper right corner blank. Although it was already dark out, she didn't want to wait for morning, so she turned on the outdoor lights and walked down to the end of the driveway. Leashless, Merlin trailed after her. She put the pink envelope into the still-pristine mailbox, closed the door and raised the flag.

"Okay, boy. We did it." Allie gave Merlin a pat and headed back up the drive with him. The black lab replied with a conversational *woof*. A moment later, he turned, bounded back down to the mailbox, and paced back and forth barking with excitement. Allie sighed. She knew she should have used the leash. "C'mon, Merlin. Time to go in." The dog shook himself all over, as if he had just emerged from a bath, gave an insistent bark, and reached up to put his front paws on the mailbox.

Allie knew when she was defeated. "Fine, boy. I'll show you what's in there, but it's just a letter, not a box of Milk-Bone treats." As if he understood, the lab sat and waited for her. When she reached his side, Allie looped an index finger under his collar and with the other hand opened the box again. "There. You satisfied? Nothing but a—" She stopped, her mouth still open. The little red flag was down, and the mailbox before her was empty.

* * *

The next morning, after a night during which excitement robbed her of a good many hours of sleep, Allie took Merlin for a walk and found a new rune crystal in the mailbox. And thus began a wonderful quill-friendship.

My Dearest Princess Allie,

Thank you for your kindness in sending such a delightful and heartfelt response. I received your reply scant hours after I sent my letter to you.

We are indeed very much alike. As you surmised, we are of an age, and my situation, too, is grave. My life, like yours, is "a mess."

My mother the queen died last year at the hands of an assassin. On the eve of the winter solstice my father the king remarried. My stepmother wishes me to marry her cousin Warlord Morwolf in order to expand her family's holdings. In return, Lord Morwolf has agreed to ally with us in times of war.

My parents, like yours, did not consult me in this matter. Alas, my father agreed to the match! I cannot love Lord Morwolf. He is a cruel, brutish man, rude of manner, and thrice our age, dearest Allie. And he has but seven of his own teeth!

When I asked my father to reconsider the match, he told me that it is my duty to take a husband who will make our kingdom more powerful. Because my father wages war each spring, this alliance is much to be desired.

Should I refuse, I will be sent into exile. Marriage, too, would be a form of exile. Since my two older sisters wed lords from the mountain reaches, I hear from them but once a year.

My heart is heavy, my future bleak. Have you any words of comfort to offer, dearest friend?

Your Quillfriend,

Avienne

P.S. I am all in wonderment at the beauty and intricacy of your portrait painting. How can I ever express sufficient gratitude for such a precious gift?

*   *   *

Dear Princess Avienne,

First off, I'm not actually a princess. I'm just sort of a normal teenage girl. I like music, mostly boy bands or divas. What kind of music do you like? Do you play an instrument? I tried playing clarinet for two years, but I was never very good at it. For fun I go to the movies, hang out with my friends, or maybe go dancing. At least I used to. I don't have any friends here yet. What do you do for fun?

Now for the serious stuff. Wow. Exile? My parents would never be able to do that. They always wanted more kids, but my mom couldn't have another one, so I know they couldn't stand to give me up.

Your country looks so pretty in your letters. Are you positive your father won't let you stay? I'm sure the king loves you more than he shows. Try talking to him. Anyway, no one here would ever make a girl our age marry *anyone*, much less such an awful-sounding man as Lord Morwolf. That sounds so medieval! They do make us go to school, though, and learn things like math and history (yuck) and science. Then we have to choose what to do with the rest of our lives. That can be pretty scary.

I hope things work out with your father.

Your friend,

Allie

* * *

My dearest Allie,

Your kind words gave me fresh hope. I must tell you that at first my father was firm in his resolve: I must marry Lord Morwolf, bear his children, and run his castle at Fleamarsh, or be cast out of my father's lands forever. When I made my appeal to him, however, his heart softened, and he relented. I now have a third choice: if I do not marry the warlord, I may enter a convent, never to leave its walls again, and take a vow of silence.

I cannot express how grateful I am to you for aiding me thus with my dilemma. Yet if I make this choice, my faithful Mythwell may not accompany me.

Perhaps you dread your choices at school even as I dread my choice between a loveless marriage, exile, and the convent. If so, my heart aches for you. Thank you for being my comfort in my time of need.

Your devoted friend,

Avienne

P.S. I adore music, and have been known to swoon when listening to a minstrel sing tragic ballads. Though I blush to admit to my skill, I am an accomplished lute player and harpist. Like you, I love to dance, but my greatest joy (or fun, as you call it) is going for long walks with Mythwell, who secretly teaches me about plants and medicine and the stars, instead of the silly needlework and simpering manners I study at court.

*   *   *

Dear Princess Avienne,

Boy, am I beat! This morning Dad got me up *before nine* and dragged me off to go shopping with Mom at the dismal little mall that is the closest thing to civilization within a half-hour's drive of where we live. I had to choose some new clothes for school, but most of the shops only carried styles I wouldn't be caught dead in. Only three stores had any clothes worth being seen wearing. I did find one cute dress, a pair of strappy spring sandals, and three tops. Oh, and a pair of tight jeans that make my legs look really long. But that was *all* I could find. I mean, I really tried, but there wasn't much to work with.

I'm sure that you never have any problem finding the right clothes. I wish I were a princess. You probably just snap your fingers and the royal tailor makes whatever you want. I know you're not happy about that warlord everyone wants you to marry, but in a lot of ways, you're really lucky. Most of the time you can just take it easy and get anything you need.

After shopping, Dad took Mom and me to Starbucks for scones and a latte, but I'm exhausted. I don't know how they expect me to walk the dog, take out the trash, and unstack the dishwasher after all that shopping. I doubt anyone would ever ask a princess to do all that! If only I could go live with you.

I think I'll take a nap now before my Dad comes up with even more chores for me to do. Write soon.

Your good friend,

Allie

P.S. I'm sorry to hear about the convent thing. What an awful choice! You'd have to give up both your family and your friends. Maybe it's better than marrying that Morwolf guy, but if I were you, I'd choose exile. I mean, at least then I could try to pick a place, kind of like here, probably, where I could enjoy living and still keep as many of the people I care about as possible. Weird, huh? I guess I never realized how much my friends meant to me until I couldn't be with them anymore. I think I'll write to Roshanda again after my nap.

* * *

My dearest Allie,

I write you today from the dungeon of my father's castle. This was the suggestion of my stepmother, to enable me to think "more clearly" until I have made my final decision about marrying Lord Morwolf. She fears I may flee (yet would this not be choosing exile?), and I believe she had a hand in an assassination attempt on Mythwell today. The plot failed, but now my loyal friend is wounded and imprisoned with me. Mythwell tells me that the queen is with child and will bear my father his first male heir. For this prize he has so long desired, the king will doubtless grant her any favor she asks. My fate may well be sealed.

But enough of my selfish thoughts. I fear I have greatly misjudged the gravity of your own situation. Am I to understand that your father beat you and then forced you to perform menial labor? I am very saddened to hear of it. Does this "shopping mall" bear any similarities to a marketplace or bazaar? If so, I shudder to think of you venturing there. The merchant stalls in our villages are dirty and dangerous, and filled with pickpockets. You must have been terrified. I can only imagine that the scones and latte you wrote of are similar to the bread and water I am being given now during my confinement. Be strong, my friend. We must both endure.

Your devoted friend,

Avienne

P.S. This may be my last opportunity to write to you, regardless of my wishes, if I am soon forced to make my choice. Live well, dearest friend.

*   *   *

Dear Princess Avienne,

Please, please don't stop writing. Your problems are far worse than mine, and I'd do anything to help you. And to answer your questions: no, my parents aren't cruel to me, and they don't force me to do dangerous work or "menial" chores. They try really hard to make a good life for all of us, not just themselves. I even showed my mom some of your letters to me (I've been writing them down like a story), and she said she wished we could give my fairytale princess the loving home and family she deserved. I thought it was kind of sweet. She doesn't even know you're real!

Guess what? I started my new school today, and it actually wasn't that bad. The campus is really pretty, with lots of trees and green fields around it. I got lost a couple of times in the halls, but most of the teachers were helpful, and an awesome-looking guy from my homeroom showed me where the chemistry lab is. I think I'm going to like my Shakespeare class best, but history is pretty interesting, too. I found out there's a spring dance coming up. I think I may be brave and go to it all by myself and see who I can meet. After all, it can't be nearly as difficult as facing an awful marriage, permanent seclusion, or exile, can it?

I think about you all day long and wonder what choice you made. I wish you could be here so we could talk face to face instead of through letters. Please take care of yourself, and try to find a way to reach me.

Your dear friend,

Allie

* * *

Days passed, and the only mail Allie received was a bright and cheery letter from Roshanda—nothing at all from Princess Avienne. Roshanda was full of gossip about familiar friends and places that Allie missed … including the news that Ian Walters had already started dating Katie Clark. Although she was happy to hear from Roshanda, Allie found she hardly cared that Ian had gotten over her so quickly. She was so preoccupied with worry about the fate of the princess, that she couldn't imagine being upset by such small concerns.

Allie checked the mailbox every afternoon. Her mother even expressed amusement at how excited Allie seemed to get "when there's usually only junk anyway." Day after day, Allie's anxiety built. She wondered how Avienne had resolved her dilemma.

Had she relented in the end and agreed to marry cruel old Warlord Morwolf? Allie couldn't imagine kissing anyone with only seven teeth—probably brown and crooked ones. And how could anybody decide on their life's mate at age fifteen?

It was possible that the princess had chosen instead to accept exile, to leave her beautiful kingdom. Even an unknown and mysterious land sounded better than a place called "Fleamarsh."

Or had she decided that her best chance was just to be locked inside a nunnery, never to speak a word again, surrendering all hope of returning to the outside world and freedom? Allie shuddered.

She had thought her own life was terrible just because she had moved to a new place and had no friends. Though she still longed for a companion, someone with whom she could share her thoughts and her dreams, Allie realized that her problems were vanishingly small compared to those of the princess.

Avienne's enchanter friend Mythwell had been wounded; maybe he was even unconscious or dead by now. What options did the princess truly have? Allie wished she could be there to comfort her friend, even if it meant sitting in a dank dungeon with her.

It was cloudy on Saturday when Allie took Merlin out to walk and to check the mailbox again. She had already tried twice that afternoon, and either the postal carrier was late, or they hadn't received any mail at all today.

Of course there were no postal delivery trucks from fantasy land. She wouldn't see anyone drive up, so she would simply keep checking.

The black lab frolicked, delighted as usual to be outside. He pulled on his leash and bounded around the mailbox as Allie opened it. She was startled to find not a rune crystal, but a smallish parcel wrapped in crinkly brown parchment and covered with arcane symbols. Still, the distinctive runes on the wrapping told her who had sent the package. Allie caught her breath. She had had so many disappointments over the past several days that she had almost given up hope. This might not be one of Avienne's beautiful holographic letters, but it was something to be treasured, nevertheless.

When Allie reached for the package, she felt immediately how strangely heavy it was. What had the princess sent her—a lead box?

She had to use both of her hands to slide it across the corrugated bottom of the mailbox, and the instant she pulled it free, it abruptly felt as if she had lifted a hundred pounds. Struggling to hold onto the package, Allie lowered it as quickly and gently as she could to the ground. Merlin sniffed at it with excitement.

Allie straightened and noticed that the parcel was obviously, and rapidly, *growing*. She took a step backward. As the package continued to expand, parchment tore away to expose a glittering crystalline crate as tall as Allie herself. A milky mist swirled within it, and more runes were etched across every exposed surface. Shadows moved in the depths of the mist, and Allie heard sounds coming from the box: a thump and then … a bark? Suddenly the crystalline cover of the crate dissolved, and a tiny white dog pranced out of the mist.

Not at all what Allie had expected. The dog looked, for all the world, like an oversized dandelion puff that had sprouted four legs, a nose, and a tail.

Merlin stepped forward and greeted the diminutive visitor by exchanging thorough sniffs and nose touches. Then the two dogs faced the open crate and barked. Its sparkling walls evaporated, and the mist cleared, revealing a startled-looking girl with raven hair, smudged cheeks, and a filth-encrusted velvet gown. "Are— are we truly here?"

Allie gasped. "Princess Avienne?"

The girl smiled. "No longer 'Princess,' I fear. Merely a 'normal teenage girl,' like you."

Allie laughed with delight and threw her arms around Avienne, ignoring the grime and the smell. She released her friend and stepped back to marvel at what had happened. This was no illusion, no sparkling hologram. Avienne was as real and solid as Allie herself. "You escaped? So you chose exile, after all."

The ex-princess gave an elegant shrug. "How can it be exile, when I have chosen to be in a beautiful land with those who mean the most to me?"

"But—" Allie said. "What about Mythwell?" The dandelion-puff barked twice.

Avienne stooped to pick up the little white dog and hugged it. "He had only enough time and strength to send one such enchanted parcel. This was the only means by which he could escape with me." She scratched the dog's head. "It is enough that we are alive and together. Can you tell me, dear friend, where we can earn food and shelter?"

Allie grinned. "Let's go talk to my parents."

*　*　*

Allie never found out how her father handled the paperwork or the explanations of why her "cousin" had come to live with them, but within three days, Avienne was a sophomore at Allie's new high school.

Allie never regretted the choice to share her parents with the gracious ex-princess. They had distinctly different personalities and rarely found themselves in competition with each other. That was why in their junior year, Avienne helped Allie become homecoming queen, complete with crown. In turn, in their senior year, Allie masterminded the campaign that got Avienne elected as student body president.

Although it seemed strange to some, since the girls had adjacent rooms, Allie and Avienne often wrote little postcards and notes, which they left for each other on beds, in backpacks or school lockers, on dressers, and on mirrors.

Rebecca Moesta (pronounced MESS-tuh) *wanted to be an author since her early teens, but it wasn't until 1991 that she began writing in earnest. Her solo novels include* Buffy the Vampire Slayer: Little Things *(2002) and three novels in the Junior Jedi Knights series. With her husband, Kevin J. Anderson, she wrote the Crystal Doors trilogy, the movie novelization of* The League of Extraordinary Gentlemen *under the pseudonym "K.J. Anderson" (2003); a movie novelization of* Supernova *(2000); a novelization of the popular StarCraft computer game* StarCraft: Shadow of the Xel'Naga, *under the pseudonym "Gabriel Mesta" (2001); and a Star Trek graphic novel,* The Gorn Crisis *(2001). The team, currently working on Star Challengers, a Young Adult science fiction series, has also written two young adult Titan A.E. novels (2000), two high-tech Star Wars Pop-up Books, and the 14-book Young Jedi Knights series of Star Wars novels. They are also co-publishers of WordFire and can be found online at wordfire.com.*

Ever since their spaceship crashed and they were stranded on The World, Bailles and Clingerts have been enemies … never intermarrying … never having anything to do with each other. But in this classic Robert Silverberg tale, it's Romeo & Juliet *in space when a Baille and Clingert fall in love …*

THE OUTBREEDERS

BY ROBERT SILVERBERG

The week before his wedding, Ryly Baille went alone into the wild forests that separated Baille lands from those of the Clingert clan. The lonely journey was a prenuptial tradition among the Bailles; his people expected him to return with body toughened by exertion, mind sharp and clear from solitary meditation. No one at all expected him to meet and fall in love with a Clingert girl.

He left early on a Threeday morning; nine Bailles saw him off. Old Fredrog, the Baille Clanfather, wished him well. Minton, Ryly's own father, clasped him by the hand for a long, awkward moment. Three of his patrilineal cousins offered their best wishes. And Davud, his dearest friend and closest phenotype-brother, slapped him affectionately.

Ryly said good-bye also to his mother, to the Clanmother, and to Hella, his betrothed. He shouldered his bow and quiver, hitched up his hiking trousers, and grinned nervously. Overhead, Thomas, the yellow primary sun, was rising high; later in the day the blue companion, Doris, would join her husband in the sky. It was a warm spring morning.

Ryly surveyed the little group: six tall, blond-haired, blue-eyed men, three tall, red-haired, hazel-eyed women. Perfect examples all of Baille-norm, and therefore the highest representatives of evolution.

"So long, all," he said, smiling. There was nothing else to say. He turned and headed off into the chattering forest. His long legs carried him easily down the well-worn path. Tradition required him to follow the main path until noon, when the second sun would enter the sky; then, wherever he might be, he was to veer sharply from the road and hew his own way through the vegetation for the rest of the journey.

He would be gone three days, two nights. On the third evening he would turn back, returning by morning to claim his bride.

He thought of Hella as he walked. She was a fine girl; he was happy Clanfather had allotted her to him. Not that she was prettier than any of the other current eligibles—they were all more or less equal. But Hella had a certain bright sparkle, a way of smiling, that Ryly thought he could grow to like.

Thomas was climbing now towards his noon height; the forest grew warm. A bright-colored, web-winged lizard sprang squawking from a tree to the left of the path and fluttered in a brief clumsy arc over Ryly's head. He notched an arrow and brought the lizard down—his first kill of the trip. Tucking three red pinlike tail feathers in his belt, he moved on.

At noon the first blue rays of Doris mingled with the yellow of Thomas. The moment had come. Ryly knelt to mutter a short prayer in memory of those two pioneering Bailles who had come to The World so many generations ago to found the clan, and swung off to the right, cutting between the fuzzy grey boles of two towering sweetfruit trees. He incised his name on the forestward side of one tree as a guide-sign for his return, and entered the unknown part of the forest.

He walked till he was hungry; then he killed an unwary bouncer, skinned, cooked, and ate the meaty rodent, and bathed in a crystal-bright stream at the edge of an evergreen thicket. When darkness came, he camped near an upjutting cliff, and for a long time lay on his back, staring up at the four gleaming little moons, telling himself the old clan legends until he fell asleep.

The following morning was without event; he covered many miles, carefully leaving trail-marks behind. And shortly before Dorisrise he met the girl.

It was really an accident. He had sighted the yellow dorsal spines of a wabbler protruding a couple of inches over the top of a thick hedge, and decided the wabbler's horns would be as good a trophy as any to bring back to Hella. He strung his bow and waited for the beast to lift its one vulnerable spot, the eye, into view.

After a moment the wabbler's head appeared, top-heavy with the weight of the spreading snout-horns. Ryly fingered his bowstring and targeted on the bloodshot eye.

His aim was false; the arrow thwacked hard against the scalelike black leather of the wabbler's domed skull, hung—penetrating the skin for an instant—and dropped away. The wabbler snorted in surprise and anger and set off, crashing noisily through the underbrush, undulating wildly as its vast flippers slammed the ground.

Ryly gave chase. He strung his bow on the run, as he followed the trail of the big herbivore. Somewhere ahead a waterfall rumbled; the wabbler evidently intended to make an aquatic getaway. Ryly broke into a clearing—and saw the girl standing next to the wabbler, patting its muscular withers and murmuring soothing sounds. She glared up at Ryly as he appeared.

For a moment he hardly recognized her as human. She was slim and dark-haired, with great black eyes, a tiny tilted nose, full lips. She wore a brightly colored sarong-like affair of some batik cloth; it left her tanned legs bare. And she was almost a foot shorter than Ryly; Baille women rarely dipped below five-ten in height.

"Did you shoot at this animal?" she demanded suddenly.

Ryly had difficulty understanding her; the words seemed to be in his language, but the vowels sounded all wrong, the consonants not harsh enough.

"I did," he said. "I didn't know he was your pet."

"*Pet!* The wabblers aren't pets. They're sacred. Are you a Baille?"

Taken aback by the abrupt question, Ryly sputtered a moment before nodding.

"I thought so. I'm Joanne Clingert. What are you doing on Clingert territory?"

"So that's it," Ryly said slowly. He stared at her as if she had just crawled out from under a lichen-crusted rock. "You're a *Clingert*. That explains things."

"Explains what?"

"The way you look, the way you talk, the way you ..." He moved hesitantly closer, looking down at her. She looked very angry, but behind the anger shone something else—

A sparkle, maybe. A brightness.

Ryly shuddered. The Clingerts were dreaded alien beings of a terrible ugliness, or so Clanfather had constantly reiterated. Well, maybe so. But, then, *this* Clingert could hardly be typical. She seemed so delicate and lovely, quite unlike the rawboned, athletic Baille women.

A blue shaft of light broke through the saw-toothed leaves of the trees and shattered on the Clingert's brow. Almost as a reflex, Ryly sank to his knees to pray.

"Why are you doing that?" the Clingert asked.

"It's Dorisrise! Don't you pray at Dorisrise?"

She glanced upward at the blue sun now orbiting the yellow primary. "That's only Secundus that just rose. What did you call it—*Doris*?"

Ryly concluded his prayer and rose. "Of course. And there's Thomas next to her."

"Hmm. We call them Primus and Secundus. But I suppose it's not surprising that the Bailles and Clingerts would have different names for the suns. Thomas and Doris ... that's nice. Named for the original Bailles?"

Ryly nodded. "And I guess Primus and Secundus founded the Clingerts?"

She laughed—a brittle tinkling sound that bounced prettily back from the curtain of trees. "No, hardly. Jarl and Bess were our founders. *Primus* and *Secundus* only mean first and second, in Latin."

"Latin? What's that? I—"

Ryly shut his mouth, suddenly. A cold tremor of delayed alarm passed through him. He stared at the Clingert in horror.

"Is something wrong?" the Clingert asked. "You look so pale."

"We're talking to each other," Ryly said. "We're holding a nice little conversation. Very friendly, and all."

She looked indignant. "Is anything wrong with that?"

"Yes," Ryly said glumly. "I'm supposed to hate you."

* * *

They walked together to the place where the waterfall cascaded in a bright foaming tumble down the mountainside, and they talked. And Ryly discovered that Clingerts were not quite so frightening as he had been led to believe.

His wanderings had brought him close to Clingert territory; Joanne had been but an hour from home when she had met him. But he nervously declined an offer to come to the Clingert settlement with her. That would be carrying things much too far.

After a while the Clingert said, "Do you hate me yet?"

"I don't think I'm going to hate you," Ryly told her. "I think I like you. And particularly every time I think of Hella—"

"Hella?" The Clingert's eyes flashed angrily.

"The Baille who was my betrothed." He accented the *was*. "Clanfather gave her to me last month. We were supposed to be married when I returned to the settlement. I thought I was looking forward to it too. Until—until—"

A wabbler mooed somewhere deeper in the forest. Ryly stared helplessly at the Clingert, realizing now what was happening to him.

He was falling in love with the Clingert.

Ever since the days when Thomas and Doris Baille first came to The World, Baille and Clingert had kept firm boundaries. Baille had mated only with Baille. And now—

Ryly shook his head sadly. In the blue-and-gold brilliance of the afternoon, this Clingert seemed infinitely more desirable to him than any Baille woman ever had.

She touched his hand gently. "You're very quiet. You're not at all like the Clingert men."

"I guess I'm not. What are they like?"

She made a little face. "Much shorter than you are, with ugly straight dark hair and black eyes. Their muscles bunch up in knots when they draw bows; your arms are long and lean. And Clingert men get bald at a very young age." Her hand lightly ruffled his Baille-yellow hair. "Do Bailles lose their hair young?"

"Bailles never get bald. Clanfather's hair is still as yellow as mine, and he's past fifty." Ryly fell silent again, thinking of Clanfather and what he would say if he knew what had taken place out here.

Not since the days when Thomas cast the first Clingert from his sight has this happened, he would probably intone in a deep, sententious voice.

Ryly remembered a time far away in his childhood when a Baille woman had birthed a dark-haired son. Clanfather had driven child and parents out into the forest, and there other Bailles had stoned them. Ryly was not anxious to share that fate. But yet—

He scrambled to his feet. The Clingert looked at him in alarm. "Where are you going?" she asked.

"Back. To the Baille settlement."

There was a moment of silence between them. Finally Ryly took a deep breath and said, "I'll return. Meet me at this place three days from now, at Dorisrise—I mean, when Secundus rises. Will you be here?"

Uneasiness glimmered in her dark eyes. "Yes," she said.

*　*　*

He reached the familiar Baille territory near nightfall the next day, having covered the outlying ground as rapidly as he could and with as few stops along the way as possible. He ducked back onto the main road around the time of Thomasset on Fiveday. He had had little difficulty in locating the tree that bore his name in its bark. Only the blue sun shone now, and it was low above the horizon; the moons were beginning their procession across the twilight dimmed sky.

Ryly stole into the settlement on the back road. That route brought him past the crude little cabin which Thomas had built with his own hands as a place for Doris and himself to live, long ago when the first Baille had tumbled out of the sky and settled on The World. Ryly quivered a little as he passed the dingy old shrine; the sort of betrayal he was contemplating did not come easy to him.

Above all, he did not want to be seen. Not until he had spoken with his phenotype-brother Davud.

A cat mewled. Ryly ducked into the concealing darkness of a vine bower and waited. A stiff-necked old man passed by: Clanfather. Ryly held his breath until the old one had entered the Clan house; he slipped out of his shelter, then padded silently across the main courtyard, and ran into the open archway that led to Davud's cabin.

The light was on. Davud was inside, drowsing in a chair. Ryly tiptoed through the rear door. He sprang across the room in four big bounds and clapped his hands over Davud's mouth before the other had fully come awake.

"It's me—Ryly. I'm back."

"Mmph!"

"Keep quiet and don't make any loud noises. I don't want people to find out I'm here yet."

He stepped back. Davud rubbed his lips and said, "What in Thomas' name made you want to scare me like that? For a second I thought it was a Clingert raid."

Ryly winced. He stared intently at Davud, wondering if it was safe to tell him. Davud, of all the Bailles, was closest to him in physique and in attitude, which was the reason Clanfather had designated them phenotype-brothers even though they had different parents. Among the Bailles, actual parentage meant little, since genetically every clan member was virtually identical to every other.

He and Davud were uncannily alike, though: both standing six-three, the Baille-norm height, both with the same twist to their unruly blond hair, the same sharpness of nose, and the same thinness of earlobe.

He poured a beaker of thick yellow bryophyte wine and sipped it slowly to steady his nerves. "I have to talk to you, Davud. Something very important has happened to me."

Ignoring that, Davud said, "You weren't supposed to come back until tomorrow morning. I saw Hella around Thomasset, and she said she couldn't wait to see you again." Davud grinned. "I told her I was enough like you to do, but she wouldn't listen to the idea."

"Don't talk about Hella. Listen to me, Davud. I went into Clingert territory on my trip. I met a Clingert girl. I … love her … I think."

Davud was on his feet in an instant, facing Ryly, brow to brow, chin to chin. His nostrils were quivering. "What did you just say?"

Very quietly Ryly repeated his words.

"I thought that was it," Davud muttered. "Ryly, are you out of your head? Marry a Clingert? That *filth*?"

"But you haven't seen—"

"I don't need to see. You know the old stories of how the first Clingert quarreled with Thomas until Thomas was forced to drive him away. You know what sort of creatures the Clingerts are. How can you possibly—"

"Love one? Davud, you don't know how easy it is. The Baille girls are so damned big and brawny! Joanne is—well, you'd have to see her to know. The fact that Thomas and the first Clingert had some silly quarrel hundreds of years ago—"

Davud's face was a white mask of indignation. "*Ryly!* Get hold of yourself! You're talking nonsense, man—absolute nonsense. Baille and Clingert must never breed. Would you want to pollute our line with theirs?"

"Yes." Defiantly.

"You're mad, then. But why did you come back here to tell me about all this? Why didn't you simply stay with your Clingert?"

"I wanted someone to know. Someone I could trust—like you."

"You made a mistake in that case," Davud said. "I'm going to tell Clanfather the whole story, and when they stone you I'll be glad to take part. That's what they did the last time this happened, fifteen years ago, if you remember. When Luri Baille had a baby that looked like a Clingert. The line has to be kept pure."

"Why?"

"It—it has to, that's all," Davud said weakly. As Ryly started to walk out, he added, "Hey! Where do you think you're going?"

"Back to the forest," Ryly said in a bitter voice. "I promised her I'd be back. I should never have come here in the first place." He was shaking and perspiring heavily; somewhat to his own surprise he realized that by this conversation he had effectively cut himself off from the Bailles forever.

"You're not going, Ryly. I won't let you."

Davud grabbed Ryly's collar, but he pulled away. "Don't try to stop me, Davud."

Without replying, Davud gripped the fleshy part of his arm. Calmly Ryly pivoted and smashed his fist into the face that was so much like his own. Davud blinked, half believing, and started to mutter something. Ryly quickly jerked his arm free and hit Davud a second time. Davud sagged to the floor.

Ryly stood poised indecisively for a second, watching with some astonishment the flow of blood from his phenotype-brother's broken nose. Then he turned and dashed through the doorway, out into the dark courtyard, and ran as hard as he could for the forest road.

He listened for the shouts of pursuers but could hear none yet. He wondered if perhaps he had hit Davud too hard.

* * *

Ryly spent an uneasy night in the forest not too far from the edge of the Baille territory; when morning came, he struck out at a rapid pace for the Baille-Clingert border. Joanne would be at the waterfall by Dorisrise—he hoped. For an instant he considered what would become of him if she had been playing him false, but he reached no answer. Could he return to the Bailles and marry Hella after all? He didn't think so.

The day grew warmer as he half trotted through the forest, following the series of trail-marks he had left to guide himself. When he reached the trysting place, it was not yet Dorisrise; Thomas alone was in the sky. Ryly sat by the water's edge and splashed himself to clean away the sweat of travel.

He heard footsteps. He looked up, hoping it might be Joanne. But it was Davud who appeared.

"So you followed me?"

Davud nodded. "I had to, Ryly."

"And I suppose you brought the whole tribe behind you, all of them foaming at the mouth and ready to stone me." Ryly sighed. "I guess I didn't hit you hard enough, then. You woke up too soon."

Davud's nose was swollen and slightly askew. He said, "I came alone. I want to try to talk you out of this crazy thing, Ryly. Nobody else knows about it yet."

"Good. Now you go back and forget anything I said to you last night."

"I can't do that," Davud said. "I can't let you mate with a—a *Clingert*. I came to bring you back to Baille land with me."

Ryly clenched his fists. He had no desire to fight with his phenotype-brother a second time, but if Davud was going to insist—

"Get away from me, Davud. Go back alone."

It was almost Dorisrise time, now. Ryly hoped he would be able to get Davud out of the way before Joanne reached their rendezvous. But Davud was shaking his head stubbornly. "Baille and Clingert shall not breed. Thomas set that law down for us in the beginning, and it can never be broken. It is—"

He stopped, jaw sagging, and pointed. Slowly Ryly turned. The first rays of Doris glinted blue in the flowing waterfall, and Joanne stood behind him.

"Which of you is Ryly?" she asked plaintively.

Ryly unfroze first. "I am," he said. "This is my phenotype-brother Davud. He came with me to—meet you. Davud, this is Joanne."

"Is *this* a Clingert?" Davud asked slowly. "But—but—Clanfather always said they were *ugly*! And—"

Joanne laughed, her special Clingert sort of laugh that Ryly had already grown to love. "He seems stunned. Just as stunned as you were, three days ago. Do all of you Bailles think we're ogres?"

Davud sat down heavily on a rotting stump. His face was very pale by the light of the double suns; he was shaking his head reflectively and seemed to be talking quietly to himself. At length he said, "All right. I apologize, Ryly. Now I see what you were talking about. *Now* I see!"

There was an overenthusiastic note in Davud's tone of voice that irked Ryly, but he refrained from voicing any annoyance. "What about Thomas and his laws now, Davud?" he said. "Now that you've seen a Clingert?"

"I take everything back," Davud murmured. "Everything."

Ryly glanced from his phenotype-brother to Joanne. "I guess we have his blessing; then. If—if you're willing to become an outcast from the Clingerts, that is."

Now it was Joanne's turn to look startled. "Outcast? For fulfilling the aim of the first Clingert?"

"What's that?"

"You mean you don't know?"

Ryly shook his head. "I don't have the faintest idea of what you're talking about."

"When it all started," she said patiently. "When the spaceship exploded and the Clingerts and Bailles were thrown free and landed on The World, hundreds of years ago, Jarl Clingert wanted to interbreed, but Thomas Baille wouldn't have any of it. He wanted to keep his line pure. So there hasn't been very much contact between Clingert and Baille since then, ever since the time the first Baille threatened without provocation to kill Jarl Clingert if he came within ten miles of—"

"Hold it," Ryly said. "It was Clingert who tried to kill Thomas Baille and marry Doris, but Thomas drove him off and—"

"No," said Joanne. "You've got it all backward. It was *Baille's* fault that—"

"Let's discuss ancient history some other time," Davud interjected suddenly. There was a curiously pained expression on his face. "Ryly, do you mind if I talk to you alone a moment?"

"Why—all right," Ryly said, surprised.

They drew a few feet farther away, and Ryly said, "Well? What do you think of her?"

"That's what I want to talk to you about," Davud whispered harshly. "I think she's far and away above the Baille women. She's so—*different.* Gentle but not weak, small but not flimsy—"

"I knew you'd like her, Davud."

"Not *like*," Davud groaned. "Love. I love her too, Ryly."

* * *

It came like a blow across the face. Ryly's eyes widened and stared into the equally blue ones of his phenotype-brother. The Baille genes had been duplicated perfectly among them, it seemed. In every respect.

"You can't mean that," Ryly said.

"I do. Dammit, I do. How can I help it?"

"We can't *both* have her, Davud. And I think I have priority. I—"

Davud gasped and seized him suddenly, spinning him around. Ryly looked, shut his eyes, touched his fingers lightly to his eyelids, and looked again. The mirage was still there. It was no illusion.

He saw two Joannes.

"Ryly? Davud? Meet Melena. Melena Clingert."

"Is she—your sister?" Ryly asked hoarsely. The two Clingerts were, at this distance, identical.

"My cousin," Joanne said. "I don't have any sisters." She grinned. "Melena was hiding near the far side of the waterfall. I brought her along to have a peek at Ryly."

Ryly and his phenotype-brother exchanged astonished glances.

"Of course," Ryly said softly. "We Bailles all look alike; why shouldn't the Clingerts? Three hundred years of inbreeding. Lord, they must all be identical!"

"More or less," Joanne said. "There are some minor variations but not many. Most of the unfixed genes in the clan were lost generations ago. As probably happened in your clan too. This was the thing that Jarl Clingert wanted to avoid, but when Thomas Baille refused to—"

"It was Clingert's treacherous ways that caused the whole thing," Ryly snapped. "Let's get that straight right now. Why, it's common knowledge!"

"Among whom? Among the Bailles, that's who—whom!" Joanne's eyes were blazing again, with the fury Ryly loved so much to see. "But why don't you listen to the Clingert side of the story for a change? You Bailles were always like that, shutting your ears to anything important. You—" She stopped in midbreath. Very quietly she said, "I'm sorry, Ryly."

"It was my fault. I started the whole thing."

"No," she said, shaking her head. "I did, when I brought up the topic of—"

He smiled and touched a finger lightly to her lips. "Look," he said.

She looked. Davud and Melena had drawn to one side, standing on a moist, moss-covered patch of ground within the field of spray and foam of the waterfall. They were talking softly. It wasn't difficult to see by their faces what the topic of discussion was.

"We'll have to forget about ancient history now," Joanne said. "Forget all about what happened between Jarl Clingert and Thomas Baille four centuries ago."

Ryly took her hand. "We'll go somewhere else on The World," he said. "Start all over, build a new settlement. Just the four of us. And maybe we can recruit some others, if I can lure a few Bailles out here to meet Clingerts."

"And vice versa. The Clingert men hate the Bailles now too, you know. But that can stop. We'll breed the feuding out."

Ryly looked over at Davud and Melena, then back at Joanne. Everything looked incredibly lovely at that moment—the angular red leaves of the overhanging trees, the white spray of the falls, prismatically colored blue and gold by the sunlight, the quiet green clouds drifting above. He wanted to fix that moment in his mind forever.

He smiled. His mind was still full of insidious Clanfather-instilled legends of the early days on The World as seen through Baille eyes. But he could start forgetting them now.

Soon there would be a third clan on The World—a hybrid clan, both fair and dark, both short and tall.

And someday his descendants would be spinning legends about *him*, and how he had helped to found the clan, back in the misty time-shrouded days of the remote past.

Robert Silverberg *is rightly considered by many as one of the greatest living Science Fiction writers. His career stretches back to the pulps and his output is amazing by any standards. He's authored numerous novels, short stories and nonfiction books in various genres and categories. He's also a frequent guest at Cons and a regularly columnist for* Asimov's. *His major works include* Dying Inside, The Book of Skulls, The Alien Years, The World Inside, Nightfall *with Isaac Asimov,* Son of Man, A Time of Changes, *and the 7 Majipoor Cycle books. His first Majipoor trilogy,* Lord Valentine's Castle, Majipoor Chronicles, *and* Valentine Pontifex, *were reissued by ROC Books in May 2012, September 2012, and January 2013.* Tales of Majipoor, *a new collection bringing together all the short Majipoor tales, followed in May 2013.*

Our next story details a pivotal event that occurred off screen just prior to key events of my debut novel, The Worker Prince. It focuses on Davi Rhii and his best friends, Farien and Yao, and how their rivalry with fellow cadet Bordox took a darker and darker turn in their days at the Boralian Military Academy and their …

RIVALRY ON THE SKY COURSE
(A DAVI RHII STORY)

BY BRYAN THOMAS SCHMIDT

BEEP! BEEP! The alarm on the targeting computer of his VS28 starfighter pounded Davi Rhii's ears as adrenaline throbbed through his veins. He glanced down to see several blips on the screen. "Incoming enemy craft," he announced into the comm, then switched on his shields and prepared for his second encounter with the enemy that day.

Body tensing and pressing back in the seat, he shifted weight and adjusted his controls as the sleek, black snub nose of another VS28 appeared beside him in the clouds, flying a little too close. "Bordox, aren't wingmen supposed to fly in formation behind their leader?"

Bordox's snapped back over the comm, "Yeah, so fall back and fly behind me then."

Davi bit back a retort and took a deep breath. "I have command, pilot."

The enemy craft appeared ahead, swooping down toward them. Davi rotated his VS28 and lined up on the lead attacker's fighter. His hands clasped the joystick as he let go with his lasers. He landed two hits on the attack leader's wings, sending him spinning toward the ground, smoke and debris trailing behind.

"Got him!" He whooped over the comm as another enemy fighter exploded nearby outside his blast shield.

"Lucky shot," Bordox sneered as another attacker's ship exploded on Davi's screen. "*That* was skill."

"Great, but stay in formation so we can protect each other," Davi ordered, but Bordox ignored him and dove off in another direction. He executed a roll with his VS28 and went in for another run. Breathing deliberately to keep himself relaxed—a trick his uncle had suggested—he fired three times in a row, sending another attacker into a smoking dive.

Bordox dove in from the opposite direction, but his lasers missed their target even as an enemy fighter braked and slid onto his tail.

Bordox cursed over the radio. "Get this guy off me, Rhii!"

"Oh, now you want teamwork," Davi snapped as he swooped down toward the fighter chasing Bordox but he was too late. The enemy fighter fired three times, hitting Bordox's engines and one of his ship's main wings. Bordox's fighter rocked and spun out of control toward the ground. Davi remained focused, lining up his sights and destroying the last two enemy fighters.

Then his console flashed and froze as klaxons blared and the cockpit shield rose automatically.

"Lights up!" Professor Orson Jonas called.

The reflector pods overhead lit the room with blinding light. Davi squinted and climbed out of the flight simulator. His best friends, Yao and Farien, raced over to pat him on the back, the shorter Farien's lighter white skin contrasting with their Tertullian friend's orangish tone, both aglow with Davi's victory.

"How many does that make?" Yao's purple eyes brightened against his dark orange-tinted skin. "Nine in a row by my count."

Davi's breathing returned to normal as he glanced over at Bordox struggling to extract his huge frame from the tight seat of another sim. "Who's counting? It's all in fun."

Bordox scowled as their eyes met.

Farien guffawed. "Don't show him any mercy he wouldn't show you."

"Just friendly competition," Davi said, figuring he'd already humiliated Bordox enough. Still, inside, his heart pounded in triumph and blood warmed his flesh.

The flight classroom was one of the largest on the military academy's campus. Occupying the bottom floor of an instruction building, it contained several rows of tan flight simulators with black seats and control panels identical to those of actual VS28 starfighters. A laser board covered most of the front wall.

Professor Orson Jonas stood behind a lectern, his black hair beginning to show strands of gray. He wore the gray uniform of the full military officer he had been until retiring to teach at the academy.

"Perhaps next time, Cadet Bordox will try and work with his leader instead of trying to compete with him and *actually* survive the battle," Professor Jonas said with a smile.

Bordox grimaced and slunk back to his desk in the classroom as Davi exchanged high fives with Yao and Farien.

*   *   *

"I failed the test!" Farien rested his dark hair on the dining hall table.

Davi chuckled and patted him on his bulky shoulder. Farien might be the shortest of the three, but he made up for it in muscle. "I think I failed, too. You're not the only one."

The glint of the gold buttons on their blue-gray uniforms teased Davi's eyes. Matching hats sat on the table next to their trays of brown Qiwi antelope meat, Gixi juice, and Jax fruit salad with fresh baked bread. They faced each other around one of the long, reddish brown tables that ran in rows down the middle of the dining hall.

Yao sipped his Gixi juice and his purplish eyes glinted as he smiled at the sweet taste Davi knew reminded him of home. "Don't be so dramatic, Farien. You could have joined the study group. We invited you several times."

"Easy for you to say, you're a genius at math," Farien growled as Yao and Davi chuckled.

"Ignore him, Yao," Davi said. Farien needed to let off steam, and Davi knew better than to interfere.

"At least you're good at something." Farien lifted his head off the table, pulled his tray back from the middle, and took a bite of Qiwi. "You impressed Professor Jonas on the simulators today. I stink at that, too."

"Bordox didn't seem impressed." Yao grinned.

Davi licked his lips in anticipation as he sliced his Qiwi, pink juice flooding out to cover his fingers. "Bordox relies on his size to intimidate people instead of developing his skills."

"Speaking of Bordox." Yao nodded toward the door.

A huge, hulking cadet with light yellowish-brown skin and a dark beard, common to colonists who'd descended from Hispanic cultures on Old Earth, Bordox walked as if he owned the place. None of the cronies who followed him matched their leader's size, but all walked with the same swagger, the same smug look on their faces.

Davi turned and his green eyes met Bordox's for a moment. His rival's brown eyes held an anger Davi hadn't expected, but his smug face never faltered.

Swallowing, Farien smiled and waved at Bordox. "Hey, Bordox, nice job on the flight simulators. So good of you to show us all how not to do it!"

Bordox struggled to maintain his composure as the cadets around them smiled and guffawed.

"Don't egg him on, Farien," Yao said as Davi nodded in agreement. Bordox didn't appear in the mood for their usual hazing.

"Mock all you want, Farien," Bordox said in his scratchy baritone as he and his friends barreled across the room, stopping at the end of their table. "You're as inept at flying as you are at math." Bordox's buddies snickered.

Farien's muscles tensed and he jumped to his feet, rattling the bench. Davi put a hand on his arm. "I'm sure everyone could use extra time on the simulators."

Still shaking, Farien frowned and sat back down.

"Like your family will allow you to be put in danger, Prince." Bordox sneered. "You're only here because of special treatment."

"At the Academy, I'm your peer, not your Prince," Davi insisted, deliberately keeping his voice even despite the embarrassment that his rival had brought it up.

"Yes, your royal peerness," Bordox snapped, and his cronies cackled as they turned away and moved off toward the serving counter.

"I'm sick of that jerk!" Farien shuffled the food on his plate with a fork.

Davi shrugged as he chewed a bite of juicy Qiwi meat. "He's never liked to lose."

"If he keeps this up, he'll be drummed out of flight school," Yao said. "His focus should be on his studies rather than humiliating you."

"He still thinks my uncle stole the throne," Davi said amused by the absurdity of it. Would Bordox and his family never let that folk tale go? "I don't think his father makes it easy on him with all the failures, either."

Farien groaned. "Don't tell me you feel sorry for him! No one deserves your sympathy less than that moron!"

Davi and Yao exchanged amused glances as they turned back to their meals.

* * *

Professor Jonas pounded a fist on the lectern, motioning for the chattering students to quiet down. "Cadets, I'm pleased to announce our annual sky course competition has been scheduled for the end of the month. You'll want to work hard in the simulators over the next few weeks to avoid embarrassing yourselves in front of your family and friends. The High Lord Counselor, along with most of the Council, will be in attendance."

"Our little Prince had better sit this one out," Bordox said raising his voice and sneering as Davi grimaced, "so he won't publicly embarrass the Royal family." Bordox and his friends guffawed as others in the class voiced their disagreement.

"I wonder what excuse your father will come up with, Bordox," Farien said, "to avoid having to see you humiliated again."

Bordox's face reddened as the cadets laughed at him again. "At least the Lords won't have to lower themselves by sitting next to commoners like your family, Farien." He and his friends sneered as Davi offered Farien a calming look.

"Cadet Bordox, Cadet Rhii followed orders well in the simulators last class, unlike yourself," Professor Jonas said, causing Bordox to sink down in the chair of his simulator. "Your own attitude and performance leave much to be desired."

Davi relished Bordox's discomfort as the other cadets snickered and elbowed each other through broad grins.

"I'd be happy to tutor him, Professor Jonas, if he'd like," Davi said with a smirk, provoking another round of laughter.

"Oh really, my Prince? You'd lower yourself to help little ole me?" Bordox said back, mimicking a small child. "Go back to your stolen palace, crown boy."

"Members of the Royal family are to be treated with respect!" Farien stood, chest puffing, fists clenched, as if preparing to rush Bordox at any moment.

Bordox's face turned dark. When their eyes met, his look was sharp as blades. "From what I hear, the royal prince's blood isn't so royal."

Yao stood and grabbed Farien's arm, trying to calm him as Davi smiled. Bordox must be really desperate to come up with something so absurd. "Who'd have known you're so fond of folk stories, Bordox."

"If it's a folk tale, I guess you're the folk lore prince," Bordox said. "A starport rumor about a baby who arrived in a courier craft from the stars and landed near the palace, adopted by a lonely princess with no offspring." Bordox's cronies chortled and sneered. "Maybe I should have my father look into it, just in case," Bordox said as Farien struggled against Yao's grip. Bordox's father, Lord Obed, headed the Lord's Special Police, an elite squad of soldiers dedicated to the High Lord Counselor's service.

"Enough!" Professor Jonas hollered then waited for them to quiet down. "Cadet Bordox, you're out of line. Impugning the reputation of another cadet without cause is enough for me to have you dismissed. Prince Rhii's heritage is not in doubt. Would you like me to take this matter before the Academic Council?"

Bordox tensed in his seat, fists clenched and just stared straight ahead but Davi felt the anger radiating from him in waves.

"Now pull up your datapads to the chapter on flight patterns and pay attention!" the Professor ordered as Bordox sank down further into his seat. His eyes held a hatred Davi had never seen.

*　*　*

The next night, Davi, Yao, and Farien gathered for dinner at the Promenade with three beautiful women they'd met at a park. Seated on the outdoor patio that overlooked a lake, the smooth, cool breeze urged them to relax and enjoy the time off.

"Would you ladies care to go for a stroll?" Warmth filled Davi as the last bite of his meal settled into his stomach.

"There he is, the adopted prince. It's sad, isn't it, hearing his blood isn't really royal? It's so charitable of the High Lord Counselor and Princess to take him in anyway so he can make something of himself."

Davi's blood temperature rose as he turned to see Bordox and his companions cackling nearby with dates of their own. People around them stared, making Davi and his friends' dates shift uncomfortably.

"A slave child sent into space in a courier to save his life adopted by a princess." Bordox's sarcasm cut Davi like shards of ice "It really is a great story, isn't it? Almost like magic."

Davi heard more guffawing around them as Farien stiffened, his face whitening in anger. "You're pushing it too far, Bordox. I'm warning you."

"Or what? Your worker prince will call his uncle?" Bordox sneered as his friends chuckled.

"It must be really humiliating to watch him keep beating you on the sims," Yao said with a grin. "Especially since his family has a history of such victories against yours."

"Let's settle this right here!" Farien's chair squeaked as he pushed back from the table and stood, fists balling at his side.

Davi stood beside him. Public disparaging was too much. He had to defend his family's honor.

"Come on, ladies, don't listen to him," Yao said from behind them.

Farien and Davi turned as their dates hurried away down the promenade.

Bordox snickered, his eyes glowing in triumph, as he and his companions turned and walked away.

"Let's go!" Farien said, stepping forward.

"He's got too many people with him, Farien. You can't take them all on," Yao said, grabbing him by the arm.

Davi stood fuming, his body stiff with tension, as he watched Bordox and his cronies walk calmly past a skitter shop along the Promenade. His instincts matched Farien's. Private teasing was one thing, but spreading lies in public was another. Especially when it cost them their dates. Who knew how far the rumor would spread now? An idea popped into his head and he smiled. "I think what I have in mind will make you feel much better."

He turned and led the way toward the skitter shop, Yao and Farien following.

They rented skitters and took off down the promenade, hovering a few feet off the ground as they weaved through the scattered pedestrians. Experienced riders, the three manipulated their vehicles smoothly around light poles, people and other objects as they sped along. One-man ground craft ridden like Old Earth motorcycles, skitters used manipulated air to hover and move above a planet's surface. They were sleek and fast, and favorites of both civilians and military.

As they rode, Davi spotted Bordox's group walking close to the edge of the water.

"There they are. Let's go say hello." The skitter's servos hummed as Davi accelerated, enjoying the vehicle's vibrations and gentle hum as he raced forward with Yao and Farien close behind.

Davi steered the skitter over behind Bordox's group. Others on the Promenade spotted them coming and jumped or stepped aside to clear a path. Davi revved the engines loudly as he came up fast from their rear, taking Bordox and his friends by surprise.

Trying to jump clear in panic, Bordox and several companions, including his date, lost their balance and fell into the river. They yelled as they fell, sputtering and cursing after splashing down in the water.

Amused by their version of revenge, Davi and his friends didn't even look back as they rode away.

"Your ideas really are the best," Farien said.

"I hope that water's cold," Yao said as they stopped and turned to watch Bordox's friends helping him and his disgusted date out of the water. "You know this will only make him madder." Yao looked at Davi.

Davi shrugged. "He's the one who made it personal. Besides, I feel better." Laughing with his friends, he revved his skitter's motor and accelerated again and they rode away.

*　*　*

Over the next several weeks, Davi and Bordox barely crossed paths; mostly during lectures or when cadets gathered and compared simulator results. Bordox jeered at him a couple of rare times when his scores outdid Davi's, but otherwise made no attempt to converse. In time, the tension between them receded to its normal level.

Two days before the competition, Davi and his fellow contestants gathered with Professor Jonas at the starport.

"You each get one practice run on the actual course before the competition," Professor Jonas explained. "You must destroy all the targets and avoid all the obstacles before reaching the finish line. Scores will be determined through combining how many obstacles and targets each of you defeats with your overall speed."

Davi glanced around at the grandstands scattered through the course, which wound over the city in a large oval. He could almost feel the history that had taken place there. Spectators could rent special goggles allowing them to see the course for the popular annual event. Adding to the challenge, the VS28s had been designed for spaceflight and didn't operate near as efficiently within the planet's atmosphere. The professors regarded it as a truer test of the cadets' piloting skills due to the added handicap.

Davi, Bordox, and Farien had been assigned to a group with six others. As they approached their fighters, Davi increased his pace to come alongside Bordox. "Good luck up there today."

Bordox looked at him a moment, as if evaluating his sincerity. "You too."

"I saw your sim scores. You've been working hard."

Bordox shrugged. "We'll see who's the hotshot pilot now."

Davi grinned and extended his hand. Bordox nodded as he shook it, then they hurried toward their assigned craft.

They launched from the starport and rendezvoused at the starting zone for the course, waiting for Professor Jonas' signal to start their run.

Davi's VS28 rose into the sky, its vibrations and hums not much different than the well-designed simulator's. Sunlight from the planet's twin suns warmed his neck and shoulders, making him feel like he belonged up here.

Listening to the hum of the engines ease as the ship's vibrations calmed beneath him, he settled onto his starting altitude and turned to each side, memorizing the wingspan and diameters. Although they'd been allowed some practice time over the past two weeks, the sky course would require them to fly in closer proximity than normal, and he wanted to feel out the fighter so he could run the actual competition on instinct. His concern for the day wasn't winning but learning how the fighter would respond and what would be required to succeed in navigating the course. He could always add speed later.

A long, high tone sounded over their comm channel as they accelerated onto the course, engine trails streaming behind them. Farien and two others accelerated far too fast for Davi's comfort. He relaxed and hung back, getting to know the fighter and the course. To his surprise, Bordox hung back with him.

Navigating the first few obstacles with ease, Davi hit three targets then accelerated, the force pushing him against his seatback.

Then his controls froze.

He wiggled the joystick and punched the fuel button. Control returned. He breathed a sigh of relief.

He'd lost sight of Bordox as they passed through some low clouds. As he emerged from the cloud cover, his controls froze again. His heartbeat pounded in his head like a bass drum, rushing adrenaline making it difficult to think and focus, even as his mind raced through troubleshooting checklists they'd memorized in class.

When every attempt he made failed to restore control, he keyed his comm. "Test Alpha Six, my controls are frozen." He breathed deeply and tried not to panic.

Professor Jonas' steady voice came back through the comm. "Test Alpha Six, attempt to reinitialize your flight computer and report the results."

Davi flipped the switches, starting the reinitialization sequence for his flight computer and controls. The whole process should take a couple of minutes, and as he waited, he flew into another series of clouds. His fighter jerked, tossing him about, and he heard metal shrieking. Turning back, he saw Bordox's fighter close on his wing, a cocky smirk on Bordox's face. Had their fighters touched?

Davi switched his comm to the private squadron channel. "Bordox, what are you doing?"

Bordox's voice came back sounding apologetic. "Sorry. It's hard to see through the clouds."

"Back off, Bordox," Farien scolded over the comm. "He's lost his controls."

Before Farien finished, Bordox accelerated up beside Davi so close, Davi feared an impact.

"More fun if I can see your eyes." Bordox looked over and smiled.

Davi tensed, glaring toward Bordox's cockpit. This wasn't the time to play.

"Test Alpha Eight," Professor Jonas said, using Bordox's call sign, "pull off so you don't get caught in the tractor beams."

Bordox sneered and put his ship into a gradual dive, allowing his left wing to scrape Davi's right wing. Startled and fearful, Davi shifted his joystick and accidentally sent his VS28 into a roll.

Davi's flight computer finished initializing and beeped, notifying him it was ready. He struggled with the controls, trying to stop spinning and regain control. Instead, his fighter pointed straight at the ground.

The g-forces pushed him back harder against his seat with every second. He struggled with the stick to no avail, then pulled a hand off the joystick and keyed the comm again. "Test Alpha Six in trouble."

"Hang on Alpha Six," Professor Jonas responded, klaxons blaring in the control room behind him.

His fighter continued spinning out of control, the ground growing nearer as he gained speed. His pulse pounded and his breathing increased. He wondered how a pilot mentally prepared to die. The ground appeared as a smeared whirl through his blast shield.

Remembering the eject system, his hand shot toward it. The fighter rocked, sending his shoulder hard against the cockpit wall, and two VS28s flown by military officers pulled even with him on either side. His fighter jerked again and stopped spinning, suspended between the other two. They adjusted direction until all three flew straight again, then turned back toward the starport.

Davi had never experienced tractor beams before. His body relaxed in the seat, as he exhaled and released the controls then said a silent prayer thanking the gods.

*   *   *

That night in his dorm room, Davi leaned back on his bed as Farien paced beside the closed door. Yao watched from the chair near the desk.

"Bordox tampered with your fighter," Farien said, still angry.

"We don't know that for sure," Yao responded.

Davi breathed deeply, thankful it was over. "It's the first time he's ever apologized to me. He made a point of asking if I was okay. The fighters are harder to maneuver than the simulators. And you know how bad Bordox was on the sims."

"What other explanation is there?" Davi exchanged a look with Yao then Farien, hoping. Neither had one.

"Did you see the look on his face at the starport after?" Farien continued.

"Tampering with fighters is serious," Davi didn't want to believe Bordox would take things so far. "Someone could get hurt or killed."

"His eyes said he knew," Farien said.

"Oh, you're an eye reader now, are you?" Yao teased.

"Come on. You both know what I mean." Farien stopped pacing and leaned against the back of the closed door, looking frustrated.

"Why would he go that far? He may be jealous of me. We give each other a hard time. But I could have been hurt or killed." Davi wondered when their friendly competition had gotten so distorted that Bordox would risk putting Davi in real danger or doing him harm? This was military training, not war.

"Bordox hates you," Farien answered. "Walz overheard him at the Bar Electric swearing he'd bring you down no matter what."

"Bordox always brags like that." Davi had heard Bordox's comments so often, he'd stopped caring. "It's just talk. He never acts on it."

"Lord Obed still claims your grandfather stole the throne." Yao was the best versed among them in history, his favorite subject.

"It's just silly jealousy." Davi scoffed at Yao's expression.

Yao shrugged. "It's a motive."

Bordox had deliberately flown too close on the practice run. That much was sure, but had the crashing been deliberate or just his usual incompetence? Davi sighed, hoping they were wrong. "Without proof there's nothing we can do."

"We can tell Professor Jonas," Farien said.

"And risk being accused of disparaging another cadet ourselves? You have enough demerits already." Yao looked at Farien, who sighed in defeat.

Davi took a slow breath, releasing tension from his body. "They always reassign fighters before the race. Professor Jonas promised to let me have another practice run alone tomorrow during afternoon break. Can you two keep Bordox occupied?"

"A request to stop by his father's office during afternoon break." His shoulders lifted as the corners of his mouth formed a smile.

"What?" Yao shook his head. "He wouldn't have time. He couldn't get to LSP headquarters and back before his break ended."

Farien nodded. "Right."

Yao stared quizzically at Farien. "You're planning to forge an official government communiqué?"

"Walz's specialty is intelligence," Farien said. "Forgeries are part of his training. He'd love to test his skills in a real life situation."

Davi laughed. "Sometimes I think you're too devious to be an officer, Farien."

Yao shook his head. "It could come back to haunt us."

"You've got a better idea?" Farien asked.

"No," Yao and said together.

"Okay, let's go see Walz," Davi said as he stood.

Farien lit up and gleefully turned to the door.

* * *

On the day of the competition, Davi walked past the grandstands and saw his mother, Miri, and Uncle Xalivar, the High Lord Councilor, talking with Bordox's father and Yao's parents. His mother spotted him and waved, smiling with pride.

Hope she's still smiling afterwards, he thought nervously and struggled to focus, trying his uncle's deep breathing again.

The VS28s waited in smooth, perfectly aligned rows, their snub noses and three wings gleaming under the light of the twin suns overhead. The transparent cockpit blast shields waited open at ninety-degree angles from the cockpits below as the pilots prepared to climb into their ships. Davi glanced over and saw Bordox sneering at him from nearby.

Professor Jonas approached. "Rhii, switch fighters with Bordox."

The smug smile vanished from Bordox's face as they both turned toward the professor. "What? Why?"

The Professor sounded irritated. "All the fighters are the same. What's the issue, Cadet?"

Davi kept his eyes on Bordox's face watching for a reaction. He saw the truth in his eyes. *You did it again, didn't you?*

Bordox ignored him, grumbling to himself.

Davi and Bordox both moved to the fighter to which the other had been assigned.

Yao climbed the ladder to help Davi strap in. "Maybe Professor Jonas suspects Bordox had something to do with what happened on your practice run."

Davi shrugged and smiled. "Doesn't matter. As long as the competition's fair, I'll leave him in the dust."

Yao chuckled and climbed down, saluting with a wink of his purple eyes.

Davi's group went through their preflight checks, then launched in pairs through the launch tubes, rendezvousing again at the sky course starting zone. He greeted the twin suns like old friends. The sky seemed clearer than usual. *A good day for a race.*

When the signal came over their comm channel, they flew into the course as fast as they could.

Bordox kept his fighter even with Davi's as they dodged the first obstacles and shot several targets, then his speed dropped off as his ship began angling downward. Davi looked over, watching him struggle with the controls.

He keyed the private comm channel. "You need help over there, Bordox?" When he got no answer, he sped on through the course. Bordox wasn't one to ignore the offer if he really needed it.

Five minutes later, Davi landed at the starport, riding the high from an almost perfect run. Once he'd gotten into it, he'd forgotten all about his competition and just done his job, enjoying the ride. Looking around, he realized Bordox and his fighter were nowhere in sight. Had he even completed the course?

Then he heard a whining overhead and turned as a VS28 arced in at an odd angle and slammed to the tarmac in a dangerously rough landing, Bordox still at the controls. The man had moxy, that was for sure. Davi would have ejected and let the ship crash. The fighters were rigged for ground-activated self-destruct if their crash trajectory took them too close to any grandstands or populated areas.

As those around him gasped and mumbled, Bordox's hateful eyes locked on Davi's own from the cockpit.

* * *

Later, Professor Jonas announced the winners. Davi had the highest score by far. As he and his friends walked back toward the grandstands, Davi overheard a commotion down an alley between buildings. As they reached the alley's mouth, they stopped and peered in.

Bordox forced one of his friends back against a wall. "You were supposed to make the fighter slow, not unflyable. I could have been killed!"

"You're the one who didn't want him humiliating you again!" The friend said.

"It's not our fault the professor switched the fighters for the first time ever," another friend said.

"You humiliated me in front of my father!" Bordox pounded a fist against the wall above his frightened friend's head.

Davi and his friends exchanged a look then hurried past before anyone spotted them, continuing toward the grandstands.

"We're so proud of you," his mother, Miri, said as she wrapped Davi in a warm embrace. Her light blue eyes radiated warmth.

"Well done, Xander," Xalivar said with pride, addressing Davi by his given name, not the nickname Davi and his mother favored. Uncle Xalivar wore his usual gold robe with a white collar and cuffs. In the center by his neck lay the jewel known as the Emperor's eye. Shorter than Davi but taller than Miri, he had a dark beard.

Davi smiled. "Thanks for coming."

"We wouldn't have missed it," Miri assured him, pride almost bursting off her face.

Davi tried not to frown as Lord Obed and Bordox approached. Obed wore a ceremonial robe similar to Xalivar's. His skin had a light yellowish brown hue with the same intense brown eyes as his son. He smiled and extended his hand to Davi. "Congratulations, Prince Rhii. A great showing."

Davi shook the proffered hand, smiling. "Thank you, sir."

Lord Obed turned and looked at Bordox, who stood there looking down at his feet. "You've embarrassed me enough today," Obed growled.

Bordox sighed and extended his own hand. Davi had to hide his surprise as he shook it. "Congratulations, Rhii. You deserve it."

Obed led Bordox away as Yao stepped away from his parents and stopped next to Davi. "That had to hurt."

Davi nodded, continued to watch Bordox for a moment. He feared things had changed forever between them. He'd never wanted to make an enemy, but it hadn't been his fault.

"Come on," Farien called, waving him over, "we've got a party to get to!"

Their hands met in a high five as Davi joined them, and they hurried off for their favorite bar.

Bryan Thomas Schmidt *is an author and Hugo-nominated editor of adult and children's speculative fiction. His debut novel,* The Worker Prince *received Honorable Mention on Barnes & Noble Book Club's Year's Best Science Fiction Releases. His short stories have appeared in magazines, anthologies and online and include entries in* The X-Files *and* Decipher's WARS, *amongst others. His anthologies as editor include* Shattered Shields *with co-editor Jennifer Brozek,* Mission: Tomorrow, Galactic Games, *and* Little Green Men—Attack! *with Robin Wayne Bailey (forthcoming) all for Baen,* Space Battles: Full Throttle Space Tales #6, Beyond The Sun, *and* Raygun Chronicles: Space Opera for a New Age. *He can be found online at bryanthomasschmidt.net.*

16-year-old Allison wants what most girls her age want: a normal life with school, boys, and fun. But due to her grandma's strange illness, she's needed at home, and being away for long poses major problems. Beth Cato has quickly become a regular in my anthologies, with this dark fantasy you'll see why. A 1970s animal rights group's sleeper curse becomes a nightmare in ...

An Echo in the Shell

By Beth L. Cato

Despite the bitter autumn chill, Jonah's kiss warmed Allison's lips and sent unaccustomed heat swirling through her belly. Gravity didn't weigh her steps as she hopped up to the front porch. He had kissed her. He had held her hand and kissed her. Allison squealed and spun in a dizzying circle.

Feet away, the walls of her house shuddered. Something heavy smacked against the inner window, unseen behind the thick cover of nailed plywood. In that instant, the heat from the kiss evaporated and reality grounded her like an anvil.

Grandma.

Allison flung open the screen and fumbled with the key to unlock the doorknob and both deadbolts. She jumped inside. Glass squealed and crunched beneath her flats.

"Shut the door!" screamed Mom.

Allison kicked the door shut and slammed the locks in place. Grandma's solid weight impacted against Allison's back, sending a gush of air from her lungs. The doorknob gouged her gut. Grandma's knobby fingers inched up her arms towards her neck. The buzzing sound grew louder; the earthy, indefinable odor more potent.

Then Mom was there. With a sharp squeal, Grandma released her hold. Allison slipped around just in time to catch Grandma as she slumped to the ground. Mom stood there, panting, her hair electrocution-wild. A syringe gleamed in her hand.

"She took an extra-long nap and was too quiet when she woke up and then I couldn't catch her." Mom blew stray hair from her lips, tears filling her eyes. "Her first Kafka rage."

"So how long were you chasing her—oh." As Allison heaved Grandma onto the couch, she finally had a good look at the room. Broken glass littered the floor. Two side-tables lay broken, one leg embedded in the wall like a spear. Through the arched doorway to the dining room, she saw more overturned chairs and the light of the gaping refrigerator door. Grandma had broken things before or tried to bust out, run towards lights outside, but nothing like this.

The rage. The next symptoms … no.

"Oh, Grandma." Allison stroked Grandma's shorn scalp.

"Looks like she has some cuts and bruises. I need to take pictures of her and the room and then I can sweep up this glass."

"You should have called me," Allison said.

"Like I had a chance," Mom snapped. "But no, you had to go on your little date. I hope you enjoyed it, because you aren't having another one for a long time. She always seems to respond best to you." Mom gnawed at her inner cheek as she stared at Grandma.

"Mom! That's not fair!"

"Life's not fair. You're sixteen, Allison. You'll have plenty of time for boys and all that nonsense later on. Go grab the digital camera for me."

Glass crunched underfoot as Allison stalked towards the hall. Like Mom had any place talking to her about boys, seeing how Dad left, seeing how Mom hadn't even attempted a date since Y2K.

But maybe Mom was right, too. Maybe Grandma had missed Allison. Maybe that was why she flipped out. Maybe this wasn't "the rage" doctors talked about. Maybe it was something … weird. A tantrum. That's all.

She made a slight detour to shut the fridge and reset the childproof latch. The office door was open, which meant Mom must have been working when Grandma's rampage started. No surprise there. Mom tried to squeeze in freelancing whenever she could. The monitor was darkened in screensaver mode, the green light beneath blinking like a heartbeat. Allison grabbed the camera from its dock.

She took pictures as she walked through the house. A new hole in the wall. She stopped in the doorway to the living room and took in an empty spot on a high bookshelf. That broken glass used to be her great-great-grandmother's vase. The one that used to be Grandma's favorite.

It was just a vase.

There were no curtains over the board-covered windows. A Plexiglas shield covered the TV, and that was frosted and scratched. Any shelves were bolted to the walls, cupboards secured with childproofing snaps and locks. Mom leaned against an open cabinet beside the TV, set something inside, and shut the door. A shot of whiskey, probably. As if Allison didn't know. Mom would probably finish off the bottle when Allison was in bed and bury the evidence at the bottom of the recycling bin, as usual.

Grandma sat up on the couch. Her eyelids blinked as she stared dully into space. Her crudely shorn hair lay flat against her skull, dull metal grey against pasty skin. Her shadow cast against the front door revealed the truth. Long antennae curved from her head and arced a foot in height. Two mandibles protruded from her face and worked at the air. From her shoulders, diaphanous wings clung to her back and stretched the length of her body and through the couch itself. None of that was visible to the human eye, of course. Not yet. Light revealed the strengthening curse, that Grandma's body had become the husk of a soul-stealing bug.

That was the proof that Grandma suffered from Kafka Syndrome.

* * *

Grandma used to be Loretta Christiansen. Retired letter carrier for the United States Postal Service. Sunday school teacher for thirty-five years. Widow of Johann Christiansen. Mother of one. Grandmother of one. Game show junkie.

Really, when Allison thought of her grandma and who she truly was, her game shows were the first thing that came to mind.

"Come on, you banana brain," Grandma would yell at the TV. "The answer's the Mississippi River! The Amazon isn't even on this continent." Grandma had declared that Alex Trebek was dead to her after he shaved off his mustache.

Funny and old game shows were the best of all. Checkered bell-bottom pants and big hair were standard issue, along with cheesy orange studio sets. Allison was crestfallen at age ten when she realized no other kids knew about *Match Game 75* and Charles Nelson Reilly or the hilarity of the Whammies on *Press Your Luck*.

Oh, how Grandma would laugh as she watched, light and feminine and free, and descend into giggles and wheezes.

One day as Grandma and Allison walked the two blocks from school, Allison saw Grandma's shadow. The horns were mere nubs then, the wings like little fists from her shoulders.

Allison wasn't scared. She reached for Grandma's hand and squeezed, and stood close enough so that the shadow couldn't be seen.

The curse had been on Grandma and others for decades and the victims never even knew. Back in the early '70s, some group of animal rights radicals laid a sleeper curse on laboratory workers in five states. Their goal: make the workers become their own test subjects. By the time the illness manifested in shadows decades later, there was nothing magic or medical science could do.

Grandma had delivered mail to all the labs within the complex. For some reason, the Asian cockroach room's curse was the one that clung to her soul. Ate it away.

But Allison swore that sometimes a flash of clarity returned to Grandma's eyes. Sure, she might not be able to talk anymore, or laugh. She ate with her fingers gathered like pincers. Sometimes she hissed when surprised. And at dusk, she fixated on the lights outside, especially the ones reflecting on the lake behind the house—so they boarded up the windows. That attraction made the Asian cockroach different from other kinds. They hungered for light.

They were also supposed to be really strong flyers.

Allison refused to think about that final stage. It was a long ways off. But there were only some five thousand people under the curse, a few hundred with the Kafka variant. No one knew the exact timeline. Doctors said that most would die during that final physical transition, anyway.

Until then, Allison had Grandma to love and care for, and that was all that mattered.

*   *   *

The next morning, the house looked normal again. Spartan. The sharp stink of fresh paint made Allison's nose run.

With the phone to her ear, Mom paced along the bay window in the dining room. "I know you're still building the Kafka wing, but this was her first big incident of the rage. Yes, I read the report—no, we aren't sending her to that lab. The whole point of that curse was to force her to be some lab animal, damn it!" She took in a deep breath. "Sorry. Sorry. She signed a living will before—uh huh. I'm sorry. Last night was just really rough and ..."

Oh. Mom was talking with the people at that special home for National Lab curse patients. It was down near the University of Washington. A really nice place. They were building it for compatibility with a dozen different curses-in-progress.

Mom's voice slurred. Maybe the person on the phone wouldn't notice. Allison's stomach clenched in a knot. She hated mornings now.

Mom trailed a hand down her face. "Yes. Yes. Thank you." She pressed a button on her phone and set it down on the table, staring at it between her fingers.

"No progress?" Allison asked.

Mom's lips worked for a second and she shook her head. "They can't build it any faster. Other than that, they said we can sedate her more if necessary. I just ..." She looked away, blinking, her head bobbing slightly. "Hey, don't you have that biology test today?"

"That was last week. But all of my homework is done. I had everything taken care of before my date, remember?"

"Oh yes. Your date. That's right, it's Monday morning." Mom stared at where the calendar used to hang. Now only a few gouges from tacks marked the spot. "I'm losing my mind."

"You could drink less." Allison tried to keep her voice light.

"That's none of your business." Mom made no such attempt at levity.

"It is if I hear you slurring like this first thing in the morning."

Mom sucked in a sharp breath, the sound so like Grandma's cockroach hiss that it sent a rush of cold along Allison's spine. "How dare you. I'm an adult. I'm in complete control of how much I drink. It helps me sleep. Last night I needed all the help I could get, after that."

Allison grabbed an apple from the fridge and made a quick retreat towards the front door. She couldn't bear to even look at Mom.

Grandma was still asleep on the couch, her jaw gaped open. Asleep, she looked so normal.

"Hey Grandma," Allison whispered, her throat hot with tension. "I've gotta go to school. I'll miss you. Maybe this afternoon we can hang out?" Without waiting for an answer, she planted a kiss on Grandma's forehead. It was a shame the game show channel had changed their whole line-up a few months before. All their old shows were shuffled around.

"Allison. She's gone. This is just a shell—"

"Don't say it. I'm sick of you saying that."

"Reality's going to crash down hard on you when it comes, Allison. You can't be in denial forever."

"Denial? I know Grandma's sick—"

"She's not sick, damn it, she's gone! Dead! That's not her on the couch, get it?"

It was the whiskey, it was that stupid whiskey that made Mom all awful every morning. Allison backed up to the front door, her nails digging into flesh of the apple in her palm. She swung her backpack onto one shoulder and fled. She hit the sidewalk running fast enough that the tears tipped from her eyes and flew away without touching her cheeks.

* * *

"Come on, Grandma. It's time to get ready for bed."

With her hand curled beneath Grandma's armpit, Allison walked her down the hall. They staggered together, Grandma's steps small and shuffling. She fitted Grandma in fresh disposable underwear and a pink paisley nightgown that snapped up the sides. Then she guided Grandma to her room. Mattresses sat on a bare concrete floor. Scratches gouged the walls. Allison tried not to see it, tried not to compare the room to how it used to be with its dense '70s wood furniture and Currier & Ives prints on the walls.

She tucked in the old woman, taking care to layer the blankets and cover her wrinkled feet.

Allison laid a hand against Grandma's cheek. By Mom's account, it had been an okay day. Nothing good, nothing bad. Allison's day—well.

"Jonah asked me to go out with him on Friday," Allison whispered. "I didn't say no, not straight out. I mean … I know how he'd react. He's a cool guy, really. But …" She could only say "no" so many times. Most of her old friends had moved on for that very reason, or were content with just hanging out at school, never mentioning the possibility of anything after.

"It's hard sometimes, you know? But I know Mom won't let me go."

Grandma's teeth bared in a grimace. If her shadow had been visible, no doubt those pincers would be working as if they could bite. But there was no shadow. Just Grandma.

"Good night, Grandma. I love you." She planted a kiss on her forehead.

Allison shut the door and bolted it on the outside.

Mom was holed up in her office, working frantically on her work backlog. Probably would be until late. Allison disgorged her backpack's contents onto the couch and turned on the TV. She had already gotten a decent start on her homework by staying late after school—not like she was in a rush to get home for more quality time with Mom—but the terrors of algebra awaited.

Out of habit, she picked up the remote and flicked it to the game show channel.

"—*Match Game* Marathon!" boomed an overly pleasant announcer.

Allison's head jerked up.

A *Match Game* Marathon this Friday. Twenty-four solid hours of bell-bottoms and orange-shag goodness. Grandma would love this!

From the office, the chatter of computer keys continued, punctuated by dark, indecipherable mutters.

Mom wouldn't agree. Mom would say it was pointless, that Grandma wasn't in there, that it was all just a waste of time. She would yell and rant and do everything she could to make sure the TV stayed off. Allison's hand clenched the remote as if she could strangle the plastic. Grandma would love this marathon. If anything could coax her out of her shell, this would be it. Mom had even said Grandma responded best to her.

Mom needed to be out of the house that night.

Grinning, she reached for the phone and dialed up Mom's best friend, a friend who'd already pestered Mom for months to cut loose and relax for sanity's sake. "Hey, Shayna?" she said. "Allison here. Mom's really needing a break. You think we can tag team her?"

A few minutes later, she hung up. A devious plot was already underway. Shayna knew how to score tickets for some overnight bed and breakfast deal over in Leavenworth this Friday night. If Shayna had already shelled out the money, Mom would be more likely to cave in and go. It'd still take a few days to wear her down, but Allison knew it would work. On some level, Mom knew she needed a break, too. This was the excuse.

Allison finished up her homework as the TV droned in the background. For the first time in ages, she hummed aloud, a smile on her lips. This Friday was going to be the awesomest night ever, for all of them.

When Allison crawled into bed, she was still smiling. An incessant buzzing sound shivered through the wall. Grandma slept one room over, her breathing like a mob of a thousand mosquitoes.

Down the hallway, the door clicked open. From the living room came the soft thud of the opening liquor cabinet and the clink of glass. Mom was getting ready for bed, then.

Allison stared at the blackness of the ceiling. Her happiness dwindled away as a sick knot resumed its normal place in her stomach. Mom was the one who was really gone, not Grandma.

The terrible susurrus continued from next door, from Grandma. "It's just buzzing," Allison whispered, as if saying it aloud made it true.

She drifted to sleep, and the buzzing droned on.

* * *

"I shouldn't go." Mom clutched her suitcase handle and paced the living room. "You know what happened on Sunday—"

"She's been fine all week. If it gets to be too much, I'll call 9-1-1," Allison said. "Now go. If Shayna has to shut off her car to come get you, the neighbors might call 9-1-1 before you even leave."

Mom laughed, the sound abrupt and nervous. "Yeah. Riding tied up in the trunk might look suspicious."

"Go." Allison held open the door and pointed to the sidewalk.

Mom ducked her head like a chastised child, casting glances over her shoulder as she walked halfway along the path. "If you need me—"

"I'll call. Go!"

Allison bolted the door and stood there, shivering. It was going to be awful cold tonight. Through the peephole, she watched the car drive away. Mom was probably crying now, apologizing to Shayna, saying she shouldn't go. Shayna would keep driving.

"Well, Grandma, this is our big night," said Allison.

Grandma sat on the couch with a slack jaw. Her dead eyes stared ahead at the television.

"That's right, it's TV time! We've already missed some twelve hours of the marathon. We're slacking." She powered on the television and squealed as she sat down beside Grandma. "Look at Charles Nelson Reilly in that snazzy red suit! Geez, I think I saw Brett Somer's dress on sale at the mall last week. And you said the '70s would never come back in fashion."

Grandma buzzed softly. Allison leaned against her knees and giggled as she watched. "Oh, gosh. I'm surprised that comment made it past the censors then. That was awfully double-edged, even for now." Rain drummed a soft rhythm above their heads. Another episode came on, then another.

"That was a cop-out answer. That could have been smarter or funnier." Allison shot a furtive glance at Grandma, in search of agreement.

"Charles Nelson Reilly! Best player ever! Remember when I showed you the song Weird Al made all about him? Wasn't it awesome?"

"That hair. Crazy. Did she stick her finger in a light socket or what?"

Buzzing answered. Only buzzing.

Two hours passed; three.

Grandma's laughter wasn't there. Grandma wasn't there.

Allison turned off the television. She stared at the black screen. Through the marred protective glass, she could see their reflections. Grandma's expression never changed.

Grandma was really gone.

The realization was quiet. Cold. Back when the diagnosis first came, Allison had tried to joke that the curse wasn't real until Grandma had wings. Now she understood. It wasn't about how Grandma looked, or even her shadow. It was about ... Grandma.

She stood. In the blank screen, she saw Grandma stand as well. Grandma pivoted, hunch-backed, and dove at the taped-together lamp on the end table. It crashed to the carpet, and in a blink, the room was cast into darkness.

"Grandma?" No. This wasn't Grandma, not really. It wore her skin, but soon, it wouldn't even wear that. Mom had injected Grandma before she left—her regular dose with a little extra.

It wasn't enough to quell the rage.

There was a long, cockroach hiss and the shuffling of feet and Grandma was there, those hands scratching at Allison's neck.

She sidestepped. Grandma grunted, swinging towards her. Allison retreated towards the TV. Lamp shards skittered and crunched underfoot. Pain pierced the sole of her right foot, followed by the intense warmth of blood.

In scant grey light, Grandma advanced, her feet wide like a sumo wrestler. Her mouth gaped, glare reflecting from her teeth.

Her gaze—empty. No hatred. No malice. Allison was just ... a thing. A target. Prey?

Grandma was gone. Dead. She was dead. She wasn't in that body anymore.

Anger rippled through Allison and clogged her throat. Anger at the hippies and their curse, anger at Mom and her alcohol and her work, anger at doctors for doing nothing. Anger at Grandma.

"You were supposed to fight this!" Allison yelled. "You're supposed to still be in ... there!"

Grandma launched herself forward. Allison slipped aside, her bloodied foot tacky on the carpet, and Grandma plowed into the liquor cabinet. It rattled, glass tinkling and liquid jostling.

Allison hated that cabinet. Hated it. She turned, throwing her shoulder into the cabinet. It rocked against the wall, unable to fall because of the straps securing it in place. She hugged it with both arms and yanked with all of her body weight. The cabinet pulled from the wall. Then Grandma was there, tackling her. Allison met the next wall with a grunt. The cabinet crashed into the carpet at Grandma's heels.

Mom could buy more alcohol. She undoubtedly would. But there was something amazing about hearing those bottles shatter. There was just enough light to see a gush of dark fluid seep through to the floor, as if the cabinet itself bled.

"You should have laughed during *Match Game*," Allison whispered. "You would have laughed."

How long would the curse drag on? How many months, years? How long would this thing wear Grandma's skin? How long until—that Asian cockroach emerged? The wings. The antennae. The shadow come to life. And Mom—how would Mom change? What facade would she wear?

Nausea punched her in the stomach. Suddenly it was all real. All too real. Grandma hissed, and Allison stepped back. Her bare feet kicked through more pieces of the lamp. Pain zinged all the way up her leg and caused her to gasp. If she made it across the room to the switch, Grandma would go for the light instead. That would distract her until ...

Light. Outside, the light would be on down at the dock. A light that attracted clouds of bugs.

The awfulness of the thought froze her for a moment. Then the fumes of weeping liquor stung at her nostrils, and she knew what she would do.

She glanced at the door to the back patio. The story poured into her head: she would say she heard that old tomcat on the porch, that she opened her door to check. That Grandma attacked her. It was close to the truth. That they had fought throughout the room and then ended up back at the door. The door that lead to the stairs and the lake and the light and the cold, rainy night.

Allison staggered across the room and towards the door. Grandma's nails gouged at her neck. An earring ripped free from Allison's lobe. She worked the locks as Grandma's body dragged from her arm. The door swung free, iciness a wave over her skin.

Grandma hissed, grabbing Allison's neck with both hands, and shoved. Allison's head met the hardness of the doorjamb. Stars danced in the middle of the room as she fell to her knees. The loosened snaps of Grandma's gown clacked at Allison's head level.

"You're free," Allison whispered. "Go."

Then, the old woman was out the door, her bare feet smacking on wet cement. Allison forced her head to turn.

Rain fell in wavering sheets. Out on the nearby lake dock, a single yellow light stood as a sentinel. Grandma, hunched, was like a gray shadow in the blackness as she scurried away. The unsnapped gown trailed behind her like wings. Then she met the stairs. She tumbled, feet over head. Allison listened to the rasps of her own breaths. Grandma's head was visible again, barely. She still worked towards that brightness below, just like the Asian cockroach she was.

Allison could have screamed for help. She would have, if Grandma had been somewhere within that frail shell.

A slow ooze of blood coursed Allison's cheek. She lowered herself to the frigid linoleum before the door. The gallop of her heart was louder than the buzzing had ever been. She quivered as she heard a distant splash, and clenched her eyes shut. The light from the dock still burned through the blackness, and as the minutes passed and the chill sank in, the relentless rhythm of the rain soothed her like a lullaby.

Beth Cato *hails from Hanford, California, but currently writes and bakes cookies in a lair west of Phoenix, Arizona. She shares the household with a hockey-loving husband, a numbers-obsessed son, and a cat the size of a canned ham. She's the author of* The Clockwork Dagger *steampunk fantasy series from Harper Voyager. Follow her at BethCato.com and on Twitter at* @BethCato.

This brand new tale is Lou Antonelli's 96th short fiction sale in 12 years and he dedicates it to Ralph K. Banks, who first told him about going out into the country with his friends in rural Texas as teens and dancing to the radio under the stars. Set in the good ole days of the 1950s, this well told tale waxes nostalgic about a boy, a girl, a dance, and a UFO encounter at ...

THE MILKY WAY DANCE HALL

BY LOU ANTONELLI

Light pollution.

We didn't have any of it back then.

Heck, we were lucky to have lights. I was still in junior high school when the REA ran electricity to the farms in Franklin County.

When I was in high school, there really wasn't anything for teenagers to do there. Drive-in movies were popular, but we were much too small to have one. The nearest was one county over, in Mount Pleasant.

There was absolutely nothing in between the two cities. There weren't even any farms; the power company held the land for the lignite underneath. So it was completely black, and boy, did the stars shine at night.

There was this one farm-to-market road than ran through that wilderness, between us and Mount Pleasant. Late at night, after all the adults thought us teenagers were in bed, a bunch of us would sneak out there. It was the flattest stretch of road anyone had ever seen—smooth as a glass dance floor. And that's what we used it for. Needless to say, there was never any traffic late at night. We'd sneak out in our jalopies and hot rods and drive to that flat and open stretch of what we called County Line Road, and park our cars along either side facing each other. Everyone would shine their headlights on the road to light up our makeshift "dance hall."

Late at night we could pick up KWKH in Shreveport loud and clear. Music was changing then, and we'd listen to Conway Twitty, Carl Perkins, Jerry Lee Lewis, and Charlie Feathers belt out rockabilly songs. There was also some new kid from Mississippi named Presley getting airplay.

It was almost like we were on another world, our little island of light in a sea of darkness. What contributed to that impression was to see the stars so bright above us, and how the Milky Way crossed the sky like a shining arch.

My steady at the time was Charlene Redfern—or so I thought. I'd just found out she was now going out with Dub Mack. He was the quarterback on the football team. I was just second string. Looking back, I think she used me to get to meet Dub. I should have known Charlene was out of my league. I was just a redneck farm boy, her daddy owned the only car dealership in town.

Still it hurt.

That afternoon, outside after school, Connie walked up to me. She looked across the books she held up against her chest.

"You going out dancing tonight?"

I started to say no, and then I looked at her and stopped. Suddenly I was ashamed. I hadn't realized it before, but Connie was sweet on me—and I had ignored her.

I was ashamed because I knew it was because of my born prejudice. Connie belonged to one of the few Mexican families in town.

Consuela Zavala was short, and cute in a well-upholstered sort of way. She looked a lot like Snow White—dark hair with big black eyes.

"I want to," I said, "but I don't have a date."

She smiled. "I'll go with you," she said.

"That'd be swell!"

"Pick me up at the corner from my house at 10:30."

"Sounds great," I said. She smiled over her books and turned to walk away.

"Wow," I thought to myself as I headed to the parking lot.

Along the way I popped into a five and dime store and bought a candy bar. I stashed it in my jacket pocket.

* * *

I picked Connie up in my weather-beaten Ford Tudor and we drove to County Line Road. We were one of the first cars out there. I parked on the side and turned off my lights.

I was amazed to see that the Milky Way was shining so brightly it reflected in the pavement. I stared, fascinated. Connie didn't say anything for a few minutes, but looked at the starshine in wonder.

Finally she said, "It's so beautiful."

Just then I saw a flash in the rear view mirror. We both turned to see a shooting star in the sky behind us.

Instead of disappearing across the sky like a shooting star normally would, this one followed a path until it reached the horizon. When I took a second look, I realized it hadn't even reached the horizon, but disappeared behind a low hill between us and Mount Pleasant.

Now you have to remember that this was the 1950s and space invader movies were all the rage. I started to get a creepy feeling and wished more of my high school pals would show up. A minute or so later the main caravan arrived.

Sure enough, Charlene was riding in Dub's car. He drove a brand new '56 Ford Crown Vic. His daddy the banker had bought it for him from Charlene's father.

Everyone parked and kept their headlights on. Dub parked directly across me and I could see Charlene glaring at Connie through the windshield. Dub wrapped an arm around her shoulder.

Connie squeezed my hand.

"I'm sorry, Don," she said. "Charlene is stuck-up. You can dance with me tonight."

The car radios were coming on and Connie took my hand.

"Come on, let's dance a little, and show them we can have fun, too."

We all began to dance in the road. I quickly forgot about Charlene.

Now, most of the songs on the radio that night were good old Rockabilly tunes, but suddenly KWKH played the Number One song on the Billboard—which happened to be one of those sad "teenager in love" songs. The slow ballad brought the dancing to a screeching halt.

When Dub let go of Charlene, she looked down the road at us and began to head in our direction. Connie looked like she didn't appreciate Charlene coming to barge in.

Charlene walked up to me.

"You think you can pretend I don't exist," she said raising her voice.

"Listen Missy, you're the one who decided to go out with someone else without even telling me," I said.

"I don't think you know what you had," said Charlene.

"Yeah, a girl who didn't appreciate him," said Connie. "Go back on down the road and dance with your rich daddy's boy. And leave us alone."

"Why you little hussy spic …"

I automatically raised my hand. Another came up from below and grabbed my wrist.

"Don't be stupid," said Connie. "They can have each other."

Charlene turned around and walked away. When she reached Dub, she turned around and glared at me as Dub wrapped his arm around her waist and took her to his car.

"Her nose is so high she'd drown in a rainstorm," said Connie.

"She shouldn't call you names."

She took my hand. "Let's go to the car and cool off. Forget about it."

I turned down the volume of my car radio as we got in. That slow song by George Hamilton IV came to an end. "That song about 'A Rose and a Baby Ruth' sure put the quietus on the dancing," I said.

Connie chuckled. "It's a nice song, but you sure can't dance to it," she said. Then she got thoughtful.

"You know, it's a song about a boy who's sorry about getting in an argument with his girl, and wants to make up," she said. "But all he can afford is one rose, and a candy bar."

She smiled. "He's poor folks, like us."

The sky was so dark and the Milky Way so bright that as I looked into Connie's big dark eyes I could actually see the archway of stars reflected in them.

Slowly, one by one the car headlights and radios began to turn off.

Connie looked at me. I didn't know what I should do next. Then I had an idea.

Because of my old car's musty smell, I had an air freshener stuck on the dashboard. It was a little glass vase with a fake cloth rose, soaked in some sweet-smelling liquid. I also remembered I still had in a pocket of my jacket hanging on the back of my seat the candy bar I picked up that afternoon after school.

I pried the air freshener from the dashboard and reached for the candy bar. Connie looked at me a bit puzzled.

"I want to give you something." I handed her the rose and the Baby Ruth. "I'm just a poor farm boy and that's all I have for you tonight."

She giggled. "You're a goofball," she said. "But a sweet goofball. That song is about a boy who's trying to make up with a girl he had a fight with. You should give these to Charlene."

"The only thing I want to give Charlene is a swift kick in the rear."

We both laughed.

When we stopped, I looked at her and she looked at me.

Suddenly, we heard the car engines around us start up. Headlights began to come on. Connie looked up the road. "Dang," she said, "there's red and blue lights coming, it's the Sheriff!"

Now, one advantage of being a farm boy is that I knew this road from whenever we went to market in Mount Pleasant. So I pulled out and floored it.

"Please be careful," said Connie as she clutched the edges of the seat.

What I hadn't counted on was that some jalopy had spilled a

crankcase of oil on the road ahead of us. I barely saw the slick before I hit it. My car spun around and we went off the road and flew through the air.

Back then, there were no seatbelts and there were no airbags, and when we landed, we landed hard.

* * *

When I came to, I was lying in mud and reeds alongside a stock pond. I wiped blood and mud from my face with a sleeve, and looked over to see the smashed car. I had a glow-in-the-dark watch, so I looked at the dial. It said 3:00 A.M., so I had been out for hours.

I had a sharp pain in my chest that hurt when I breathed. I stood up in the mud and reeds and realized they had broken my landing when I flew out the car window.

We were so far off the road nobody could see us, and I couldn't see the road; the stock pond was in a hollow.

Then I thought of Connie. I went over to the car, and looked inside. It was lying upside down, and she was on the inside of the roof. The bloody foam running from her nostrils told me she was still alive but barely.

Remember, this was 1956—there were no paramedics, no EMTs, no emergency rooms. Ambulances came to take you to the funeral home—which was where Connie would be going. I began to bang my fists on the side of the wrecked car.

"Dammit, dammit the first girl who's ever been nice to me, and I've got her killed."

I just didn't cry, I wailed. My heart absolutely broke. And in the dark in the middle of nowhere someone—or something— heard me.

Even though my eyes were full of tears I could still see those brilliant stars in the Milky Way. Suddenly a black cloud appeared among them. I heard a low whistling kind of sound, and I realized that something was coming down from the sky towards me. I wiped my eyes and saw an outline of soft lights. It set down alongside the stock pond. I thought I was hallucinating, but I noticed the lights were reflected in the water.

I began to get very lightheaded. Whatever it was that came up to me had some way keep me from looking directly at it. I looked at the ground and pointed to the car.

"Help her please, please help her. I did this. I'm so sorry."

A voice came on in my head like a drive-in radio speaker.

"We can heal her, but we must go. She must go. With us."

"It doesn't matter, she'll die anyway," I said out loud. "Please save her life."

Then I thought: "We are not dumb animals, she doesn't deserve to die like this."

My chest hurt, and I realized I had been injured more seriously than I thought. I began to pass out, but as I did the voice came in my head:

"You do not need us, you will not die. We will save her."

As I blacked out I heard the sound of screeching metal as if the car door was being forced open.

* * *

When I woke up, I was in the hospital in Mount Pleasant. My parents were there. My mother so relieved to see me awake she started to cry. My father looked stern, but I could tell he was also relieved to see me awake.

The doctor stood by my bed, and picked up my patient chart as he tipped his cigarette into an ashtray. "You are a very lucky young man," he said. "You have a mild concussion, and three broken ribs. You've been out for over 24 hours."

"Connie was with me," I rasped. "Is she okay?" I was afraid of the answer.

"You're lucky we found you at all," said my father. "You were so far off the road."

I had noticed a sheriff's deputy sitting in the corner. He came over to the bed.

"Connie must've been ejected, like you, when your car crashed. But we still haven't found her."

"The last time I saw Connie," I said. "She was lying in the car."

"They didn't find anybody in the car," said the deputy.

My father glared at me. "You got that poor girl killed," he said.

I began to cry.

"Stop it," said my mother to my father. "Hasn't he been hurt enough?"

They didn't realize the reason I was crying was because I was happy there was hope that someone, anyone, whoever had been out there in the dark had taken Connie away to save her.

*   *   *

Of course I recovered or I wouldn't be here talking to you today, officer. I appreciate you coming over and sharing these pictures with me. I didn't realize that the church across the street has cameras in its parking lot that show the front of my house.

Now that I've seen them, I'm sorry that I wasn't here when whoever it was broke into the house. You see, officer, I've lived here all my life. Of course my parents passed a long time ago, and so did my wife a few years back. My children have all grown up and moved away.

Back in 1956, this house was pretty much the only one on this road. All the other houses around here have been built since then. I appreciate that my neighbors noticed someone breaking in and called 911. I know you're staring at me, puzzled why I told you the story about that night when I went out dancing with Connie, and the other kids, in our Milky Way dance hall. But you see, although the photos are taken from far away, I recognize the person busting in the front door.

It looks like she's still short and cute, from what I can tell. I certainly can't see any gray. I'm happy she still remembered where I lived.

Now I know what you're thinking, there's no way it could be Connie. But her body was never recovered—everyone puzzled over that, the best they could figure it sank to the bottom of the stock pond. They drained it and dredged it, and still never found a body. No one ever had a final answer about what happened—until now.

If by chance there were visitors from outer space who were moved by my plea, and took her with them to heal her, we could assume—couldn't we?—their space travel might involve near light speed. That would explain her appearance. If you don't understand my point, google "time dilation."

I noticed you haven't written anything down for a while. I don't blame you. I'm not sure I believe this all myself. But here's one thing. On the report you had me fill out, there's a space to list stuff that was stolen. But you don't have anywhere to put things that were left behind.

When I came home, I found on the kitchen table a couple of things that looked like they were dropped in haste. She probably dropped them and left quickly when she saw your car. But she still was able to leave me a message that makes me happy. After all those years, I know she's ok.

This is the rose, and this is the Baby Ruth.

As fresh as the day I bought it.

A life-long science fiction reader, **Lou Antonelli**'s *first story was published in 2003 when he was 46. Since then he has had 96 short stories published in the US, UK, Canada, and Australia in venues such as* Asimov's Science Fiction, Jim Baen's Universe, Dark Recesses, Andromeda Spaceways In-Flight Magazine, Greatest Uncommon Denominator (GUD), *and* Daily Science Fiction, *among others. He has received honorable mentions in* The Year's Best Science Fiction *volumes edited by Gardner Dozois in 2010, 2008, 2006, 2005 and 2004. His steampunk short story, "A Rocket for the Republic," was the last story accepted by Dozois before he retired as editor of* Asimov's Science Fiction *after 19 years. It was published in* Asimov's *in September 2005 and placed third in the annual Readers' Poll. His four collections include* Fantastic Texas *published in 2009 and* Texas & Other Planets *published in 2010, and the Hugo-nominated* Letters from Gardner, *2015. He is a professional journalist and lives with his wife and dog in Mount Pleasant, Texas.*

Our next debut story is another dark tale, this one set in the universe of Kate Corcino's Progenitor novels, including Spark Rising *(2014) and the just released* Spark Awakening. *In it, young Lucas faces a difficult choice between love and family....*

BLOOD AND WATER
(A SPARK STORY)

BY KATE CORCINO

Z one Four

"He won't do it, Grandfather. He's weak." The loathing in Jacob's voice had never been more clear. "He's a blight on our family."

Lucas bit his cheek until he tasted blood. His questions had already disappointed the old man perched behind the desk in front of them, and he knew better than to speak out of turn. God forbid he should ever forget his place and argue in front of the man. Jacob might have earned those privileges. Lucas certainly hadn't.

Their grandfather's head slowly turned. His pale, icy eyes—the color Lucas had inherited—were frigid as he regarded Jacob for a long, silent moment. When he spoke, however, his voice was soft and encouraging. "A blight? How so?"

Lucas turned his head to look at his brother, who stood at attention beside Lucas.

"Yes, sir. A blight. For as long as I can remember, you've always taught us that Sparks are demons, living proof of the times of Tribulation. Why else would they have power over energy, over fire? That Lucas was born to our family is a sign of our shame."

"Our shame? Stupid boy, Lucas is a sign of our favor." Grandfather's stare bored into Jacob.

Lucas's stomach dropped in shock.

Does he mean it?

"Our family's birth record has been spotless—not a single stain of Spark blood. Lucas was born a Spark, yes, but he was born only a month after I was blessed with weeks of visionary dreams that showed me I needed to send a Spark forth to infiltrate the enemy." The old man leaned back in his chair, steepling his hands. "But where would I get such a creature? A loyal Spark? A man with the abilities that would gain him access to their world while retaining the conscience and piety, the humanity, of ours?" Grandfather shook his head. He reached out to spin the teacup in front of him, a meditative movement.

"I had done my work too well," he continued. "Our Sparks live apart. They know their place, even those that come to us as agents from the Ward School. Our Reintegration Program guarantees that. We don't have a single Spark who could meet the eyes of the non-powered, who could manage to pass as one of *them.*

"I knew what I needed. I prayed for guidance. And I was gifted Lucas. Why do you think I sent him away as a child?"

Lucas's mouth opened and closed. Jacob stood motionless. Was he as shocked as Lucas? He must be.

Grandfather turned to Lucas. "You're surprised. Tell me why *you* think I sent you away."

Lucas cleared his throat. "You sent me away because you could not bear the sight of me, but you could not stand having one of your family living in the Kennels." Lucas repeated the line his mother had told him, using the colloquial term for the Spark village that was set apart. She'd told him her version of the truth on one of her rare visits to faraway Zone Six where Lucas was fostered. And as if telling him the truth had set her free, she'd never returned. Even as a boy, he'd justified her absence for her. It was a long journey from the Pacific Northwest to the far side of the Great Plains.

Only Grandfather had ever made the trip after that.

"If I could not bear the sight of you, Lucas, then why did I travel there twice every year, at my age and in my health? Why spend weeks with a caravan just to see you?" Grandfather wore a soft smile.

"But …" Lucas found himself shaking his head. "When you brought me home last autumn, you told me I should never use the Spark. Never mention it. I thought—I thought you were ashamed of me."

Lucas had violated that secrecy. He'd told Meredith.

She was the first person who'd ever loved him. She loved him even after he told her. She'd been shocked, of course. A thing like that? Your secret boyfriend, the grandson of your Councilor, is a *Spark*? But it hadn't taken more than a few minutes for her to smile up at him, green eyes glowing with her belief in him, and tell him that he was still her Lucas. She felt no shame toward him.

And no … Grandfather, too?

"Lucas. I have never been ashamed. I have been proud every day that my grandson was chosen. Where others will see a mere Spark, I see a flaming sword of righteousness."

"I don't understand," Jacob dared to whisper.

Grandfather returned his gaze to Lucas's brother. "Lucas is not a curse, Jacob. Lucas is a blessing, a tool, given to us to show favor." Grandfather looked again at Lucas. "And *that* is why you must go away again. I arranged this position for you at the Zone Three Post-Secondary Training Facility so you could be fast-tracked into the mid-range Agent branch. Zone Three is our next target, and I am counting on you to lay the foundation for us. Do you understand?"

Lucas nodded, but he knew it was slow. Too slow. His grandfather's eyes narrowed, prompting a verbal response.

"I do. But I—are you certain I'm the one to do this?" Panic fluttered in his chest. He couldn't leave. All the way to Zone Three, across the Rocky Mountains and south, deep in the high desert? That was even further than Zone Six had been. It was a month of travel by caravan. What about Meredith? Lucas grasped at the first logical argument he could. "Couldn't Jacob go? He's been trained for this sort of thing."

It was a mistake.

"Fool." Grandfather spat at him. "Only Sparks are permitted to be Agents. You were created for this. You will not disappoint me." Grandfather took a deep, calming breath, and his snarling lips trembled back into their usual ascetic expression. He leaned forward, his eyes steady on Lucas's. "You are the only Spark born to our family. The only Spark I would trust with my fortune, with my future, with my life. Or is that a mistake?"

Lucas's head shook quickly now. He had no idea he was so important to his grandfather. "No, sir," he whispered, "it's not a mistake."

Grandfather settled back again. He turned his gaze to a report before him. Lucas was too tall and too far back from the desk to read the scrawled words upside down.

"I believe you, grandson. But this mission is too important for you to go without demonstration of your devotion. Are you ready to prove yourself?"

"Yes, sir."

"As devoted as your brother Jacob?"

"Of course, Grandfather."

Jacob shifted restlessly beside Lucas, but Lucas couldn't turn his gaze from his grandfather now. He was going to give Lucas a trusted mission, meant only for him, one only he could achieve. Lucas struggled to reign in his quickening breath.

Once I've proved myself, I can ask to marry Meredith. Maybe Grandfather will send her with me? Or she can join me later.

"Edgar has betrayed me." Grandfather tilted his head as he looked at Lucas and paused.

His most trusted aide, Meredith's father, was a traitor?

"But I find that I still have use of his particular skills, so I cannot rid myself of him. Not yet. Still, he must be punished. His oldest daughter must die."

Lucas's breath caught, strangled by his closing throat.

His oldest—Meredith?

"Kill her, Lucas. Your early training is complete. It is time for me to take up the weapon that has been provided and strike out at evil. It is time for you to earn your place at my side, by smiting sinners. Do you understand, Lucas?"

Lucas's head swam. He clenched the muscles in his back and around his knees, determined to keep his feet under him. Kill Meredith? Killing her would somehow show he was worthy of the holy mission for which he'd been born?

"Yes. Exactly." It wasn't until Grandfather beamed at him that he realized he'd spoken the words aloud. "Edgar has sinned against us, consorting with Sparks. Conspiring. He is a trusted member of my team, Lucas, and I cannot lose his skills. But he must be brought up short. He must know the cost of righteousness and bear it. Kill his daughter. And then I'll know you're ready to begin your work."

Lucas was still. When he'd been summoned, he'd decided to take the opportunity to ask Grandfather for permission to marry Meredith. That wasn't happening now. It wasn't ever happening!

I am a flaming sword of righteousness. He said it. It's truth.

Lucas waited for the wave of despair that he expected to swamp him. He couldn't be this calm. He should be reeling. Hysterical.

I am a flaming sword of righteousness. I am meant to cut down sinners.

How could he—?

He couldn't. Perhaps that was why he felt nothing? He had nothing to fear. He had no intention of doing as he'd been told. Grandfather expected him to kill Meredith?

Never.

Grandfather clearly took his silence as confirmation. He dismissed Lucas, holding up his cheek so Lucas could skirt the desk between them, bend down, and offer his grandfather a kiss. As Lucas started to withdraw after pressing his lips to the thin, delicate skin, Grandfather whispered to him, "Do it quickly, Lucas. I've waited so long for you to come back to me. I'm eager to get started."

Lucas nodded, his heart steady inside his chest. "Yes, Grandfather."

As Lucas backed away, Jacob leaned in to take Lucas's place and offer farewell respect, but Grandfather turned from him.

"We are not finished, Jacob. Stay. We must talk."

Lucas stepped backward again, pulled the door open, and backed out, closing it again behind him.

Am I a tool? A weapon?

Lucas turned his body, his gaze sliding over a pair of the vicious, fanatically-devoted teenagers his Grandfather used as guards. He had no reason to fear them.

Or did he?

Lucas shivered and glanced over his shoulder at the young men behind him now. If he failed to do as he'd been told, would he be given over to the Youth Guard? They lived together like a pack, in a separate barracks. They attacked with the feral ferocity of a pack, as well.

Leaving Grandfather's administrative suite behind, he entered the halls of the main Council building and had to weave between the plainly dressed people making their way to appointments. The thought of their ordinary errands juxtaposed against the horror grandfather had just asked of him made him wish nothing more than to flee.

I'll go get Meredith. We'll get away.

But instead of taking him from the building, his feet carried him to the little chapel tucked into a corner. It was dark inside the windowless room.

Lucas's foster family had been almost as devout as Grandfather. They'd taken him to services, and when they traveled, they made certain to find a shrine or church for holy days. This room had little in common with those places. In other zones, churches were places of light and fellowship. Here, Grandfather decreed that their prayer spaces should reflect the state of the times they lived in. The room was dark, the ceiling low and oppressive. The only light filtered in from the hall behind him. Only a minimal amount leaked from the censer on the low altar ahead.

Lucas hovered in the doorway, momentarily confused. Why had he come?

Murder.

He blinked back the sudden flow of tears. The last thing he needed was anyone witnessing and reporting his weakness to Grandfather. He took a long, ragged breath and started forward, stopping only when he was in front of the altar. Lucas took up one of the long, skinny splinters of wood and fed it through a gap in the censer to light it. His shaking hand lit a beeswax candle before shaking the flame from the splinter.

The little flame burned tall and steady.

The way I'm meant to stand with my burdens. Lucas swallowed and glanced around, self-conscious. He'd never been good at prayer. He bowed his head.

I try. You know I try. Believing is hard for me. I'm not like Grandfather. But if there's a purpose for me, I have to see it. I have to know it. Show me. Please. Show me the path. I know Grandfather is worthy. I know he's chosen. But I—I'm just me. If you don't show me, I cannot do this. I can't.

A vision of Meredith swam into his mind's eye. How could this be expected of him? Lucas thought about that for a moment. He was a Spark, by definition soiled. If he'd been chosen to bear that burden, what was to say he wasn't expected to bear more, so that others wouldn't have to? As soon as he acknowledged the thought, he felt sick. He couldn't seriously entertain doing what he'd been asked. He couldn't.

I need something clear. Something real. Shame combined with his nausea. His cheeks flamed. *Show me what to believe. Show me what is true.*

He waited. Nothing happened. He wasn't gifted with a vision like his grandfather had been. He didn't experience sudden clarity. He was just as lost as he'd been when he walked in. His head dropped in disappointment, Lucas turned away from the altar and left.

He walked aimlessly. He hadn't been asking for proof of existence or anything like that. He'd only wanted a sign to hold to, something to fuel him. Something to show him that the path Grandfather set before him wasn't as wrong as it felt, curdled in his belly.

How can you even think about this? Go get Meredith and run!

The sound of a raised voice brought him out of his reverie, and he lifted his head. Blinking, he looked around. He'd left the building by the rear door that emptied into the wide square with barracks, stable, and storage. He must have turned off into the alleys beside the administration building, because he stood in a narrow passage.

Lucas glanced either way. There was no one. Had he heard a voice? He'd heard his name.

Now there was the sound of frantic, hoarse voices. They pulled him forward. He eased up to the corner of the nearest building and peered around the edge. Two men held a furious, low conversation as they huddled back against the far wall.

One of the men was a Spark. Lucas could see the faint halo of power that hazed out the air around him. Only other Sparks could see it. It was a reminder of Lucas's difference.

The other man was hidden behind the Spark for several moments. When he finally stepped around the other man, making an emphatic gesture with his hands, Lucas sucked in a breath. Edgar.

The man Lucas's grandfather had told him was conspiring against them. The man Lucas was meant to punish. Meredith's father. What was it Grandfather had said? *He is consorting with Sparks.* Lucas's gaze moved between the two men. They certainly seemed to be conspiring, whispering in a back alleyway.

You asked for a sign.

Lucas swallowed.

No.

Just as he was about to pull his head back into his own alley and slink away, Lucas heard his name again. This time, there was no question. He listened hard to hear the hoarse words that followed his name.

"—don't know how you can be sure. I'd *see* it. There's no sign at all," the Spark protested.

"I'm telling you, he's a Spark. I don't care what the old man says, he's not going to move against his grandson. Once we have Lucas, we can move. It's our time." Edgar's words were filled with confidence.

Lucas felt a chill. *He knows I'm a Spark. How does he know?*

There was only one way—Meredith had told him. Lucas rejected the thought, pushing it whole from his mind. He wouldn't consider it. He had told her she could not share his secret. He'd told her how important it was. She would never betray him.

There was no sign, merely coincidence. And Lucas was no weapon.

He hurried away from the alley, moving as silently as possible until he was sure he'd not been heard making his escape. Then he ran. He had to see Meredith.

Lucas made a beeline for the Council Administrators' Housing Area. The three concentric rings of small houses were testimony to the importance and purity of the families that lived within them, just as the immaculate roads and buildings within the walls demonstrated mastery over the wild, lush growth of the rainforest that crept over the old cities outside.

Lucas, newly returned from Zone Six, lived in the family compound at the center. Meredith's family lived in the first ring surrounding the center. It meant they were, literally, inner circle. Those who lived there were the most trusted of those tasked with assisting Councilor Four. They should have been the most trustworthy.

What do I do? How was it I got lost and wound up right there, right then? How did he know about me?

It was too much. Betrayal. Murder. Signs. His future assignment, so far away. And the one thing he wanted, the only thing he wanted for himself, possibly tainted. How did it all get so mixed up?

His mind circled back around to the horror of his most immediate mission.

It didn't matter. None of it mattered.

He pounded on her door. Meredith opened it, her little sister hovering behind her.

"Hi." Her round face spread with a broad smile, dimples appearing. The dimples had caught his eye and done him in. Well, the dimples and assets just south. "We're just about to go—"

"No, no. Come with me." Lucas reached out and took her hand. "Come with me." He drew her out after him.

"But where—? What's wrong?"

"It's a secret. Just come with me." He knew that he'd have to do a better job of planning if they were to actually make it away.

He wasn't a murderer. He couldn't do what Grandfather wanted. He'd run away to another Zone, hide in plain sight doing whatever it was that Sparks did for a living. He could learn to work a power plant as well as he could learn to be an agent, couldn't he? If he had to, he could even pretend to be normal. If he didn't use the Spark—if he never, ever reached out to the Dust—then he'd never show the latent energy-signature that other Sparks could see. No one would ever know what he was, not even another Spark.

They could do it. He just had to convince her. But for now, he needed to know that she'd marry him.

Meredith glanced back over her shoulder at her sister. "Tell Mama that I've gone with a friend."

"A friend?" Her sister's singsong question was cut off by the door slamming shut behind Meredith.

He pulled her away from her home, away from the compound at the center of the circle, and toward the Northern gate. He needed to be free of the city, and anyone who might be watching or listening, before he spoke to her.

The closer they came to the gate, the more they had to dodge those on bicycles, horses, and horse-drawn carriages of refashioned old combustion-engine car frames. Unlike in Zone Six, there weren't electric cars in the mix. Sparks weren't permitted to own vehicles here in Zone Four, and the Councilor made certain that his upper-level administrators shared his worldview. The use of Spark power in the zone was to be severely limited. Lucas's grandfather would not have his people dependent upon aberrations.

Unless the aberration is a weapon of God?

His breathing increased, hitching in his throat with his panic. He wasn't a weapon. He wasn't a sword.

Lucas led Meredith through the gate for foot traffic. They followed the road out for fifteen minutes, through the area that had been slashed and burned back from the city wall for visibility. Finally, the road entered the forest, and they were plunged into twilight coolness as they wound deeper, away from view of the gates. He stepped off the road, circling around a large, unruly hedge of wild roses that bordered the road.

It was cool under the canopy of evergreens and wide, leafy, deciduous trees. Meredith laughed behind him now as he pulled her through the ferny undergrowth. They wove between trees, slipping on bright mossy growth, and wound down deeper into the forest. Finally, when he figured they were far enough from the road and any other humans, he pulled her behind a stand of honeysuckle-tangled maple and turned to her.

"Marry me, Merry," he blurted.

Her eyes went wide. "What?"

"Marry me. I just—I spent this morning talking to my grandfather. And I—" Lucas shook his head, trying to put it all into words that she could understand, that wouldn't terrify her. He couldn't. "Marry me."

"You talked to the Councilor?" Her eyes had gone wide and soft. A little hopeful smile lifted her lips and lit her face.

Did she think he meant that he'd talked to Grandfather about her? That he'd asked permission to marry?

Lucas didn't have it in him to hurt her. He didn't want to see the disappointment and pain in her eyes. Instead of telling her that the marriage was his own idea and that they'd have to run to be together, he took her hand and pulled her to him. He loved the feel of her lush body crushed against his thin frame and the contrast of her darker skin and hair against his uniform paleness.

They tumbled to the ground together, arms and tongues and legs already tangled. He shouldn't. He had no real plan to get away. He had nothing but the hope that he could convince her to come with him before his grandfather realized Lucas was too weak to be a holy weapon and decided to send Jacob to finish Lucas and the job he should be plotting. Lucas shouldn't be here, with Meredith of all people, indulging in the comfort of her soft body and gentle touch.

Even if he hadn't been hiding from his responsibility, shame would still coat him with every touch. The pleasure of the moment washed it away for now, yes, but they'd both pay for it later. They'd each have to spend time in seclusion, repenting.

But knowing that hadn't stopped them on any other night they'd stolen away to be together since they'd met. Lucas slid his hand inside her loose shirt to trail up her soft skin until he was cupping the heavy, warm flesh that had caught his attention in the first place. He lifted and kneaded the flesh that overflowed his hand, and his own body responded. He used one leg to spread her thighs apart so he could reach between and pull up on her skirt and then settle between the softness of her thighs. They wouldn't be stopping today, either.

Lucas lifted his mouth from Meredith's to look down at her. Her hands, busily unfastening his pant buttons, finished. She slid one hand inside to stroke and play while she brought the other up to cup the back of his head. She tried to draw his head back down to hers, her lips parting again, but they continued the movement to a grin instead of a kiss when he resisted her. He wanted to look at her. He lived for looking at her.

"Can't help it, Merry," he told her, voice rough in his own ears as he whispered to her, "I love the way you look." He spread her shirt apart so he could feast his eyes and give her a soft, breathless laugh while he skimmed the fingertips of one hand over her wide, peachy nipple. "I love *you*, Merry. I love you."

And he did.

They weren't just words. They hadn't been from the beginning. He'd never loved anyone like this, with this depth. With ... such devotion.

Except Grandfather. The whisper of thought made him shiver. His hand stopped.

"Lucas," Meredith stopped, her hand curving around to his cheek, "what?"

His eyes had filled. He blinked back the moisture. "I love you," he said, his voice rough.

Meredith's lips curved up in a smile, but her eyes filled with tears, too. "I love you, too," she managed to choke out. "And I will marry you, Lucas."

Lucas's head swam. He lowered his head to rest his forehead against hers in gratitude. She was meant for him. It was the only explanation for the instant connection they'd both felt when they'd met on his first day back in the Zone. Grandfather always spoke of the divine hand touching lives.

Meredith was proof of that touch in his life. She was his reward for not giving up after being abandoned by everyone else. He could make this work. He had to. But first, he had to finish. Lucas closed his eyes so he could focus on what he was doing.

When he lay next to her again, gasping and puffing, he managed, "Okay. Okay. We're getting married."

Meredith laughed beside him. He joined her, giddy and happy. The sound died away, leaving just the two of them curled around each other in the leaves. Long before he was ready, she pushed at him, sitting up with mischief on her broad, happy face. She buttoned her shirt and straightened her clothes, nudging at him with her hip to do the same.

"Come on, lazy bones. Come on." She jumped up. "If we're going to be married—"

"Wait." Lucas sat up, buttoning his pants. "Merry, it's—this is a secret for now. This is just for us." He had to tell her. They needed to make their plans to run. They'd have to go soon. Maybe in the morning?

How long do I have?

Instead of being upset, she just laughed and nodded. "I know. But you've trusted me with so much. Telling me about your Spark. Talking to your grandfather. If we're going to get married, it's time for you to know *our* secret, too."

"Our secret?" They had a secret? He racked his brain. Was she pregnant?

"No, silly. Not *our* secret, you and me. *Our* secret, my family."

Lucas went cold. Her *family* had a secret?

Pay attention, Lucas. This is important.

The voice in his head sounded different. Deeper, heavier, like Grandfather's voice, but more solemn. His breath slid between his lips like the last gasp of a dying man.

Meredith took his hand and dragged him deeper into the forest.

The world went silent. He was certain she was still talking. She turned back to him as she led him through the trees and brush. Her lips were moving. She even laughed, but he didn't hear any of it. He didn't hear the wind or the insects or the sound of their feet moving through the undergrowth.

He tried to focus again on that inner voice, to call it back. He needed to question it.

Instead, all he heard was the memory of Grandfather's words, "You mustn't disappoint me, Lucas. So much is riding on you."

I have to pay attention.

He stared at Meredith's back. She'd spoken of a family secret. Was she a traitor?

How did her father know about me?

There was only one way. He tried to find calm. He failed. "What secret?"

What does it matter? We're running away together. The thought was like a desperate scrabble inside his head, so different from the authoritative boom of moments before.

It mattered. If there really were secrets and plots, it meant Grandfather might not be wrong. It meant that voice in his head might not be his own. He'd asked for proof, after all.

Meredith wove them through the trees as they headed downhill now, gathering speed until they splashed into the shallow edge of the river. She snatched up a branch and began pushing it into the water, feeling along the bottom.

"Here," she finally said. "There's a sandbar. The river's deep, but it isn't fast. We can cross on the sandbar."

"Cross to where? Merry—" Lucas looked around, trying to get his bearings in the dappled light filtering through the trees. He hadn't been back long enough to know the city well, much less the surrounding countryside. All he knew was that the moss-coated humps of the ruins of old buildings made his heart thump in his chest and his mouth go dry. The remnants of the world that had been before were now draped with vines and hidden by ferns. The hidden ruins were a reminder of the evil of the world that had come before. They were a reminder of his place in the world that was now.

He wanted the ordered, clean lines of the city around him. "Where are we going?"

Before she could answer, he realized where she was taking him. It wasn't anything directional. No more than a feeling, like an echo of his grandfather's words. Those conspiring against him consorted with Sparks. His mind flashed to the scene in the alley.

And isn't she already guilty of the same? His mind hissed the thought. *She loves you, after all.*

"Merry, are you taking me to the Kennels?"

Her happy expression flashed into irritation. "Don't call it that. It's a village. A community, just like the one we live in."

"Okay," he said. A feeling of wrongness worked through his belly like spreading fingers. What business did she—did either of them—have in the Spark village? "But are we?"

Meredith smiled and glanced over her shoulder at the far shore, still focused on luring him onward.

Was she a lure? What had Edgar said? Once they had Lucas, they had his grandfather?

How had Edgar known he was a Spark? Lucas had told only one person....

"Why?"

She let an impatient huff of breath escape and tilted her head. "I wanted to surprise you. Dad said to wait, he was afraid ... but the Councilor knows now. You talked to him, and we're getting married!" She let a giddy laugh escape and threw her arms to the side, gesturing her happy disbelief with the long stick. "He knows about us, and of course, he knows about you. The Councilor's own grandson is a Spark. Dad couldn't even hardly believe it when I told him."

Lucas felt a sick sort of spinning in his midsection, as if something—his breath, his understanding—was being sucked down into a death spiral.

He'd told her she had to keep that between them. It was his deepest secret. It was his shame. He'd shared it with her because her love somehow eased it....

What had she done?

She'd given his weakness to her father as a weapon.

A rush of heat suffused his face. His pulse throbbed in his temple. He could hear the pounding in his ears, the force of his blood echoing the anger that flashed through him.

"Yes, we're going to the village." Her voice was breathless, excited. "We're going to see my niece. She's strong, so strong. Stronger than any of the men. Do you know the Council policy on girls like that?"

He nodded automatically. Lucas had heard Grandfather discussing policy with aides. But what difference did the stupid policy make? Why was she even talking about this? She'd *betrayed* him. And she was babbling on like it didn't matter.

"They take them away," he said. "Because the Council believes they're a danger to the delicate balance of freedom and production." It was easy to parrot what he'd heard. The Council wanted Sparks just strong enough to power the cities but not so strong that they could do more. Not so strong that they could want more. With a matrilineal power, that was dangerous. The rare strong girls, a one-in-a-thousand evolutionary slip, would grow into women who'd pass on their strength. They'd create a generation of monsters just like them.

He didn't tell Meredith that, though. Something in him was pulling back, watching. Wary. Doing exactly what the voice in his head had told him.

Meredith nodded. "You do understand. But now we don't have to hide Emma anymore. Your grandfather will stand for us in the Council. He'll protect Emma. And we owe it all to you."

Lucas struggled to follow her leaps. He'd never said that. He'd never promised any of that. All he'd wanted was someone to share his secret.

"No," he said softly. Then, again, louder, "No. I didn't say that—any of that. You want my grandfather to stand up to the rest of the Councilors against *his* policy? No, Merr. Grandfather didn't even give me permission to marry you. That wasn't what we talked about. He told me to—asked me to—"

Her smile died. "He asked you to what?"

Lucas shook his head. He couldn't tell her. "I want to marry you, Meredith, but he wants to send me away." A partial truth was better than nothing. His next words tumbled out, a rush of air to push the sin of disobedience from him. "I want us to go away, instead, start new somewhere else where we don't have to pretend anymore. Somewhere neither of us has to be a secret."

"You're a Spark," she whispered. "It doesn't matter where we go. It'll always have to be secret."

"No. Not every Zone is like this." This was where he could convince her. She hadn't been outside Zone Four before. Lucas had. Whether it was biblically right or not, he knew there were places where Sparks were as free as any other citizen. His grandfather was determined to change that. But it hadn't happened yet. "My foster family took me to other—"

"Lucas. No." Her voice was firm. "We stay. My place is here. Fighting with my family."

"Fighting my family?" He snapped the question.

Meredith's chin lifted. "If necessary. Your grandfather is right about one thing. We do have to stand on faith. Some things are righteous, Lucas. Sometimes God requires us to do things we'd never consider, because they are right."

Including betraying the man who loves you? The anger beat strong in his temples again.

Her words echoed his grandfather's, yet her meaning was a world apart. Both of them couldn't be right. One of them must be a pretender. One of them was using faith to further an agenda. He loved them both. How was he to know who was wrong?

"No. It isn't right. No matter how hard it is on any of us, Grandfather is the one true path."

"No. No! Lucas, Sparks aren't aberrations. They're not subhuman. They're not dogs, either. And they sure as Dust aren't a sign of the end times. Your grandfather is twisting something good and true to suit his own purposes, and it's wrong!" She lifted her arms again, but the stick shook this time. "We are alive, right now. And we are people, both of us. It's just that one of us can make the Dust do what he wants. Are you less of a person, Lucas?"

No. But I'm chosen. I'm different than the other Sparks. You should know that! If she loved him, truly loved him as Grandfather did, shouldn't she see that he was special? Was this what the voice had wanted him to realize?

The truth hit him like a fist. She didn't. She couldn't. She was working against his grandfather. Lucas was just a means to an end.

She wouldn't leave with him because she didn't love him. She would never marry him.

"All I wanted was you." He hated that his voice sounded so broken.

She shook her head, her eyes going soft again. She stepped closer, dropping the stick into the water to dip below the surface, then bob back and spin slowly away. Meredith reached out to him. "I want you, too."

He wanted to believe her. He just didn't. Not anymore. Her fingers left a cold trail down his cheek to his chin then dropped to his chest. Her eyes followed them.

She can't even meet my eyes. How could I have been such a fool? The thought of how desperately he'd wanted to run away with her made his stomach clench.

"I'm right," she said. She raised her gaze to his briefly then moved it over his face. "You know I'm right. Come with me so you can see. Let us convince you. Being a Spark isn't a curse. It's a gift."

It was the exact word his grandfather had used. Except his grandfather hadn't used it to manipulate Lucas. He'd used it to shame Jacob, to show him the divine in Lucas—the divine Meredith could not see.

That was why he'd given Lucas this assignment. It wasn't merely so Lucas could prove himself to Grandfather. Jacob sneered at Lucas at every opportunity. He expected Lucas to screw up. Jacob expected Lucas's defect to stain everything he did.

With sudden icy clarity, Lucas realized it might already have done so.

He'd sworn to keep his Spark a secret. Not a single member of the Brayer family had been born a Spark in the two hundred years since Sparks were engineered, until Lucas. If it had been up to his mother, he'd have been left at the edge of the contained Spark community as a foundling. Or drowned.

Grandfather had saved him. He wanted Lucas. He needed him. And Lucas had repaid Grandfather's devotion by sharing his secret with the family intent on destroying Grandfather's legacy.

"You know I'm right." Her hand rested on his stomach, her fingers curling into his shirt. "Baby, you're not a curse."

His nerves fluttered under her touch, his body trying to respond, even as his stomach curled with nausea. Lucas swallowed, his mouth suddenly dry. She had been using his weakness for her this whole time.

He looked away from her, turning his head back to the shoreline behind him. His gaze swept along the tangled forest, looking for an answer, a path.

He found it.

Two men crouched in the underbrush up the shore from them. One of them was Jacob. How had he and Meredith not heard them?

You were too focused on your plans to betray the only man who has ever believed in you. And she was focused on plans of her own, wasn't she?

Lucas was certain Jacob watched not only to ensure Lucas acted, but to complete the task himself if Lucas failed. The men were following her. They must know she was being used as a lure to corrupt Lucas. He had his answer. All he'd had to do was listen.

And believe.

Meredith really was the key to Lucas's future. He was chosen.

Tears of gratitude welled in his eyes. Was this what righteousness felt like? The making of impossible decisions? "No," he said. "It's not a curse. It's a weapon."

He felt a wave of serenity settle over him, easing into him through his skin like a misty cloak of virtue that cooled away the anger. Lucas knew what he was now, even as he turned back to look down at the only person he'd thought had loved him in spite of what he was—

No, he corrected himself sternly. *That's wrong. Grandfather loves me. Even when Mother rejected me, he always came for me.*

"Maybe you're right, Meredith." He soothed away the confusion in her eyes after his last words. He lifted her hand from his stomach and gave each knuckle a soft kiss then settled it back by her side. "But you're a gift, too. You were meant for me."

It was true. Just not in the way that either of them had thought.

"You were always meant to show me the right way...." He'd just had to see her through faith instead of desire. He bent and touched his lips to hers.

Meredith rose on her toes to meet him, lifting her arms to his shoulders.

It made sweeping her under easier. He wrapped his hands tight around her neck and pushed her beneath the water.

Her hands clutched at his shoulders at first, as if she thought it might be a game. After a moment, she fought him. Her fingers curled into claws that strafed his neck and chin. His height kept his eyes from her nails. His long legs set wide gave him stability, even as her own legs kicked.

The water boiled around her from her desperate flailing. Her hands suddenly gripped the front of his shirt and then slid loose. Her arms fell to the water and bobbed under and back up again, just as the branch had moments before.

Her long black hair swirled around his wrists, an inky cloud that helped him focus. He held her under, waiting. He had to be thorough. Grandfather would expect no less.

Two crimson drops dripped from the gouges she'd opened on his chin. They settled on the surface of the water then slowly distorted with the lazy swirling of the water around his wrists. The blood caught in the floating strands of her hair and separated, spreading in the water until they couldn't be seen. They were still there, he knew. Still Lucas. But hidden.

He took a deep, cleansing breath and lifted Meredith from the water. Her green eyes stared up. Water drained from her nostrils and mouth, poured off her hair. Somehow heavier now, her body resisted him. He pulled her to him, crushing her softness to his chest a last time.

Lucas turned, dragging her with him. He trudged the few steps back to the shore to settle his accomplishment in the detritus of the river's narrow beach. A slender thread of grief fluttered in some wind within him. Soon, it would be gone, as ephemeral as the life of the traitor he'd loved.

The footsteps of the two men crunched closer and then stopped. Lucas took two steps back, allowing them in. His brother would want to check her, to be certain Lucas had done as he'd been told.

Edgar's oldest daughter was dead. The family would know the cost of their betrayal.

As Jacob inspected the body on the beach, Lucas turned his impassive gaze to the other man. He could see the energy haze of the man's Spark. Jacob was partnered with a Spark? Jacob detested Sparks.

But we do what we must for the good of the family, no matter how unpalatable.

"Who are you?"

The other man gave him a cocky dip of his head as his lips curved up in an expression halfway between a grin and a smirk. "I'm the man who's going to train you to be the best damn mid-range agent-in-training Zone Three has ever seen."

"You're an agent?" It was less a question than a confirmation. His grandfather used the tools that God provided, as Lucas himself had finally done.

"Marreau." The man stuck out his hand as he offered his name.

Lucas calmly took it, offering a firm shake. "You'll be training me?"

"And escorting you down there, yes. Looking forward to a little dry heat." The man shivered at the damp coolness of the Pacific Northwest's version of summer.

Beside Marreau, Jacob shifted, his hand dropping from the dead girl's neck. He nodded over his shoulder at Marreau then flicked a warily respectful gaze over Lucas.

"Maybe there's hope for you yet, Spark." The words were grudging, but honest.

Lucas nodded. "We're not done today."

Jacob cocked his head at his brother.

"There's a little girl being hidden in the Kennels. A strong one. Emma."

Jacob's brows lifted. "We can run a sweep now." He finally offered his brother a smile.

Lucas felt his lips curving in response.

"Grandfather will be proud," Jacob said, "especially because of the relationship."

Lucas let the curve become a full smile. Yes. That was the feeling that had blown through him, a wind to push away the grief, leaving behind the purity of their goal. That was the feeling surging in his chest. Pride.

Kate Corcino *writes adult speculative fiction. Her debut novel,* Spark Rising, *placed second in the Paranormal, Futuristic and Fantasy category of the Toronto RWA Catherine Award for 2014. It also won the 2015 National Excellence in Romance Fiction Award for Paranormal/Futuristic.*

Kate Corcino

Her latest novel, Spark Awakening, *has just released. Her short stories include "Border Time," a forthcoming story set in The X-Files universe of the TV show. She has also released* Ignition Point, *a collection of related short stories set in the same story world as the novel. Find her on Twitter as @KateCorcino or at KateCorcino.com.*

Mike Resnick, one of the most successful science fiction and fantasy storytellers working today, brings us our next tale, the fable of a boy and a dragon. We've all heard the story of the boy who cried, "wolf," but maybe not the one about the dragon who cried, "boy" or …

THE BOY WHO YELLED "DRAGON"
(A FABLE)

BY MIKE RESNICK

You've all heard the story about the boy who yelled "Wolf!"

Teachers and parents have been using it to teach children a lesson for centuries now. It's become a part of our culture. *Everybody* knows about the boy who yelled "Wolf," just as they know about the three blind mice and the little Dutch boy who put his finger in the dike and the day Michael Jordan scored 63 points in a playoff game.

But would you like to know the *real* story?

* * *

It began a long, long time ago, in a mythical land to the north and west which, for a lack of a better term, we shall call The Mythical Land To The North And West.

Now, this Land was the home of exceptionally brave warriors and beautiful damsels (and occasionally they were the same person, since beautiful damsels were pretty assertive back then). Each young boy and girl was taught all the arts of warfare, and were soon adept with sword, mace, lance, bow and arrow, dagger, and the off-putting snide remark. They were schooled in horsemanship, camouflage, and military strategy. They learned eye-gouging, ear-biting, kidney-punching, and—since they were destined to become knights and ladies—gentility.

So successful was their training that before long enemy armies were afraid to attack them. Within the borders of the Land justice was so swift that there was not a single criminal left. It would have been a very peaceful and idyllic kingdom indeed—except for the dragons.

You see, the Land was surrounded by hundreds of huge, red-eyed, razor-toothed, fire-breathing dragons, covered with thick scaly skin and armed with vicious-looking claws, and just as 50 years ago a Maasai warrior became a man by slaying a lion with his spear, and today you are hailed as an adult when you can break through Microsoft's firewall, back in the days we are talking about a boy or girl would be recognized as a young man or woman only after slaying a dragon.

Okay, you've got enough background now, so it's time introduce Sir Meldrake of the Shining Armor. Well, that's the way he envisioned himself, and that's the name he planned to take once he had slain a dragon and found someone who could actually make a suit of shining armor, but for the moment he was just plain Melvin, tall, gangly, a little underweight, shy around damsels, more worried about pimples than mortal wounds received in glorious battle. His number had come up in the draft, and it was his turn to sally forth and slay a dragon.

He climbed into his older brother's hand-me-down armor, took out the garbage, kissed his mother good-bye (but only after he made sure none of his friends were watching and snickering), climbed aboard the family horse, and armed with lance, sword, mace, and a desire to show Mary Lu Penworthy that he was everything she said he wasn't, he set off to slay a dragon, bring back both ears and the tail (or whatever it was one brought back to prove he had been victorious), and become a knight rather than a skinny teen-aged boy who couldn't get a date for the prom.

Soon the city was far behind him, and before long he had crossed the border of the Land itself, and was now in unknown territory. He hummed a little song of battle to keep his spirits up, but he was tone-deaf and his humming annoyed his horse, so finally he fell silent, scanning the harsh, rocky landscape for dragons. He found himself wishing he had paid a little more attention in biology class, so he would know what dragons ate when they weren't eating people, and where they slept (if indeed they slept at all), and especially what kind of terrain they liked to hide in when preparing to ambush young men who suddenly wished they were back home in bed looking at naughty illuminated manuscripts beneath the covers.

At night he found a cozy cave and, lighting a fire to keep warm and ward off anything that might want to annoy him—like, for example, a pride of dragons (or did they come in flocks, or perhaps gaggles?)—he sang himself to sleep, which kept his spirits up but almost drove his horse to distraction.

When morning came he peeked out of the cave, just to be certain that nothing lay in wait for him. Then he peeked again, to be doubly certain. Then he thought about Mary Lu Penworthy and decided the mole on her chin that had seemed charming only two days ago was really rather ugly in the cold light of day, and hardly worth slaying a dragon for. The same could be said for her eyes (not blue enough), her lips (not rosy red enough), and her nose (which seemed to exist solely to keep her eyes from bumping into each other).

One by one he considered every young lady of his acquaintance. This one was too tall, that one too short, this one too loud, that one too quiet, and to his surprise he decided that none of them were really worth risking his life in mortal combat with a dragon. In fact, the more he thought about it, the more he couldn't come up with a single reason to seek out a dragon. It was a silly custom, and when he returned to the Land, which he planned to do the moment his horse calmed down and stopped looking at him as if he might burst into song again, he would seek out the Council of Elders and suggest that in the future the rite of passage to adulthood should consist of slaying a chipmunk. They were certainly more numerous, and what purpose was served by slaying a dragon anyway?

His mind made up, Melvin climbed atop his steed and turned him for home—and found his way barred by a huge dragon, 20 feet high at the shoulder, with little beady eyes, thin streams of smoke flowing out of his nostrils, claws the size of butcher knives, and a serious case of halitosis.

"Why have you come to my kingdom?" demanded the dragon.

"I didn't know dragons could talk," said Melvin, surprised.

"I don't mean to be impertinent," said the dragon, "but I could probably fill a very thick book with what you don't know about dragons."

"Yes, I suppose you could," admitted Melvin. He didn't quite know what to say next, so he finally blurted: "By the way, my name is Sir Meldrake of the Shining Armor."

"Are you quite sure?" asked the dragon. "No offense, but you look rather rusty to me."

"My own armor's in the shop getting dry-cleaned," said Melvin, starting to feel rather silly.

"Oh. Well, that explains it," said the dragon charitably. "And since we're doing introductions, my name is Horace. Spelled H-O-R-A-C-E, and not to be mistaken for Horus the Egyptian god."

"That's a strange name for a dragon," said Melvin.

"Just how many dragons do you know on a first-name basis?" asked Horace.

"Counting you, one," admitted Melvin. "Just out of curiosity, how many men have you encountered?"

"The downstate returns aren't all in yet, but so far, rounded off, it comes to one." Horace paused uneasily. "What do we do now?"

"I don't know," said Melvin. "I suppose we battle to the death."

"We do?" said the dragon, surprised. "Why?"

"Those are the ground rules. You meet a dragon, you slay him."

"That's the silliest thing I ever heard!" protested Horace. "I meet dragons all the time, and I've never slain one. In fact, I plan to marry one when I'm an adult, and sire twenty or thirty thousand little hatchlings."

"Had you someone in mind?" asked Melvin, interested in spite of himself.

"Nancy Jo Billingsworth," said the dragon with a sigh. "The most beautiful 17 tons of wings and scales I've ever seen." He looked at Melvin. "How about you? Have you picked out your lady yet—always assuming you survive our battle to the death?"

"I'm playing the field at the moment," said Melvin.

"So you can't get a date either," said Horace knowingly.

"It's these darned zits," said Melvin, trying not to whine.

"Take off your helmet and let me get a good look at you," said Horace.

"You'll be disgusted," said Melvin. "Everyone is."

"Try me," said the dragon.

Melvin removed his helmet.

"God, I would *kill* for zits like those!" said Horace fervently.

"You would?" said Melvin. "Why?"

"Look at this hideous smooth skin on my face," said Horace, holding back a little whimper of self-loathing. "Let's be honest. Nancy Jo Billingsworth winces every time she looks at me. She'd die before she'd go out with me."

"I know exactly how you feel," said Melvin sympathetically.

"It's not just my face," said Horace, a tear rolling down his smooth green cheek. "It's *me*. Whenever we choose up sides for basketball, I'm always the last one picked. When it's Girls' Choice at the dance, I'm the only one who's never asked."

"They won't even let me in the locker room," Melvin chimed in. "They say I'm just wasting space. And the girls draw straws in the cafeteria, and the loser has to sit next to me."

Before long the young man and the young dragon were pouring out their hearts to each other, and because no one had ever listened before, they continued until twilight.

"Well, we might as well get on with it," said Horace when they had finished their litany of misery.

"Yeah, I suppose so," said Melvin unenthusiastically.

"I want you to know that if you win, I won't hold it against you," said the dragon. "No one will miss me anyway. I haven't got a friend in the world."

"That's not true," protested Melvin. "*I* like you."

Horace's homely green face lit up. "You do?"

Melvin nodded. "Yes, I do." He paused thoughtfully. "You know, I've never had a real friend before. It seems a shame that one of us has to kill the other."

"I know," said the dragon. "Still, rules are rules."

Suddenly Melvin stood up decisively. "Who says so?"

Horace looked around, confused. "I think I just did."

"Well, I'm going to break the rules. You're my only friend, and I'm not going to kill you."

"You're *my* only friend, and I'm not going to kill you either." Horace paused, as if considering what to do next. "Let's kill the horse. At least we'll have something to eat."

Melvin shook his head. "I need him to get home."

"I kind of thought we'd stay out here and be friends forever," said Horace in hurt tones.

"Oh, we'll be friends forever," promised Melvin. "And as my first act of friendship, I'm going to save your life."

"That's very thoughtful of you," said Horace. "But don't be so sure I wouldn't have killed you instead."

"I'm not talking about me," said Melvin. "But every week a new candidate is chosen to go forth and slay a dragon, and next week it's Spike Armstrong's turn."

"Who is Spike Armstrong?" asked Horace.

"He's everything I'm not," said Melvin bitterly. "He's the captain of every sports team, he's the most handsome boy in the Land, and even though he has the brains of a newt all the cheerleaders fight to sit near him in the cafeteria."

"I dislike him already," said Horace.

"Anyway, if he finds you, he'll kill you," concluded Melvin.

"So you're going to fight him in my place?" asked Horace. "I call that exceptionally decent of you, Melvin. I'll always honor your memory and put flowers on your grave."

"No, I'm not going to fight him," replied Melvin. "I wouldn't fare any better against him than you would. But any time I know he's sallying forth in your direction, I'll go to the far side of the city and tell everybody that a dragon is approaching, and Spike will immediately head off in that direction and you'll be safe."

"That's a splendid idea!" enthused Horace. "And whenever Thunderfire goes out hunting for a man to eat, I'll do the same thing to him."

"Thunderfire?" repeated Melvin.

Horace grimaced. "Females swoon over him. He's got lumps the size of baseballs all over his face, and his flame shoots out ten feet, and he just struts around like he owns the place. But I'll see to it that he never finds you."

"You know," said Melvin, "I *like* having a friend."

"Me too," said Horace. "My mother says one should always seek out new experiences."

Their ruses worked. Spike Armstrong never did slay Horace, and Thunderfire never did eat Melvin. As for Melvin and Horace, they continued to sneak away and meet every Saturday afternoon except when it was raining, and although neither of them ever did become king or marry the damsel of their dreams, they each had a friend they could trust and confide in, which in many ways is better than being a king or marrying a dream.

And that is the story of the boy who yelled "Dragon!"

Of course, when dragons sit around the campfire at night, or tuck their children into bed, they tell the story of the dragon who yelled "Boy!"

Mike Resnick *is, according to Locus, the all-time leading award winner, living or dead, for short science fiction. He is the winner of five Hugos from a record 37 nominations, a Nebula, and other major awards in the United States, France, Spain, Japan, Croatia, Catalonia, and Poland, and has been short-listed for major awards in England, Italy, and Australia. He is the author of 76 novels, 275 stories, and 3 screenplays, and is the Hugo-nominated editor of 42 anthologies. His work has been translated into 26 languages. He was the Guest of Honor at the 2012 Worldcon and can be found online as @ResnickMike on Twitter or at* <u>mikeresnick.com</u>.

In the war torn future of our next tale, families gather for the annual celebration of their Independence Day and to mourn the loss of far too many youths on a colony that was once designed to be a "model society." Rex is someone whose duty is to perform functions in hard vacuum, well-educated and even-tempered even in crisis. Not a lover nor a fighter, instead he's part of a special class known as …

NEWTS

BY KEVIN J. ANDERSON

During what should have been the ring colony's Independence Day celebration, the mood in the family habitat was somber. Rex Hollings stared through the viewing window toward the pastel clouds of Saturn. Thanks to the mellowing influence of his implant, he wore a placid smile, aware of and yet immune to the misery and dread all around him. The others were incapable of being so stable in a time of crisis.

Rex admired the planet's gentle beauty. The majestic ring arced up and caught sunlight, glittering with a spray of rocks where the tightly knit group of Worthies had built habitation modules, storage depots, greenhouse domes. All those artificial structures should have formed the backbone of a carefully engineered society. A magnificent colony. Standing alone, Rex considered the grand aspirations of visionary Ardet Hollings, who had founded the Worthies.

Now there were three empty seats at the dinner table. All families had suffered similar losses in the recent space battle.

As the emotional currents moved around him, Rex imagined himself as a rock in a fast-flowing stream, as in the library images he liked to view. Images of natural beauty were the only parts of Earth that Ardet had allowed them to see, claiming that everything else was too corrupt. He found the lovely landscape scenes very soothing, the rushing waters, the crashing ocean waves, the silvery waterfalls. Rex had never visited Earth, and he never would, especially not now.

Though he could not personally experience extreme moods, he still recognized the agitation from his mother and his two sisters-in-law. It was like learning a foreign language. Even little Max was affected by the tension; the boy clung fussily to his Uncle Rex, who was two years younger than his father. Rex picked up his unsettled nephew, whispering soft words that soothed him. Max stopped crying, giggled once, then played with his uncle's hair. They both looked out the window. "See the planet? Isn't it pretty?" As a first-born, Max would never be subjected to the implant, or the operation. If Rex hadn't been so calm, he might have envied the little boy.

Mother emerged from the kitchen unit, forcing a bright smile. She looked wrung-out and pale, overworked, overwhelmed, but not willing to surrender any ground to Fate. She would keep doing what she must, regardless of the circumstances. As the wife of Ardet Hollings, she had always been an excellent example for other Worthy women to emulate, filling her role, doing her tasks, never overstepping the boundaries. Rex thought she was perfect. Even knowing the terrible things that had happened to the colony, and what they could expect from the Earth military forces, her job was to manage their home and keep the family unit intact. Mother would die before she gave up any of those tasks, no matter what outside threat might be coming their way.

"Today is our special day, so we have a feast. Twenty-one years ago today Ardet led us away from Earth and brought us here to form our model society." She said the phrases she had memorized. Her husband had written the original Independence Day speech, and the words had become canon. "We came here to find peace, despite the hardships we knew we would have to face and without interference from outsiders."

Rex intoned the benediction along with his two sisters-in-law, "Peace despite hardship." He handed the now-happy toddler back to Ann, tapping Max on the nose and making him giggle one last time before the meal.

Mother brought out platters of fresh vegetables grown in the greenhouse domes. At the end of his shift that day, Rex had brought home the best from the harvest, far more than they really needed to eat. There were ears of bright yellow corn, bowls of green beans, leafy salads dressed with spicy herbed sauces. Tofumeat added extra protein.

With all greenhouse systems perfectly functional, at last, the productivity in the domes was enough to feed a population beyond even Ardet's greatest dreams—and now that so many colonists had died, there was extra food for the table. *Silver linings.* Rex smiled at the thought. He served himself sliced tomatoes so red they made the eyes ache.

"There isn't much reason to celebrate," grumbled Ann as she took her seat next to one of the empty spots. When Max fussed, she set the toddler on her knee and absently shushed him. Rex offered to take the boy, but Ann shook her head.

Mother would not let anything derail her purpose. "It is still our Independence Day. We have always celebrated it, and we'll do so again this year. Our men would want it that way."

"Who knows what will happen next year?" Rex said, meaning to be optimistic. He let events flow toward him and accepted whatever came. He, like so many others of his generation, was kept on an even keel, cooperative, causing no trouble. Ardet had wanted it that way.

Instead, his comment stung the others there. Rex could see expressions fall and felt their turbulent anxiety: grief for lost husbands, fear of the inevitable end of their way of life, anger at the enemy that had robbed the Worthies of their future. No matter how brave their deaths had been while standing against the invaders, the men were still dead.

"I'm … sorry for what I said. It was insensitive."

"That's all right, Rex. You can't help it," Mother said.

Dark-eyed Jen, the widow of his brother Ian, took a seat across from Rex, moving as if in a daze. She had full lips, a lush figure, and a once-sparkling personality that had made her an extremely desirable mate. Ian had been the envy of many

Worthies when she'd accepted his proposal of marriage, and Ardet himself had blessed the union. Rex had been very pleased for both of them, hoping they would have many children ... but there hadn't been time. He could sense Jen's sorrow at that now, the suffocating weight of lost opportunities.

It all flowed past him. He was a rock in a stream. That was as much as the implant, and his altered body, allowed him to be.

Since Rex was the only "man" there, Mother asked him to say a brief prayer for Lee and Ian, as well as their father and all of the fallen heroes. Rex mouthed the memorized words in his thin, piping voice. Then they all joined in an uninspired but adequate recitation of Ardet's traditional Independence Day benediction. When he finished speaking, everyone murmured, "As Ardet said."

Giving him a shy smile, Jen served Rex one of the ears of corn, took a smaller one for herself, then passed the plate down to where Ann was struggling with Max while scooping up some beans. Ann had a round face and curly brown hair. When her husband was still alive, she had kept herself beautiful for him, but in the months since Lee had fallen, she'd had little opportunity to do so, especially with caring for Max.

Rex knew that Ann struggled to be strong, to follow Mother's example; Worthy women were groomed to be exceptionally competent in their well-defined areas of responsibility, and to rely on the men to fulfill their own duties. But not even Ardet, with his grand dreams and detailed societal models, had envisioned the possibility of an entire stratum vanishing practically overnight.

Ann asked, "How soon do you suppose the DPs will be here?" She spoke as if it were casual mealtime conversation, though Rex could hear the tension, like brittle glass in her voice.

"I'll have no such talk at the table." Mother passed the salad bowl around again and urged them to eat. "This isn't the time for it."

"I'm afraid," Jen said in a small voice, looking directly at Rex. He glanced away, knowing what she wanted from him but unable to give it. He felt so sorry for her.

The Democratic Progressives had dispatched a retaliatory force to crush them, and everyone knew it was only a matter of time. The Worthies had already sacrificed all their fighting men against the first small exploratory force that had come to Saturn. Ardet, Lee, Ian, and the other men in the Worthy settlement had defeated the enemy that day, but at incredible cost to themselves. The remaining colonists would have no chance when Earth's reinforcements arrived at Saturn. For months now, Rex had felt the uneasy panic wafting among the colony survivors like the wind from a laboring air recycler.

But he remained calm. All newts remained calm. Ardet had thought it for the best.

After the meal, his belly full, Rex helped out in the kitchen unit, cleaning dishes, recycling scraps. Though Worthy men did not do such work, newts were allowed to perform some duties traditionally reserved for women. Besides, Rex had designed or refined some of the household recycling systems himself, and he knew how to keep them functioning at peak efficiency.

Jen offered to help him while Ann and Mother played with Max in the main living area. One of Ardet's old recorded speeches played on the screen; crowds of exuberant new colonists cheered, giddy with their recent separation from Earth and assured of a bright future if only they followed the rigid Worthy plan.

Jen stood uncomfortably close to Rex in the cramped kitchen unit. He used a squeegee to scrape food into a compost-recycler and stored the serving plates in the sanitizer, which used water reclaimed from the abundant ice in Saturn's rings. For a while, she made light conversation, though he could hear a deep and desperate huskiness to her voice, a longing and a need. After a long pause, Jen said in a very low whisper, "Rex, I ache every time I see you. Do you know how much you remind me of Ian? You look so much like him."

"I *am* his brother. We've always looked a lot alike."

She slipped her arms around his waist. "Face me."

He felt awkward, interrupted in his work, but he dutifully turned. He looked at Jen's oval face, her delicate chin. Both of his brothers' wives were beautiful women, yet Rex felt no desire for his sisters-in-law. Still, he loved them deeply. Jen must have seen it on his face. He stroked her hair, trying to calm her, as he had done with Max.

Growing bolder, she pressed her soft breasts against his chest, then tilted her face. She kissed him, at first tentatively, then ferociously. Her lips were moist and pleasant, warm, wanting more than he was capable of giving. "I miss him so much, Rex. I'm so lonely."

"We're all lonely." He gently extricated himself, patted her on the shoulder, as a brother would, and reminded her of what she already knew. "I'm not entirely like Ian. I'm missing some of my parts."

Though he had not intended to upset her in any way, he experienced her reaction like whitecaps crashing against a sea cliff. *Another library image from Earth* ... Rebuffed, Jen backed to the door of the kitchen unit. He could not experience the same reactions, with all the highs and lows of passion clipped from him, but he very much wanted to understand. "I'm sorry," he said automatically, hoping it would defuse the tension simmering in her. "Don't be angry."

Dark hair swirled around her as she tossed her head and looked at him with a flicker of ... disgust? "How can you keep us safe from the DPs? They're coming! You know what they're like. They'll destroy us all."

Rex blinked at her, struggling to quell the situation. Yes, he had heard Ardet's speeches on the evils of Earth, the manic greed and violence of the Democratic Progressives. Rex, born here in the new colony, had never experienced Earth except through his father's harsh descriptions, but he believed the stories of a lawless society in which no member knew his or her place. After great struggle and persecution, the Worthies had broken away from that, coming far enough out here into unclaimed territory that they could achieve their potential, following Ardet's social map. Rex was part of that; they all were.

"We all have our tasks, Jen. I'm a newt. You know that being a fighter—or a lover—is not one of my duties." He offered a comforting smile. "I can do many things, Jen, just not what you're looking for right now." Rex squared his shoulders, as he had seen his brothers do. "But if we don't stay the course in our darkest hour, then we dishonor Ardet. He gave us our instructions. If we cast them aside now, then we are no better than the people from Earth."

It was an intellectual argument, the kind Rex was best at, and he could see that it did not convince Jen's heart. After she left him in a swirl of anger and fear, he went back to finish the kitchen chores by himself.

* * *

The handful of intact Worthy men insisted they would go down fighting for their principles, their way of life. Rex was physically, and chemically, prevented from feeling the same passionate resolve, but he could admire their determination, their bravery, their refusal to give up. He was sure Ardet Hollings would have been proud.

Shortly after their independence day, Rex and a dozen newts were removed from their daily assignments and sent out into the space rubble field with Commander Joseph Heron. Heron was old, scarred, and impatient, one of only twenty-three male survivors of the initial battle against the Democratic Progressives. Listening to him rail against Fate, Rex wondered if Heron had spent the last several months wishing that he too had died in the conflict. But if he had, who would defend the Worthies against the decadent and despicable DPs?

From the time he was child, Rex had been trained how to suit up and how to perform outside functions. He was perfectly capable of performing tasks out in hard vacuum, as were his fellow newts. They were well-educated, even-tempered workers who remained unruffled in a crisis. They would complete their tasks as required, no matter how anxious and uptight Commander Heron and his desperate soldiers might be.

Scouts had already combed the space battlefield for any wreckage they could salvage, but Heron insisted on trying again and again. The vagaries of gravity in the rings churned up new discoveries, like repressed emotions coming to the surface. Rex was sure nothing remained to be found, but the commander had nothing to cling to but dogged optimism. Rex was surprised, and pleased, when the searches paid off: Far from where anyone expected gravity and momentum to have carried it, they discovered a nearly intact DC ship.

Leaving Heron in charge was yet another example of Ardet's great wisdom: No newt would have bothered to keep searching.

"This is our greatest break yet, men," the commander said over the suit intercom as their shuttle approached. Heron allowed only a small touch of irony when he said "men." His voice held an edge, as if anger could inspire the newts to greater dedication, but the implants continued to keep them controlled, calm. It was the most reasonable way to get a tough job done. After the Worthies' early years of near-starvation, Ardet had based much of his plan on that basic idea....

Heron named the wreck *Flying Dutchman* after an old Earth ghost story. The *Dutchman*'s hull had been breached in several places, venting its atmosphere and killing the small crew. When their shuttle circled the derelict, Rex studied the configuration, making mental notes about what needed to be repaired. Decades ago, when leaving their tainted planet behind, Ardet's followers had purchased brute-force commercial vessels to haul people and equipment on a one-way trip to Saturn. This DC exploratory ship was faster, its lines sleeker, its potential greater than anything the colonists had used.

When the shuttle docked against the *Dutchman*'s cold hull, Heron addressed his men and the newts. "Inside this wreck, there may be energy weapons, explosive projectiles, something we can use. It's my aim to get this vessel up and running. Then we'll have five ships, and we can make a good accounting of ourselves when the DPs come."

"Can we even understand the systems, sir?" Rex asked. "This technology far surpasses what we're used to."

The older commander turned to him. Behind the reflected glimmer on the curved faceplate, Rex could see his frown. "Just because you don't have any balls, doesn't mean you don't have any brains. I'm counting on you to figure this out, Rex. It's the only way we can survive."

Rex didn't think they would survive in any case, but he made no further comment. The other newts waited to receive instructions.

After they broke into the *Dutchman*, the salvagers separated into teams and methodically moved from deck to deck. They discovered the iron-hard bodies of six DC soldiers, expressions frozen as if surprised that a tiny group of isolationists had fought so bitterly against their impressive ship. Two of Heron's men let out defiant cries of triumph; the others were queasy and silent. The newts were put on corpse detail, gathering and ejecting the dead soldiers. They didn't mind.

On the bridge, Commander Heron and his men studied the dead ship's systems. Rex stepped up to the engine controls and navigation modules, and peered down to read the labels on each station. He knew how to fix familiar systems—recyclers, irrigators, and lighting—but these looked different.

"Don't just stand there and make this place crowded," Heron said. "Not much time left!" The other newts spread out and began to make repairs.

With so many unknown factors, the Worthies had no way of determining exactly when the retaliatory ships would arrive. After receiving distress signals from the battle in the rings six months ago, Earth should have taken at least a month to gather a new fleet, which would take five or more months in transit. But if the DC military had modified their engines, improved their speed or fuel efficiency, they could fly to Saturn more swiftly than expected.

By any calculation, the DPs could be here any day.

Rex used a circuit mapper and command-train isolator to check the station panels, one row after another. He documented which modules were functional and which needed to be routed around or replaced. Even if the *Dutchman* were completely repaired, though, the new DC ships were bound to be far superior.

That first engagement had been unintentional, at least on Earth's part. The Democratic Progressives had sent an exploratory force through the solar system, mapping resources, choosing possible locations for new colonies and outposts.

"It's what so-called 'progressives' do," Ardet had said in a speech to every member of the Worthy colony. "They spread, and exploit, and take what they want. We cannot let them steal our homes! We dare not let them disrupt our grand experiment. We must prove the strength of our principles." His voice grew deeper and more powerful; it had been so stirring that Rex found himself moved in spite of the implant. "The DPs are barbarians—they will pillage, and rape, and destroy everything we hold dear!"

The Worthy men had howled, the women had cringed, and the newts had listened carefully. The men gathered every possible ship, cobbled together anything that could be used as a weapon, then set an ambush in the rings to protect their way of life.

The DC exploratory force had come to Saturn with escort ships and scientific vessels, intending to use the plentiful ice in the rings to replenish their fuel and water supplies. Rex had studied the records of their arrival, and (as far as he could tell) the DPs had taken no aggressive action; it seemed possible that they hadn't even known about the tiny hidden colony. But fiery-eyed Ardet called it an incursion, a criminal trespass by plunderers. After overcoming birth pains and terrible difficulties, the colony had begun to thrive, exactly according to the design. They wanted nothing to do with the people of Earth.

The DC scientists and pilots were astonished when the Worthy men attacked. Though the DC exploratory fleet was not a military force, they had fought back, killing most of the young men and Ardet Hollings himself before being destroyed themselves.

"Nothing here we can't fix," Commander Heron said, rapping on the arm of the captain's chair. "We can get the *Dutchman* flying again!" He looked around the bridge as if expecting the newts to cheer, but they continued their tasks with silent efficiency. He turned to Rex. "*You*. You're Ardet's own son. Doesn't anything get you riled up?"

Rex shrugged in his bulky suit. "That's not possible, sir." He reset a panel and was gratified to see that all systems were now functional. "But I do my job to the best of my abilities. Is there something inadequate about my performance?"

Discouraged, the commander let out a long sigh that was audible across the helmet radio. "We won't be able to last five minutes against the forces from Earth."

* * *

Back at his familiar work in the greenhouse domes, comfortable with the routine despite the imminent arrival of the

DPs, Rex was glad to be doing something worthwhile. "There is no more glorious work than providing food for our people," Ardet had said to all greenhouse workers. And since Rex also worked on the illumination and irrigation systems, he felt he was doing even more than his part. It gave him a warm satisfaction to know he fit in so well.

Overhead, bright stars and outlying ring fragments moved like fireflies. Some of the women harvesting produce looked up nervously, as if expecting them to be braking jets from Earth ships; Rex saw only lovely lights as bright as diamonds.

He hummed a tuneless song to relax himself, though the implant did most of the job. Crews of newts and women picked ripe vegetables and fruits, never letting anything go to waste. The recycled air smelled fresh, moist, mulchy. Overhead lamps poured out warm, buttery light to nourish the plants. Coming around the gauzy limb of Saturn, the sun also rose, adding its distant light and life. Bees transported from Earth buzzed around the flowers, sexless drones doing their work for the betterment of the hive.

Two years ago, encouraged by his father, Rex had improved the hydroponic trays and then the nutrient-delivery irrigators in the planted rows. Now he drew a deep breath and sighed as he looked out at the colorful patterns of growth, all the shades of green. Each species was planted in the proper order for optimal food production, everything in its place, everything productive. Ardet Hollings had been such a genius.

Rex ruffled his fingers through the velvety leaves of enhanced strawberries. Ripe and red, they would make a sweet dessert; perhaps Mother would serve some tonight. She had been more extravagant with her cooking in the past few weeks, as if to reassure everyone that nothing was wrong.

As he moved the leaves aside, Rex spotted a darting lizard. The original colonists had brought no large animals with them from Earth, but along with the bees they had released numerous small animals such as birds, shrews, and tiny lizards. The birds and rodents had died; only the lizards had survived, and thrived, finding an entire ecological niche for themselves.

Rex tried to catch it, but he wasn't quick enough. The lizard vanished among the strawberry plants, showing only a flicker of a tail that was a different color—obviously broken off and then regrown. Lizards had that amazing regenerative ability. Rex went back to his work picking the berries.

In the beginning, Worthies had planted only the fastest growing and highest-energy-density foods, then used reprocessing chemistry to break down even the waste vegetation into edible mass. They'd had nothing else to eat. Because of Ardet's innovative survival measures, that crisis had passed when Rex was just a child, and now the Worthies had the luxury and the inclination to plant decorative flowers and ornamental shrubs from stored genetic samples.

This place had become a home instead of just a subsistence colony. But it wouldn't last.

In their fourth year away from Earth, one of the three primary greenhouses had failed; a piece of rogue stony debris thrown from an impact in the rings had sailed at high velocity into the armored dome, shattering several panes and hemorrhaging atmosphere. Most of the air was gone, the temperature plunged, the greenhouse sent into an unstable wobble. Seven people died, and all the plants perished—one third of the crops to feed the settlement. Adding to the disaster, a blight had swept through the corn crop in one of the other greenhouses, decimating that harvest as well.

On the relatively new colony, their survival had already been hanging by a thread. Most of their preserved supplies were already gone. Devastated by the loss, the Worthies watched their perfectly planned future crumble. Though workers scrambled to build another greenhouse dome and create subsidiary growing areas, they faced the very real prospect of dying—or returning, beaten, to repressive Earth.

Ardet rallied them. "Return is never an option! We have fought too hard to establish a perfect society. I have provided the road map. Do we dare take our children back to that hellhole? How could we betray them in such a way?" He had lifted his young son Rex for all his followers to see. Now, when Rex watched the tapes and studied his father's words, he was glad that in his small way he had helped Ardet make his point. "We have given our citizens their places, defined their roles, offered them security instead of cultural pandemonium. Men and women fill the niches for which they were bred, without the confusion of too much freedom and too many pressures." It was a famous speech that all students were required to memorize. In the recording, the people were bleak, gaunt and hollow-eyed—with fear, as much as from hunger.

After the greenhouse failure, knowing they would barely have enough to eat for the next few years, Ardet had assessed the big picture and repainted his grand social landscape. "As Worthies, we must watch ourselves. We did not ask for an easy life, nor will we ever have one. Our population must always be carefully controlled. We will grow, and we will triumph, but out here we must do it in a properly planned fashion. This is not Earth."

"Peace, despite hardship," the crowd had mumbled.

"Thus, for the time being, we must stabilize our population. We must shore up our society, keep our roles intact, keep our people happy. We cannot have strife, nor can we have uncontrolled breeding. Thus, as a gesture to strengthen all of us in our resolve, we must make sure that no more than two children in each family will reproduce."

This announcement had been met with dismay, since Worthies had, until now, been encouraged to have large families in order to increase their numbers. The people muttered. "Most of us already have more children than that, Ardet. Do you … want us to kill them?" someone asked from the audience. Watching that interchange over and over, Rex was sure that the questioner would have done it, if Ardet had asked.

Their leader shook his head and gave a broad, paternal smile. "Of course not. We love our children. They are the building blocks of our great society. But, we must use them with great care, to a noble purpose." Ardet had looked at them all with his intense visionary glare. "While I am confident we have the strength to survive, this crisis is only an example of our possible tribulations. By our own design, we are in a new situation here at Saturn. We came to escape the anarchy and gluttony of Earth, and to do that we must change ourselves … and that is a good thing, though it will be hard.

"For this generation, we must take interim measures. Difficult measures, but vital ones. After the first two children, our extra sons and daughters will remain important parts of our perfect society, but they will also make the sacrifice so that we can remain strong and stable." He had looked at them all. Rex still felt a chill when he recalled the historical tapes. "They must be neutered."

As an educated adult, when Rex considered the details of the solution, he didn't think the mathematics worked out. Neutering the additional children had not decreased the number of mouths to feed. But, as became clear later, that had only been the first part of Ardet's brilliant plan. Using the greenhouse accident as a springboard, he had led his people past another watershed, pushed his new society to an entirely new level.

Because he was their leader, because his followers would do anything he asked, they had not argued. To show his sincerity, Ardet had won their hearts by offering up his own young son as the first to be castrated. Rex was told again and again what a great thing he was doing, though being only four years old at the time he had understood nothing about what was really being taken from him.

After a large group of children was neutered and properly raised—girls as well as boys—Ardet had quietly revealed his deeper motivation to create an entire layer of society without aggression, without destructive competitiveness. Newts were cooperative and friendly, productive, and completely reliable, if not ambitious; the boys being the most prominently changed. The castration itself was not sufficient for Ardet's purpose, though. With carefully metered implants, the newts remained on an even emotional footing, causing no trouble. Each family was allowed two viable children, and the rest became a new caste, the strong and stable foundation for a great Worthy civilization. Rex had listened to the rationales over and over. He thought it was breathtaking....

Now, as Rex and the newts continued their work in the greenhouse, the women reacted to a signal piped in over the dissemination channel. The words were spoken in a crisp voice with just a tinge of fear. "An outpost on the fringe of the outer ring has picked up radio chatter, and long-distance sensors have just discovered the Earth military force on its way. The Democratic Progressives will arrive at the rings of Saturn within a week, two at the most."

Hearing this, Rex missed his brothers more than ever. He had never understood them, but he loved them nevertheless. In their youth, Lee and Ian had fought and wrestled with each other, so full of life. Fairly bursting with energy, they had always exhausted their little brother. They had tried to include Rex in their roughhousing play, but even as a boy he had never enjoyed it— due more to the implant than the actual neutering. What if he had been more like them?

As he finished filling his container with strawberries, Rex looked up through the transparent dome. He thought about Jen, desperate for him to be something he wasn't, then felt sorry for Ann and her little boy. For their sakes, he tried to imagine himself in a Worthy soldier's uniform. What if it came down to that?

Would he grab a projectile repeater rifle and stand at the habitat doorway with Mother, Ann, and Jen behind him? Snarling, would he point the hot barrel of the weapon toward oncoming DC invaders, scream like a madman and blast away one enemy after another? Maybe he would use the weapon as a club if he ran out of ammunition. He would bare his teeth. He would claw at them with his hands. The women would treat Rex as a hero, a savior. Then he would hop aboard the *Flying Dutchman* and streak off into space, using the ship's weapons to destroy more of the DC attackers. He would make them pay dearly....

Rex wiped away the faint sweat that had broken out on his forehead, shaking his head at the strange ideas. The implant struggled to banish the thoughts as fast as they came into his head. None of it felt like something he could do, something he *should* do. Rex was a newt, with his specific role to play—just like every Worthy. Ardet would have been gravely disappointed to learn his son had even entertained such fantasies. It was not at all what the great leader had designed newts to do. They served another purpose.

Rex emptied his container of strawberries, then went to pick soybeans. Even after the women had rushed off, he and four newt companions stood together chatting. Their conversation didn't touch on the approaching Democratic Progressives. Rex was confident that everything would work out for the best.

*   *   *

The family huddled together in the living quarters for their final hours. Rex held a squirming Max as he stood at the window, but even his uncle's attentions could not calm the boy against the palpable storm of panic. Rex felt the boy's misery and held him close, but they could not help each other.

Intellectually, he knew their dire straits, though the implant worked overtime to keep him quiet and anchored. Now he needed it more than ever. With a glance at the pale, wide-eyed faces of his mother, of Ann and Jen, Rex wondered if they envied him his calm.

With Max clinging to him, he pondered what it might have been like if he'd had a child of his own. If things had been different, would he have felt the longing to reproduce, the endless ticking of a biological clock?

Rex kissed the toddler's cheek, then looked toward the upswept rings, where he could see the glimmers of inbound DC ships. Some families were using telescopes to watch the defensive measures Commander Heron was struggling to implement. Rex saw all he needed to see with his own eyes.

Each weapons launch, each explosion, was a tiny spark. The Earth forces had come with more than a hundred fully armed military vessels, more than enough to overwhelm any resistance the Worthies could mount. Even so, Heron had taken the *Flying Dutchman* into battle; the other intact men had a few ships, little more than tiny cargo shuttles loaded with explosives. They faced off against the DPs in a brave but hopeless last stand. Fifteen newts had been recruited to man some of the defensive posts, but the Worthies did not have enough weapons for them. Rex wondered if his neutered comrades were experiencing any fear in their extreme circumstances. Was this what Ardet would have wanted them to do?

As they approached, the DC ships issued numerous warnings—they sounded like pleas—for the Worthies to stand down. From listening to the battle chatter, it seemed to Rex that the enemy fired only after Commander Heron had launched his weapons. Once the battle began, however, the DPs quickly obliterated the resistance.

The Earth ships were visible now as distinct blips closing in on the isolated colony. There seemed to be as many hospital ships as armed military vessels. Decoys? With their superior forces, why would the DPs expect so many casualties? And if they meant to slaughter the Worthies, why bother with medical aid?

"We do not intend to harm you," said a strangely accented but gentle-sounding voice over the dissemination channel. A *female* voice, in command. That startling fact alone demonstrated to Rex how different these invaders were.

"They're lying," Ann growled. Now she tried to take Max, but the boy clung to his uncle. Rex soothed him, and Ann withdrew to her terrified pacing.

As the DPs passed the outer supply depot, it exploded, booby-trapped with proximity bombs. Flying shrapnel tore open one of the Earth battleships. Rex knew that the depot had been manned by two newts assigned there by Commander Heron.

Tears streaked Jen's lovely face. "That one was for Ian," she whispered, her voice cold and bitter.

Mother sat grimly in her favorite chair. "At least the damned Capitalists won't be able to take our supplies."

"Cease your resistance!" The female commander's voice sounded sterner now. "We cannot allow you to threaten peaceful ships. After you are disarmed, you will be given an opportunity to explain yourselves and air any grievances in world courts. But we must protect ourselves."

"Then stay away!" Jen shouted. Her once-luxuriant dark brown hair was stringy; her eyes grew red as she kept crying. Rex was sure his brother would still have found her beautiful.

When the ships surrounded the habitation complex, there were no more flashes, no more desperate attempts to block them. The crackling accented voice continued, "Please stand down. We do not wish to hurt anyone else. We will not harm you. You have our word."

Jen moaned from the other side of the room. "They're going to kill us all! They'll drag us back to Earth and make us their slaves." Ardet had painted that picture many times, convinced his followers what monsters the DPs were. Rex couldn't let himself believe that his father might have distorted the truth, exaggerated the threat.

Little Max continued to squirm, and Rex set him down. "It's already over."

Ann glared at him. "Don't you even care? Don't you realize what they'll do to us?"

Reaching an impossible decision, Mother disappeared into the sleeping quarters, then returned holding a heavy pulse rifle. Both Ann and Jen saw the weapon and cringed. Even Rex could barely cope with his surprise.

Ardet Hollings had wanted a peaceful society. He had reconfigured the human structure to guarantee there would be no conflict, only order and productivity. By using his followers as human building materials, by creating the unshakeable and diligent newts to be the backbone of a strong and satisfying life, he had intended to make such weapons unnecessary. The pulse rifle had no purpose other than to shed blood.

"Mother, we can't do that! It is forbidden," Ann said, though her voice held a rough hunger. Rex could see the raw conflict in her mind.

"The men are our defenders," Jen said.

"All our men are dead," Mother said. "We have no choice. We have to defend ourselves." She lifted the weapon, and it was obvious she already knew how to use it. Rex wondered where she had gotten the practice, why she had ever considered it necessary. "Unless Rex will do it."

She held the pulse rifle forward, and Rex found that he was unable to move. "I can't. I'm a newt. Our father made it so—"

"Do you believe in Ardet's teachings? Do you truly trust his words?"

He shied away from the weapon, shaking his head. "The implant, the operation—our father forced me not to be a man. How can you demand it of me now?"

"Because times demand it." Mother's eyes were sharp and hard. "You know what you have to do." She placed the rifle in his hands. It felt heavy and cold. He stared at the firing controls.

The DC ships clustered around the colony domes and locked themselves down. Rex's family members all jumped upon hearing a loud thump as the invaders forced open the access airlocks. "They're coming!" Ann said.

Rex stood with the rifle like a dead weight in his arms. Yes, he did believe what Ardet had told them. He had listened to all the speeches, enough to memorize most of them. He knew what the Worthies stood for. He accepted everything Ardet had claimed, though the actions of the DC invaders were not what he had expected.

The implant helped him to consider his thoughts, to see them objectively, without the disturbing backwaters and eddies of unruly emotions. He had no testosterone-induced distractions, no aggression, no wild mating drive. In this impossible situation, only the newts among the Worthies could remain solid and true to Ardet's principles.

Yes, he believed. He knew what his father would have wanted of him. Ardet had made it plain in his teachings, in his speeches, and in his actions. How else could Rex accept what had been done to him?

Mother looked at her only remaining son, her face full of emptiness. Jen and Ann stared at him, perhaps seeing echoes of his brothers.

The female DC spokesman broadcast another message. "You will not be harmed. You will be taken care of. If some of you wish to come back to Earth, we will arrange safe passage."

"Don't believe them," Jen cried. "They're barbarians."

Heavy footsteps came down the halls. Rex stood like a rock in a fast-moving stream, feeling the weight of great events all around him. He was a Worthy, a vital component of Ardet's vision. He had his role, he was a newt. He believed in what they stood for.

The pulse rifle in his hands was armed. The DPs were coming closer.

He set the weapon aside. Behind him, someone moaned in fear or disappointment. Mother, perhaps?

If he truly believed in his father's plan, then he had to accept what he was—and what he was supposed to do.

Newts were made to be teachers, listeners, faithful workers, a stable class without violent tendencies. If Ardet had wanted his son and all those like him to be heroes, he would never have cut them off at the ... knees. Rex didn't need the implant to tell him that this was for the best.

As the DC consolidation parties moved toward the family habitat, Rex faced them. He experienced no despair or panic, neither elation nor fear. Just an unending sense of calm....

Kevin J. Anderson *is the author of more than 125 books, 54 of which have appeared on national or international bestseller lists; he has over 23 million copies in print in thirty languages. He has won or been nominated for the Nebula Award, Hugo Award, Bram Stoker Award, Shamus Award, the SFX Reader's Choice Award, and New York Times Notable Book. He and his wife Rebecca Moesta are the publishers of WordFire Press.*

In this tale set in an urban fantasy retelling of Peter Pan, a Salvation Army store worker discovers a doll in a donation box that she just can't let go … but what if it's alive? Urban fantasy meets horror in K.D. McEntire's fascinating Lightbringer series, with …

BABYDOLL
(A LIGHTBRINGER TALE)

BY K.D. MCENTIRE

The screen door screeched shut behind me. Across the street, my neighbor Manny's old tom slunk beneath the snarl of dead bushes bracketing his front porch and the branches rattled like bones, catching at his fur. The tom hissed, exposing yellow, blunted teeth. He was old. I didn't take it personally.

Carmen's Camry ground into life as I rushed down the front steps. No sooner had I slammed the passenger door than Aunt Carlie strode onto the porch, robe flapping around her knees, screaming fit to wake the dead.

"YOU GET BACK IN THIS—"

Carmen didn't let Carlie finish, she peeled out, and in minutes, we were out of the sad wreck of our neighborhood, heading south toward San Jose. Her engine rattled oddly when we hit the highway.

I glanced at the dash out of habit—Carmen's gas gauge has been busted for months, pointing to full even when the car is coasting.

"We're early. Wanna stop?" I dug in my pocket for a couple of ones, almost all I had left until payday but payday was today, so it was kind of kismet. I waved the bills under her nose and Carmen laughed, thanking me, and jamming the dollars into her cup holder.

We stopped at the Mom'n'Pop close to work. I was thirsty but figured on snagging a dented Dew at work. I'd run through my savings going up to the City, so soda was a couple bucks I couldn't afford.

"Hey," Carmen said, poking her head through my window. "You feel up to blowing off the Army today? We can snag a Redbox and head back to my place. Pop popcorn and veg."

Carmen's fingers brushed against my elbow. She had a zit on her jaw beneath her ear, small now, but I knew it'd be a whitehead by the end of the day. Her diet was terrible.

I hesitated. I'd had the nightmare again last night and Thursdays were always slow; bailing on our shift at the Salvation Army was super tempting but, then again, that meant I'd have to spend the whole afternoon with Carmen.

This wasn't normally a problem. Carmen and I have been best friends forever, but since Juan and I split up two months back Carmen's been touching me more—a poke on the shoulder, fingers skimming my elbow—and inviting me out more than usual. One-on-one stuff.

If I'd asked her straight out, she'd have laughed in my face and called me a lez, but it wouldn't be personal. Carmen's closet-case had always just been this aspect of her that didn't bug me until now. Now, though—now I'm stuck. Carmen's smart, she probably knows what I did and is trying to make up for it—to make me feel better, or take care of me—but I don't need her help.

I'm not ashamed.

I'm just tired.

If I went with her we could talk, maybe air out stuff. Maybe if I weren't still bare over the whole mess, I'd consider it, consider her, but not now. I need her friendship and Carmen has to know that, to understand it, before she gets resentful and weird.

I swallowed, about to agree on faking sick, but then I remembered that I'd called out three times last month when I'd had to go up to the City. If I bailed again, I'd get fired for sure.

A sane person would've told bosslady Jackie about my medical thing, but she was kind of a prig and a gossip. I did *not* want everyone at the Salvation Army to know I'd been up to San Francisco for a hoovering. I needed this gig to start fresh, get out of this town. Be the badass I know is hiding somewhere inside me.

"Nah," I said flippantly, inhaling the diesel-stench and prodding a piece of peeling rubber peeking out from the doorframe. "Jackie'll hold our checks if we try to pick them up and buzz off."

"Point," Carmen sighed.

We were ten minutes early to work.

I promised myself that I'd talk to Carmen soon, maybe during our shift, if we could find a corner to clean together, but luck wasn't with me.

It never is.

Slow doesn't even cover how dead it was. Jackie runs a tight ship; most of the night there was jack-all for us to do except keep the browsers from shoplifting.

Carmen'd been assigned the register and wasn't allowed to leave the front, so it was a long, lonely night. I organized the clearance bins.

Just when I thought my head would explode from boredom, Jackie dumped a box in my arms. "Come on," she said, bustling past the jeans without looking to see if I was following, "your pick: scrub the toilets or stocking?"

"Stock," I said automatically, hefting the box. I'd already had to bleach the dressing rooms once tonight. I didn't want to have to do the same to the bathroom.

"Thought so. Let's get ahead on the new stock then and save the morning crew the hassle."

Working the back has its benefits—you have to lift the heavy crap and scrub off the ick, but you also get first crack at the donations. Our store's got a bunch of dads in receiving, so the toy section's usually pretty sparse.

I was pretty startled to find that the box weighing me down was filled with delicate dolls—not Barbie or American Girl but real, old-fashioned dolls with brittle curls, frilly dresses, and thin porcelain skin. Some of the dresses were still dusted with cobwebs.

Jackie saw me assessing the stash. "I used to collect dolls like that when I was a kid," she said. "Kept 'em for when I had a little girl." She patted her sloping gut. "Joke's on me, huh?"

I kept quiet. Another reason I didn't want to fess up to my visit to the clinic was Jackie's fertility struggles. She was done now but Carmen'd warned me off talking babies my first week on the job. Twenty years of trying and four miscarriages had left Jackie bitter.

"If I had any sense I'd buy them myself," Jackie continued, oblivious to my discomfort. "Dolls that old, you know one's gotta be *Antique Roadshow* quality." Patting me on the shoulder, she headed for the back.

The front door dinged as I set down the box and a regular customer—this goth redhead that goes to my school, name of Wendy—wandered in. Normally she's got her buddy Eddie with her, but I couldn't see his faded-out dye-job anywhere.

Carmen shot Wendy a wave, and Wendy idly wagged her fingers back; she seemed distracted, looking around the place like she'd never seen it before. Wendy does that a lot around town, striding past dangerous stuff like it's not there, or crouched on a bench muttering to herself, pausing like she's talking to someone else. People used to call her Wacky Wendy, but she's gotten stranger lately, conspicuous to the point where she makes most of our class uncomfortable. No one jokes around her much anymore, you never know when she might snap and haul a handgun to gym or something.

Whatever. I had more important stuff to do than wonder about that weirdo. I unpacked the dolls, examining each one before setting it on the toy shelf, turning the idea of antiques over in my head. Most of the dolls were old but not in pristine, eBay-ish condition—some had cracks and others were water stained or moth-eaten.

Ten minutes to closing, I was down to the last doll in the box. This one was different, I could sense it the second I laid eyes on her. Tentatively, I reached into the box, and it was like sticking my arm in an icebox, cold eddying around my fingers in waves.

The doll was more than gorgeous. She was exquisite.

Coppery red curls, springy and firm, clustered around a heart-shaped face. Her features weren't the typical button nose and bee-stung mouth most of the others sported—less child-like, more adult, with sharp, precisely shaped features—and her eyes were completely unlike the sleepy blue and green marbles set in the other doll faces. These were almond-shaped and pale brown, amber-hued, flecked with gold. Even her clothing was different. It was an older linen piece that reminded me of the Avonlea books cluttering my bookcase.

I flipped the doll over, looking for the price tag, and sighed. The others topped out at twenty bucks but my doll had been priced at a hundred-fifty, easily half my paycheck, and an obscene amount for furniture from our store, much less a toy aisle baby doll.

Still, I knew I had to have her. Owning her wasn't a choice; it was *need*, stark and raving, clawing at my insides. The thought of putting her down was a painful pressure behind my eyes, a pounding in my pulse, as if I was meant for this dainty, precise thing or like she, inexplicably, had chosen me.

Across the store, Wendy turned my way, and for the first time in months, I paused to really *look* at her. She's always been scrawny but now Wendy was much too thin, her skin so pale I could make out the tracing of blue veins along her temples against her faded black dye and grown out roots. Scabs laddered across the ink that curled and curved across her collarbone and wrists.

She looked sick but that didn't change the queasy, taut feeling I got in my gut when I realized that I had her full, undivided attention. Wendy's eyes seemed to *glow*, like she was looking inside me. Instinctively, I cupped a hand across my belly.

When she blinked, the glow was gone.

Uneasily, I tucked the doll beneath my arm, backing toward the break room. Carmen and Jackie, eager to go home, were both too busy counting down the register to realize that Wendy hadn't left or that I wasn't in the back closing up.

I ought to ignore the clenching in my gut, the fluttering of my heart—what could weirdo Wendy do anyway? Nothing. I should rush up to the front with the doll and ask if Jackie could put her on hold for me, or keep her in the office or something until I could figure a way to afford her. I should put her down. I should go talk to Carmen, rent a Redbox—

Wendy started toward me.

All the *shoulds* vanished immediately.

Panicking, I bolted, the doll still gripped tight in my arms.

Behind me I heard shouting—Carmen and Jackie realizing that something was wrong as the fire door burst open, and I darted into the alley—Wendy yelling incoherently, and the blare of an alarm that both seemed loud and muffled at the same time.

There was a bus closing its doors at the bus stop on the corner. I raced up and pounded once. The driver glared but popped the door to let me board before pulling away.

Behind me, the yells faded as I fed the very last of my cash into the till and then, exhausted, drifted further into the bus with the doll tight in my grip. The bus was empty for a Thursday—a homeless dude drooled in his sleep on the back seat, a couple Asian tweens mid bus whispered together, and a prim old Indian lady avidly read *Fifty Shades* behind the driver.

I sat between the old lady and the kids as the bus pulled away from San Jose toward the highway.

I didn't even know where we were going, only that I'd forgotten to pick up my check at the start of my shift and that if I went back I was risking getting arrested for shoplifting the doll. I couldn't go home—even if Wendy didn't know exactly where I lived, she'd be able to find out easily enough. We weren't allowed our cells on the floor, so my phone was in my locker at work. I couldn't call Carmen for a ride.

Hell.

But I had the doll. There was that at least.

"Thank you for saving me," said the girl in the seat beside me. I hadn't heard her board the bus or settle down, she was just *there*, subtle as smoke, and when her hand cupped my elbow, her fingers were cold and thin, pale, tipped with blue.

She had the most beautiful amber eyes. Her name was Joyce. I don't know how I knew that, but I did.

"No problem," I whispered, closing my eyes as Joyce leaned over and whispered quickly to me, enveloped in her sickly sweet scent, cradled in a swiftly rising fog.

* * *

It'd been a huge mistake to let the girl realize she was watching, Wendy knew, but she was off her game tonight, had been for weeks. She knew the two employees vaguely, they went to school with her; she'd had Carla or Corrie, or whatever her name was, last year in Art, and the other girl, Lucy or Lana or Lorrie, in English.

C-whatever was yelling now, but Wendy had tuned her out, trying to follow the dimming scent of the dead, squinting through the grey and wasted Never after the bus as it pulled away.

Wendy knew that she didn't need to rush off and catch up with the ghost clinging to the girl. She just needed to get an idea where they were going and stalk them from there. The bus line would be able to give her the next few stops, but ever since their spat, Eddie'd been avoiding her, so he was out for a ride up to the City, especially to chase down a ghost.

Not for the first time that day, Wendy wished she hadn't lied to Piotr for so long about her reaping. He'd have busted ass to chase the bus and jump aboard; would have dragged the Walker out by its stinking, rotting cloak and held the bastard down while Wendy called the Light and sent it back to whatever god would accept a Walker's cannibal soul.

Ignoring the girl still hysterically yelling at her, Wendy tucked her hands in her pockets and walked back to her father's car. In theory, *she* could drive the sedan up to the City, but lately she'd been lifting his ride too often as it was, and she wasn't sure she felt confident enough to handle San Francisco's twisting, cluttered streets on her own without wrecking the sedan.

Then again, that Walker had seemed pretty damn intent on following L-girl closely. She moved, it moved. It was the damndest thing. In all the time she'd been reaping, Wendy'd never seen the like. Living human body heat burned the dead, so souls avoided the living and humans never had a clue that the dead were nearby. It was a win-win situation all around as far as she was concerned. Fewer people to observe her doing her thing, for one.

The thing that ate at her was the way the girl had seemed *protective* of the Walker, like it wasn't just trying to tick itself into a nibble off her soul ... like she could *see* it. But that was ridiculous. The living—the regular, normal living, at least—couldn't see the dead.

Wasn't it?

"Mom would know what to do," Wendy muttered to herself as she slid behind the steering wheel. What she wouldn't give to be able to talk to her mom just once more. Advice. Any advice would do.

Without her mother, Wendy felt like she was barely treading water, constantly threatened by the tidal pull of her "job" and the rest of her ridiculous, confusing life. She'd never wanted this burden she'd inadvertently inherited from her mom, and now she was left to sink or swim all alone.

"Okay," Wendy muttered. "Okay. Risk the City? Or try to catch her at home or at school? *What is her name?!*" Wendy pounded the steering wheel and rested her head against the top curve. The shouting had stopped. The thrift store was now dim and quiet.

"Lucky," she recalled suddenly, and it *felt* right. It was such a bizarre name for a girl Wendy vaguely remembered had been given nothing but crap hand after crap hand her whole life. Jerk boyfriend who even oblivious Wendy knew cheated on her, orphaned in the same ice storm that took Eddie's dad, crashed out with family in those teeny little studios four blocks from Wendy's place.

Lucky fell in gym and broke her nose. Lucky went to Homecoming in a borrowed white dress and got her period. Lucky took the class pet home over the weekend, and it came back squashed by her aunt.

Lucky, Wendy thought, flicking on the engine and pointing the sedan toward the City, *has never been lucky.* And now she was in the worst scrape of her life, though she probably had no clue. That Walker was different from the others. Wendy didn't know why or how, just that it was, and that if she didn't fall into a little luck of her own, then Lucky might be joining her parents sooner than she ever imagined.

* * *

The bus let off near the wharf. I got off, clutching the doll to my chest, and drifted toward the piers—normally thrumming with tourists all times of day and night, but a cool fog licked my ankles, eddying across the water.

Everyone else must have bailed, I reasoned, and felt more than heard the chuckle as my new friend walked beside me. The world seemed so different now that she was here—everything clearer and at the same time darker, harder, swathed in grey and glimmering with faint, distant lights, pinpricks like dying stars guiding my steps down alleys I'd have never dared after dark before, invisible fingers tugging at my pants as I passed.

Maybe it was because it was long past sunset, but I didn't recall this part of the City being paved with cobblestones. There was a wall up ahead, black-spotted with mold like watching eyes, and on the breeze tendril-drooped blossoms like cobwebs sifted on the breeze, caught in the rising wind, buffeted by the oncoming storm.

I shivered and tucked the doll closer into my arms, cradling her tight, and bent to brush a kiss against her forehead. She was warm in my arms, her miniscule nails sharper than I expected, pressing into the curve of my elbow. I gripped her tighter; if I dropped her, she'd crack against the cobblestones, brittle bone china turned to dust and dismay.

"Keep walking," the whisper behind me said, and I nodded. Joyce knew best. She'd found me, hadn't she? She would save me.

There. We were closer now, and I could see it even through the rising fog—the bridge rising up, decrepit and rotting and new and yet not.

I didn't know how or why I was seeing these two places overlaid against one another like pictures from another time imposed on the world I knew, but there was gravity to the grey place, somber solemnity, and I was just so *tired* of the struggles of the bright world, my world.

If given an opportunity, I'd dive into the mist and never come back.

"Soon," Joyce promised me, and I dared a glance back at her. Her amber eyes filled my vision, so bright, so big, but at the same time there seemed to be something subtly wrong with her face.…

I shook my head, breaking the hallucination. *Idiot*, I berated myself. Joyce was exquisitely shaped, sharp and pristine and beautiful. Her skin was smooth, poreless, and moonlight pale, and her hair hung in perfect corkscrew ringlets. I stank like sweat and dust and bleach. Joyce smelled charnel sweet, overblown roses and midsummer honey.

But the skull, the rot, a whisper like a sob came from the back of my mind. *Didn't you see the loose flap of her tongue?* I pushed the voice down, burying it deep. Joyce, I knew, was flawless, inside and out. Not like me.

Not like me at all.

Joyce took my hand in hers, careful of my doll—*her doll* I knew now, fashioned with her bones and blood and hair and dust—and together we drifted toward the bridge.

* * *

Wendy wasn't even out of the parking lot when C-girl pounded on her passenger side window, startling the hell out of her. "LET ME IN!"

Flipping the girl the bird, Wendy was about to drive off when the passenger door, treacherous, faulty thing, popped open. C-girl dove into the seat and slammed the door shut. "Drive! Follow that bus!"

"That's what I was *doing*!" Wendy retorted waspishly but accelerated anyway. If she had any sense at all, she'd kick C-girl out, but Wendy was tired of handling every emergency on her own. Without her mom or Eddie, she was kind of at a loss with dealing with normal people. The dead were more her forte, and before Piotr, she'd just send them into the Light without bothering to learn their names.

"Look, Lucky's been having a shit time of it," C-girl said. "I know you're all holier-than-thou and don't follow gossip ..."

"I am not!" Wendy protested.

"But she's been kind of miserable for weeks now," C-girl continued, ignoring her. "Did you see the way she was holding that doll? I think she snapped."

"Snapped?" Wendy said, turning the idea over in her head. She didn't know a whole lot about the more esoteric side of the reaping business—her overprotective mom had kept her in the dark half the time—but every now and then Mom'd let slip about a wily ghost who broke the rules in a righteously awful way.

"Yeah. Look, if you breathe a word of this to anyone I will personally eviscerate you," C-girl swore, "but Lucky had to go up to Planned Parenthood a bit back."

Wendy nodded, keeping her lip zipped. She had enough trouble handling the drama of the dead, there was zero room for opinions about living decisions that didn't concern her.

C-girl paused, waited for Wendy to comment, and when she didn't, smiled briefly. "She tried to hide it from everyone but I'm—*we're*—not stupid. It's been eating at her. It wasn't a hard choice, it's not like she's mourning it, but still ... Lucky's got a very 'what if?' kind of brain. She broods even when she doesn't realize it."

Wendy cleared her throat. "You think she's off to do something drastic?"

"She was holding that thing like a baby," C-girl said flatly.

Wendy thought of the Walker hanging over Lucky's shoulder, a grey and rotting shroud urging her to flee as soon as Wendy'd turned their way, and bit back her own theory. Lucky might be brooding, sure, depression was an easy way for certain ghosts to worm their way in, but the only reason a Walker would have to drive her like a donkey toward the City was for personal gain.

Skinwalker, Wendy thought bitterly. She'd never encountered one, but they were just as nasty as the name implied—a Walker soul who'd found an abandoned human shell to ride around in, working the body from the inside like a grisly puppet. The flesh protected them from the likes of Wendy and her mom, and once they were in a shell, it was nearly impossible to pry them out again. Skinwalkers had no compunctions about killing anyone they could get their hands on, tearing humans and souls alike into shreds for the fun of it all.

If Wendy didn't get to Lucky before the Walker found a way to convince her to abandon her body, then they were all very screwed.

* * *

The wind was cold. It was nearly Thanksgiving, the weather wasn't that big a surprise, but I worried that the little girl would catch a chill.

"Keep going," Joyce whispered from my arms, her huge eyes opening and shutting sleepily. She was tired, I could sense it. Of course she was, it'd been a century of silence and pain, of sorrow and loss for her.

I couldn't remember when the figure at my side had vanished into the doll, but they were merged now, waiting for me to complete the circuit.

"You're lucky," Joyce murmured as I stepped up on the bridge and hesitated at the fence blocking the edge. It was so foggy I'd have time to climb it before anyone spotted me and butted in, but how to do so without breaking Joyce? "You're still young enough. Still pure."

Was I? Despite everything that'd happened, I still felt very young and very alone, aching for the comfort of Dad's loose arm around my shoulder, missing sips of strawberry lemonade Mom'd make in June.

Juan'd made my missing lesser for a while but then—

"What are you doing to me?" I asked as I began my ascent. My head felt alternately fuzzy and sharp, my palms slicked with sweat as that muffled voice in the back of my mind screamed itself hoarse.

"Just clearing the way, dear," the doll murmured and I knew what it intended, clear as day. We were connected and I could feel her preparing to hollow me out.

Problem is, I couldn't quite make myself care.

It's not like I hadn't gone through it once before.

I swung a leg over the edge of the fence and the rain began. It pattered around us, little drops at first, but soon pounding my shoulders and head, soaking my socks. I reached the bottom of the fence and looped my fingers into the chain link, relishing the numbness.

If it were a little colder, just a little, it would ice the way it had the night my parents died. The streets would grow slick. People would die.

Joyce was crooning at me, singing a sweet siren song, but all I could recall was the silence of my room the day of the funeral. The dark. The quiet. The space that was all mine before I'd moved in with Carlie in her cramped studio.

Carlie wouldn't miss me. Carmen would.

As if I'd pulled her from thin air, suddenly there was a screech of tires and Carmen was there, Wendy right behind her, scrambling up the fence, and screaming—no, *shrieking*—my name.

She shouldn't be here, I thought. *She shouldn't have to see this.*

In the back of my brain Joyce was howling, cursing, and Wendy was glowing, ribbons of the whitest, purest light pouring out of her chest, yet Carmen didn't seem to notice, and I couldn't really make myself care …

there was a pressure and a pinch and I was so, so cold …

and the two worlds bled together, grey over black, Light sluicing over me, hotter than fire, *burning, searing* the cold away …

but the cold fought back and Joyce's howl turned triumphant. She sank into me and jostling at my soul, pushing it nearly out of me, joining her spirit to mine for better control. I could feel the pressure of her, the frozen chill of her dead and decaying mind and I just … *knew.*

I could clearly see—no, *recall*, we were so close as to be one person now—every awful thing Joyce was responsible for, every casual cruelty in life and death, every terrible, nasty deed, every child soul she'd devoured to stave off the inevitable fading away. In a flash like lightning I understood about the limbo, the Never, and Wendy, the Lightbringer, the terror of the dead, the reaper of souls.

Carmen was stuck on the fence. A break in the chain-link had snagged her hem. She was sobbing openly, her mascara black rivulets snaking down her cheeks.

Wendy wasn't crying. I think she knew that I knew about her now. There was such a look of sadness to her, a well of grief that stunned me with its depth.

I writhed; Joyce was in me like fishhooks dug deep.

But I was in her as well.

"Don't," I heard Wendy say into the storm, not a cry, but a whisper. She knew, or thought she did, what I had to do now, but it was a futile request. I knew all about her and Wendy wasn't a fool; allowing a dead woman to ride around in my body would damn so many more than just me.

I smiled. "I'm pure," I said, and despite the storm I knew that she had heard me. "I guess it's my lucky day."

Unwilling to waver any longer, I wrestled Joyce for control of my limbs. It would be easy to give up, to let her use me, squashed small in my own skin. Or I could go and take her with me. Joyce had refused the Light when she died before, scared of Hell or the nothing of the after, existing as a carrion feeder ever since. So many would die if I let her go on. I wouldn't make that mistake.

I pushed off the bridge. Joyce shrieked. But it didn't matter, I was rising on the tide of Wendy's grief and acceptance. I hit the water. I didn't struggle.

It filled me. And when the Light came ... I smiled.

K.D. McEntire *is the author of the* Lightbringer *YA urban fantasy trilogy from PYR Books. She lives in Kansas where between raising her two young sons, she is working on another novel, and can be found online at kdmcentire.com.*

A boy in a refugee camp fighting for water to keep his family alive, encounters Jumpers David and Millie in this tale from Steven Gould's bestselling and brilliant Jumper series, the basis for the movie starring Hayden Christensen.

SHADE
(A JUMPER STORY)

BY STEVEN GOULD

Xareed had been waiting for the water truck for two days, seated in the dirt at the edge of the camp, his family's plastic ten-liter water-jug tied to his ankle.

He didn't like being on the edge of the camp.

Except for the piece of cardboard he carried impaled on a stick there was no shade. The poet Sayyid had said, "God's Blessing are more numerous than those growing trees," and Xareed hoped so, for there were no trees in the camp or outside. So the blessings had better be more numerous, not less.

Being on the edge of the camp, especially on this side, was also bad because rebels would occasionally fire into the tents from the far side of the old lakebed, or set up mortars among the folds and gullies in the bottom.

Bad enough, but when the government troops came in response, the rebels would be long gone, and the troops would say they were hiding in the camp and there would be searches and arrests and summary executions.

It was safer deep inside the camp where Xareed lived with his mother and grandfather and sisters. Back when they'd come here, after the rebels had killed his father and burned their farm, there'd still been a little water in the lake and a lot of mud, so his family actually had a house, just a one-room building, but made of thick sun-dried bricks that kept the family cool in the heat and which had, on more than one occasion, stopped stray bullets and shrapnel that tore through the tents that most of the refugees lived in.

It had been Xareed's idea, one of the few things he'd gotten from school that meant anything here. That, and enough English to talk to the foreigners who helped at the camps.

But Xareed really missed the shade of trees. His last memory of their farm, as they fled, was not the burning house and fields, but the flames consuming the wide canopy of their umbrella thorn acacia tree.

When the strangers showed up at the clinic tent, rumors and questions flew up and down the water line.

"How did they get here?"

"I don't know. Maybe a truck on the far side of the camp?"

"Maybe they came on a water truck?"

This was nonsense since the entire camp knew within minutes when the water truck had been sighted.

"Could it be a new supplies convoy?"

"Maybe a new drilling machine?"

The camp's three wells, drilled two years before, had dried up in the previous month. There was still some water in the clinic's tanks but it was being strictly rationed. One of the NGOs had sent a new drilling rig but it had been confiscated by the government and sent south.

Everyone was dry-mouthed and angry and all the young ones kept saying *"Waan domonahay"* (I'm thirsty) over and over again. Many had woken to find their water bottles stolen and accusations had flown, followed by fists.

"Maybe there was a helicopter?"

Sometimes the IRC got copters in with medical supplies.

"I heard they walked."

Xareed peered across the baked earth toward the nurse's station. The strangers were a white man and woman, wearing practical khakis and baseball caps. They didn't look like they'd walked. It was possible, but it was thirty dry kilometers to the next village. These people looked fresh, almost moist, like the reeds that grew by the stream in his old village.

"It's like they sprouted from the ground."

There was laughter at this, but only quiet laughter. Everyone was too hot and thirsty to laugh loudly.

"Xareed," one of his friends said, "you go ask."

Xareed translated to English for anyone. "They could be French or German or Norwegian. You go ask. Nurse will know."

A boy further down the line saw the tanker truck first, by the dust it threw up, while it was still kilometers away. It was coming by the lake road, winding along the old shoreline. Some of the newer refugees surged to their feet, but the old hands sat stoically. Time enough to stand when you could hear the diesel motor, hear the creaks of the springs as it bounced in and out of the road's potholes. Even then there would be some delay as they put the dispenser hose on the tank and filled the clinic's tanks first.

Xareed shifted his cardboard parasol as the sun tracked across the sky. It was one of the few things he owned and he had to watch it carefully. As shade it was valuable enough but during the cold nights any number of his campmates would steal it to burn. Fuel was not quite as rare as water. You could get it by walking far enough from the camp but the rebels or government troops might find you and that never ended well.

The sound of grinding gears was plainly audible and he had untied the string around his ankle and was thinking of standing when the truck hit the mine.

He jumped to his feet, his mouth open in dismay. The rebels must've planted it in the last two days. This same truck had used the same route the week before with no problem. The diesel was burning and he was pretty sure he'd seen water spray from a tank rupture before the swirling dust had engulfed the vehicle.

He was running, sprinting forward, almost without thought. The water. Even ruptured, the tanker could take some time to drain, if he could get to it in time—

It was at least six hundred meters to the truck and he slowed almost immediately to a steady jog. While speed was of the essence, it would do no good if he collapsed on the way to the truck or was too weak to carry his filled water can back.

Or if I step on a mine, he thought, and shifted his course off the dirt road.

If he could just fill his can. His sisters complained all day long about the thirst but his grandfather, who never complained, was weak and feverish.

He glanced behind. He'd clearly had the element of surprise but now a general rush was on, other boys and men and a few girls, enough that dust was rising into the air from their passage. *Ignore them*, he told himself.

A tall thin boy sprinted past Xareed, running for all he was worth, a twenty-five liter can in each hand and two more slung over one shoulder, banging against his back and chest.

For an instant Xareed was tempted to match his speed, to sprint as he did, but he kept himself to the steady jog. His resolve was tested as two more men dashed past. He was over halfway now, but the truck still seemed small in the distance, shrouded in dust and dark smoke, and the tall, skinny sprinter seemed almost there, but that had to be an illusion.

He *hoped* it was an illusion.

It was. The tall sprinter collapsed a hundred meters short of the truck and the other fast men were reduced to a staggering walk. They were bent over, gasping for air as Xareed jogged past them.

Xareed was also gasping for air by the time he reached the truck. He circled wide around the front where the fuel tank, behind and below the driver's side, had been ruptured by the mine and a puddle of diesel burned, flames licking up the driver's door. Even from eight meters away the waves of heat were painful and he held his cardboard parasol out to keep the worst of it off his face.

He glanced back. The rest of the crowd was still coming and the cloud of dust had grown but he still had a fifty-meter lead over the closest. As he got around to the passenger side his eyes were on the water pouring out of the rents in the tank and he dropped the parasol and began fumbling with the screw cap on his jug.

And that's when he heard the cries.

Someone was still alive in the truck cab.

The water was already slowing as it poured out of the ruptured tank and the others were so close. With a curse, he dropped the water jug and scrambled up on the step and clawed for the door handle.

The door came open about six inches and jammed. He braced his foot against the side of the truck and pulled and it creaked, then gave way suddenly and he fell to the ground, but he was back up on the truck step without thinking about it.

On the far side the driver was clearly dead, his clothes aflame, but there was a woman in the passenger seat moaning and staring about with wide eyes. Her face was bloody and her clothes too, but he couldn't tell if it was her blood or the driver's. She was fumbling with her right hand, reaching across her body, trying to reach her seat belt release. Her other arm was hanging, apparently useless, and her shirtsleeve was starting to smoke.

Xareed reached for the buckle and screamed as it burned him. He reached again, and instead of grabbing it, punched two fingers into the release button. The tab slid out and he pulled her, by her good arm, and, toppled back down onto the ground, her weight pinning him to the ground.

"Christ, she's on fire."

The weight came off of him and he saw the stranger, the white man, stripping off his shirt and smothering the flames that had started on the passenger's sleeve. Then the other stranger, the woman, was there suddenly. Xareed thought he must've passed out; for one moment she wasn't there and then she was. She looked angry and scared.

"You're going to get yourself killed!" she said fiercely, but then added, "She better go straight to hospital. One with a good burn unit."

Xareed blinked. What were they talking about? The nearest hospital was over three hundred kilometers away. Even if they could get a helicopter in, the chances of it being shot down were high.

The man nodded. "Right. I'll take her. Check on him, okay?" He jerked his chin toward Xareed. "He pulled her out."

The heat from the burning cab was increasing and the white woman pulled him further away.

There was shouting from the end of the truck. The ruptured tank was empty now and they were trying to get the other compartments open but it was crowded. Xareed looked around for his jug but it was gone. Someone in the crowd had snatched it up.

He tried to scramble to his feet but the woman pressed him down. The man and the injured passenger were gone. He must've carried her around the end of the truck and back to the camp.

"My water can!" Xareed said, struggling against her. "My can she is gone!"

"Ah, good. You have some English," the woman said, clearly relieved. She still kept her hand on his shoulder, though.

"I must find my can! My family needs water!"

She nodded. "Water is important. I'll get you some water but let me see if you're hurt."

Xareed looked at her. "Are you *crazy*! They will take all the water. There isn't enough." He tried to get up again but his six-hundred-meter run, the heat, the lack of water, the fire, his burnt hand—it was all too much. She was able to hold him down easily.

"Shhhh. I promise I'll get you some water. What's wrong with your hand?"

Xareed was cradling his right hand. "I, uh, fire, uh hot, it. On the belt seat."

"Ohhh. Burned? When you got her out? That was very brave of you. Let me see." She held his hand lightly by the wrist and looked closely without touching it. "Ow. Looks like you'll blister. Wait here."

She stepped back around the front of the truck, where the smoke still billowed. Xareed tried to get up again but he was suddenly overwhelmed by it all. They were pushing and shoving at the other end of the truck. His hand hurt. The water jug was gone and his mother and grandfather and sisters would go thirsty.

The woman stepped back around the front of the truck. She had a cloth in her hand wrapped around something. She crouched again, beside him, and said, "Put this against your fingers—it will help."

He held out his burnt hand, cautiously. He thought maybe she had some salve, some ointment, but she gently pressed the entire cloth against his hand.

The relief was sudden and shocking. It was ice, like they used to have at his old school, like the tops of distant mountains. She opened the cloth a little and took a chunk, a cube, from inside and mimed putting it in his mouth.

He did. So cold. So good. He sucked greedily at it.

"Rest here a few minutes. I'll go get your water."

She brought him back a jerry can, plastic, with "5 gal" embossed on the side. It was full. More shocking, it was cold— beads of water were condensing on the sides and it felt almost as good on his burn as the ice.

He looked around for his makeshift parasol and it was there, but the crowd had trampled it flat and the stick was broken and the cardboard torn.

He couldn't help it. He cried.

The woman picked up the scraps of cardboard. "Ah, I saw this, when you were sitting in line. Clever."

He nodded. "My parasol."

"A nice bit of shade. What's your name?"

"Xareed, Miss."

"Call me Millie."

The crowd around them was growing and on the other side, someone was throwing dirt on the burning diesel oil. He put an arm around the jerry can, holding it close.

The woman eyed the growing crowd uneasily. "Come on, Xareed. I'll help you carry this back to the camp, all right?"

They walked side by side, the can between them. She was only a little taller than he was and they shared the handle, his left hand, her right touching.

"Where are you from, Miss Millie?"

"Canada," she said. "How long have you been here?"

"Three years. We were firstcomers." He told her about their mud brick house and his mother, grandfather, and sisters. "Is that man your husband?"

"Yes. David."

"Why did you come here?"

"To help, if we can," she said.

She was sweating now, and Xareed was relieved. He hadn't been sure if she was human or not. He asked his next question nervously. "*How* did you come here?"

She glanced sideways at him and then back at the dirt they were trudging across. "Why do you ask?"

"It's hard to get here. Sometimes helicopters come but the rebels have rock … ats?"

"Rockets."

"Rockets. And the roads have mines. And there is no convoy." He peered at her. "And I do not think you walk."

She sighed. "No. We came our own way." She did not elaborate, but instead asked him what circumstances had brought him to the camp.

He found himself telling her the entire story, right up to looking back at the burning farm, the burning tree.

"Ah," she said. "Shade."

"Yes."

She left him at the edge of the camp where he was able to get one of his trusted neighbors to carry the water can the rest of the way in return for a liter of its contents. By the time he'd reached the mud brick house, the ice was reduced to a handful of small chips but there was still enough for his sisters, mother, and grandfather to each have a small mouthful.

It was a miracle. A small miracle, but still a miracle.

* * *

Later, that afternoon, the next miracle happened.

"The tanks are full! The tanks are full."

"Are the wells working?"

"Did more trucks come?"

Wildly different stories swept the camp. He got one version from Yahay, who lived in a tent near Well #2. "It was that stranger, the man who came with the woman, without a car."

"What did he do?"

"He climbed up onto the water tower." The water tower was a metal tank on legs three meters above the ground. A petrol wellpump filled it so gravity could drain it. It was three meters across and four meters tall and held 38,000 liters when full. Since the well had gone dry the month before, it had been mostly empty.

"So?"

"He opened the inspection hatch and climbed down into it. I was standing near. I heard water rushing and then the tank began to creak. I ran to the tap and cold, cold water came out when I held the valve open. I cried out in surprise and everyone came running. In the excitement, I didn't see him come out of the tank. Maybe he didn't," Yahay said, wide-eyed. "Maybe he turned into the water."

Xareed remembered the man disappearing with the injured passenger. He didn't think the man had turned into water. Especially when the other two tanks were found to be full very soon after.

Xareed went looking and found the strangers sitting with the French IRC nurse and watching the sunset in front of the clinic intake tent. He crouched down behind the tent flap and listened.

"It's a respite. How often can it be done? We've been short for a month now. Forty-five hundred people go through a lot of water."

The man—David—looked at his wife. "Can't keep it up. It will attract too much attention and it will be bad for us and for the camp. But, I do have a longer-term solution, I think."

"Yes?"

"Let me try it. You'll know if it works."

They left after that, walking out into the sudden dusk, and Xareed watched carefully. He was wondering if he would see another miracle when he saw another man leave the edge of the camp and drift after the strangers.

While it was true that the rebel troops did not hide in the camp, it didn't mean that they didn't have their spies among the refugees. This man was a bit too well fed, a bit too well dressed. He wore boots and pants, not sandals and the robe, and his shoulder-slung bag was shiny new.

Perhaps he too was interested in the miracle of the water.

Xareed looked around and then followed, swinging wide to the north. He kept his head down, like someone looking for firewood. Anything near the camp was long gone, but that didn't keep people from looking.

David and Millie kept moving, crossing quickly over the dip that marked the old lakeshore and then down the slope. They were moving by feel and starlight now.

Xareed found a shallow gully that marked an old streambed and ran down it, using it to hide his passage. He passed David and Millie and crouched low as they walked closer.

Millie was saying, "—find Canadian salmon here and it will blow the whole thing."

David said, "Yeah. Pity. There's an awful lot of snowmelt going to waste up there. But you're right. And there's the hypothermia danger. BBC Meteorological says it's raining around Lake Tanganyika. That'll do."

From Xareed's position in the gully they were all silhouetted against the fading sunlight on distant wisps of clouds, so he saw the follower close the distance and take the gun and something else from his bag.

Xareed felt a rock under his knee and dug it out of the dried mud. It was bigger than his fist and sharp cornered. He threw it as hard as he could, aiming behind and above the gun.

Light from a flashlight stabbed out and then there was a smacking sound and a cry. The flashlight tumbled to the ground where it shone across the submachine gun lying by itself in the dirt. Then he saw a hand, a white man's hand, reach into the light and pick up the gun. The flashlight came up and shone down on the man who'd followed them from the camp.

The man was clutching his head with his hands and blood stained the side of his face. He was groaning and Xareed said, "It is deserved."

The flashlight turned his way and he blinked in the sudden glare. "Ah. You, eh? From the truck? What did Millie say ... Jareed?"

"Xareed. Where is Miss Millie?"

The flashlight swept around in a circle. There was no sign of anyone else.

"Ah, well, she'll be back." David's voice didn't sound puzzled at all by the woman's disappearance. "What are you doing out here?"

"I saw him follow you from the camp."

Millie was there, then, wild-eyed, a baseball bat raised high and swinging.

The flashlight moved sideways three meters. No. It was suddenly three meters to the side—there was no movement. Just as Millie had not been there and then she was, the flashlight was one place and then another.

"Whoa, Millie. It's okay!" David turned the flashlight on himself, then pointed it at the man on the ground, then at Xareed. "Xareed got 'em. With a rock?"

Xareed's mouth was open and he felt numb. With some effort he said, "Yes. I throwed a rock. How did you do that?"

"Don't think about it, Xareed. It'll only make you crazy," said David.

"I think maybe crazy is what I am."

Millie lowered the bat. "No. David is the crazy one." She glared in the light. "You scare me like that again and I'll …"

"It wasn't me," David said in an offended voice.

The man on the ground had stopped moaning and was looking at them all, wide-eyed. Suddenly he jumped to his feet and ran out into the darkness, down the slope into the lake bottom. David swiveled the light to follow his flight but the man didn't turn back and soon dropped out of sight into one of the gullies below.

"You did not shoot him," Xareed observed.

David looked down at the submachine gun dangling in hand, as if he were surprised he still held it. "No. Not me."

"He is a rebel. He may bring back more. Sometimes they hide down there."

David looked vaguely concerned. "Oh."

There was a flash from several hundred meters ahead of them followed by a loud noise. Ten seconds later there was an explosion in the camp behind them, followed by distant screams.

Xareed shuddered. "Mortars. They're firing on the camp. Give me the gun. I will go stop them."

David looked down at the gun in his hand. Another mortar went off. He shifted the gun in his grip and Millie said, "No! That's not the way!"

"Then what?"

"Water runs downhill."

David blinked. "Oh. So it does."

He handed the flashlight and the gun to Millie and vanished.

Xareed recoiled and fell backwards, then scrambled back to his feet.

Millie gestured with the flashlight. "We need to get up the hill a bit."

"Why?"

She pulled the clip from the gun and threw it out into the darkness, then worked the slide, ejecting another bullet from the chamber before she threw it in the other direction. "You'll see."

They backed up the hill, toward the camp. Another mortar shell exploded in the camp and Xareed thought of his sisters, probably tucked in the corners of the house, their one mattress pulled up around them. The house would be proof against anything but a direct hit or near miss. Then the bricks would go from being protectors to projectiles.

David was back, but then gone, like he'd blinked into existence then left. Then he was back again. Then gone. Then it was as if he was blinking. There, not, there, not, but the time between slowly decreased and then there was a David-shaped hole and water flooded out of it in all directions, fast and furious, like a river torrent after a heavy rain.

Even up the hill, it washed all the way up to Xareed's knees, warm water, not too cold, and then it flowed away, into the gullies and down the hill.

There was one more mortar flash from the bottom of the old lakebed before the rushing water arrived. The rush of the water drowned out most noise but he thought he heard distant shouts and cries.

He and Millie backed further up the hill until they reached dry ground, then sat. Millie turned the flashlight off but the sound of the water was overwhelming. Xareed could even feel it through the ground, a thrumming vibration against the soles of his feet and the palms of his hands.

The smell of it, wet and rich, permeated the air, turning the normally dry, searing air into a moist and heady mix of half-familiar smells.

"It smells like ... like rain."

"Yes," agreed Millie. "Like rain after a long dry spell."

* * *

Xareed woke to the morning light, which, magnified, reflected off wavelets on the surface of a lake stretching two kilometers to the far shore.

He sat up and looked around. He was above the shoreline, barely, and his head had been pillowed on a rolled up jacket. It was Millie's, he realized, but he did not remember falling asleep.

He wondered if they'd taken him someplace far away, but when he looked around, the sleeping camp was stirring. People stood at the edge of the camp, staring at the water, taking a few tentative steps forward, as if they thought it was a mirage that would vanish when they walked toward it.

Maybe it was. He reached out a hand and trailed his fingers through the water, then held them up and let them trickle into his mouth. An empty mortar casing bobbed on the wavelets, a few feet out from the shore, and he remembered the night before. He imagined the rebels trying to get up the wet slopes weighed down by their guns and mortars and ammunition, and, though he hoped they'd made it out, he felt confident they'd had to leave the heavy metal tools of war behind.

He got up and went to see how his family was.

* * *

It could've been far worse. The mortar had hit in the square, a stretch of empty dirt where people with things to trade or sell sat in the morning and where the men sat in the evening discussing the Qur'an. There was a small crater and shrapnel had killed a woman across the way, but the nearest structure was Xareed's house.

"She's fine," his mother said, though she kept her arm around his youngest sister and wouldn't let her go play with the other girls.

Xareed nodded. Awrala really *was* fine. She'd woken from the loud noise and the weight but it really hadn't even frightened her.

She'd been far more worried by her mother's frantic cries and when her mother and grandfather had pulled her from under the pile of collapsed bricks, her mother had run her hands over and over her arms and legs and back and front, looking for some hurt, some wound.

Awrala was fine but it would take some time for his mother to believe it.

They were making bricks. They'd separated out the unbroken ones from the collapsed wall and the rest they'd thrown into the mortar crater. Xareed spent his time walking back and forth to the lake, carrying water and mud for the crater. His sisters trod and stirred the sludge and his grandfather formed the bricks and set them out in neat rows. It would take a few weeks but the wall would be good as ever and they were making enough bricks to add another room.

He was on his way back to the lake, his back sore and the buckets light and empty, when Millie fell into step beside him, looking cool and comfortable in the heat, her eyes shaded by gleaming sunglasses. "Hallow," she said, trying to say it like they did locally, but she still sounded foreign-alien.

"Hello." He tried to act relaxed but he couldn't help looking at her from the corners of very wide eyes.

"I wanted to thank you, for the other night. For helping us."

He shrugged. "I have been thinking that maybe, perhaps, you did not need help."

She smiled. "You didn't know that. I don't know that, for that matter. Who knows what would have happened?"

Xareed snorted. He knew what *he* thought. "You are kind."

"We are grateful. We could take you out of here. There is a large community of your people in Minnesota. In the United States."

He had heard this. It was cold there. "How many could you take? Could you take my sisters? My mother and grandfather?"

Millie licked her lips. "Yes."

"How long would it take? The journey?"

She half-smiled. "No time, really. A few minutes for all of you and your things."

"Then you could take all of us, yes?" He sketched his arm around in a large circle, encompassing the entire camp.

She frowned. "No. I don't think we could. People would come and stop us. We have enemies."

"The rebels? The government troops?"

She shook her head. "Ah … no. That's local. Our enemies have a very long reach. We could take your family, though."

He looked around. The water had changed things. There were waterfowl on the lake. Someone had seen fish. An NGO had gotten a food convoy through and, hearing of the lake, they'd included seeds: maize, beans, and wheat. All over the camp people had started gardens, putting children to work scaring off the birds who might eat the seed. The wells were no longer dry as the water from the lake seeped into the water table.

"We are here. This is where we have come and, thanks to you, there is hope now. As long as the lake does not dry up again." He glanced at her again and raised his eyebrows.

She looked at the lake, her hands on her hips, and smiled. "Perhaps that can be avoided."

She flicked away and he blinked, surprised. He thought she would've said goodbye.

He bent down to drag the buckets through the water and she was back. She had a Chinese parasol, bamboo and bright blue paper with a sprinkling of red and pink flowers, and she held it out to him. "To replace your old parasol."

He took it without thinking, then said, "No." He tried to hand it back to her but she stepped back and put her hands behind her back.

"No, it's yours."

His face contorted. He wanted the parasol with all his heart. He ran up over the rise and handed it to the first person he saw, a young girl carrying a baby on her hip.

He went back to the water buckets and Millie looked at him, then disappeared again, coming back immediately with another umbrella.

This one was pink with white hyacinths. He took it from her and gave it to an old woman washing clothes at the water's edge. He began walking with the buckets back toward the center of camp.

Millie walked out from behind a tent and held out a green umbrella. Xareed gave it to a boy chasing a grasshopper. Millie stepped out from another corner with another parasol and Xareed gave it to a woman weaving mats out of plastic and cardboard. By the time they reached Xareed's house, he'd given away twenty-three umbrellas and a long line of people was following them.

Millie shook her head. "You are very stubborn."

He smiled.

"All right, you win," she said.

"No more umbrellas?"

"Not exactly."

* * *

The word spread quickly and the lines formed at the edge of the square. There was much scrambling to keep the new bricks from being ground into the dirt. His entire family stood there, taking the umbrellas out of the cardboard boxes and handing them out and giving the boxes away, too, when they were empty. Then they would go into the mud brick house and bring out more boxes.

"Where are they coming from?" asked his friend, Yahay. "Your house could not hold a tenth of those boxes."

"Where did the water in the lake come from? Where did the water in the tanks come from?" he asked back. "It is as the poet said, *God's Blessing are more numerous than those growing trees.*"

* * *

He saw Millie one more time after the crowds had been shown that the "miracle house" was empty once more. She was sitting by his grandfather, helping him pat the bricks into shape, accepting feedback; laughing as the old man make invisible corrections to every brick she'd formed.

Xareed crouched on his heels and watched.

Millie looked sideways at him, "Did you take one for yourself?" She lifted her arm and gestured around. As far as you could see, the camp had blossomed with color. People were laughing, people were singing, and people were dancing, bright canopies of color twisted and whirled.

Xareed smiled and stepped into the house and then came back. The shaft was from one of the broken umbrellas—you open enough crates and you run across some breakage—but the top was a circle of cardboard, cut from one of the boxes.

Millie stared at it, her mouth dropping open. Then she fell onto her back and laughed and laughed.

He stood there and watched, dignified.

In the shade.

Steven Gould *is the author of* Jumper, Wildside, Helm, Blind Waves, Reflex, Jumper: Griffin's Story, 7th Sigma, Impulse, *and* Exo *as well as short fiction published in* Analog, Asimov's, *and* Amazing, *and other magazines and anthologies. He is the recipient of the Hal Clement Young Adult Award for Science Fiction and has been a Hugo, Nebula, Prometheus, Locus List, and Compton Crook finalist, but his favorite distinction was being on the ALA's list of Top 100 Banned Books 1990-1999. Steve lives in New Mexico with his wife, writer Laura J. Mixon (M. J. Locke) and their two daughters, two dogs, and three chickens. He has practiced aikido and Japanese sword for the last two decades, and has recently served two terms as president of the Science Fiction and Fantasy Writers of America. He can be found on Twitter as @stevengould and on Facebook at Steven Gould.*

Our last original story written for this volume is a charming fantasy about a young girl who innocently rescues a fairy godmother and receives a wishing stone with one wish, which she must then decide how to use ...

GRANTED

BY JODY LYNN NYE

The tiny woman leaned against the trunk of the beech tree, gasping. Water ran from her fine blue dress and long golden tresses, pooling around her delicate little shoes. She looked up at Abigail with green eyes larger than any woman had a right to have. In fact, she was downright beautiful.

"You saved my life!"

Abigail Baker wrung out her own skirt and the ends of her camisole's sleeves. The sturdy maiden's clothes were caked with flour, now turned to paste by the water. Her mouse-brown hair looked like the tail of a water rat, and her hands were chafed from climbing over the stone banks of the River Avon with the woman in her arm. Lucky it was a warm spring day. She'd dry quickly enough. She slipped her wooden clogs back on.

"It's all right. Thank God I saw you fall. That bridge is slippery, and the weir's sucked many to their doom. Not all can swim. I can," Abigail added proudly.

"Well, you must be rewarded, girl!"

No one with any sense turned down a reward. Abigail put out her hand for a coin.

Let it be silver, she thought fervently. To her outrage and dismay, what the petite lady placed on her palm was a blue glass sphere the width of her thumb.

"What's that? I can't spend that!"

"It's a wish, my dear," the lady said, kindly. "It's worth more than any coin."

"Go on!" Abigail said, snorting. "Like in my nan's stories? I'm not a child any more. I don't believe in wishes."

"Oh, yes. You can have whatever you wish for." The lady flourished her hands, and her silken gown became as dry as a bone and spotlessly clean. Her hair waved and flowed over her shoulders. "I'm a fairy godmother. I was on my way to the earl's mansion to bless his new daughter."

Now Abigail gasped. Magic, that was what it was! She'd listened close to the tales, and knew all the ways of getting the most out of a pixie, a leprechaun or a fairy. She grinned.

"Then, I wish for seven more wishes," she said. Seven was a lucky number. But the pebble remained cold in her hand.

"No!" the lady said, lowering her bright brows. Evidently, she knew all the ways, too. "One wish. That is what you may have. Don't be greedy. That's all the earl's daughter will have, too. You can have anything you ask for."

Abigail felt a pang of disappointment.

"Just one thing?"

The lady laughed, crinkling her beautiful eyes. "You can make the wording as complicated as you like, as long as you remember that everything you say will come true."

"What's 'complicated'?" Abigail asked, frowning. Sounded like a word the dean of the cathedral would know.

The fairy godmother sighed.

"Never mind. If you can say your wish in one breath, I'll grant it. Now, I must go. The others will be waiting."

Abigail watched the fairy shimmer her way past the masons carving decorative capstones and segments of pillars for the new nave in Salisbury's grand cathedral, where she had just brought bread from her father's bakery for the men's midday meal. More than one of the workers had tried to pinch Abigail. But not one looked up at the passing lady's marvelous beauty. They must not be able to see her! Magic again! Abigail clutched her marble in her fist.

What to do with it, what to do? she pondered as she started toward home.

The men could see *her*, all right. They leered and laughed. Big, black-haired Pieter Harwood tried for a kiss as she passed.

"You're wet as a fish," he said.

She pushed him back and sashayed away, swaying her hips. The men cat-called behind her. Pieter would be a master mason one day, then maybe she'd marry him. He was good-looking enough.

Ah, but with the marble, Abigail could look higher than a mason! The earl had a son, Gwillim. He looked like a frog, but he'd be earl in his turn. If she wished for lots of gold, she could attract Gwillim's eye. No, that wouldn't do. Her father would just take it away and spend it as *he* chose. She might get a handful of silver for her dowry. She'd have to be cannier than that.

Wishes at christening! Noblemen got so many better things than ordinary folk did. Abigail threw the marble into the air and caught it again. Here was her chance to live like a lord. The possibilities tumbled over and over in her mind, like kittens in a basket.

Tall, narrow, fine stone houses rose on either side of the cathedral close. They had glass windows made up of small, sparkling, diamond-shaped panes. Her house, adjacent to the bakery in the small lanes beyond the market, wasn't big or grand. She had to share a small attic room with her two little sisters. The blue marble could change that! Da would like it if they suddenly owned a mansion with lots of land and gardens. Then, she wouldn't wake up to the acrid smell of dung and rotten food on the middens at the street corners.

"Maybe I'll just get rid of the stink," Abigail said aloud. A sharp itch erupted just under her wet bodice. She wriggled her free hand underneath the stiffened fabric to scratch. Her struggle elicited ripe chuckles from the lads watching her from the shop doors and barrows. She made a face at them. The itch moved upward between her breasts. She plunged her fingers in and drew out a wriggling black spot, which she cracked with her nails and cast down into the reeking gutter. "Or fleas. I'll get rid of every flea in England!" Oh, the bliss of never rolling over in bed to scratch! That would be better than any riches.

But why not have all? she mused, as she wove her way in among the crowd of shoppers and the trestle tables set out for market day. To be able to buy anything she chose, with no pestilence or stink anywhere, would be bliss. Could this little stone bring her everything she asked for?

It was so hard to choose. The good Lord knew that she had trouble keeping to one idea. Her best friend Madeline Prout, the dyer's daughter, was much better at thinking. Abigail's father would be looking for her to make more deliveries, but if she surprised him at the end of the day with a grand estate and servants, he wouldn't mind if she was a bit late returning.

On such a fine day, Madeline was out in the busy courtyard of the dyer's shop with her brothers and her father's apprentices, a kerchief over her curly brown hair. They were hanging up swathes of freshly-dyed colored fabric on the ropes that stretched across the space like a giant spider's web. The colorful cloth smelled of hot cow's piss. Abigail grasped her friend around the waist and pulled her toward a bench in the corner of the yard where no one else could hear. Madeline lifted sad eyes to her.

"What's wrong?" she asked.

"Nothing's wrong," Abigail said, with a wide grin, showing her the blue marble on the palm of her hand. "I've got a *wish*. I rescued a fairy godmother from the river, and she gave it to me as a reward! I need you to help me work out how to say what I wish for."

"A wish? That's just dreaming," Madeline said, with a sharp wave of her hand. "I'll tell you what's real…!"

"No, but listen," Abigail interrupted. Her plans spilled out in a torrent of words. "… So, I'm going to make my father the richest man in Salisbury. I thought about a lot of things first, like I might have wished that I could fly. Then I could go see London. A girl such as me is never likely to get farther than Amesbury. Or I might have asked for a carriage and horses, but I'd have to be careful to ask for the stable to keep them and the oats to feed them. I think I can say that all in one breath. So, I've decided. My wish will be for a mansion with fifty acres and all the servants I'd need to run it, and fine bedchambers for my Mam and Da and me. You could come to stay in your own special room. Wouldn't that be grand? We could ride out on my horses—" She nodded sharply. "I'll have to remember to say horses, and stable, and an ostler. It will be hard to get that all in." The marble caught silver lights from the sun. "You're the smartest person I know. Can you help me get all that into one breath?"

She beamed at Madeline. Instead of sharing her excitement, Madeline stared at the ground, her hands listless on her lap. Abigail finally broke out of her dream and focused upon her friend's face. In between the usual odd dye streaks, this time ochre yellow and bittersweet orange, Madeline's eyes and nose were red. She squeezed the other girl's hand.

"What's the matter, Maddy?"

Madeline fetched in a deep breath. A sob caught in her throat.

"It's my ma. You know she's been poorly since winter." Abigail nodded. "Three days ago she started coughing up blood. The healer says it's the crab. It's eaten up her whole insides. She's just waiting now for the angels. And *that's* just a marble," she said bitterly, knocking Abigail's hand back with a scornful gesture. "Not magic. There's no magic in this world, for lords or anyone else."

Abigail was too shocked to protest.

"I thought it was just spring ague." She loved Mistress Prout like a second mother. Half her life had been spent running in and out of the dyer's shop and home, with Maddy's mother cuffing or cuddling them both as needed. "Oh, my poor dear. I'm so sorry." She put her arms around Madeline and drew her head to her shoulder. Madeline burst into tears.

"I've got to be the woman of the house. Ma is counting on me to care for everyone."

She wasn't ready. Abigail knew that, just as she knew she didn't know all the ins and outs of her own home. If *her* mother was taken from her—what a horrible thing that would be. She would add a learned doctor to live in her mansion, so nobody would die of the crab. The marble would see to it.

Abigail rocked Madeline. No sparkling glint of fantasy was

enough to dispel the reality of losing her mother so soon. All Madeline's own plans would be put to one side, for who knew how long? She had six younger brothers and sisters. Two of them were tearaways whom only her mother could control. Her father's business was thriving, but he needed a secure and well-run household behind him. How terrible to pile all that on Maddy's slender young shoulders.

Abigail let out the deep breath she'd been holding, and drew in another one. If it would do any good, she'd gladly sacrifice her own dreams.

"I wish your Mam was well and healthy, and would go on living many more years," Abigail said, with all her heart in her words, "so she'll see you married and in a house with your own children one day."

The hard, cold marble in her fist popped like a snapdragon's jaw. She opened her hand to see the blueness dissipate in the air like a puff of flour. *Ah, well. Easy come, easy go.*

"Thanks, Abby," Madeline said, hugging her best friend. "I love you for saying that. I wish it would come true, too. We both know it can't. But, come say goodbye to her." She rose to her feet and held out a hand to help Abigail up. "God alone knows how long it will be until He calls to her."

"Maddy!" a voice shrieked. "Maddy, come up quick! Hurry!"

The girls looked up at the high, narrow windows of the second story. Gillian, Madeline's seven-year-old sister, waved to them. Without a word, they made for the stairs.

* * *

"It's a miracle," the stout little herbwoman said, piling her muslin bags of leaves and roots into her wicker basket on the foot of the bed with her neat little hands. "I would I could credit my potions and tinctures, but before God I cannot. Not a trace of the fever, and her chest is clear and sound as a bell. One moment there's blood coming out with every breath, and the next, she's asking for soup!"

Propped up with feather-stuffed pillows against the head of the bed and wrapped in woolen blankets and eiderdowns,

Mistress Prout smiled. Her narrow face was pale, but color was returning to it.

"It was a simple request," she said, looking around at her children and her terrified husband, who had been summoned to his wife's bedside from his dye pots. Master Prout clutched her hand as if he couldn't believe that it was still warm. "Why is everyone so excited about it?"

Madeline laughed for pure joy, and hugged her mother.

"I'll get some soup for you, Ma," she said. She headed for the kitchen stairs. Abigail followed her. "Oh, thank God! Thank God in all the highest for sparing her! I'll spend all evening on my knees in church."

Abigail thought it was better not to say anything more about her wish as they filled a crockery bowl with hot soup from the stove and added the softest of the new bread spread with honey alongside the spoon on a wooden tray.

"Take it up, will you?" Madeline asked. Her face was flushed with joy as she bustled around the big worktable in the center of the small kitchen. "I'll warm some bits of meat to see if she can manage them."

"Gladly," Abigail said. She took up the heavy tray and began to edge her way up to the bedchamber.

"Well!" a voice said, at her elbow. Abigail jumped, nearly spilling the soup. The fairy godmother stood in the turn of the stairwell, glowing like a taper. "That wasn't at all what I expected of you. You had such big dreams!"

"Yes, well," Abigail said, blushing. "It just slipped out."

"I don't think so," the fairy said, opening her enormous green eyes wider. "You've a kind heart. This is the second life you've saved in a single day, though you wasted your wish. Just think what you could have done if you'd been able to exercise your imagination. I was waiting to see!"

"It wasn't wasted!" Abigail exclaimed, glaring at the little woman. "Maddy's my best friend. Her mother's always been good to me!"

"I was teasing," the fairy said, in a kinder voice. "You're a generous soul. It just tells me that perhaps I should have granted your request when you asked for more wishes." She held out her dainty palm, and another blue marble appeared on it. She set it down on the tray next to the bread and patted Abigail's cheek. "Try to do something more interesting with this one, will you? I'll be looking forward to what you come up with next."

Abigail looked at her, and mischief and joy rose in her soul. "Then, I wish …"

The fairy put her finger over her mouth.

"Later," she said. "Don't let the soup get cold."

Abigail sprang up the stairs, grand plans already swirling in her mind.

Jody Lynn Nye *lists her main career activity as "spoiling cats." She lives northwest of Chicago with one of the above and her husband, author and packager, Bill Fawcett. She has written over forty books, including* The Ship Who Won *with Anne McCaffrey, eight books with Robert Asprin, a humorous anthology about mothers,* Don't Forget Your Spacesuit, Dear!, *and over 140 short stories. Her latest books are* Rhythm of the Imperium *(Baen Books), and* Wishing on a Star *(Arc Manor Publishing).*

One of my favorite science fiction novels ever, Ender's Game, gave birth to a whole series of which our final story is a part. Originally published in slightly longer novella form as a standalone by Tor Books, we present it here in its first anthology appearance, slightly abridged by the author, Orson Scott Card. Set in the same Battle School where Ender's Game is set, this series follows students as they come to term with cultural and religious differences surrounding the celebration of Christmas in ...

THE WAR OF GIFTS
(AN ENDER STORY)

BY ORSON SCOTT CARD

Zeck Morgan sat attentively on the front row of the little sanctuary of the Church of the Pure Christ in Eden, North Carolina. He did not fidget, though he had two itches, one on his foot and one on his eyebrow. He knew the eyebrow itch was from a fly that had landed there. The foot itch, too, probably, though he did not look down to see whether anything was crawling there.

He did not look out the windows at the falling snow. He did not glance to left or right, not even to glare at parents of the crying baby in the row behind him—it was for others to judge whether it was more important for the parents to stay and hear the sermon, or leave and preserve the stillness of the meeting.

Zeck was the minister's son, and he knew his duty.

Reverend Habit Morgan stood at the small pulpit—really an old dictionary stand picked up at a library sale. No doubt the dictionary that had once rested on it had been replaced by a computer, just one more sign of the degradation of the human race, to worship the False God of Tamed Lightning. "They think because they have pulled the lightning from the sky and contained it in their machines they are gods now, or the friends of gods. Do they not know that the only thing written by lightning is fire? Yea, I say unto you, it is the fire of hell, and the gods they have befriended are devils!"

It had been one of Father's best sermons. He gave it when Zeck was three, but Zeck had not forgotten a word of it. Zeck did not forget a word of anything. As soon as he knew what words were, he remembered them.

But he did not tell Father that he remembered. Because when Mother realized that he could repeat whole sermons word for word, she told him, very quietly but very intensely, "This is a great gift that God has given you, Zeck. But you must not show it to anyone, because some might think it comes from Satan."

"Does it?" Zeck had asked. "Come from Satan?"

"Satan does not give good gifts," said Mother. "So it comes from God."

"Then why would anyone think it comes from Satan?"

She frowned her forehead, though her lips kept their smile. Her lips always smiled when she knew anyone was looking. It was her duty as the minister's wife to show that the pure Christian life made one happy.

"Some people are looking so hard to find Satan," she finally said, "that they see him even where he isn't."

Naturally, Zeck remembered this conversation word for word. So it was there in his mind when he was four, and Father said, "There are those who will tell you that a thing is from God, when it's really from the devil."

"Why, Father?"

"They are deceived," said Father, "by their own desire. They wish the world were a better place, so they pretend that polluted things are pure, so they don't have to fear them."

Ever since then, Zeck had balanced these two conversations, for he knew that Mother was warning him about Father, and Father was warning him about Mother.

It was impossible to choose between them. He did not *want* to choose.

Still … he never let Father see his perfect memory. It was not a lie, however. If Father ever asked him to repeat a conversation or a sermon or anything at all, Zeck would do it, and honestly, showing that he knew it word for word. But Father did not ask anybody anything, except when he asked God.

Which he had just done. Standing there at the pulpit, glaring out at the congregation, Father said, "What about Santa Claus! Saint *Nick*! Is he the same thing as 'Old Nick'? Does he have anything to do with Christ? Is our worship pure, when we have this 'Old Saint Nick' in our hearts? Is he really *jolly*? Does he laugh because he knows he is leading our children down to hell?"

He glared around the congregation as if waiting for an answer. And finally someone gave the only answer that was appropriate for this point in the sermon:

"Brother Habit, we don't know. Would you ask God and tell us what he says?"

Whereupon Father roared out, "God in heaven! Thou knowest our question! Tell us thine answer! We thy children ask thee for bread, O Father! Do not give us a stone!"

Then he gripped the pulpit—the dictionary stand, which trembled under his hands—and continued glaring upward. Zeck knew that when Father looked upward like that, he did not see the roof beams or the ceiling above them. He was staring into heaven, demanding that all those hurrying angels get out of his way so his gaze could penetrate all the way to God and *demand* his attention, because it was his right. Ask and it shall be given, God had promised. Knock and it shall be opened! Well, Habit Morgan was knocking and asking, and it was time for God to open and give. God could not break his word—at least not when Habit Morgan was holding him to it.

But God took his own sweet time. Which was why Zeck was sitting there on the front row, with Mother and his three younger siblings beside him, all perched on chairs so wobbly they showed the slightest trace of movement. The other children were young, and their fidgets were forgiven. Zeck was determined to be pure, and his wobbly chair might have been made of stone for all the movement it made.

When Father stared into heaven this long it was a test. Maybe it was a test given by God, or maybe Father had already received his answer—received it perhaps the night before when he was writing this sermon—and so the test was from him. Either way, Zeck would pass this test as he passed all the tests laid before him.

The long minutes dragged. One itch would fade, only to be replaced by another. Father still stared into heaven. Zeck ignored the sweat trickling down his neck.

And behind him, somewhere among the seventy-three members of the congregation who had come today (Zeck hadn't counted them, he had only glanced, but as usual he immediately knew how many there were), someone shifted in his seat. Someone coughed. It was the moment Father—or God—had been waiting for.

Father's voice was only a whisper, but it carried through the room. "How can I hear the voice of the Holy Spirit when I am surrounded by impurity?"

Zeck thought of quoting back to him his own sermon, given two years ago, when Zeck was only just barely four. "Do you think that God cannot make his voice heard no matter what other noise is going on around you? If you are pure, then all the tumult of the world is silence compared to the voice of God." But Zeck knew that to quote this now would bring down the rod of chastisement. Father was not really asking a question. He was pointing out what everyone knew: That in all this congregation, only Habit Morgan was really, truly pure. That's why God's answers came to him, and only to him.

"Saint Nick is a mask!" roared Father. "Saint Nick is the false beard and the false laugh worn by the drunken servants of the God of frivolity. Dionysus is his name! Bacchus! Revelry and debauchery! Greed and covetousness are the gifts he instills in the hearts of our children! O God, save us from the Satan of Santa! Keep our children's eyes averted from his malicious, predatory gaze! Do not seat our children upon his lap to whisper their coveting into his stony ear! He is an idol of idolatry! God knows what spirit animates these idols and makes them laugh their ho, ho, whoredoms and abominations and braying jackassery!"

Father was in fine form. And now that he was bellowing the words of God, striding back and forth across the front of the sanctuary, Zeck could scratch the occasional itch, as long as he kept his gaze locked on Father's face.

For an hour Father went on, telling stories of children who put their faith in Santa Claus, and parents who lied to their children about Saint Nick and taught their children that all the stories of Christmas were myths—including the story of the Christ child. Telling stories of children who became atheists when Santa did not bring them the gifts they coveted most.

"Satan is a liar every time! When Santa puts a lie on the lips of parents, the seed of that lie is planted in the hearts of their children and when that seed comes to flower and bears fruit, the fruit of that lie is faithlessness. You do not deserve the trust of your children when you lie for Satan!"

Then his voice fell to a whisper. "Jolly old Saint Nicholas," he hissed. "Lend your ear this way. Don't you tell a single soul what I'm going to say." Then his voice roared out again. "Yes, your children whisper their secret desires to *Satan* and he will answer their prayers, not with the presents they seek, and certainly not with the presence of God Immanuel!—no, he will answer their prayers with the ashes of sin in their mouths, with the poison of atheism and unbelief in the plasma of their blood. He will drive out the hemoglobin and replace it with hellish lust!"

And so on. And so on.

In Zeck's mind, the clock that kept perfect time went round the full forty minutes of the sermon. Father never repeated himself once, and yet he also never strayed from the single message. God's message was always brief, Father said, but it took him many words to translate the pure wisdom of the Lord's language into the poor English that mere mortals could understand.

And Father's sermons never ran over. He wrapped them up right in time. He was not a man who talked just to hear himself talk. He labored his labor and then he was done.

At the end of the sermon, there was a hymn and then Father called upon old Brother Verlin and told him that God had seen him today and made his heart pure enough to pray. Verlin rose to his feet weeping and could hardly get out the words of the prayer of blessing on the congregation, he was so moved at being chosen for the first time since he confessed selling an old car of his for nearly twice what it was worth, because the buyer had tempted him by offering even more for it. His sin was forgiven, more or less. That's what it meant, for Brother Habit to call on him to pray.

Then it was done. Zeck leapt to his feet and ran to his father and hugged him, as he always did, for it felt to him when such a sermon ended that some dust of light from heaven must linger still on Father's clothing, and if Zeck could embrace him tightly enough, it might rub off on him, so that he could begin to become pure. Because heaven knew he was not pure *now*.

Father loved him at such times. Father's hands were gentle on his hair, his shoulder, his back; there was no willow rod to draw blood out of his shirt.

"Look, son," said Father. "We have a stranger here in the House of the Lord."

Zeck pulled free to look at the door. Others had noticed the man, too, and stood looking at him, silent until Habit Morgan declared him to be friend or foe. The stranger wore a uniform, but it wasn't one that Zeck had seen before—not the sheriff or a deputy, not a fireman, not the state police.

"Welcome to the Church of the Pure Christ," said Father. "I'm sorry you didn't arrive for the sermon."

"I listened from outside," said the man. "I didn't want to interrupt."

"Then you did well," said Father, "for you heard the word of God, and yet you listened with humility."

"Are you Reverend Habit Morgan?" asked the man.

"I am," said Father, "except we have no titles among us except Brother and Sister. 'Reverend' suggests that I'm a certified minister, a hireling. No one certified me but God, for only God can teach his pure doctrine, and only God can name his ministers. Nor am I hired, for the servants of God are all equal in his sight, and must all obey the admonition of God to Adam, to earn his bread by the sweat of his face. I farm a plot of ground. I also drive a truck for United Parcel Service."

"Forgive me for using an unwelcome title," said the man. "In my ignorance, I meant only respect."

But Zeck was a keen observer of human beings, and it seemed to him that the man had already known how Father felt about the title "reverend," and he had used it deliberately.

This was wrong. This was a pollution of the sanctuary.

Zeck ran from Father to stand a few feet in front of the man.

"If you tell the truth right now," Zeck said boldly, fearing nothing that this man could do to him, "God will forgive you for your lie and the sanctuary will be purified again."

The congregation gasped. Not in surprise or dismay; they assumed that it was God speaking through him at times like this, though Zeck never claimed any such thing. He denied that God ever spoke through him, and beyond that he could not control what they believed.

"What lie was that?" asked the man, amused.

"You know all about us," said Zeck. "You've studied our beliefs. You've studied everything about Father. You know that it's an offense to call him 'reverend.' You did it on purpose, and now you're lying to pretend you meant respect."

"You're correct," said the man, still amused. "But what possible difference does it make?"

"It must have made a difference to you," said Zeck, "or you wouldn't have bothered to lie."

By now Father stood behind him, and his hand on Zeck's head told him he had said enough and it was Father's turn now.

"Out of the mouths of babes," said Father to the stranger. "You've come to us with a lie on your lips, one which even a child could detect. Why are you here, and who sent you?"

"I was sent by the International Fleet, and my purpose is to test this boy to see if he is qualified to attend Battle School."

"We are Christians, sir," said Father. "God will protect us if that is his will. We will lift no hand against our enemy."

"I'm not here to argue theology," said the stranger. "I'm here to carry out the law. There are no exemptions because of the religion of the *parents*."

"What about for the religion of the child?" asked Father.

"Children have no religion," said the stranger. "That's why we take them young—before they have been fully indoctrinated in any ideology."

"So you can indoctrinate them in yours," said Father.

"Exactly," said the man.

Then the man reached out to Zeck. "Come with me, Zechariah Morgan. We've set up the examination in your parents' house."

Zeck turned his back on the man.

"He does not choose to take your test," said Father.

"And yet," said the man, "he *will* take it, one way or another."

The congregation murmured at that.

The man from the International Fleet looked around at them. "Our responsibility in the International Fleet is to protect the human race from the Formic invaders. We protect the whole human race—even those who don't wish to be protected—and we draw upon the most brilliant minds of the human race and train them for command—even those who do not wish to be trained. What if this boy were the most brilliant of all, the commander that would lead us to victory where no other could succeed? Should everyone else in the human race die, just so you in this congregation can remain ... *pure?*"

"Yes," said Father. And the congregation echoed him. "Yes. Yes."

"We are the leaven in the loaf," said Father. "We are the salt that must keep its savor, lest the whole earth be destroyed. It is our purity that will persuade God to preserve this wicked generation, not your violence."

The man laughed. "Your purity against our violence." His land lashed out and he seized Zeck by the collar of his shirt and dragged him sharply backward, toward him. Before anyone could do more than shout in protest, he had torn Zeck's shirt from his body and then whirled him around to show his scarred back, with the freshest wounds still bright red, and the newest of all still beading with blood from this sudden movement. "What about *your* violence? We don't raise our hands against children."

"Don't you?" said Father. "To spare the rod is to spoil the child—God has told us how to make our children pure from the moment they achieve accountability until they have mastered their own discipline. I strike my son's body to teach his spirit to embrace the pure love of Christ. You will teach him to hate his enemies, so that it no longer matters whether his body is living or dead, for his soul will be polluted and God will spit him out of his mouth."

The man threw Zeck's shirt in Father's face. "Come back to your house and you'll find us there with your son, doing what the law requires."

Zeck tore away from the man's grip. The man was holding him very tightly, but Zeck had a great advantage: He didn't care how much it hurt to pull himself free. "I will not go with you," said Zeck.

The man touched a small electronic patch on his belt and immediately the door burst open and a dozen armed men filed in.

"I will place your father under arrest," said the man from the fleet. "And your mother. And anyone in this congregation who resists me."

Mother came forward then, pushing her way past Father and several others. "Then you know nothing about us," said Mother. "We have no intention of resisting you. When a Roman demands a cloak from us, we give unto him our coat also." She pushed the two older girls toward the man. "Test them all. Test the youngest, too, if you can. She doesn't speak yet, but no doubt you have your ways."

"We'll be back for them, even though the two youngest are illegal. But not till they come of age."

"You can steal our son's body," said Mother. "But you can never steal his heart. Train him all you want. Teach him whatever you want. His heart is pure. He will recite your words back to you but he will never, never believe them. He belongs to the Pure Christ, not to the human race."

Zeck held himself still, so he could not shudder as his body wanted to. Mother's boldness was rare, and always chancy. How would Father react to this? It was *his* place to speak, to act, to protect the family and the church.

Then again, Father had said several times that a good helpmeet is one who is not afraid to give unwelcome counsel to her husband, and a man so foolish that he can't hear wisdom from his wife is not worthy to be any woman's husband.

"Go with the man, Zeck," said Father. "And answer all questions with pure honesty."

* * *

Zeck got into a hovercar with the man. There was one soldier driving; the rest of the soldiers got into a different vehicle, a larger one that looked dangerous.

"I'm Captain Bridegan," the soldier said.

"I don't care what your name is," said Zeck.

Captain Bridegan said nothing.

Zeck said nothing.

They got to Zeck's house. The door was standing open. A woman was waiting inside, with papers spread out on the kitchen table, along with a pile of blocks and other paraphernalia, including a small machine. She must have noticed Zeck looking at it because she touched it and explained, "It's a recorder. So other people can hear our session and evaluate it later."

Captured lightning, though Zeck. Just another device used by Satan to snare the souls of men.

"My name," she said, "is Agnes O'Toole."

"He doesn't care," said Bridegan.

Zeck extended his hand. "I'm pleased to meet you, Agnes O'Toole." Didn't Bridegan understand the obligation of kindness and courtesy that all men owed to all women, since women's destiny was to go down into the valley of the shadow of death in order to bring more souls into the world to become purified so they could serve God? What tragic ignorance.

"I'll wait out here," said Bridegan. "If that's all right with Zeck, here."

He seemed to be waiting for an answer.

"I don't care what you do," said Zeck, not bothering to look at him. He was a man of violence, as he had already proven, and so he was hopelessly impure. He had no authority in the eyes of God, and yet he had seized Zeck by the shoulders as if he had a right. Only Father had a duty to purify Zeck's flesh; no other had a right to touch him.

"His father beats him," said Bridegan. And then he left.

Agnes looked at him with raised eyebrows. But Zeck saw no need to explain. They had known about the chastisement of the impure flesh before they came—how else would Bridegan have known to take off his shirt and show the marks? Bridegan and Agnes obviously wanted to use these scars somehow. As if they thought Zeck wanted to be comforted and protected.

From Father? From the instrument chosen by God to raise Zeck to manhood? As well might a man raise his puny hand to prevent God from working his will in the world.

Agnes began the test. Whenever the questions dealt with something Zeck knew about, he answered forthrightly, as his father had commanded him. But half the questions were about things completely outside Zeck's experience. Maybe they were about things on the vids, which Zeck had never watched in his life; maybe they were things from the nets, which Zeck only knew about because they were damnable webs made of lightning, laid before the feet of foolish souls to snare them and drag them down to hell.

Agnes manipulated the blocks and then had him answer questions about them. Zeck saw at once what the purpose of the text was. So he reached over and took the blocks from her. Then he manipulated them to show each and every example drawn on two dimensions on the paper. Except one. "You can't make this one with these blocks," he said.

She put the blocks away.

The next test was entitled "Worldview Diagnostics: Fundamentalist Christian Edition." Since she covered this title almost instantly, it was obvious Zeck wasn't supposed to know what he was being tested on.

She began with questions about the creation and Adam and Eve.

Zeck interrupted her, quoting Father. "The book of Genesis represents the best job that Moses could do, explaining evolution to people who didn't even know the Earth was round."

"You believe in evolution? Then what about Adam as the first man?"

"The name 'Adam' means 'many,'" said Zeck. "There were many males in that troop of primates, when God chose one of them and touched him with his Spirit and put the soul of a man inside. It was Adam who first had language and named the other primates, the ones that looked like him but were not human because God had not given them human souls. Thus it says, 'And Adam gave names to all cattle, and to the fowl of the air, and to every beast of the field; but for Adam there was not found an help meet for him.' What Moses originally wrote was much simpler: 'Adam named all the beasts that were not in the image of God. None of them could speak to him, so he was utterly alone.'"

"You know what God originally wrote?" asked Agnes.

"You think we're fundamentalists," said Zeck. "But we're not. We're Puritans. We know that God can only teach us what we're prepared to understand. The Bible was written by men and women of earlier times, and it holds only as much as they were capable of understanding. We have a greater knowledge of science, and so God can clarify and tell us more. He would be an unloving Father if he insisted on telling us only as much as humans could understand back in the infancy of our species."

She leaned back in her chair. "So then why does your father call electricity 'lightning'?"

"Aren't they the same thing?" asked Zeck, trying to hide his contempt.

"Well, yes, of course, but—"

"So Father calls it 'lightning' to emphasize how dangerous it is, and how ephemeral," said Zeck. "Your word 'electricity' is a lie, convincing you that because it runs through wires and shifts the on-off state of semi-conductors, the lightning has been tamed and no longer poses a danger. But God says that it is in your machines that lightning is at its most dangerous, for lightning that strikes you out of the sky can only harm your body, while the lightning that has tamed you and trained you through the machines can steal your soul."

"So God speaks to your father," said Agnes.

"As he speaks to all men and women who purify themselves enough to hear his voice."

"Has God ever spoken to you?"

Zeck shook his head. "I'm not yet pure."

"And that's why your father whips you."

"My father is God's instrument in the purification of his children."

"And you trust your father always to do God's will?"

"My father is the purest man on Earth right now."

"Yet you have never trusted him enough to let him know you have a word-for-word memory."

Her words struck him like a blow. She was absolutely right. Zeck had heeded Mother and never let Father see his unnatural ability. And why? Not because Zeck was afraid. Because *Mother* was afraid. He had taken her faithlessness inside himself as if it were his own, and so Father could not purify him. Could never purify him, because he had been deceiving Father for all these years.

He rose to his feet.

"Where are you going?" asked Agnes.

"To Father."

"To tell him about your phenomenal memory?" she asked pleasantly.

Zeck had no reason to tell her anything, and so he didn't.

Bridegan was waiting in the other room, blocking the door. "No sir," he said. "You're going nowhere."

Zeck went back into the kitchen and sat back down at the table. "You're taking me into space, aren't you," he said.

"Yes, Zeck," she said. "You are one of the best we've ever tested."

"I'll go with you. But I'll never fight for you," he said. "Taking me is a waste of time."

"Never is a long time," she said.

"You think that if you take me far enough from Earth, I'll forget about God."

"Not *forget*," she said. "Perhaps you'll transform your understanding."

"Don't you understand how dangerous I am?" said Zeck.

"We're actually counting on that," she said.

"Not dangerous as a soldier," he said. "If I go with you, it will be as a teacher. I'll help the other children in your Battle School see that God does not want them to kill their enemies."

"Oh, we're not worried about you converting the other kids," said Agnes.

"You should be," said Zeck. "The word of God has power unto salvation, and no power on earth or in hell can stand against it."

She shook her head. "I might worry," she said. "*If* you were pure. But you're not. So what power will you have to convert anybody?" She piled up the test booklets and stuffed them in the briefcase with the blocks and the recorder. "I have it on tape," she said loudly, for Bridegan to hear. "He said, 'I'll go with you.'"

Bridegan came into the kitchen. "Welcome to Battle School, soldier."

Zeck did not answer. He was still reeling from what she had said. *How can I convert anyone, when I'm still impure myself?*

"I have to talk to Father," said Zeck.

"Not a chance," said Agnes. "It's the impure Zechariah Morgan that we want. Not the pure one who confessed everything to his father. Besides, we don't have time to wait for another set of lash wounds to heal."

Bridegan laughed harshly. "If that bastard raises his hand against this boy one more time, I'll blast it off."

Zeck whirled on him, filled with rage. "Then what would that make *you*?"

Bridegan only kept on laughing. "It would make me what I've always been—a bloody-minded soldier. My job is defending the helpless against the cruel. That's what we're doing, fighting the formics—and it's what I'd be doing if I took off your Father's hands up to the elbows."

In reply, Zeck recited from the book of Daniel. "A stone was cut out without hands, which smote the image upon his feet that were of iron and clay, and brake them in pieces."

"Without hands. A neat trick," said Bridegan.

"And the stone that smote the image became a great mountain, and filled the whole earth," said Zeck.

"He's got the whole King James version by heart," said Agnes.

"And in the days of these kings," recited Zeck, "shall the God of heaven set up a kingdom, which shall never be destroyed: and the kingdom shall not be left to other people, but it shall break in pieces and consume all these kingdoms, and it shall stand for ever."

"They're going to love him up in Battle School," said Bridegan.

So Zeck spent that Christmas in space, heading up to the station that housed Battle School. He did nothing to cause disturbance, obeyed every order he was given. When his launch group first went into the Battle Room, Zeck learned to fly just like all the others. He even pointed his weapon at targets that were assigned.

It took quite a while before anyone noticed that Zeck never actually hit anybody with his weapon. In every battle, he was zero for zero. Statistically, he was the worst soldier in the history of the school. In vain did the teachers point out that it was just a game.

"Neither shall they learn war anymore," quoted Zeck in return. "I will not offend God by learning war." They could take him into space, they could make him wear the uniform, they could force him into the Battle Room, but they couldn't make him shoot.

It took many months, and they still wouldn't send him home, but at least they left him alone. He belonged to an army, he practiced with them, but on every battle report, he was listed with zero effectiveness. There was no soldier in the school prouder of his record.

* * *

Dink Meeker watched as Ender Wiggin came through the door into Rat Army's barracks. As usual, Rosen was near the entrance, and he immediately launched into his "I Rose de Nose, Jewboy extraordinaire" routine. It was how Rosen wrapped himself in the military reputation of Israel, even though Rosen wasn't Israeli and he also wasn't a particularly good commander.

Not a bad one either. Rat Army *was* in second place in the standings. But how much of that was Rosen, and how much was the fact that Rosen relied so heavily on Dink's toon—which Dink had trained?

Dink was the better commander, and he knew it—he had been offered Rat Army and Rosen only got it when Dink turned down the promotion. Nobody knew that, of course, but Dink and Colonel Graff and whatever other teachers might have known. There was no reason to tell it—it would only weaken Rosen and also make Dink look like a braggart or a fool, depending on whether people believed his claim. So he made no claim.

This was Rosen's show. Let him write the script.

"*That's* the great Ender Wiggin?" asked Flip. His name was short for Filippus, and, like Dink, he was Dutch. He was also very young and had yet to do anything impressive. It had to gall a young kid like Flip that Ender Wiggin had been placed into the Battle Room early and then rose to the very top of the standings almost instantly.

"I told you," said Dink, "he's number one because his commander wouldn't let him shoot his weapon. So when he finally did it—disobeying his commander, I might add—he got this incredible kill ratio. It's a fluke of how they keep the stats."

"Kuso," said Flip. "If Ender's such a big nothing, why did you go out of your way to get him in your toon?"

So somebody had overheard Dink ask Rosen to assign Ender to his toon, and word had spread. "Because I needed somebody smaller than you," said Dink.

"And you've been watching him. I've seen you. Watching him."

It was easy to forget sometimes that every kid in this place was brilliant. Observant. Clear memory and sharp analytical skills. Even the ones who were still too timid to have done much of anything. Not a good place for doing anything surreptitious.

"É," said Dink. "I think he's got something."

"What's he got that I don't got?"

"Command of English grammar," said Dink.

"Everybody talks like that," said Flip.

"Everybody's a sheep," said Dink. "I'm getting out of here." Moments later, Dink pushed past Rosen and Ender and left the room.

He didn't want to talk to Ender right away. Because this genius kid probably remembered the first time they met. In a bathroom, right after Ender was put in Salamander Army's uniform, his first day in the game. Dink had seen how small he was and said something like, "He's so small he could walk between my legs without touching my balls." It didn't mean anything, and one of his friends had immediately said, "Cause you got none, Dink, that's why," so it's not like Dink had scored any points.

But it was a stupid thing to say, which was fine, you could be stupid around new kids. Except it had been Ender Wiggin, and

Dink now knew that this kid was something else, someone important, and he deserved better. Dink wanted to be the guy who knew right away what Ender Wiggin was. Instead, he'd been the idiot who made a stupid joke about how short Ender was.

Short? Ender was small because he was young. It was a mark of brilliance, to be brought to Battle School a year younger than other kids. And then he was advanced to Salamander Army while all the rest of his launch group were still in basic. So he was really under age. And therefore small. So what kind of idiot would mock the kid for being smarter than anybody else?

Oh, suck it up, oomay, he told himself. What does it matter what Wiggin thinks of you? Your job is to train him. To make up for the weeks he wasted in Bonzo Madrid's stupid Salamander Army and help this kid become what he's supposed to become.

Not that Wiggin had really wasted the time. The kid had been running practice sessions for launchies and other rejects during free time, and Dink had come and watched. Wiggin was doing new things. Moves that Dink had never seen before. They had possibilities. So Dink was going to use those techniques in his toon. Give Wiggin a chance to see his ideas played out in combat in the Battle Room.

I'm not Bonzo. I'm not Rosen. Having a soldier under me who's better than I am, smarter, more inventive, doesn't threaten me. I learn from everybody. I help everybody. It's about the only way I can be rebellious in this place—they chose us for our ambition and they prod us to be competitive. So I don't compete. I cooperate.

Dink was sitting in the game room, watching the other players—he had beaten all the games in the room, so he had nothing left to prove—when Wiggin found him. If Wiggin remembered Dink's first dumb joke about his height, Wiggin didn't show it. Instead, Dink let him know which of Rosen's rules and orders he had to obey, and which he didn't. He also let him know that Dink wouldn't be playing power games with him—he was going to get Ender into the battles from the start, pushing him, giving him a chance to learn and grow.

Wiggin clearly understood what Dink was doing for him. He left, satisfied.

There's my contribution to the survival of the human race, thought Dink. I'm not what great commanders are made of. But I know a great commander when I see one, and I can help get him ready. That's good enough for me. I can take this stupid, ineffective school and accomplish something that actually might help us win this war. Something real.

Not this stupid make-believe. Battle School! It was children's games, but structured by adults in order to manipulate the children. But what did it have to do with the real war? You rise to the top of the standings, you beat everybody, and then what? Did you kill a single Bugger? Save a single human life? No. You just go on to the next school and start over as nothing again. Was there any evidence that Battle School accomplished anything?

Sure, the graduates ended up filling important positions throughout the fleet. But then, Battle School only admits kids that are brilliant in the first place, so they would have been command material already. Was there any evidence that Battle School made a *difference*?

I could have been home in Holland. Walking by the North Sea. Watching it pound against the shore, trying to wash over and sweep away the dikes, the islands, and cover the land with ocean, as it used to be, before humans started their foolish terraforming experiment.

Dink remembered reading—back on Earth, when he could read what he wanted—the silly claim that the Great Wall of China was the only human artifact that could be seen from space. In fact the claim wasn't even true—at least not from geosynchronous orbit or higher. The wall didn't even cast enough of a shadow to be seen.

No, the human artifact that could be seen from space, that showed up in picture after picture without exciting any comment at all, was Holland. It should have been nothing but barrier islands with wide saltwater sounds behind them. Instead, because the Dutch built their dikes and pumped out the salt water and purified the soil, it was land. Lush, green land—visible from space.

But nobody recognized it as a human artifact. It was just land. It grew plants and fed dairy cattle and held houses and highways, just like any other land. But we did it. We Dutch. And when the sea levels rose, we raised our dikes higher and made them thicker and stronger, and nobody thought, Wow, look at the Dutch, they created the largest human artifact on Earth, and they're *still making it*, a thousand years later.

I could have been home in Holland until they were actually ready to have me do something real. As real as the land behind the dikes.

Free time was over. Dink went to practice. Then he ate with the rest of Rat Army—complete with the ritual of pretending that all their food was rat food. Dink noticed how Wiggin observed and seemed to enjoy the game—but didn't take part. He stayed aloof, watching.

That's something else we have in common.

Something *else*? Why had he thought of it that way? What was the first thing they had in common, that made it so standing aloof was something else?

Oh, that's right. I almost forgot. We're the smartest kids in the room.

Dink silently laughed at himself with perfect scorn. Right, I'm not competitive. I know I'm not the best—but without even thinking about it, I assume that I'm therefore *second* best. What an eemo.

Dink went to the library and studied a while. He hoped that Petra would come by, but she didn't. Instead of talking to her— the only other kid he knew who shared his contempt for the system—he actually finished his assignments. It was history, so it mattered that he do well.

He got back to the barracks a little early. Maybe he'd sleep. Maybe play some game on his desk. Maybe there'd be somebody in a talkative mood and Dink would have a conversation. No plans. He refused to care.

Flip was there, too. Already getting undressed for bed. But instead of putting his shoes in his locker with the rest of his uniform and his flash suit and the few other possessions a kid could have in Battle School, he had set his shoes down on the floor near the foot of his bed, toes out.

There was something familiar about it.

Flip looked at him and smiled wanly and rolled his eyes. Then he swung up onto his bed and started reading something on his desk, scrolling through what must be homework, because now and then he'd run his finger across some section of the text to highlight it.

The shoes. This was December fifth. It was Sinterklaas Eve. Flip was Dutch, so of course he had set out his shoes.

Tonight, Sinterklaas—Sint Nikolaas, patron saint of children—would come from his home in Spain, with Black Peter carrying his bag of presents, and listen through the chimneys of the houses throughout Holland, checking to see if children were quarreling or disobedient. If the children were good, then they would knock on the door and, when it was opened, fling candy into the house. Children would rush out the door and find presents left in baskets—or in their shoes, left by the front door.

And Flip had set his shoes out on Sinterklaas Eve.

For some reason, Dink found his eyes clouding with tears. This was stupid. Yes, he missed home—missed his father's house near the strand. But Sinterklaas was for little children, not for him. Not for a child in Battle School.

But Battle School is nothing, right? I should be home. And if I were home, I'd be helping to make Sinterklaas Day for the younger children. If there had been any younger children in our house.

Without really deciding to do it, Dink took out his desk and started to write.

> *His shoes will sit and gather moss*
> *Without a gift from Sinterklaas*
> *For when a soldier cannot cross*
> *The battle room without a loss*
> *Then why should Sinterklaas equip*
> *A kid who cannot fly with zip*
> *But crawls instead just like a drip*
> *Of rain on glass, not like a ship*
> *That flies through space: I speak of Flip.*

It wasn't a great poem, of course, but the whole idea of Sinterklaas poems was that they made fun of the recipient of the gift without giving offense. The lamer the poem, the more it made fun of the giver of the gift rather than the target of the rhyme. Flip still got teased about the fact that when he first was assigned to Rat Army, a couple of times he had bad launches from the wall of Battle Room and ended up floating like a feather across the room, a perfect target for the enemy.

Dink would have written the verse in Dutch, but it was a dying language, and Dink didn't know if he spoke it well enough to actually use it for poem writing. Nor was he sure Flip could read a Dutch poem, not if there were any unusual words in it. Netherlands was just too close to Britain. The BBC had made the Dutch bilingual; the European Community had made them mostly anglophone.

The poem was done, but there was no way to extrude printed paper from a desk. Ah well, the night was young. Dink put it in the print queue and got up from bed to wander the corridors, desk tucked under his arm. He'd pick up the poem before the printer room closed, and he'd also search for something that might serve as a gift.

In the end he found no gift, but he did add two lines to the poem:

> *If Piet gives you a gift today,*
> *You'll find it on your breakfast tray.*

It's not as if there were a lot of *things* available to the kids in Battle School. Their only games were in their desks or in the game room; their only sport was in the Battle Room. Desks and uniforms; what else did they need to own?

This bit of paper, thought Dink. That's what he'll have in the morning.

It was dark in the barracks, and most kids were asleep, though a few still worked on their desks, or played some stupid game. Didn't they know the teachers did psychological analysis on them based on the games they played? Maybe they just didn't care. Dink sometimes didn't care either, and played. But not tonight. Tonight he was seriously pissed off. And he didn't even know why.

Yes, he did. Flip was getting something from Sinterklaas—and Dink wasn't. He should have. Dad would have made sure he got something from Black Piet's bag. Dink would have hunted all over the house for it on Sinterklaas morning until he finally found it in some perverse hiding place.

I'm homesick. That's all. Isn't that what the stupid counselor told him? You're homesick—get over it. The other kids do, said the counselor.

But they don't, thought Dink. They just hide it. From each other, from themselves.

The remarkable thing about Flip was that tonight he didn't hide it.

Flip was already asleep. Dink folded the paper and slipped it into one of the shoes.

Stupid greedy kid. Leaving out both shoes.

But of course that wasn't it at all. If he had left only one shoe, that would have been proof positive of what he was doing. Someone might have guessed and then Flip would have been mocked mercilessly for being so homesick and childish. So ... both shoes. Deniability. Not Sinterklaas Day at all—I just left my shoes by the side of my bed.

Dink crawled into his own bed and lay there for a little while, filled with a deep and unaccountable sadness. It wasn't home-sickness, not really. It was the fact that Dink was no longer the child; now he was the one who helped Sinterklaas do his job. Of course the old saint couldn't get from Spain to Battle School, not in the ship *he* used. Somebody had to help him out.

Dink was being, not the child, but the dad. He would never be the child again.

*　*　*

Zeck saw the shoes. He saw Dink put something into the shoe in the darkness, when most kids were asleep. But it meant nothing to him, except that these two Dutch boys were doing something weird.

Zeck wasn't in Dink's toon. He wasn't really in *any* toon. Because nobody wanted him, and it wouldn't matter if they had. Zeck didn't play.

Which made it all the more remarkable that Rat Army was in second place—they won their battles with one less active soldier than anybody else.

At first Rosen had threatened him and tried to take away privileges—even meals—but Zeck simply ignored him. Ignored other kids who shoved him and jostled him in the corridors. What did he care? Their physical brutality to him, mild as it might be, showed what kind of people they were, the impurity of their souls, because they rejoiced in violence.

Genesis, chapter six, verse thirteen: And God said unto Noah, The end of all flesh is come before me; for the earth is filled with violence through them; and, behold, I will destroy them with the earth.

Didn't they understand that it was the violence of the human race that had caused God to send the Buggers to attack the Earth? This became obvious to Zeck as he was forced to watch the vids of the Scouring of China. What could the Buggers represent, except the destroying angel? A flood the first time, and now fire, just as was prophesied.

So the proper response was to forswear violence and become peaceful, rejecting war. Instead, they sacrificed their children to the idolatrous god of war, taking them from their families and thrusting them up here into the hot metal arms of Moloch, where they would be trained to give themselves over entirely to violence.

Jostle me all you want. It will purify me and make you filthier.

Now, though, nobody bothered with Zeck. He was ignored. Not pointedly—if he asked a question, people answered. Scornfully, perhaps, but what was that to Zeck? Scorn was merely pity mingled with hate, and hate was pride mixed with fear. They feared him because he was different, and so they hated him, and so their pity—the touch of godliness that remained in them—was turned to scorn. A virtue made filthy by pride.

In the morning he had forgotten all about Flip's shoes and the paper that Dink had put into one of them the night before.

But then he saw Dink step out of the food line with a full tray, and walk back to hand the tray to Flip.

Flip smiled, then laughed and rolled his eyes.

Zeck remembered the shoes then. He walked over and looked at the tray.

It was pancakes this morning, and on the top pancake, everything had been cut away except a big letter *F*. Apparently, this had some significance to the two Dutch boys that completely escaped Zeck. But then, a lot of things escaped him. His father had kept him sheltered from the world, and so he did not know many of the things most of the other children knew. He was proud of his ignorance. It was a mark of his purity.

This time, though, there was something about this that seemed wrong to him. As if the letter *F* in the pancake was some kind of conspiracy. What did it stand for? A bad word in Common? That was too easy, and besides, they weren't laughing like that—it wasn't wicked laughter. It was ... sad laughter.

Sad laughter. It was hard to make sense of it, but Zeck knew that he was right. The *F* was funny, but it also made them sad.

He asked one of the other boys. "What's with the *F* Dink carved into Flip's pancake?"

The other kid shrugged. "They're Dutch," he said, as if that accounted for any weirdness about them.

Zeck took that solitary clue—which he had already know, of course—and took it to his desk immediately after breakfast. He searched first for "Netherlands F." Nothing that made sense. Then a few more combinations, but it was "Dutch shoes" that brought him to Sinterklaas Day, December sixth, and all the customs associated with it.

He didn't go to class. He went to Flip's tidily made bed and unmade it till he found, under the sheet and next to the mattress, Dink's poem.

Zeck memorized it, put it back, and remade the bed—for it would be wrong to put Flip at risk of getting a demerit that he did not deserve. Then he went to Colonel Graff's office.

"I don't remember sending for you," said Colonel Graff.

"You didn't," said Zeck.

"If you have a problem, take it to your counselor. Who's assigned to you?" But Zeck knew at once that it wasn't that Graff couldn't remember the counselor's name—he simply had no idea who Zeck was.

"I'm Zeck Morgan," he said. "I'm a spectator in Rat Army."

"Oh," said Graff, nodding. "You. Have you reconsidered your vow of nonviolence?"

"No sir," said Zeck. "I'm here to ask you a question."

"And you couldn't have asked somebody else?"

"Everybody else was busy," said Zeck. Immediately he repented of the remark, because of course he hadn't even tried anybody else, and he only said this in order to hurt Graff's feelings by implying he was useless and had no work to do. "That was wrong of me to say that," said Zeck, "and I ask your forgiveness."

"What's your question," said Graff impatiently, looking away.

"When you informed me that nonviolence was not an option here, you said it was because my motive is religious, and there is no religion in Battle School."

"No open observance of religion," said Graff. "Or we'd have classes constantly being interrupted by Muslims praying and every seventh day—not the *same* seventh day, mind you—we'd have Christians and Muslims and Jews celebrating one Sabbath or another. Not to mention the Macumba ritual of sacrificing chickens. Icons and statues of saints and little Buddhas and ancestral shrines and all kinds of other things would clutter up the place. So it's all banned. Period. So please get to class before I have to give you a demerit."

"That was not my question," said Zeck. "I would not have come here to ask you a question whose answer you had already told me."

"Then why did you bring up—never mind, what's your question."

"If religious observance is banned, then why does Battle School tolerate the commemoration of the day of Saint Nicholas?"

"We don't," said Graff.

"And yet you did," said Zeck.

"No we didn't."

"It was commemorated."

"Would you please get to the point? Are you lodging a complaint? Did one of the teachers make some remark?"

"Filippus Rietveld put out his shoes for St. Nicholas. Dink Meeker put a Sinterklaas poem in the shoe and then gave Flip a pancake carved with the initial *F*. An edible initial is a traditional treat on Sinterklaas Day. Which is today, December sixth."

Graff sat down and leaned back in his chair. "A Sinterklaas poem?"

Zeck recited it.

Graff smiled and chuckled a little.

"So you think it's funny when they have *their* religious observance, but *my* religious observance is banned."

"It was a poem in a shoe. I give you permission to write all the poems you want and insert them into people's wearing apparel."

"Poems in shoes are not my religious observance. Mine is to contribute a small part to peace on Earth."

"You're not even *on* Earth."

"I would be, if I hadn't been kidnapped and enslaved to the service of Mammon," said Zeck mildly.

You've been here almost a year, thought Graff, and you're still singing the same tune. Doesn't peer pressure have *any* effect on you?

"If these Dutch Christians have their St. Nicholas Day, then the Muslims should have Ramadan and the Jews should have the Feast of Tabernacles and I should be able to live the gospel of love and peace."

"Why are you even bothering with this?" said Graff. "The only thing I can do is punish them for a rather sweet gesture. It will make people hate you more."

"You mean you intend to tell them who reported them?"

"No, Zeck. I know how you operate. You'll tell them yourself, so they'll be angry and people will persecute you and that will make you feel more purified."

For a man who didn't recognize him when he came in, Graff certainly knew a lot about him. His face wasn't known, but his ideas were. Zeck's persistence in his faith *was* making an impression.

"If Battle School bans my religion because it forbids all religion, then all religion should *be* forbidden, sir."

"I know that," said Graff. "I also know you're an insufferable twit."

"I believe that remark falls under the topic of 'The commander's responsibility to build morale,' is that correct, sir?" asked Zeck.

"And that remark falls under the category of 'You won't get out of Battle School by being a smartass,'" said Graff.

"Better a smartass than an insufferable twit, sir," said Zeck.

"Get out of my office."

*   *   *

An hour later, Flip and Dink had been called in and reprimanded and the poem confiscated.

"Aren't you going to take his shoes, sir?" asked Dink. "And I'm sure we can recover his initial when he shits it out. I'll reshape it for you so there's no mistaking it, sir."

Graff said nothing, except to send them back to class. He knew that word of this would circulate throughout Battle School. But if he hadn't done it, then Zeck would have made sure that word of how this "religious observance" had been tolerated would spread, and then there really would be a nightmare of kids demanding their holidays.

It was inevitable. The two recusants, Zeck and Dink, both of whom refused to cooperate with the program here, were bound to become allies. Not that they knew they were allied. But in fact they were—they were deliberately stressing the system in order to try to make it collapse.

Well, I won't let you, dear genius children. Because nobody gives a rat's ass about Sinterklaas Day, or about Christian nonviolence. When you go to war—which is where you've gone, believe it or not, Dink and Zeck—then childish things are put away. In the face of a threat to the survival of the species, all these planetside trivialities are put aside until the crisis passes.

And it has not passed, whatever you little twits might think about it.

*   *   *

Dink left Graff's office seething. "If they can't see the difference between praying eight times a day and putting a poem in a shoe once a year ..."

"It was a great poem," said Flip.

"It was dumb," said Dink.

"Wasn't that the point? It was a *great* dumb poem. I just feel bad I didn't write one for you."

"I didn't put out my shoes."

Flip sighed. "I'm sorry I did that. I was just feeling homesick. I didn't think anybody would do anything about it."

"Sorry."

"We're both so very, very sorry," said Flip. "Except that we're not sorry at all."

"No, we're not," said Dink.

"In fact, it's kind of fun to get in trouble for keeping Sinterklaas Day. Imagine what would happen if we celebrated Christmas."

"Well," said Dink, "we've still got nineteen days."

"Right," said Flip.

By the time they got back to Rat Army barracks, it was obvious that the story was already known. Everybody fell silent when Dink and Flip stood in the doorway.

"Stupid," said Rosen.

"Thanks," said Dink. "That means so much, coming from you."

"Since when did you get religion?" Rosen demanded. "Why make some kind of holy war out of it?"

"It wasn't religious," said Dink. "It was *Dutch.*"

"Well, eemo, you be Rat Army now, not Dutch."

"In three months I won't be in Rat Army," said Dink. "But I'll be Dutch until I die."

"Nations don't matter up here," said one of the other boys.

"Religions neither," said another.

"Well it's obvious religion *does* matter," said Flip, "or we wouldn't have been called in and reprimanded for cutting a pancake into an *F* and writing a funny poem and sticking it in a shoe."

Dink looked down the long corridor, which curved upward toward the end. Zeck, who slept at the very back of the barracks, couldn't even be seen from the door.

"He's not here," said Rosen.

"Who?"

"Zeck," said Rosen. "He came in and told us what he'd done, and then he left."

"Anybody know where he goes when he takes off by himself?" asked Dink.

"Why?" said Rosen. "You planning to slap him around a little? I can't allow that."

"I want to talk to him," said Dink.

"Oh, *talk*," said Rosen.

"When I say talk, I mean talk," said Dink.

"I *don't* want to talk to him," said Flip. "Stupid prig."

"He just wants to get out of Battle School," said Dink.

"If we put it to a vote," said one of the other boys, "he'd be gone in a second. What a waste of space."

"A vote," said Flip. "What a military idea."

"Go stick your finger in a dike," the boy answered.

"So now we're anti-Dutch," said Dink.

"They can't help it if they still believe in Santa Claus," said an American kid.

"Sinterklaas," said Dink. "Lives in Spain, not the North Pole. Has a friend who carries his bag—Black Piet."

"Friend?" said a kid from South Africa. "Black Piet sounds like a slave to me."

Rosen sighed. "It's a relief when Christians are fighting each other instead of slaughtering Jews."

That was when Ender Wiggin joined the discussion for the first time. "Isn't this exactly what the rules are supposed to prevent? People sniping at each other because of religion or nationality?"

"And yet we're doing it anyway," said the American kid.

"Aren't we up here to save the human race?" said Dink. "Humans have religions and nationalities. And customs. Why can't we be humans too?"

Wiggin didn't answer.

"Makes no sense for us to live like Buggers," said Dink. "*They* don't celebrate Sinterklaas Day, either."

"Part of being human," said Wiggin, "is to massacre each other from time to time. So maybe till we beat the Formics we should try *not* to be so very very human."

"And maybe," said Dink, "soldiers fight for what they care about, and what they care about is their families and their traditions and their faith and their nation—the very stuff they don't allow us to have here."

"Maybe we fight so we can get back home and find all that stuff still there, waiting for us," said Wiggin.

"Maybe none of us are fighting at all," said Flip. "It's not like anything we do here is real."

"I'll tell you what's real," said Dink. "I was Sinterklaas's helper last night." Then he grinned.

"So you're finally admitting you're an elf," said the American kid, grinning back.

"How many Dutch kids are there in Battle School?" said Dink. "Sinterklaas is definitely a minority cultural icon, right? Nothing like Santa Claus, right?"

Rosen kicked Dink lightly on the shin. "What do you think you're doing, Dink?"

"Santa Claus isn't a religious figure, either. Nobody prays to Santa Claus. It's an *American* thing."

"Canadian too," said another kid.

"Anglophone Canadian," said another. "Papa Noel for some of us."

"Father Christmas," said a Brit.

"See? Not Christian, *national*," said Dink. "It's one thing to stifle religious expression. But to try to erase nationality—the whole fleet is thick with national loyalties. They don't make Dutch *admirals* pretend not to be Dutch. They wouldn't stand for it."

"There aren't any Dutch admirals," said the Brit.

It wasn't that Dink let idiotic comments like this make him *angry*. He didn't want to hit anybody. He didn't want to raise his voice. But still, there was this deep defiance that could not be ignored. He had to do something that other people wouldn't like. Even though he knew it would cause trouble and accomplish nothing at all, he was going to do it, and it was going to start right now.

"They were able to stifle our Dutch holiday because there are so few of us," said Dink. "But it's time for us to insist on expressing our national cultures like any other soldiers in the International Fleet. Christmas is a holy day for Christians, but Santa Claus is a secular figure. Nobody prays to Saint Nicholas."

"Little kids do," said the American, but he was laughing.

"Santa Claus, Father Christmas, Papa Noel, Sinterklaas, they may have begun with a Christian feast day, but they're national now, and people with no religion at all still celebrate the holiday. It's the day of gift-giving, right? December 25th, whether you're a believing Christian or not. They can keep us from being religious, but they can't stop us from giving gifts on Santa Claus day."

Some of them were laughing. Some were thinking.

"You're going to get in such deep doodoo," said one.

"É," said Dink. "But then, that's where I live all the time anyway."

"Don't even try it."

Dink looked up to see who had spoken so angrily.

Zeck.

"I think we already know where you stand," said Dink.

"In the name of Christ I forbid you to bring Satan into this place."

All the smiles disappeared. Everyone fell silent.

"You know, don't you, Zeck," said Dink, "that you just guaranteed that I'll have support for my little Santa Claus movement."

Zeck seemed genuinely frightened. But not of Dink. "Don't bring this curse down on your own heads."

"I don't believe in curses, I only believe in blessings," said Dink. "And I sure as hell don't believe I'll be cursed because I give presents to people in the name of Santa Claus."

Zeck glanced around and seemed to be trying to calm himself. "Religious observances are forbidden for everybody."

"And yet *you* observe your religion all the time," said Dink. "Every time you don't fire your weapon in the Battle Room, you're doing it. So if you oppose our little Santa Claus revolution, eemo, then we want to see you firing that gun and taking people out. Otherwise you're a flaming hypocrite. A fraud. A pious fake. A liar." Dink was in his face now. Close enough to make some of the other kids uncomfortable.

"Back off, Dink," one of them muttered. Who? Wiggin, of course. Great, a peacemaker. Again, Dink felt defiance swell up inside him.

"What are you going to do?" said Zeck softly. "Hit me? I'm three years younger than you."

"No," said Dink. "I'm going to bless you."

He set his hand in the air just over Zeck's head. As Dink expected, Zeck stood there without flinching. That was what Zeck was best at: taking it whatever anybody dished out without even trying to get away.

"I bless you with the spirit of Santa Claus," said Dink. "I bless you with compassion and generosity. With the irresistible impulse to make other people happy. And you know what else? I bless you with the humility to realize that you aren't any better than the rest of us in the eyes of God."

"You know nothing about God," said Zeck.

"I know more than you do," said Dink. "Because I'm not filled with hate."

"Neither am I," said Zeck.

"No," murmured another boy. "You're filled with kuso."

"Toguro," said another, laughing.

"I bless you," said Dink, "with love. Believe me, Zeck, it'll be such a shock to you, when you finally feel it, that it might just kill you. Then you can go talk to God yourself and find out where you screwed up."

Dink turned around and faced the bulk of Rat Army. "I don't know about you, but I'm playing Santa Claus this year. We don't own anything up here, so gift giving isn't exactly easy. Can't get on the nets and order stuff to be shipped up here, all gift-wrapped. But gifts don't have to be toys and stuff. What I gave Flip here, the gift that got us in so much trouble, was a poem."

"Oh how sweet," said the Brit. "A love poem?"

In answer, Flip recited it. Blushing, of course, because the joke was on him. But also loving it—because the joke was on *him*.

Dink could see that a lot of them thought it was cool to have a toon leader write a satirical poem about one of his soldiers. It really *was* a gift.

"And just to prove that we aren't celebrating actual Christmas," said Dink, "let's just give each other whatever gifts we think of on any day at all in December. It can be Hanukkah. It can be … hell, it can be Sinterklaas Day, can't it? The day is still young."

"If Dink would give us all a gift," intoned the Jamaican kid, "that would give our hearts a lift."

"Oh how sweet," said the Brit.

"Crazy Tom thinks everything's sweet," said the Canadian, "except for Tom's own mold-covered feet."

Most of them laughed.

"Was that supposed to be a *present*?" said Crazy Tom. "Father Christmas is doing a substandard job this year."

"It would be pleasant to get a present," said Wiggin. Everybody laughed a little. Wiggin went on. "It would be better to get a letter."

Only a few people chuckled at that. Then they were all quiet.

"That's the only gift *I* want," said Wiggin softly. "A letter from home. If you can give me that, I'm with you."

"I can't," said Dink, now just as serious as Wiggin. "They've cut us off from everything. The best I can do is this: At home you know your family's doing Santa stuff. Hanging up stockings, right? You're American, right?"

Wiggin nodded.

"Hang up your stocking this year, Wiggin, and you'll get something in it."

"Coal," said Crazy Tom, the Brit.

"I don't know what it is yet," said Dink, "but it'll be there."

"It won't really be from them," said Wiggin.

"No, it won't," said Dink. "It'll be from Santa Claus." He grinned.

Wiggin shook his head. "Don't do it, Dink," he said. "It's not worth the trouble it'll cause."

"What trouble? It'll build morale."

"We're here to study war," said Wiggin.

Zeck whispered: "Study war no more."

"Are you still here, Zeck?" said Dink, then pointedly turned his back on him. "We're here to build an army, Wiggin. A group of men who work together as one. Not a bunch of kids hammered down by teachers who think they can erase ten thousand years of human history and culture by making a rule."

Wiggin looked away and said, sadly, "Do what you want, Dink."

"I always do," answered Dink.

"The only gift that God respects," said Zeck, "is a broken heart and a contrite spirit."

A lot of kids groaned at that, but Dink gave Zeck one last look. "And when were you ever contrite?"

"Contrition," said Zeck, "is a gift I give to God, not to you." Only then did Zeck walk away, back toward his bed, where he'd be hidden behind the curvature of the barracks room.

* * *

Rat Army was only a small percentage of the population of Battle School, but word spread quickly. The other armies began picking it up as a joke. Someone would pick up some scrap of leftover food and drop it on someone else's meal tray, saying, "There you are, from Santa with love." And everybody at the table would laugh.

But even as a joke, it was a gift, wasn't it? Santa Claus was giving gifts all over Battle School within days.

It was more than just gifts. It was stockings. Nobody could say who started it, but after a while it seemed that the giving of every gift was accompanied by a stocking. Rolled up, hidden inside something else, but always a stocking. Nobody hung the stocking up in hopes of getting it filled, of course. It was the other way around—the stockings were being given as part of the gift.

And the recipient of the stocking found a way to wear it, whether it fit or not. Dangling from a sleeve. On a foot, but not matched with the other sock. Inside a flash suit. Sticking out of a pocket. Just for a day, the sock was worn, and then it was given back. It was the stocking more than the words now that said, *This is from Santa Claus.*

The stockings were needed, because what were the gifts? A few were poems, written on paper. Some of them were food scraps. As the days passed, however, more and more of the gifts took the form of favors. Tutoring. Extra practice time in the Battle Room. A bed that was already made when somebody came back from the showers. Showing somebody how to get to a hidden level in one of the video games.

Even when it wasn't a tangible gift, there was the stocking to make it real.

Father was right, thought Zeck. The parents of these children put the lie of Santa in their hearts, and now it bears fruits. Liars, all of them, giving gifts as homage to the Father of Lies. Zeck could hear his father's voice in his memory: "He will answer their prayers with the ashes of sin in their mouths, with the poison of atheism and unbelief in the plasma of their blood." These children were not believers—not in Christ, and not in Santa Claus. They knew they served a lie. If only they could see that when you do charity in the name of Satan it turns to sin. The devil cannot do good.

Zeck tried to go see Colonel Graff, but he was stopped by a Marine in the corridor. "Do you have an appointment with the commandant of Battle School?"

"No, sir," said Zeck.

"Then whatever you have to say, say it to your counselor. Or one of the teachers."

The teachers were no help. Few of them would talk to him anymore. They'd say, "Is this about algebra? No? Then tell it to somebody else, Zeck." The words of Christ had long since worn out their welcome in this place.

The counselor did listen—or at least sat in a room with him while he talked. But it came to nothing.

"So what you're telling me is that the other students are being kind to each other, and you want it stopped."

"They're doing it in the name of Santa Claus."

"What, exactly, has anyone done to you—in the name of Santa Claus?"

"Nothing to me, personally, but—"

"So you're complaining because they're being kind to other people and *not* to you?"

"Because it's in the name of—"

"Santa Claus, I see. Do you believe in Santa Claus, Zeck?"

"What do you mean?"

"Believe in Santa Claus. Do you think there's really a jolly fat guy in a red suit who brings gifts?"

"No."

"So Santa Claus isn't part of your religion."

"That's exactly my point. It's part of *their* religion."

"I've asked. They say it isn't religion at all. That Santa Claus is merely a cultural figure shared by many of the cultures of Earth."

"It's part of Christmas," insisted Zeck.

"And you don't believe in Christmas."

"Not the way most people celebrate it, no."

"What do you believe in?"

"I believe Jesus Christ was born, probably not in December at all anyway, and he grew up to be the Savior of the world."

"No Santa Claus."

"No."

"So Santa Claus *isn't* part of Christmas."

"Of course he's part of Christmas," said Zeck. "For most people."

"Just not for you."

Zeck nodded.

"All right, I'll talk about this to my superiors," said the counselor. "Do you want to know what I think? I think they're going to tell me it's just a fad, and they're going to let it run itself out."

"In other words, they're going to let them keep doing it as long as they want."

"They're children, Zeck. Not many of them are as tenacious as you. They'll lose interest in it and it will go away. Have patience. Patience isn't against your religion, is it?"

"I refuse to take offense at your sarcasm."

"I wasn't being sarcastic."

"I can see that you also are a true son to the Father of Lies." And Zeck got up and left.

"I'm glad you didn't take offense," the counselor called after him.

There would be no recourse to authority, obviously. Not directly, anyway.

Instead, Zeck went to several of the Arab students, pointing out that the authorities were allowing a Christian custom to be openly practiced. From the first few, he heard the standard litany: "Islam has renounced rivalry between religions. What they do is their business."

But Zeck was finally able to get a rise out of a Pakistani kid in Bee Army. Not that Ahmed said anything positive. In fact, he looked completely uninterested, even hostile. Yet Zeck knew that he had struck a nerve. "They say Santa Claus isn't religious. He's national. But in your country, is there any difference? Is Muhammed—"

Ahmed held up one hand and looked away. "It is not for you to say the prophet's name."

"I'm not comparing him to Santa Claus, of course," said Zeck. Though in fact Zeck had heard his father call Muhammed "Satan's imitation of a prophet," which would make Santa and Muhammed pretty well parallel.

"You have said enough," said Ahmed. "I'm done with you."

Zeck knew that Ahmed had gotten along well enough in Battle School. Their home countries were powerless to insist on religious privileges, so the children in Battle School had been granted exemptions from the obligations of Muslims to pray. But what would he do now that the Christians were getting their Santa Claus? Pakistan had been formed as a Muslim country. There was no distinction between what was national and what was Muslim.

It apparently took Ahmed two days to organize things, especially because it was impossible to ascertain at any given time which earthside time zone they were in—or directly above—and therefore what times they should pray. They couldn't even find out what time it was in Mecca and use that schedule.

So Ahmed and other Muslim students apparently worked it out so that they would pray during times when they were not in class, and would continue to use the exemption for those students who were in an actual battle at a prayer time.

The result was a demonstration of piety at breakfast. At first it seemed only a half-dozen Muslims were involved, the students prostrating themselves and facing—not Mecca, which would have been impossible—but to portside, which faced the sun.

But once the praying began, other Muslim students took note and at first a few, then more and more, joined in the praying. Zeck sat at the table, eating without conversation with his supposed comrades in Rat Army. He pretended not to notice or care, but he was delighted. Because Dink grasped the meaning almost at once. The prayer was a Muslim response to Dink's Santa Claus campaign. There was no way the commandant could ignore this.

"So maybe it's a good thing," Dink murmured to Flip, who was sitting next to him.

Zeck knew it was not a good thing. Muslims had renounced terrorism many years ago, after the disastrous Sunni-Shiite war, and had even reconciled with Israel and made common economic cause. But everyone knew how much resentment still seethed within the Muslim world, with many Muslims believing they were treated unfairly by the Hegemony. Everyone knew of the imams and ayatollahs who claimed, loudly, that what was needed was not a secular Hegemony, but a Caliph to unify the world in worship of God. "When we live by Sharia, God will protect us from these monsters. When God sends a warning, we are wise to listen. Instead, we do the opposite, and God will not protect us when we are in rebellion against him."

It was language Zeck understood. Apart from their religious delusions, they had the courage of their faith. They were not afraid to speak up. And they had numbers enough to force people to listen to them. They would be heard by those who had long since stopped even pretending to listen to Zeck.

The next prayer time was at the end of lunch. The Muslims had spread the word, and all those who intended to pray lingered in the mess hall. Zeck had already heard that the same thing happened in the commanders' mess at breakfast, but now most of the Muslim commanders had come into the main mess hall to join their soldiers in prayer.

Colonel Graff came into the mess hall just before the announced time of prayer.

"Religious observance in Battle School is forbidden," he said loudly. "Muslims have been granted an exemption from the requirement of daily prayers. So any Muslim student who insists on a public display of religious rituals will be disciplined, and any commanders or toon leaders who take part will immediately and permanently lose their rank."

Graff had already turned to leave when Ahmed called out, "What about Santa Claus?"

"As far as I know," said Graff, "there is no religious ritual associated with Santa Claus, and Santa Claus has not been sighted here in Battle School."

"Double standard!" shouted Ahmed, and several others echoed him.

Graff ignored him and left the mess hall.

The door had not closed when two dozen Marines came through the door and stationed themselves around the room.

When the time for prayer came, Ahmed and several others immediately prostrated themselves. Marines came to them, forced them to their feet, and handcuffed them. The Marine lieutenant looked around the room. "Anyone else?"

One more soldier lay down to pray; he was also handcuffed. No one else defied them. Five Muslims were taken from the room. Not roughly, but not all that gently, either.

Zeck turned his attention back to his food.

"This makes you happy, doesn't it?" whispered Dink.

Zeck turned a blank face toward him.

"You did this," said Dink softly.

"I'm a Christian. I don't tell Muslims when to pray." Zeck regretted speaking as soon as he finished. He should have remained silent.

"You're not a good liar, Zeck," said Dink. And now he was talking loud enough that the rest of the table could hear. "Don't get me wrong, I think it's one of your best points—you're used to telling the truth, so you never learned the skill of telling lies."

"I don't lie," said Zeck.

"Your words were literally true, I'm sure. Our Muslim friends did not consult you on the timetable. But as an answer to my accusation that you did this, it was such a pathetically obvious lie.

A dodge. If you really had nothing to do with it, you wouldn't have needed a dodge. You answered like someone with something to hide."

This time Zeck said nothing.

"You think this will help your chances of getting out of Battle School. Maybe you even think it will disrupt Battle School and hurt the war effort—which makes you a traitor, from one point of view, or a hero of Christianity, from another. But you won't stop this war, and you won't hurt Battle School in the long run. You want to know what you really accomplished? Someday this war will end. If we win, then we'll all go home. The kids in this school are the brightest military minds of our generation. They'll be running things in country after country. Ahmed—someday he'll *be* Pakistan. And you just guaranteed that he will hate the idea of trying to live with non-Muslims in peace. In other words, you just started a war thirty or forty years from now."

"Or ten," said Wiggin.

"Ahmed will still be pretty young in ten years," said Flip, chuckling a little.

Zeck hadn't thought of what this might lead to back on Earth. But what did Dink know? He couldn't predict the future. "I didn't start promoting Santa Claus," said Zeck, meeting Dink's gaze.

"No, you just reported a little private joke between two Dutch kids and made a big deal out of it," said Dink.

"You made a big deal out of it," said Zeck. "You made it into a cause. You."

Zeck waited.

Dink sighed. "É. I did." He got up from the table.

So did everyone else.

Zeck started to get up too.

Two hands on his shoulders pushed him back down. Hands from two different kids from Rat Army. They weren't rough. They were just firm. *Stay here for a while. You're not one of us. Don't come with us.*

* * *

The Santa Claus thing was over. Dink didn't imagine that he controlled it any more—it had grown way past him now. But when the Muslim kids were arrested in the mess hall, it stopped being a game. It stopped being just a way to tweak the nose of authority. There were real consequences, and as Zeck had pointed out, they were more Dink's fault than anyone else's.

So Dink asked all his friends to ask everybody they knew to stop doing the stocking thing. To stop giving gifts that had anything to do with Santa Claus.

And, within a day, it stopped.

He thought that would be the end of it.

But it wasn't the end. Because of Zeck.

Nothing Zeck did, of course. Zeck was Zeck, completely unchanged. Zeck didn't do anything in practice except fly around, and he didn't do anything in battle except take up space. But he went to class, he did his schoolwork, he turned in his assignments.

And everybody ignored him. They always had. But not like this.

Before, they had ignored him in a kind of tolerant, almost grudgingly respectful way: He's an idiot, but at least he's consistent.

Now they ignored him in a pointed way. They didn't even bother teasing him or jostling him. He just didn't exist. If he tried to speak to anybody, they turned away. Dink saw it, and it made him feel bad. But Zeck had brought it on himself. It's one thing to be an outsider because you're different. It's another thing to get other people in trouble for your own selfish reasons. And that's what Zeck had done. He didn't care about the no-religion rule— he violated it all the time himself. He just used Dink's Sinterklaas present to Flip as a means of making a lame point with the commandant.

So I was childish too, thought Dink. I knew when to stop. He didn't.

Not my fault.

And yet Dink couldn't stop observing him. Just glances. Just ... noticing. He had read a little bit about primate behavior, as part of the theory of group loyalties. He knew how chimps and baboons that were shut out of their troop behaved, what happened to them. Depression. Self-destruction. Before, Zeck had seemed to thrive on isolation. Now that the isolation was complete, he wasn't thriving anymore.

He looked drawn. He would start walking in some direction and then just stop. Then go again, but slowly. He didn't eat much. Things weren't going well for him.

And if there was one thing Dink knew, it was that the counselors and teachers weren't worth a bucket of hog snot when it came to actually helping a kid with real problems. They had their agenda—what they wanted to make each kid do. But if it was clear the kid wouldn't do it, then they lost interest. The way they had lost interest in Dink. Even if Zeck asked for help, they wouldn't give it. And Zeck wouldn't ask.

Despite knowing how futile it was, Dink tried anyway. He went to Graff and tried to explain what was happening to Zeck.

"Interesting theory," said Graff. "He's being shunned, you think."

"I *know*."

"But not by you?"

"I've tried to talk to him a couple of times, he shuts me out."

"So he's shunning *you*."

"But everybody *else* is shunning him."

"Dink," said Graff, "ego te absolvo."

"Whatever you might think," said Dink, "that wasn't Dutch."

"It was Latin. From the Catholic confessional. I absolve you of your sin."

"I'm not Catholic."

"I'm not a priest."

"You don't have the power to absolve anybody from anything."

"But it was worth a try. Go back to your barracks, Dink. Zeck is not your problem."

"Why don't you just send him back home?" asked Dink. "He's never going to be anything in this army. He's a Christian, not a soldier. Why can't you let him go home and be a Christian?"

Graff leaned back in his chair.

"OK, I know what you're going to say," said Dink.

"You do?"

"The same thing everybody always says. If I let *him* do it, then I have to let everybody else do it."

"Really?"

"If Zeck's noncompliance or whatever it is gets him sent home, then pretty soon you'll have a lot more kids being noncompliant. So they can go home, too."

"Would you be one of those?" asked Graff.

"I think your school is a waste of time," said Dink. "But I believe in the war. I'm not a pacifist, I'm just anti-incompetence."

"But you see, I wasn't going to make that argument," said Graff. "Because I already know the answer. If the only way a kid can go home is acting like Zeck and being treated like Zeck, there's not a kid in this school who'd do it."

"You don't know that."

"But I *do*," said Graff. "Remember, you were all tested and observed. Not just for logic, memory, spatial relationships, verbal ability, but also character attributes. Quick decision-making. Ability to grasp the whole of a situation. The ability to get along well with other people."

"So how the hell did Zeck get here in the first place?"

"Zeck is brilliant at getting along with people," said Graff. "When he wants to."

Dink didn't believe it.

"Zeck can handle even megalomaniacal sociopaths and keep them from harming other people. He's a natural peacemaker in a human community, Dink. It's his best gift."

"That's just kuso," said Dink. "Everybody hated him right from the start."

"Because he wanted you to. He's getting exactly what he wants, right now. Including you coming here to talk to me. All exactly what he wants."

"I don't think so," said Dink.

"That's because you don't know the thing that I was debating with myself about telling you."

"So tell me."

"No," said Graff. "The side arguing for discretion won, and I won't tell."

Dink ignored the obfuscation. Graff wanted him to beg. Instead, Dink thought about what Graff had said about Zeck's abilities. Had Zeck somehow been playing him? Him and everybody else?

"Why?" asked Dink. "Why would he deliberately alienate everybody?"

"Because nobody hated him enough," said Graff. "He needed to be so hated that we gave up on him and sent him home."

"I think you give him credit for more plans than he actually has," said Dink. "He didn't know what would happen."

"I didn't say his plan was conscious. He just wants to go home. He believes he *has* to go home."

"Why?"

"I can't tell you."

"Why not?"

"Because I can't trust you."

"If I say I won't repeat a story, I won't repeat it."

"Oh, I know you can be discreet. I just don't think I can trust you to do the job that needs doing."

"And what job is that?"

"Healing Zeck Morgan."

"I tried. He won't let me near him."

"I know," said Graff. "So the thing you want to know, I'm going to tell to someone else. Someone who is also discreet. Someone who *can* heal him."

Dink thought about that for a few moments.

"Ender Wiggin."

"That's your nominee?" asked Graff.

"No," said Dink. "He's yours. You think he can do anything."

Graff smiled a little Mona Lisa smile, if Mona Lisa had been a pudgy colonel.

"I hope he can," said Dink. "Should I send him to you?"

"I'll bet you," said Graff, "that Ender never needs to come to me at all."

"He'll just know what to do without being told."

"He'll act like Ender Wiggin, and in the process he'll find out what he needs to know from Zeck himself."

"Wiggin doesn't talk to Zeck either."

"You mean that you haven't *seen* him talk to Zeck."

Dink nodded. "OK, that's what I mean."

"Give him time," said Graff.

Dink got up from his chair.

"I haven't dismissed you, soldier."

Dink stopped and saluted. "Permission to leave your office and return to my barracks to continue feeling like a complete shit, sir."

"Denied," said Graff. "Oh, you can feel like whatever you want, that's not my business. But your effort on behalf of Zeck has been duly noted."

"I didn't come here for a commendation."

"And you're not getting one. All you're getting from this is my good opinion of your character. It's not easily won, but once won, my good opinion is hard to lose. It's a burden you'll have to carry with you for some time. Learn to live with it. Now get out of here, soldier."

* * *

Zeck came upon Wiggin at one of the elevator wells. It wasn't one much used by students—it was out of the normal lanes of traffic, and mostly teachers used it, when it was used at all. Zeck used it precisely for that reason. He could wait in line at the busier elevators for a long time, but somehow he never got to the front of the line until everyone else had gone. That was usually fine with Zeck, but at mealtime, when everyone was headed for the same destination, it was the difference between a hot meal with a lot of choices and a colder one with almost no choices left.

So there was Wiggin, sitting with his back to the wall, gripping his left leg so tightly that his head rested on his own knee. He was obviously in pain.

Zeck almost walked past him. What did he owe any of these people?

Then he remembered the Samaritan who stopped for the injured man—and the priest and the Levite who didn't.

"Something wrong?" asked Zeck.

"Thinking about something and didn't watch where I was stepping," said Wiggin through gritted teeth.

"Bruise? Broken skin?"

"Twisted ankle," said Wiggin.

"Swollen?"

"I don't know yet," said Wiggin. "When I move it, it throbs."

"Bring your other leg up so I can compare ankles."

Wiggin did. Zeck pulled his shoes and socks off, despite the way Wiggin winced when he moved his left foot. The bare ankles looked exactly alike, as far as he could tell. "Doesn't look swollen."

"Good," said Wiggin. "Then I guess I'm OK." He reached out and grabbed Zeck's upper arm and began to pull himself up.

"I'm not a firepole," said Zeck. "Let me help you up instead of just grabbing my arm."

"Sure, sorry," said Wiggin.

In a moment, Wiggin was up and wincing as he tried to walk off the injury. "Owie owie owie," he breathed, in a parody of a suffering toddler. Then he gave Zeck a tiny smile. "Thanks."

"Don't mention it," said Zeck. "Now what did you want to talk to me about?"

Wiggin smiled a little more broadly. "I don't know," he said. No attempt to deny that this whole thing had been staged to have an opportunity to talk. "I just know that whatever your plan is, it's working too well or it isn't working at all."

"I don't have a plan," said Zeck. "I just want to go home."

"We all want to go home," said Wiggin. "But we also want other things. Honor. Victory. Save the world. Prove you can do something hard. You don't care about anything except getting out of here, no matter what it costs."

"That's right."

"So, why? And don't tell me you're homesick. We all cried for mommy and daddy our first few nights here, and then we stopped. If there's anybody here tough enough to take a little homesickness, it's you."

"So now you're my counselor? Forget it, Wiggin."

"What are you afraid of?" asked Wiggin.

"Nothing," said Zeck.

"Kuso," said Wiggin.

"Now I'm supposed to pour out my heart to you, is that it? Because you asked what I was afraid of, and that shows me how insightful you are, and I tell you all my deepest fears, and you make me feel better, and then we're lifelong friends and I decide to become a good soldier to please you."

"You don't eat," said Wiggin. "Humans can't live in the kind of isolation you're living in. I think you're going to die. If your body doesn't die, your soul will."

"Forgive me for pointing out the obvious, but you don't believe in souls."

"Forgive me for pointing out the obvious," said Wiggin, "but you don't know squat about what I believe. I have religious parents too."

"Having religious parents says nothing about what you believe."

"But nobody here is religious *without* religious parents," said Wiggin. "Come on, how old were we when they took us? Six? Seven?"

"I hear you were five."

"And now we're so much older. You're eight now?"

"Almost nine."

"But we're so ma*ture*."

"They picked us because we have a mental age much higher than the norm."

"I have religious parents," said Wiggin. "Unfortunately not the same religion, which caused a little conflict. For instance, my mother doesn't believe in infant baptism and my father does, so my father thinks I'm baptized and my mother doesn't."

Zeck winced a little at the idea. "You can't have a strong marriage when the parents don't share the same faith."

"Well, my parents do their best," said Wiggin. "And I bet your parents don't agree on *everything*."

Zeck shrugged.

"I bet they don't agree on *you*."

Zeck turned away. "This is completely none of your business."

"I bet your mother was glad you went into space. To get you away from your father. That's how much they disagree on religion."

Zeck turned around to face him, furious now. "What did those bunducks tell you about me? They have no right."

"Nobody told me anything," said Wiggin. "It's you, oomay. Back when people were still talking to you, when you first came into Rat Army, it was always, *your father this, your father that.*"

"You only just joined Rat yourself."

"People talk outside their armies," said Wiggin. "And I listen. Always your father. Like your father was some kind of prophet. And I thought, I bet his mother's glad he isn't under his father's influence anymore."

"My mother wants me to respect my father."

"She just doesn't want you to live with him. He beat you, didn't he?"

Zeck shoved Wiggin. Before he even thought of doing it, there was his hand, shoving the kid away.

"Come on," said Wiggin. "You shower. People see the scars. *I've* seen the scars."

"It was purification. There's no way a pagan like you would understand that."

"Purification of what?" asked Wiggin. "You were the perfect son?"

"Graff's been feeding you information from their observation of me, hasn't he! That's illegal!"

"Come on, Zeck. I know *you*. If you decide something's right, then that's the thing you'll do, no matter what it costs you. You believe in your father. Whatever he says, you'll do. So what have you done wrong that makes it so you need all this purification?"

Zeck didn't answer. He just closed down. Refused to listen. He let his mind go off somewhere else. To the place where it always went when Father purified him. So he wouldn't scream. So he wouldn't feel anything at all.

"There it is," said Wiggin. "That's the Zeck he made you into. The Zeck who isn't really here. Doesn't really exist."

Zeck heard him without hearing.

"And that's why you have to get home," said Wiggin. "Because without you there, he'll have to find somebody else to purify, won't he? Do you have a brother? A sister? Some other kid in the congregation? Or ... oh, I know. It's your mother, isn't it?

Do you think he'll try to purify your mother?"

Zeck really was tuning out everything Wiggin said, yet something must have gotten through, because now, at Wiggin's cue, he started thinking about his mother. And not just any picture of her. It was his mother saying to him, "Satan does not give good gifts. So your good gift comes from God."

And then Father, saying, "There are those who will tell you that a thing is from God, when it's really from the devil."

Zeck had asked him why.

"They are deceived by their own desire," Father had said. "They wish the world were a better place, so they pretend that polluted things are pure, so they don't have to fear them."

He couldn't let Father know what Mother had said, because it was so impure of her. Can't let Father know.

If he whips Mother I'll kill him.

The thought struck him with such force he gasped and stumbled against the wall.

If he whips Mother I'll kill him.

Wiggin was still there, talking. "Zeck, what's wrong?" Wiggin touched him. Touched his arm. The forearm.

Zeck couldn't help himself. He yanked his arm away, but that wasn't enough. He lashed out with his right leg and kicked Wiggin in the shin. Then shoved him backward. Wiggin fell against the wall, then to the floor. He looked helpless. Zeck was so filled with rage at him that he couldn't contain it. It was all the weeks of isolation. It was all his fear for his mother. She really wasn't pure. He should hate her for it. But he loved her. That made him evil. That made him deserve all the purification Father ever gave him—because he loved someone as impure as Mother.

And for some reason, with all of this rage and fear, Zeck threw himself down on Wiggin and pummeled him in the chest and stomach.

"Stop it!" cried Wiggin, trying to turn away from him. "What do you think you're doing, *purifying* me?"

Zeck stopped and looked at his own hands. Looked at Wiggin's body, lying there helpless. The very helplessness of him, his wormlike, fetal pose, infuriated Zeck. He knew from class what this was. It was blood lust. It was the animal fever that took a soldier over and made him strong beyond his strength.

It was what Father must have felt, purifying him. The smaller body, helpless, complete subject to his will. It filled a certain kind of man with rage that had to tear into its prey. That had to inflict pain, break the skin, draw blood and tears and screaming from the victim.

It was something dark and evil. If anything was from Satan, *this* was.

"I thought you were a pacifist," said Wiggin softly.

Zeck could hear his father going on and on about peace, how the servants of God did not go to war.

"Beat your swords into ploughshares," murmured Zeck, echoing his father quoting Micah and Isaiah, as he did all the time.

"Bible quotations," said Wiggin, uncurling himself. Now he lay flat on the ground. Completely open to any blows Zeck might try to land. But the rage was dissipating now. Zeck didn't want to hit him. Or rather, he wanted to hit him, but not more than he wanted *not* to hit him.

"Try this one," said Wiggin. "Think not that I am come to send peace on earth: I came not to send peace, but a sword."

"Don't argue scripture with me," said Zeck. "I know them all."

"But you only believe in the ones your father liked. Why do you think your father always quoted the ones about hating war and rejecting violence, when he beat you the way he did? Sounds like he was trying to talk himself out of what he found in his own heart."

"You don't know my father." Zeck hissed out the words through a tight throat. He could hit this kid again. He could. But he wouldn't. At least he wouldn't if the kid would just shut up.

"I know what I just saw," said Wiggin. "That rage. You weren't pulling your punches. That hurt."

"Sorry," said Zeck. "But shut up now, please."

"Oh, just because it hurt doesn't mean I'm afraid of you. You know one of the reasons I was glad to leave home? Because my brother threatened to kill me, and even though I know he probably didn't mean it, my guts didn't know that. My guts churned all the time. With fear. Because my brother liked to hurt me. I don't think that's your father, though. I think your father *hated* what he did to you. And that's why he preached peace."

"He preached peace because that's what Christ preached," said Zeck. He meant to say it with fervor and intensity. But the words sounded lame even as he said them.

"The Lord is my strength and song," quoted Wiggin. "And he is become my salvation."

"Exodus fifteen," said Zeck. "It's Moses. Old Testament. It doesn't apply."

"He is my God, and I will prepare him an habitation; my father's God, and I will exalt him."

"What are you doing with the King James version anyway?" said Zeck. "Did you learn these scriptures just to argue with me?"

"Yes," said Wiggin. "You know the next verse."

"The Lord is a man of war," said Zeck. "Jehovah is his name."

"The King James version just says 'the Lord,'" said Wiggin.

"But that's what it means when the Bible puts it in small caps like that. They're just avoiding putting down the name of God."

"The Lord is a man of war," said Wiggin. "But if your dad quoted *that*, then he'd have no reason to try to control this bloodlust thing. This berserker rage. He'd kill you. So it's really a good thing, isn't it, that he ignored Jesus and Moses talking about how God is about war *and* peace. Because he loved you so much that he'd build half his religion up like a wall to keep him from killing you."

"Stay out of my family," whispered Zeck.

"He loved you," said Wiggin. "But you were right to be afraid of him."

"Don't make me hurt you," said Zeck.

"I'm not worried about you," said Wiggin. "You're twice the man your father is. Now that you've seen the violence inside you, you can control it. You won't hit me for telling you the truth."

"Nothing that you've said is true."

"Zeck," said Wiggin, "'It were better for him that a millstone were hanged about his neck, and he cast into the sea, than that he should offend one of these little ones.' Did your father quote that very much?"

He wanted to kill Wiggin. He also wanted to cry. He didn't do either. "He quoted it all the time."

"And then he took you out and made all those scars on your back."

"I wasn't pure."

"No, *he* wasn't pure. *He* wasn't."

"Some people are looking so hard to find Satan that they see him even where he isn't!" cried Zeck.

"I don't remember that from the Bible."

It wasn't the Bible. It was Mother. He couldn't say that.

"I'm not sure what you're saying," said Wiggin. "That *I'm* finding Satan where he isn't? I don't think so. I think a man who whips a little kid and then blames the kid for it, I think that's exactly where Satan lives."

The urge to cry was apparently going to win. Zeck could hardly get the words out. "I have to go home."

"And do what?" asked Wiggin. "Stand between your mother and father until your father finally loses control and kills you?"

"If that's what it takes!"

"You know my biggest fear?" said Wiggin.

"I don't care about your fear," said Zeck.

"As much as I hate my brother, what I'm afraid of is that I'm just like him."

"I don't hate my father."

"You're terrified of him," said Wiggin, "and you should be. But I think what you're really planning to do when you go home is kill the old son of a bitch."

"No I'm not!" cried Zeck. The rage filled him again, and he couldn't stop himself from lashing out, but at least he aimed his blows at the wall and the floor, not at Wiggin. So it hurt only Zeck's own hands and arms and elbows. Only himself.

"If he laid one hand on your mother," said Wiggin.

"I'll kill him!" Then Zeck hurled himself backward, threw himself to the floor away from Wiggin and beat on the floor and kept beating on it till the skin of the palm of his left hand broke open and bled. And even then, he only stopped because Wiggin took hold of his wrist. Held it and then put something in his palm and closed Zeck's fist around it.

"You've done enough bleeding," said Wiggin. "In my opinion, anyway."

"Don't tell," whispered Zeck. "Don't tell anybody."

"You haven't done anything wrong," said Wiggin, "except try to get home to protect your mother. Because you know your father is crazy and dangerous."

"Just like me," said Zeck.

"No," said Wiggin. "The opposite of you. Because you controlled it. You stopped yourself from beating the little kid. Even when he deliberately provoked you. Your father couldn't stop himself from beating you—even when you did absolutely nothing wrong at all. You are not alike."

"The rage," said Zeck.

"One of the soldierly virtues," said Wiggin. "Turn it on the Buggers instead of on yourself or your father. And especially instead of me."

"I don't believe in war."

"Not many soldiers do," said Wiggin. "You could get killed doing that stuff. But you train to fight well, so that when a war does come, you can win and come home and find everything safe."

"There's nothing safe at home."

"I bet that things are fine at home," said Wiggin. "Because, see, with you not there, your mother doesn't have any reason to stay with your father, does she? So I think she's not going to put up with any more crap from him. Don't you think so? She can't be weak. If she were weak, she could never have produced somebody as tough as you. You couldn't have gotten your toughness from your father—he doesn't have much, if he can't even keep himself from doing what he did. So your toughness comes from her, right? She'll leave him if he raises his hand against her. She doesn't have to stay to look out for you anymore."

It was as much the tone of Wiggin's voice as the words he said that calmed him. Zeck pulled his body together, rolled himself up into a sitting position. "I keep expecting to see some teacher rush down the corridor demanding to know what's going on."

"I don't think so," said Wiggin. "I think they know exactly what's going on—probably watching it on a holo somewhere—

and maybe they're keeping any other kids from coming along here to see. But they're going to let us work it out on our own."

"Work what out?" said Zeck. "I got no quarrel with you."

"You had a quarrel with everybody who stood between you and going home."

"I still hate this place. I want to get out of here."

"Welcome to the club," said Wiggin. "Look, we're missing lunch. You can do what you want, but I'm going to go eat."

"You still planning to limp on that left ankle?"

"Yes," said Wiggin. "After you kicked me? I won't have to act."

"Chest OK? I didn't break any ribs, did I?"

"You sure have an inflated opinion of your own strength," said Wiggin.

Then he stepped into the elevator and held the bar as it drifted upward, carrying him along with it.

Zeck sat there a while longer, looking at nothing, thinking about what just happened. He wasn't sure if anything had been decided. Zeck still hated Battle School. And everybody in Battle School hated him. And now he hated his father and didn't believe in his father's phony pacifism. Wiggin had pretty much convinced him that his father was no prophet. Hell, Zeck had known it all along. But believing in his father's spirituality was the only way he could keep himself from hating him and fearing him. The only way he could bear it. Now he didn't have to bear it anymore. Wiggin was right. Mother was free, now that she didn't have to look out for Zeck.

He unclenched his fist and saw what Wiggin had stuffed into it to stanch the bleeding. One of his socks, covered in blood.

* * *

Dink saw how Wiggin walked with his food tray and knew something was wrong. And it wasn't just because his tray was double-loaded. Who was he getting lunch for? Didn't matter— what mattered was that Wiggin was in pain. Dink pulled out the chair beside him.

"What happened?" he asked as soon as Wiggin sat down.

"Got lunch for Zeck," said Wiggin.

"I mean what happened to *you*," said Dink.

"Happened?" Wiggin's voice was all innocence, but his eyes, lasering in at Dink's eyes, were telling him to back off.

"Suit yourself," said Dink. "Keep your dandruff to yourself for all I care."

The conversation at the table flowed around them after that. Dink joined in now and then, but he noticed that Wiggin just ate, and that he was careful about how he breathed. Something had injured his chest. Broken rib? No, more likely a bruise. And he'd been favoring one leg when he walked. Trying not to show it, but favoring it all the same. And he was saving lunch for Zeck. They'd had a fight. The pacifist and the genius? Fighting each other? That was stupid. But what else could it have been? Who else but a pacifist would attack somebody as little as Wiggin?

Half the soldiers were gone from the table by the time Zeck came in. The food line had already closed down, but Wiggin saw him and stood up and waved him over. He was slow raising his hand to wave, though, what with his chest hurting and all.

Zeck approached. "Got lunch for you," said Wiggin, stepping away from his chair so that Zeck could sit in it.

The other kids at the table were obviously poising themselves to leave if Zeck sat down there.

"No, I'm not hungry," said Zeck.

Had he been crying? No. And what was with his hand? He kept it in a fist, but Dink could see that it had been injured. That there had been blood.

"I just wanted to give you something," said Zeck.

He laid a stocking down on the table beside Wiggin's tray.

"Sorry it's wet," said Zeck. "I had to wash it."

"Toguro," said Wiggin. "Now sit and eat." He almost pushed Zeck down into the chair.

It was the stocking that did it. Wiggin had given Zeck a gift— a Santa Claus gift, of all things—and Zeck had accepted it. Now Wiggin stood with his hands on Zeck's shoulders, staring at each of the other Rat Army soldiers in turn, as if he was daring them to stand up and go.

Dink knew that if *he* got up, the others would too. But he didn't get up, and the others stayed.

"So I've got this poem," said Dink. "It really sucks, but sometimes you just gotta say it to get it out of your system."

"We've just eaten, Dink," said Flip. "Couldn't you wait till our food is digested?"

"No, this will be good for you," said Dink. "Your food's turning to shit right now, and this will help."

That got him a laugh, which bought him enough time to finish coming up with the rhymes he needed.

"What do you do with Zeck?

You want to break his neck.

But I warn you not to try

Cause Zeck's too stubborn to die."

As poems go, it was pretty weak. But as a symbol of Dink's decision that Zeck should be given another chance, well, it did the job. Between Wiggin's stocking and Dink's poem, Zeck had returned to his previous status: barely tolerated.

Dink looked up at Wiggin, who was still standing behind Zeck, who now seemed to be eating with some appetite.

"Merry Christmas," Dink mouthed silently.

Wiggin smiled.

Orson Scott Card *is the author of the novels* Ender's Game, Ender's Shadow, *and* Speaker for the Dead, *which are widely read by adults and younger readers, and are increasingly used in schools. His most recent series, the young adult Pathfinder series (*Pathfinder, Ruins, Visitors*) and the fantasy Mithermages series (*Lost Gate, Gate Thief*) are taking readers in new directions. Besides these and other science fiction novels, Card writes contemporary fantasy (*Magic Street, Enchantment, Lost Boys*), biblical novels (*Stone Tables, Rachel and Leah*), the American frontier fantasy series, The Tales of Alvin Maker (beginning with* Seventh Son*), poetry (*An Open Book*), and many plays and scripts.*

Card was born in Washington and grew up in California, Arizona, and Utah. He served a mission for the LDS Church in Brazil in the early 1970s. Besides his writing, he teaches occasional classes and workshops and directs plays. He frequently teaches writing and literature courses at Southern Virginia University. Card currently lives in Greensboro, North Carolina, with his wife, Kristine Allen Card, where his primary activities are writing a review column for the local Rhinoceros Times and feeding birds, squirrels, chipmunks, possums, and raccoons on the patio.

ABOUT THE EDITOR

Bryan Thomas Schmidt is an author and Hugo-nominated editor of adult and children's speculative fiction. His debut novel, *The Worker Prince* received Honorable Mention on Barnes & Noble Book Club's Year's Best Science Fiction Releases. His short stories have appeared in magazines, anthologies and online and include entries in *The X-Files* and *Decipher's WARS*, amongst others. His anthologies as editor include *Shattered Shields* with co-editor Jennifer Brozek, *Mission: Tomorrow*, *Galactic Games*, and *Little Green Men—Attack!* with Robin Wayne Bailey (forthcoming) all for Baen, *Space Battles: Full Throttle Space Tales #6*, *Beyond The Sun*, and *Raygun Chronicles: Space Opera for a New Age*. He can be found online at bryanthomasschmidt.net.

IF YOU LIKED ...

If you liked *Decision Points*, you might also enjoy:

The Worker Prince

Best of Penny Dread

Launch Pad

Other WordFire Press Titles by Bryan Thomas Schmidt

The Worker Prince

The Returning (Forthcoming)

Our list of other WordFire Press authors and titles is always growing. To find out more and to see our selection of titles, visit us at:

wordfirepress.com